A Home at Trail's End

MELODY CARLSON

HARVEST HOUSE PUBLISHERS
EUGENE, OREGON

Cover by Koechel Peterson & Associates, Inc., Minneapolis, Minnesota

Cover photos © Koechel Peterson & Associates / iStockphoto / Thinkstock

Backcover author photo Ruettgers Photography

A HOME AT TRAIL'S END
Copyright © 2013 by Melody A. Carlson
Published by Harvest House Publishers
Eugene, Oregon 97402
www.harvesthousepublishers.com

Library of Congress Cataloging-in-Publication Data
    Carlson, Melody.
    A home at trail's end / Melody Carlson.
       pages cm—(Homeward on the Oregon Trail Series; Book 3)
    ISBN 978-0-7369-4875-3 (pbk.)
    ISBN 978-0-7369-4876-0 (eBook)
    1. Widows—Fiction. 2. Women pioneers—Fiction. 3. Oregon Territory—History—Fiction.
    I. Title.
    PS3553.A73257H56 2013
    813'.54—dc23

                          2012044765

Printed in the United States of America

13 14 15 16 17 18 19 20 21 / LB-CD / 10 9 8 7 6 5 4 3 2 1

Primary Returning Characters from
A Dream for Tomorrow

Elizabeth Anne Martin
  JT (12) and Ruth Anne (8)

Eli Kincaid, *former wagon train scout*

Asa and Clara Dawson, *Elizabeth's parents*

Matthew and Jess Dawson, *Elizabeth's brother and sister-in-law*

Brady, *Elizabeth's farmhand and a freed slave*

Malinda Martin, *Elizabeth's widowed sister-in-law*
  Todd (15), Emily (13), Bart (12), and Susannah (9)

William Bramford, *a widowed lawyer from Boston*
  Jeremiah (18), Belinda (17), and Amelia (16)

Hugh and Lavinia Prescott, *friends of William Bramford, also from Boston*
  Julius (19), Evelyn (16), and Augustus (13)

Bert and Florence Flanders
  Mahala (18), Ezra (16), Hannah (13), Walter (11), and Tillie (8)

Jane Taylor, *fellow emigrant whose husband was killed on the wagon train*

Chapter One

October 1857

Elizabeth felt a spring in her step as she guided Eli around the borders of her property. At the corner, she paused to point out the land adjoining hers. "That section combined with my acreage equals a whole parcel. But because I'm single, I could only file for a half parcel."

"I see." He surveyed the meadow that ran clear down to the river and then up into the wooded hills behind it.

"John and Malinda had been saving a whole parcel for us…" She stopped herself. "I mean, for James and me."

He nodded. "I understand."

"And of course, both John and James are gone now." She didn't want to dwell too much on this sad fact. It seemed more important to go forward than to look back. "So I claimed this half when we arrived." She waved her hand toward her land. "Because it was closer to Malinda as well as my family's parcels. But the other half is still available."

He smiled at her. "So you don't mind if I file a claim on it."

She laughed. "Being that you've filed a claim on my heart, it seems you are entitled to the land as well."

"This is fine land, Elizabeth. I can see why you and your family felt it was worth the effort to come out this way."

"Father thinks the meadows along the river are perfect for grazing."

"Yes." Eli's brow creased. "It's hard to believe the government is selling this land for so cheap. But I know they want it settled." He glanced over to the river. "Are there any Indians around here? I know that's the Coquille River, and I heard the Coquille tribe is friendly. This looks like the kind of place Indians would be quite comfortable in."

"To be honest, I haven't seen a single Indian since we left Empire City," she told him. "But Malinda wrote to me, saying there had been trouble in these parts. Perhaps the Indians have moved on." For some reason this wasn't a topic that many of the settlers spoke of…whether it was because it made them uncomfortable or because the Indians were not a problem was unclear.

"I know the ocean isn't too far away. It's possible they've gone over there to fish for salmon or collect clams."

"I'm looking forward to seeing the ocean," she told him.

He grinned. "Yes, we'll have to do that together." He looked intently into her eyes. "Now that you've agreed to become my bride, is there anyone I should see to get permission? Asa perhaps?"

She laughed. "No, I do not need my father's permission to marry, but I would like my parents' blessing. However, there is someone you should ask. Rather, two someones. And school let out a bit ago, so I'm sure they'll be here soon."

"I can't wait to see them."

Now she told him about JT helping to drive the livestock along the Columbia River. "It was almost as if he left a boy and grew into a man while he was gone. He's still talking about the adventures they had."

"Did he take his Bowie knife?"

6

"He certainly did. And I let him take your canteen as well."

Eli chuckled. "I'm glad you did."

"And Ruth is turning into quite an artist. You'll have to ask her to show you the drawings she did while we traveled down the Columbia River. She says she's saving them for her children." She laughed. "Can you imagine? Ruth planning for her own children?"

"I think we would make fine grandparents."

Elizabeth was touched but didn't respond as she pointed to where her horse Molly, with JT and Ruth on her back, was coming toward them. "There they are." She clutched her hands together anxiously. What if the children were unhappy about her engagement to Eli? Perhaps this was a conversation she should have privately with them. And yet she knew they needed to hear this news now—she had promised them that they would be the first to know.

"Oh, dear," she said quietly to Eli as she smiled and waved to Ruth and JT. "I'm feeling extremely nervous right now."

"So am I," Eli admitted.

"*Eli!*" JT yelled from the horse, nudging Molly to go faster.

Eli went to meet them, helping Ruth from the horse as JT hopped down. Both children hugged Eli. "When did you get here?" JT asked with enthusiasm.

"Just now," Eli told him.

"How long will you stay?" Ruth asked.

"That depends," he told her.

"On what?" JT peered curiously at him.

"Well…your mother and I want to ask you both about something." He tossed her an uneasy glance.

"That's right," she added. "Eli has asked me a very important question." She looked back at him, hoping he'd take it from here.

"I came here to ask your mother to become my wife," he said bravely.

JT looked stunned, but Ruth just grinned. "I knew it!" she exclaimed.

7

"But your mother said she can't marry without her children's approval. What do you think about me marrying your mother… and hopefully becoming your father?" He cleared his throat. "Someday…"

"I like it!" Ruth declared. "I wanted Mama to marry you a long time ago, back on the wagon train. Didn't I, Mama?"

Elizabeth just chuckled and nodded. But her eyes were fixed on JT. He was being awfully quiet just now. And his expression was very somber and hard to read. What was he thinking?

"I appreciate you giving your consent, Ruth. But we need the approval of both of you." Eli looked at JT now. "What do you think about this, JT? I realize you've been the man of the house." Eli glanced over to the stone foundation. "Well, there's not much house yet, but you've been playing the role of the man in this family. And doing an excellent job of it too." He grinned. "Your ma told me about how you helped drive the livestock through the Columbia Gorge. Takes a man to do that."

JT nodded proudly. "I know."

"So, JT," Elizabeth began, "what do you think? And please be honest."

JT looked from Eli to Elizabeth, and then a slow smile broke over his face. "I think it's a good idea. I approve." He stuck out his hand to Eli, and they shook on it.

"I appreciate that," Eli told him. "You had me worried there for a bit."

JT chuckled. "Sorry. I just wanted to give it my careful consideration."

Elizabeth laughed, patting him on the back. "I appreciate that, son."

"Does anyone else know about this?" Ruth asked. "Grandma and Grandpa or—"

"Nobody but you two," Elizabeth assured her. "Remember what I told you—you and JT would be the first to know."

"Can we go tell them now?" Ruth asked.

Elizabeth glanced at Eli, and he just shrugged. "Don't see why not."

"Yes, but let's ask them to keep it to themselves until after Malinda and Will's party tomorrow. I don't want to steal their thunder."

"Good thinking," Eli agreed.

And so they all headed over to share the good news with Asa and Clara and Matthew and Jess and Brady. Naturally, everyone was nearly as happy as Elizabeth and Eli, and they all promised to keep it under their hats.

"We don't see anyone out here much anyway," Jess assured her. "Besides our own family, that is."

"And now our family is getting bigger," Ruth said proudly.

"In more ways than one," Elizabeth added mysteriously. She glanced at Jess, who was expecting her first baby in the spring. However, other than immediate family, Jess was keeping this to herself. "How are you doing?"

Jess grinned. "I've never felt better."

"And the house is coming along nicely?" Elizabeth asked. Since Matthew and Jess' house was farther away, she hadn't been out there in a few weeks.

"Oh, yes! Matthew and Pa and Brady are quite the carpenters."

"So when is the big date?" Matthew asked Elizabeth. "I'll need to warm up my fiddle for the dancing afterward."

"I'm not sure," Elizabeth admitted.

"We haven't really discussed that yet," Eli told them. "But I say the sooner the better." He looked at Elizabeth again. "But I don't want to rush you."

She laughed nervously. "I don't really know. Maybe we should think on that a bit. And let's not forget that we don't even have a place to live yet."

"I s'pect Lizzie told you we were making her wait until last for her house," Asa told Eli. "We hadn't really planned it that way. We thought she was going to live with Malinda."

"And I don't know why you and the children don't do that," Clara told Elizabeth. "Seems you could stay up there—at least until the wedding."

"Except that Malinda will have a full house before long. I heard that Will's girls are going to move in with her soon. Will and Jeremiah will keep working on the cabin on his unit...although it sounds like that house might go to Jeremiah now that he and Mahala are planning to wed."

"So many weddings." Clara rubbed her hands together. "Won't it be fun!"

Elizabeth looked at Eli. "Maybe we shouldn't make plans for our wedding until after we get our cabin built."

He just nodded. "That makes sense."

She was glad he agreed, but she also wondered how good a plan it really was. Having a cabin finished sounded like a long way down the road. Still, she wasn't going to worry about it today.

"Where will you stay?" Asa asked Eli.

Eli scratched his chin. "I hadn't given it much thought. But I can camp most anywhere."

Clara made a concerned frown. "Anywhere...except on Elizabeth's land."

"But we have lots of room," Ruth injected.

Asa tweaked one of her braids and then grinned. "Why don't you stay here with us?" he asked Eli.

"I'd be much obliged."

"Watch out," Elizabeth teasingly warned Eli. "They'll probably try to put you to work if you're living here."

"No," Asa assured her. "I'll bet Eli will want to get to work on your place as soon as possible."

"Elizabeth has already made a nice start with that stone foundation," Eli said with pride. "It looks good and square."

"'Ceptin' that she made it a might too big," Matthew teased. "Did you notice?"

Eli shook his head. "I thought it was a good size for a family—with room to grow."

⚜

For the past couple of weeks, Elizabeth had capitalized on the good weather by sprouting seeds. As a result she now had dozens of tiny delicate plants—apples, peaches, pears, plums, and berries that were nearly ready to be planted in soil. JT was helping his uncle today, but Ruth was on hand to help Elizabeth with the task of planting. Their first task was to finish the stick fence they'd been building to protect the plants from foraging critters. Elizabeth was well aware of the damage deer and rabbits could do to young plants.

"Is this going to be high enough to keep deer out?" Ruth asked as they pounded sticks into the ground.

"No," Elizabeth admitted. "But I plan to put tall poles every few feet. I'll string wire about this tall." She held her hand up as high as she could reach. "And then I'll tie colorful rags that will flutter in the wind. Hopefully they will dissuade the deer from jumping the fence."

"And Flax will help too. He's a good watchdog."

As she and Ruth worked, Elizabeth was surprised that Eli didn't come by to say hello. In fact, as she strung the wire, she realized how much she would have appreciated his help. Even so, they were making good progress. And by late afternoon, not only was the seedling fortress fairly secure, but she and Ruth had planted most of the young plants as well. How many would survive remained to be seen. But hopefully by next fall, she would have enough little trees to transplant into a small fruit orchard.

Just as she and Ruth were finishing, JT came home from helping with the men. "We started putting up Uncle Matthew's roof," he told her as he came over to see the progress in the seedling garden. "Eli was there to help, and that made it go lots faster."

11

"So that's where Eli was today." She stood up straight and brushed the dirt from her hands.

"He said he'll be here around six to take us to the barn dance at Aunt Malinda's," JT told her as he dipped a cupful of water from one of the buckets she'd been using to water the seedlings.

"Yes." She rubbed the sore spot in her back and nodded. "He told me he would." She pointed to the water buckets. "Why don't you run down to the creek and refill those. Then you can help us water the seedlings and we'll call it a day."

"And then I'll jump in the creek and take a bath," he called out as he grabbed both buckets.

"Me too," Ruth called out.

Elizabeth looked up at the clear sky overhead. "You might as well make the most of this summerlike weather while we have it."

When JT returned, the three of them finished watering the seedlings. "Just enough to moisten the soil," Elizabeth reminded JT. "We don't want to drown them."

"Eli had to quit working early in order to go to town and buy some tools from the Prescotts," JT explained as he dropped the water cup into the nearly empty bucket. "I reckon he got tired of having to borrow tools from everybody."

"The Prescotts aren't open for business yet," Elizabeth said as she dripped some water on the last tiny seedling. "I hope Hugh will have some tools available to sell to him."

"Oh, I'm sure they do," JT assured her. "According to Augustus they have a little bit of everything."

"Wait until you see their mercantile," Ruth said as she wiped her dirty hands onto her work dress. "We've been watching it get bigger and bigger every day on our way to school. It looks just like a real building."

"A real building?" Elizabeth frowned.

"I mean with real wood," Ruth explained. "Not just logs, like Grandpa and Uncle Matthew are using."

"Augustus said his pa went to the lumber mill in Empire City and brought back a bunch of milled wood. That's why they were able to build it so fast."

"I'll bet that cost a lot of money," Ruth added.

"You're probably right about that." Elizabeth led the way out of their seedling garden, latching the stick gate behind them. She hoped it would keep the critters out. "Well, I'm happy for the Prescotts. I can't wait to see the mercantile after church tomorrow." And truly, it would be interesting to see a "real" building out here in the frontier, where everything else seemed to be made of logs and twigs and bark.

While the children bathed in the creek, Elizabeth gave herself a bucket bath in the tent shelter that her father and brother had constructed for her and the children to use as a temporary house. The tent was attached to the wagon, and compared to conditions while coming over the Oregon Trail, it was spacious and comfortable, albeit rather rustic. She had no idea what it would be like once the rains came—probably very damp. She was just finished getting dressed when Ruth and JT returned, shivering from their cool dip in the creek. But at least they were clean. And their good clothes were clean and dry and ready for them to wear.

Elizabeth went outside to survey the seedling garden. The poor tiny plants looked a little worse for wear, but that was to be expected. With sunshine and moisture, they would perk up. And with the mild winter in this region, they would probably be several inches tall by spring—and twice that by next fall. The ones that survived.

She returned to the tent to check on the children's progress.

"Here, Mama." Ruth handed her the hairbrush and her blue satin ribbon and then turned around. Elizabeth sat down on the rocker and brushed out Ruth's honey-colored hair. It was still damp from the creek as she separated it into three parts and then smoothly plaited one long braid, tying the ribbon into a nice big bow. "All done."

"There's Eli," JT called from outside.

Elizabeth reached up to her own hair, smoothing the bun she'd made earlier into place.

"You look beautiful, Mama," Ruth assured her.

Elizabeth laughed. "Thank you."

"Are we all ready to go now, Ma?" JT reached for his guitar case, which was resting as usual next to his bedroll.

"Yes." Elizabeth handed Ruth a kerosene lantern. "We'll need this on our way back."

"I wish we could take the wagon," JT told her.

"It's not that far to walk," she reminded him. She wished they could take the wagon too, but that would mean taking down their tent and breaking camp. Besides, they'd have to unload the wagon and load it all back in later. She picked up the basket containing the two berry pies she and Ruth had made the night before. One of them had gotten a little blackened on the edge of the crust, but the blackberries had been tasty, and hopefully no one would complain. Elizabeth tried not to miss her oven back in Kentucky, reminding herself that pies could burn in it too.

"Hello there," Eli called as he came into their camp. Instead of his usual buckskins, he had on his Sunday-go-to-meeting clothes, and Elizabeth could tell by the shine on his chin that he was freshly shaved. "Now, what can I carry for you?"

Elizabeth handed him the basket, and he rewarded her with a kiss on the cheek. Naturally the children giggled—and Elizabeth's cheeks blushed.

"Where's your guitar?" JT asked Eli.

"Back at camp," Eli told him. "Didn't know I was supposed to bring it tonight."

"That's all right," Elizabeth assured him.

"Maybe next time."

"Uncle Matthew will have his fiddle," JT told them. "And the McIntires will be ready to play music too."

"This will be so much fun!" Ruth clapped her hands and skipped along as if she hadn't worked hard all day.

Elizabeth smiled at Eli as she linked her arm into his. "You look mighty handsome tonight, Mr. Kincaid."

He grinned at her. "I was about to tell you that you look pretty as a picture." He nodded to Ruth. "As do you, Miss Ruth."

"What about me?" JT joked. "Do I look pretty too?"

Eli chuckled. "Well, looks to me like you're fixing to break some young girls' hearts tonight."

"Hannah Flanders wants to dance with JT at the party," Ruth teased.

"I've got an idea," Eli said. "How about if we sing our way to the barn dance?"

"Yes! Yes!" Ruth agreed. "Let's sing 'Coming Round the Mountain.'"

And so they did, going through all the choruses and even making up a few new ones until they got to Malinda's place. It was amazing how singing made the trip go much more quickly.

"As soon as we get the pies set out, I want you to meet Malinda," Elizabeth told Eli. "She's my very best friend."

It wasn't long until Elizabeth got the chance to introduce Eli to Malinda. But they were both careful not to mention their engagement. Still, Elizabeth could tell by Malinda's questions that she was suspicious. When Will came over to join them, politely greeting Eli with a curious expression, Elizabeth grew uncomfortable. It was the first time all four of them had been together, and she so wanted them all to be friends—though she knew that was probably unlikely. Will and Eli...they were so different. Even so, they exchanged polite greetings, and Eli congratulated Will and Malinda and made a respectable attempt at small talk.

"I just know something is up with these two," Malinda said suddenly to Will.

"What do you mean?" Will gave her a perplexed frown.

"I mean something is going on here. I can see it in my best friend's eyes." Malinda grasped both Elizabeth's hands and stared intently at her. "What is it? Tell me."

Elizabeth suppressed a nervous giggle and looked away, attempting to avoid Malinda's probing stare.

"I know it!" Malinda declared. "I know exactly what is going on!"

Elizabeth gave her a warning glance, but Malinda ignored it.

"I don't believe in betting, but I would wager that you two have gotten yourselves engaged." Malinda tilted her head to one side. "I just know it. And if I'm wrong, I challenge you to be forthcoming and set me straight."

"All right," Elizabeth said quietly. "You figured us out. But we wanted to keep this a secret for the evening. This is your night, Malinda. Yours and Will's."

"I just knew it!" Malinda clapped her hands. "I'm so happy for you!"

Elizabeth made a nervous smile. "Thank you."

"Congratulations," Will told Eli.

Eli gave him a slightly uneasy smile. "Well, truth be told, I reckon I owe you my gratitude, Will Bramford."

Will looked confused. "How so?"

"I'm obliged to you for not stealing my girl." Eli chuckled. "It took me a while to figure things out. But I'm sure thankful you left her for me."

Will's brow creased, but then he chuckled too. "Now that you mention it, Eli, I can see that I should be equally grateful to you."

"How is that?" Now Eli looked confused.

"I'm obliged that you had already stolen Elizabeth's heart." Will looked at Malinda with real tenderness. "That allowed me to wait for this one."

"And all's well that ends well," Elizabeth proclaimed with relief.

"Oh, no," Eli told her. "This is just the beginning."

Chapter Two

I insist that you and the children come stay at my house until Will and I wed in December," Malinda told Elizabeth as they gathered in front of the small building that functioned as both the school and the church. The service had just ended, but as usual the congregation continued to visit outside in the autumn sunshine.

"But I thought Will's girls were going to be staying with you."

"They will be, starting this week. But Emily and Amelia came up with a delightful idea." Malinda pointed to where the older girls were circled together, chattering among themselves like a flock of chickens. "They suggested that the boys sleep in the loft of the barn like they did a couple of weeks ago. They all claimed it was very comfortable. Then you and I and Ruth will share my room. And Emily, Susannah, Amelia, and Belinda can share the sleeping loft in the house—we already have enough beds up there."

Elizabeth did the arithmetic in her head. "That's ten people," she told Malinda. "Won't that be crowding your little house?"

"Not at all. Besides, it's only temporary. For the next few months, we'll make the most of it and have fun," Malinda assured her.

"That would be wonderful," Elizabeth confessed. "Especially when the weather gets wetter and colder. I'm sure Ruth and JT would enjoy being there, and they'll appreciate being closer to school. If you're certain we won't be a burden…" Elizabeth tried to imagine everyone at mealtime. "Ten hungry people at suppertime might be a challenge."

"We'll all work together." Malinda nudged Elizabeth's elbow, nodding over to where Belinda was talking with one of the Levine boys. "And unless I'm mistaken, it's only a matter of time before Belinda will be living under someone else's roof."

"*Really?*" Elizabeth glanced over to where Belinda was chatting with the tall, serious-looking young man. "Which one is he anyway?"

"That's the oldest boy, Jacob. He's twenty-three, I believe, and as dependable as the sun. He really stepped up after his father died." Malinda shook her head. "The second son, Charles…well now, he's another story."

"What do you mean?"

Malinda frowned and then lowered her voice. "Charles took an Indian woman for his wife several years ago…although they're not legally married." She made a tsk-tsk sound. "But I think they have a child."

"Oh…" Elizabeth thought of Eli's previous wife. She shuddered to think what Malinda would say if she knew about that. And yet at the same time, she had the strangest urge to just blurt it out.

"Hello, hello!" Lavinia called out as she hurried over to join them. "I missed church this morning because Augustus was feeling under the weather."

"Nothing serious, I hope," Elizabeth said.

"No, I don't think so."

"Because, as you know, my mother is good with herbal medicines." Elizabeth looked over to where Clara and Asa were visiting with a couple about their age.

"Yes, I'll keep that in mind. Evelyn is with him now." Lavinia looked up at the sky. "It's another marvelous day. If this weather keeps up we will have the mercantile completely finished soon."

"I saw it on my way to church this morning," Elizabeth said. "It's just like Ruthie told me—it looks like a *real* building."

Lavinia laughed. "It *is* a real building. And we're getting the store all set up downstairs. Now if only we can get the living quarters finished before the rains come. I hear the rain in this region can be relentless."

"It's what makes things grow and keeps it green," Malinda told her.

"And wet," Lavinia added.

"I wonder what the men are discussing so intently," Malinda said with a tinge of concern in her voice. "I hope there isn't any trouble brewing somewhere."

"Trouble?" Lavinia's brows arched. "What sort of trouble?"

"Oh, nothing." Malinda waved her hand dismissively, but Elizabeth could see the fear in her eyes.

"Well, I'll be pleased to take you up on your offer," Elizabeth told Malinda.

"What offer?" Lavinia asked.

So Malinda explained the plan to take in Elizabeth and the children along with Will's daughters.

"Oh, my. You will have a full house," Lavinia said.

"A full house and a full barn," Malinda told her.

"And everyone will help with the work," Elizabeth said. "Many hands make light work."

Malinda laughed. "Yes...perhaps I will become a lady of leisure soon."

"Out here in the West?" Lavinia scowled. "I don't believe any of us will ever experience leisurely living again. Sometimes I dream about life back in Boston. It seems so far away…like a different country."

Malinda grew serious. "Do you regret your emigration?"

Lavinia pursed her lips as she looked around at the young people talking and frolicking about. "No, no…for the sake of my children and my husband…I think we made the right decision." She gave Elizabeth a sheepish smile. "Although I'm sure there were times on the trail when I highly regretted it—many, many a time."

Just as Malinda and Elizabeth were confirming plans to join households later in the day, Eli and Will and Hugh came over to join the women. "I've been promised a sneak peek into the mercantile," Eli told Elizabeth. "Would you like to come with me?"

"Yes," she said eagerly. "Very much so."

"Oh, good," Lavinia told her. "I've been so eager to show it off to my friends." She lowered her voice. "However, we can't make it appear as though we are open for business yet. Especially since it's the Sabbath. But do come and see what we've done."

They called out to the children, explaining where they were going and that they'd be back shortly. And then they all trekked down the street to where the most impressive and most talked-about building was progressing nicely. Like so many buildings in the frontier towns they'd passed through on the Oregon Trail, the mercantile had a false front, which made it seem even taller than its two stories. Hugh unlocked and opened the front doors, and Lavinia hurried in to light some kerosene lamps.

"You even have a glass window," Elizabeth said. "So nice to get that sunlight in here. And it faces south too. Very smart."

"And we hope to put in a few more glass windows next year," Lavinia gushed. "Now if anyone would have told me a year ago that I would be swooning over glass windows, I would have thought they were daft." She laughed. "But, oh my, how times have changed."

Elizabeth looked at the wooden shelves that were being loaded with provisions and supplies. Many crates were still unopened, stacked in the back of the room. "I can see you're getting ready for business," she told Lavinia. "When will you be officially open?"

"We've actually been serving a few customers already," Lavinia confided. "But we plan to have a grand opening ceremony next Saturday. Isn't that so, Hugh?"

"That's right," he called from where he was showing the men something over in the tool section. "I expect to receive another shipment from Empire City midweek. Hopefully we'll have most of the stock unloaded and put out by then."

"It looks like you've got plenty of goods already," Elizabeth said after they'd browsed a bit. "If today wasn't Sunday I'd be doing some shopping."

"So would I," Malinda said eagerly. "It's so wonderful to have a real store in our settlement."

"Well, you two come on over tomorrow afternoon if you like," Lavinia told the women as they were preparing to leave. "Invite Clara to come too. I'll open the doors especially for you folks."

Before long the children were gathered, and Elizabeth and Eli and the children began the walk back to their homesteads. But they hadn't gone far when her parents and Matthew and Jess came along in their wagon, offering a ride. The children, acting as if they were worn out, happily hopped in the back.

"I don't mind walking," Elizabeth called out to her parents.

Asa winked at her and nodded at Eli. "I'm sure you don't."

By now most of the settlement seemed well aware that Elizabeth and Eli were betrothed, which made having some time alone with the man who would one day be her husband even more precious. "I miss having the use of my wagon," she told Eli as they walked down the rutted road. "But I'm still using it to store our goods, and it seems silly to drive it around fully loaded like it is. But maybe once the house is built...maybe this winter we'll have it to use."

"From what I hear it's hard to drive a wagon in these parts once

the rains start. It doesn't take long for these roads to turn to mud."
He nodded toward the river lazily meandering alongside the road.
"Seems the best way to travel might be the river. That's what the
coastal Indians do to get around."

"My father has wondered about that very thing," she told him.
"He's talked about using the oxen team to pull a barge up the river
from the ocean. But as far as I know, no one has tried that yet."

"The Prescotts would benefit from that kind of venture," he said
as he reached for her hand. "As it is, they have to go all the way
to Empire City to get their shipments, and that will be difficult
once the rains come. From the looks of the mercantile, Empire
City has been a good resource for them. Hugh tells me there's an
enterprising family running a sawmill up there on the bay. Having
access to milled lumber has hastened the Prescotts' building process considerably."

Elizabeth nodded. "I was trying not to feel envious at how
quickly they've been able to get their store built." She turned to
look at him, still feeling slightly amazed that he was here with her
now...that they would be married in the not-so-distant future. "But
money is not everything."

He laughed as he squeezed her hand warmly in his own. "No, it
certainly is not."

"And there are many families with more challenges than ours,"
she confessed. "I worry that the Flanders household will suffer
this winter. They seem so ill prepared. And yet Flo seems utterly
unconcerned."

"This land is generous," he said. "Those who are willing to work
hard will benefit from the natural resources." Again he pointed to
the river. "I hear the fishing is good this time of year."

"That's for certain." She nodded. "Father and Matthew and JT
have had some good luck catching salmon. Father has been running
his smoker almost continuously."

"He's a wise man. And the woods abound with deer and bear and other sources of meat, if a man is good with a gun."

"Yes." She smiled at him. Eli was an excellent hunter and fisherman. She couldn't even remember how many times he'd shared game with them on the Oregon Trail.

"And Bert has a useful trade with blacksmithing," Eli added. "Surely he can trade for food and provisions for his family. I know I'd be happy to trade with him."

Certain that no one was around to see them now, she stopped walking and turned to look into his face. "I'm so very grateful you're here, Eli." She felt her heart fluttering. "I feel very blessed to know you will be my husband."

His eyes glimmered as blue as the river as he leaned down to tenderly kiss her. "I feel equally blessed, Elizabeth," he said quietly. "More than equally. By marrying you I get a wonderful family as well. Do you know how much that means to me?" He embraced her now, holding her close. Elizabeth couldn't remember the last time she'd felt this incredibly happy...she didn't even want to.

As they continued walking, Elizabeth told him the news that she and the children would be moving in with Malinda. "I have to admit that I won't miss camping," she told him. "I won't miss waking up with everything damp from dew."

"Well, if you're not going to be camping there, maybe I should camp there myself. That way I could work on the house without having to go back and forth to your parents' place. It might speed up the process."

"Yes," she said eagerly. "That's a wonderful idea."

"And I could take care of the livestock if you like."

Elizabeth considered this. "I already arranged to bring them over to Malinda's," she said. "She has fencing for the horses and cows. And the hens are just starting to lay, and I figure with ten people in the house, we could use the eggs."

He nodded. "Yes, that's a good plan. But perhaps I can keep your team to help with the logging."

"Yes, of course," she told him. "You keep the Percherons here and put them to good use."

"That should help speed things along." He peered up at the sky. "As it is, we're getting a mighty late start, Elizabeth."

She nodded somberly. "I know. Believe me, I know."

"I hear that building becomes quite challenging once the rains start. Mud makes everything much more difficult and slow. Some of the men think we're foolish to start building at all this late."

"What do you think?" she asked.

He grinned. "I think I'd better get busy."

She smiled back at him. "We'll use the team and the wagon to get our things moved over to Malinda's this afternoon. And then I'll send them back with JT."

JT and Ruth were both eager to relocate to Malinda's. Not only did it mean being with cousins, it also made the trek to school a little shorter. The three of them worked together to break down their camp. Then they packed and loaded their wagon—almost like they used to do each morning while traveling the Oregon Trail. Elizabeth drove the wagon, and JT drove the livestock. The plan was to let their animals share the pasture with Malinda's, and perhaps Goldie would be with calf by the time they moved back to their own property.

At Malinda's they unloaded everything they felt they'd need for their stay. And while JT returned the wagon back to the property so that Eli could have use of the team for logging, Elizabeth helped Malinda to get supper started and Ruth went outside with Bart and Susannah to help get the chickens situated.

"Oh, Malinda," Elizabeth said happily. "It is so lovely to prepare food indoors again." She didn't even mind that Malinda cooked over an open fire or that her kitchen setup was much more rustic than what Elizabeth had left behind in Kentucky. She knew Malinda had made similar sacrifices years earlier.

"I remember that feeling well," Malinda told her. "The first time I cooked inside my house after so many months of cooking outside over a campfire—it was simply wonderful."

"And I don't even have to wipe the grit out of the bowl before I mix up the biscuits." Elizabeth laughed as she peered inside a clean yellow bowl. "What a treat!"

"We decided that Will's children won't move in here until next weekend," Malinda told Elizabeth. "I thought that would give us time to get settled a bit. Plus we can get some things moved around and prepare for our additional household members." Now she explained how she wanted to transform a section of the barn loft into the boys' bedroom. "We'll put clothing hooks on the wall, and I have a rather worn commode we can put up there with a pitcher and basin—although I expect the boys will do most of their washing up on the porch. I thought we could put some crates up there for storage and seating. And I want to make sure there are safe places to hang lanterns. We don't want them burning down the barn."

Elizabeth blinked. "No, we certainly do not."

"Also, I hoped to get some produce put up for winter. And I have a quilt to finish and...well, so many, many things. Trust me, we will have our work cut out for us, my friend. I hope you don't mind."

"I'm so happy to be of any help—and so grateful to have a roof over my head."

Malinda beamed at her. "It's wonderful to have you here. You know, Elizabeth, it reminds me of when we were young women... remember how we helped each other with our trousseaus before our marriages?" She shook her head. "Did you ever dream we would do it all over again?"

"Make trousseaus?" Elizabeth looked up from measuring the flour.

"No, that's not what I meant." Malinda chuckled. "But do you remember how our families thought we were so silly for wanting to imitate Queen Victoria's wedding back in those days?"

"Looking back...I think I understand their perspective now."

Malinda paused from chopping an onion. "But we did have fun, didn't we?"

"We did." Elizabeth sighed to remember what felt like a lifetime ago.

"And it feels like we will have a bit of fun again."

Elizabeth held up the spoon she was using to measure salt. "I suppose fun is similar to salt...a little bit goes a long way...but it does make life tasty."

"You and me, Elizabeth, marrying two fine men...all over again. Did you ever think this would happen?"

"Never in a hundred years." Elizabeth stirred the batter.

They worked quietly together for a while. Then as Elizabeth was rolling out the biscuit dough, Malinda spoke up again.

"God truly is the giver of second chances," she said quietly. "For both you and me. I am so grateful."

Elizabeth nodded. "Yes...so am I." As she used a water glass to cut the biscuits, Elizabeth pondered Malinda's words. It truly was ironic that she and Malinda found themselves in this position again—except now they weren't starry-eyed young girls trying to imitate a royal wedding. Now they were two widowed mothers... frontier women who were preparing to wed men who had both had previous marriages. Strange.

Maybe it was just a fact of life that one never knew what was coming around the next corner. Perhaps the only thing you could fully expect was the unexpected. Anyway, it certainly provided ample opportunity to trust God.

Chapter Three

The next couple of days seemed to fly past. And, as much as the two women accomplished, it seemed that Malinda's chore list seemed to get longer by the end of each day. Elizabeth knew this was partly because Malinda had let so much go after losing John last winter. And there was so much she wanted done before her wedding in mid-December. But Elizabeth enjoyed pitching in. Many hands truly did make light work.

"I think I'll go over to check on my property today," Elizabeth told Malinda on Wednesday morning.

"Don't you mean to check on Eli?" Malinda teased.

Elizabeth grinned. "As a matter of fact, I wouldn't mind saying hello to him."

"Why don't you take him his dinner," Malinda suggested. "I'm sure he'd enjoyed some of that bread you baked yesterday."

"A very good idea." Elizabeth took care as she prepared a basket of food for Eli. Perhaps he would want to have a picnic with her.

Because JT and Ruth had used Molly to ride to school, Elizabeth walked. But it felt good to walk. She could feel autumn in the air, and she noticed more leaves were turning lovely shades of yellow, orange, and red. And although it was cooler, it was still a pleasant sunny day. Perfect for an impromptu picnic. Feeling excited to see what sort of progress Eli was making, she hastened her pace. How many logs would he have cut by now? She doubted any of them would be laid on the foundation yet. But perhaps they would be cut to length and notched. She knew that Brady planned to go over and help Eli once he was ready to start setting the logs in place. It was only a matter of time.

She listened as she walked, wondering if she was hearing the ring of Eli's ax, or perhaps the sound was coming from Matthew's or Father's projects. She did hear birds chirping merrily and the gurgle of the creek flowing to the river. But as she got closer to her property, she heard no sounds of sawing or chopping or anything.

Finally at the homesite, she looked around in dismay. Eli was nowhere to be seen. Neither was his Appaloosa. Not only that, but her beloved Percherons, Beau and Bella, were gone too. Perhaps he'd taken them into the woods to pull some logs. But now she noticed something else. Her wagon was missing from where she normally kept it parked near the house. In its place was a pile that was neatly covered in tarps. On closer inspection, she discovered that this pile was all the goods and supplies she'd been storing in the wagon. Was Eli using the wagon to carry logs?

She walked over to the section of woods that they'd both decided had the best selection of trees to fell and called out Eli's name. No answer. She went a bit farther, calling for him every once in a while, but still no answer. She paused to listen, but again heard only the birds and the creek.

Returning to the homesite, she sat down on the foundation and pondered this. Where was Eli? And where was her team and her wagon? Of the few possessions that she'd been able to bring across the Oregon Trail, none were more valuable than her team and her wagon. And now they were gone…

She opened the basket and broke off a piece of bread, munching on it as she considered the possibilities. Perhaps Eli had taken the team and the wagon over to help Matthew or her father. She stood and smoothed her skirt. Of course, that had to be it. Eli had recently mentioned that the sooner they finished their houses, the more help he and Elizabeth would have to finish their own. Perhaps he was using the wagon to help them in some way. However, as she walked, she couldn't think of how.

Arriving at her parents' homesite, she discovered Matthew and Brady helping her father set the rafters in place for his roof. They were all perched up high, and not wanting to distract them, she decided to seek out her mother instead.

She found Clara over by their wagon and tent, hanging some clothes on the line to dry. Elizabeth greeted her and then inquired about Eli.

"I haven't seen him since Sunday." Clara frowned as she pushed a strand of graying hair back into her bonnet. "Is something wrong?"

Elizabeth forced a smile as she reached for one of her father's shirts, giving it a good shake before she pegged it to the line. "Not really. I just couldn't find him and I thought he might have come over here."

"No. Your father thought maybe he was going to give a hand with the rafters, but he hasn't been by." Clara pegged the last damp towel up.

"Oh…" Elizabeth tried to conceal her concern.

"Are you all settled in at Malinda's?"

"Yes. It's been lovely having a real roof overhead." Elizabeth held up the basket. "Would you folks like some bread? It comes out a little nicer than what you can make in the outdoor oven."

"That would be lovely. Jess is making blackberry jam today. Perhaps we can enjoy some on this. Which reminds me, did Jess tell you that she got a letter from Ruby?"

"No. So how are Ruby and Doris doing?" Elizabeth still missed these two women, but she did understand their decision to remain in Empire City for the winter. Their plan was to open a restaurant, and according to Matthew, they wanted to liquidate some of the merchandise they brought with them from St. Louis. They hoped to make enough money in Empire City to join the others next summer, stake a claim, and build a house.

"It sounds like they're off to a good start," Clara told her. "They've opened their restaurant in a little cabin that's down near the docks, and it sounds like they're making good money."

Now Elizabeth updated her mother on all that she and Malinda had been doing the past couple of days, as well as all the plans that Malinda had for them yet to do. "I think she's trying to catch up with everything she'd let go after John died." She sighed. "I remember how that was." She smiled. "Thank goodness you were nearby when I needed you."

"Well, I'm sure Malinda is happy to have you with her now. But it'll be a busy place with all those children staying there. You two will certainly have your hands full. Although the older girls should be of some help around the house. I assume they're done with their schooling by now."

"Amelia is still in school, and Belinda has been helping Mrs. Taylor with the younger children. So the girls won't be around very much during the weekdays."

"Perhaps that will be nice for you and Malinda. I'm sure you both have plenty to do to prepare for your upcoming nuptials and whatnot." Clara made a happy sigh.

"So when does Father think your cabin will be finished?" Elizabeth asked as a distraction from speaking of weddings. She didn't want her mother to guess she was worried about Eli.

"Your father still thinks we'll be able to move indoors by mid-November. I sure hope he's right. Once the rains we keep hearing about start to come…well, I'm afraid that living in the tent will turn into a rather soggy affair." She scowled at the tent. "I told Asa that I might move into the house whether it's finished or not."

"Poor Mother." Elizabeth put a hand on her shoulder. "You have been very patient through all this."

"I suppose my patience is starting to wear a bit thin." She rubbed the small of her back and sighed. "Or else I'm just getting too old for all this outdoor living."

"You are not too old." Elizabeth thought for a moment. "And I'll tell you what. If the weather changes and you're still not in your cabin, I'm sure Malinda will be glad to take you in."

Clara made an amused smile. "That's sweet, dear. But poor Malinda—her house will be full to overflowing."

"She has a barn too," Elizabeth reminded her. "I'm sure we could make room for you in there. Maybe I'd join you."

Clara laughed. "Well, I suppose if it comes down to that…I might be willing to sleep in a barn."

They went into the tent, making themselves comfortable in the chairs and visiting a while longer, but the whole time Elizabeth's missing betrothed was lodged firmly in the back of her mind. Where was Eli? Why wasn't he working on their house? Where was her team? And what about her wagon?

"Well, I should get back to Malinda's." Elizabeth slowly stood. "She's probably added half a dozen more chores to her list by now."

Her mother chuckled as she hugged Elizabeth. "Thanks for the bread, dear. And don't worry about Eli. He's a good man."

Elizabeth smiled. "I know he is. I just wish I knew *where* he is."

"Well, if anyone can take care of himself, he can."

"That's true enough."

As they emerged from the tent, Elizabeth could see that the men were still intently getting a rafter into place. "If I do see Eli, I'll encourage him to come over here to help Matthew and Father," she promised.

"And the sooner they get these houses finished, the more help Eli will have for your house." Clara's eyes twinkled. "And the sooner you two can have that wedding."

"I suppose. But getting started so late in the year…" Elizabeth shook her head. "Well, the children and I might be the ones who end up living in Malinda's barn this winter. At this rate, our wedding might not be until the end of next summer."

"Oh, dear." Clara frowned. "I hope not. Let's pray that house goes up quickly, Elizabeth."

"Well, God willing…maybe that will happen."

Elizabeth did pray as she walked back to Malinda's. She prayed that Eli was all right. She knew it was senseless to be worried about him. Her mother was correct about Eli. If anyone could take care of himself, it was Eli. He'd proven that to them on the trail over and over. Not only did he take care of himself, he helped take care of all the travelers as well. Surely, Eli was just fine.

"So how was your little picnic?" Malinda asked when Elizabeth came into the house.

Elizabeth set the empty basket on the table and sighed. "Actually, I didn't see him." She explained that the wagon and team were gone. "So I dropped the bread and other food at my parents'. My mother was most appreciative."

Malinda looked up from where she was sewing on the quilt she hoped to finish before Will's girls arrived. She planned to put it on the bed that Belinda and Amelia would share upstairs. "Where do you suppose he went?"

"Maybe he found a better section of land to get timber for the house." Elizabeth removed her bonnet.

"Yes…that must be it."

Elizabeth sat down beside her and threaded a needle, and for a while the two of them just stitched together in silence. "Malinda…?" Elizabeth began tentatively.

"Yes?" Malinda kept her eyes on her sewing.

"You wrote about the Indian skirmishes…that happened last year. Remember? In the letter I received while we were traveling."

"Yes." She nodded as she tied a knot and then clipped the thread.

"Well…I haven't seen a single Indian since I arrived here. I assumed that they've moved on. Is that right?"

Malinda frowned as she measured of a new length of thread. "Yes…that's mostly right."

"Mostly?"

"It's not something people care to speak of much, Elizabeth. But yes, the Indians have been relocated."

"Relocated?"

"Yes. After the troubles…well, the army came out and rounded them up. They took them up north I believe."

Elizabeth felt a mixture of emotions now. Her first feeling was one of relief. Her fears that Eli had been ambushed by savages who had stolen her horses and wagon seemed to be unfounded. But her next concern was for the Indians. "All of the Indians were rounded up?" she asked. "Even the women and children?" She thought about some of the Indian women she'd seen along the way. She remembered the old woman that she and Ruth had purchased moccasins from. And she remembered Eli telling her about many of them being so peaceful…about them taking him in…about his wife.

"That's what I understand. Well, except for Charles Levine. Remember I told you about him—the one who took up with the Indian woman. From what I've heard, those two are hiding out somewhere. But if the army finds them, she'll probably be taken up north too."

"Do you think that's fair?" Elizabeth asked quietly.

"Fair?" Malinda looked up. "Some of those Indians ambushed settlers, Elizabeth. Do you not recall those stories?"

"Yes…I do recall." Elizabeth nodded. "But that was only *some* of the Indians, right? And certainly not the women and children. Wouldn't that be like some of our men doing something wrong or illegal and then all of us being rounded up and put in prison with them? Would that be fair?"

Just then the children came bursting into the house, and the question and the conversation became lost in the noise and commotion. Elizabeth tried to console herself that Eli was safe—he hadn't been taken by Indians. But at the same time, she felt disconcerted to think that Indian women and children had been forced off their land. Furthermore, she knew that Eli would feel even more upset to hear of this…or perhaps he already knew. After all, it was an old story in this new country…a very old story.

Chapter Four

On Thursday morning Elizabeth convinced JT that it was time for him and Ruth to start walking to school with their cousins. "It was one thing to ride Molly from our property, but you're much closer to school here at Malinda's," she told them. "If Susanna can make the walk, then it seems Ruth is big enough as well." Of course, her real reason for this was so that she would have the use of Molly. Her plan was to ride to her property, and if Eli wasn't working on the house as she expected he would be, she would ride all around the area to search for him.

After helping Malinda with the morning chores, Elizabeth saddled Molly and set out. She had been unable to sleep the night before, worried that Eli had been injured while felling timber or attacked by a wild animal or possibly even a renegade Indian. In the dark of the night, anything seemed possible. But now, by daylight, she felt more hopeful. In all likelihood she would arrive at her homesite and find that Eli was busily at work on the house. If that was the situation, she would simply act as if she were out for a ride, spend some time with him, and then return to Malinda's.

However, when she arrived on her property, everything looked exactly as it had the previous day. Eli, the team, and the wagon were nowhere to be seen. So she rode Molly all about the property, sometimes calling out for Eli. She even followed the creek to the river, thinking perhaps he'd been fishing and had fallen in. But her searching was in vain. Eli seemed to have vanished into thin air—along with her beloved team and her wagon.

"I don't know what to make of it," she told Malinda after she'd turned Molly out to pasture. "Eli was nowhere to be found."

Malinda looked up from her churning with concerned eyes. "What do you suppose has become of him?"

Elizabeth removed her riding jacket and just shook her head. "I have no idea."

"How well do you know Eli?" Malinda asked.

"How well?" Elizabeth hung her jacket on a peg on the door. "He was our scout coming across the Oregon Trail...I'm sure I mentioned that to you already."

"Yes, I know. But before that. What sort of life had he lived?"

"He'd been a trapper," Elizabeth said absently. "So he definitely knows how to live off the land and survive."

Malinda frowned. "I don't want to sound critical, Elizabeth, but trappers are an unusual sort. Very independent of society. And some of them seem to live by their own rules."

"What do you mean?"

"Is it possible that Eli is a dishonest man?"

"No," Elizabeth said quickly. "Of course not. I trust Eli implicitly."

"Well, your team and your wagon are very valuable around here. Mrs. Levine's husband traded his team of horses for 500 acres of valuable river land several years ago, and I'm sure your lovely Percherons would bring—"

"No." Elizabeth firmly shook her head. "Eli would not do that. I know it for a fact. Eli is a good man."

Malinda focused her attention on the churn, and Elizabeth went outside to check on her livestock. At least that is what she told herself as she left the house. Mostly she wanted to get away from Malinda's suspicious accusations. Malinda did not know Eli the way Elizabeth did. As Elizabeth went out to the chicken coop, she tried not to let Malinda's words do any more damage. Still she felt perplexed. Where was he?

Elizabeth hadn't told Malinda about Eli's previous marriage to an Indian woman. Just hearing Malinda speaking of the local Indians convinced Elizabeth where Malinda's sympathies lay. And if Malinda was suspicious of Eli now, how much more so would she be if she knew everything about him? Which brought Elizabeth back to Malinda's piercing question—how well did she know Eli?

Was it possible she had agreed to marry a man of low character? Had her heart tricked her? Eli was certainly handsome and charming, and she was definitely attracted to him. But really, how well did she know him? And yet she had accepted his proposal of marriage. She had allowed him into her world—and her children's. Was it possible that she'd made an enormous mistake?

No, no, no, she told herself as she worked on mending the bit of chicken-coop fence that Ruth had mentioned to her this morning. Eli was a good man. She knew it. And yet…where was he? Why would he leave—taking her horses and wagon without saying a word to her? It made no sense. Absolutely none.

Elizabeth kept her concerns to herself as the house grew busy and noisy with the children coming home from school. She remained quiet as she helped Malinda with supper preparations. She feigned intent interest as she listened to her children's stories of school. And she pretended to be absorbed in mending a pair of JT's torn trousers as the children headed off to bed.

Finally, it was just Elizabeth and Malinda sitting by the fireplace, neither of them speaking. Elizabeth was just tying off the last thread on her mending when Malinda cleared her throat. "I know you are fretting about Eli," she said quietly. "And I fear I may have overstepped my bounds when I spoke of him earlier."

"I'm convinced it was only because you love me," Elizabeth said quietly. "And you love my children. You are concerned for our welfare."

"Yes," Malinda said eagerly. "That is exactly right. But I realize that you know Eli much better than I do. I feel certain that your instincts about him are correct, Elizabeth. Please, forgive me for casting any shadow of doubt upon him. I'm so sorry."

Her unexpected apology caught Elizabeth off guard, and she felt tears filling her eyes. "Of course I forgive you," Elizabeth said in a tear-choked voice. "But perhaps you were right. It's possible I don't know Eli as well as I'd like." Elizabeth looked up to the open sleeping loft, knowing that it was possible that the older girls could hear her words. But at least Ruth wasn't sleeping up there. She was in Malinda's bedroom with the door closed. Even so, Elizabeth lowered her voice. "I can't imagine he would have taken my wagon and my team," she whispered. "But I would be so devastated if that was so. Not just for my heart's sake, but because that is such a big part of our livelihood, Malinda. I would feel as if I had robbed my own children." She looked at her with tear-filled eyes. "Do you understand what I'm saying?"

Malinda nodded solemnly. "Being a widowed mother of children is an enormous responsibility. Especially out here in the wilderness."

"Do you think I've made a grave mistake?" Elizabeth whispered as she reached into her skirt pocket for her hanky. "In trusting Eli as I have?"

Malinda set her knitting aside. "Oh, Elizabeth, I don't know what to say." She reached over and grasped her hand. "But whatever happens, you know that you have your family nearby to help you through it. That is so important."

"Yes…that is true." Elizabeth wiped her eyes. "If Eli is still missing tomorrow, I will go and speak to my father."

"That would be wise." Malinda squeezed her hand. "In the meantime we will both be praying for Eli's welfare…and his safe return." Malinda released Elizabeth's hand and then pursed her lips. "I know I assured you that all the Indians had been cleared from this area," she said very quietly. "But it is possible that some of the renegades are still at large."

Elizabeth considered this. "But Eli is very smart about Indians. He got along quite well with the plains Indians. Besides, I thought the coastal tribes were peaceful. That's what Eli told me."

"Perhaps that was partly true. But those Rogue warriors were unpredictable. Just two years ago, there was such a bloody battle. Nearly thirty Indians were killed by the gold miners, and the remaining warriors retaliated against settlers with great aggression. We lived in fear of attacks in these parts. It's only been within the past year, since the tribes were removed, that life quieted down. But you never know…you just never know."

"I understand your fear of the Indians," Elizabeth said slowly. "But do you ever feel sympathy for them? Do you ever consider that they were living here…relatively peaceably until the white settlers came? Do you ever wonder how you would feel if we were in their place?"

Malinda made a tired sigh. "Sometimes John and I spoke of this very thing. We even had Joel Palmer as a guest in our home. He was the Oregon Superintendent of Indian Affairs. And John felt Mr. Palmer was a fair man in regard to the Indians. Mr. Palmer opposed the hostility that some of the settlers were demonstrating toward the Indians. But then General Lane came along. Most of the settlers favored General Lane's approach. However, John felt the general's answer to the Indian troubles was extreme and…well, John felt it was unjust."

"I always admired John," Elizabeth declared, "but now I admire him more than ever. I'm sure Eli would have liked him too."

"Yes, that's good and well, but John's views on the Indians were not typical of settlers, Elizabeth. And it did not win him friends. To be honest, he and I often disagreed. But in all fairness, my concerns were for the safety of my family. And the truth is I was greatly relieved when the Indians were removed."

"Even the women and children?" Elizabeth challenged. "Were you fearful of them too?"

Malinda gave Elizabeth a somewhat exasperated look. "If the women and children remained, the men would want to return. Also, who would hunt and provide for the women and children? Have you considered these things?"

Elizabeth admitted she had not, and then both women agreed they were tired and began to get ready for bed. But once again, Elizabeth found herself unable to sleep.

On Friday morning, Elizabeth hurried to finish her morning chores, saddled up Molly, and once again rode over to her property. She didn't even feel surprised when it looked the same as before. And she knew what she had to do, but it was with heavy heart that she rode over to speak to her father. She knew this news would be nearly as disturbing to him as it was to her. Eli was gone. Her team was gone. Her wagon was gone. In all likelihood, she and the children would need to stay with her parents during the winter—all five of them in the small one-room cabin.

She braced herself as she dismounted from her horse. The men were still on the roof, but it appeared that they were nearly finished with the rafters. Instead of disturbing them, she set off to find her mother. Clara and Jess were at their campsite, preparing the midday meal. "Hello," Elizabeth called in a falsely cheery voice.

"Welcome," Clara said as she replaced a lid on the big cast-iron pot.

"You're just in time for dinner," Jess said warmly.

Elizabeth joined them by the fire, feeling again as if she were on the verge of tears. Telling them this bad news was going to be so hard. She prayed God would give her strength not to break down. She needed to be strong.

Now Clara peered curiously at Elizabeth's face. "Is something wrong?"

Elizabeth nodded. "Yes. As a matter of fact—"

"The children?" Clara said urgently. "Are they—"

"Ruth and JT are fine," she assured her. "At school."

"Oh." Clara made a relieved sigh.

"It's Eli," Elizabeth began slowly, wondering how to say this.

"Oh, no," Jess exclaimed. "Has he been hurt—"

"He's gone," Elizabeth said solemnly.

"Gone?" Jess looked confused.

"How long has he been gone?" Clara asked. "Since the last time I saw you?"

"Yes...although it's possible he was gone before that." She shrugged. "I actually have no idea."

"Do you think he went hunting?" Jess asked hopefully. "Matthew and Pa have been wishing they could do some serious hunting, but they need to get the roofs on first."

"No, I doubt he would take my wagon and team to go hunting," Elizabeth told her. "Along with his own horse."

Jess' eyes grew wide. "He took your wagon and team?"

Elizabeth simply nodded, swallowing the lump in her throat.

"Perhaps he's felling timber," Clara suggested. "Would he use the wagon to bring it back?"

"What do you think?"

Clara frowned. "Your father and brother didn't use the wagons..."

"And I searched all over my property. He's not there. He's gone."

"But that makes no sense," Jess said.

"I know." Elizabeth sat on one of the chairs by the fire, putting her elbows on her knees and her head in her hands.

Clara placed a hand on Elizabeth's shoulder but said nothing.

"I just thought you should know," Elizabeth said quietly. "I'd tell Father, but I don't want to interrupt their work."

"They'll be quitting soon...for dinner," Clara told her as she went over to tend the fire.

"There must be some logical explanation for this." Jess sat next to Elizabeth, putting her arm around her shoulders. "Eli wouldn't just take off like that. He loves you, Elizabeth."

Elizabeth turned to look at her. "What makes you so sure?"

"I've seen him looking at you," Jess said. "Dozens of times. Starting out on the trail. And since he got here. He looks at you the same way Matthew looks at me."

The lump in her throat seemed to be growing. "Maybe…but he's still gone."

"I cannot believe he would run off with your wagon and your team," Clara said a bit sharply. "I just cannot believe it."

Elizabeth stood now. She knew if she remained she would break into tears. Mother and Jess didn't need that. Neither did the men. "I just wanted you to know," she said sadly to her mother. "Please tell Father for me. And Matthew and Brady."

"But don't you want to stay for—"

"No thank you." Elizabeth adjusted the brim of James' old hat and stood straight. "I need to get back to help Malinda."

Jess gave her a sympathetic look. "You're all right?"

Elizabeth nodded firmly. "I'm a frontier woman," she declared. "Just like you two. And we all need to be strong. I'll get past this…in time." Then she turned on the heel of her boot and marched over to where she'd tethered Molly to a tree. She quickly climbed into the saddle and nudged the horse with her knees, biting back tears and steadying herself in the saddle as Molly broke into an awkward trot.

What she'd just told Clara and Jess was true…or rather, she wanted it to be true. She would make it true. She was a frontier woman, and she would be strong. With God's help, even with her heart breaking, she would remain strong.

Chapter Five

Elizabeth had just turned onto the road that ran past Malinda's farm when she noticed a wagon in the distance. Few of the settlers had wagons, and that in itself was enough to get her attention. However, it wasn't really the wagon that drew her eye—it was the team of handsome black horses. Beau and Bella!

She kneed Molly to a gallop, hurrying to see who was driving her wagon. But then she pulled back on the reins, slowing the strong horse. What if it was a thief...or a band of renegades? She wasn't armed. She didn't want a confrontation. So she simply walked Molly slowly down the road, narrowing her eyes as she attempted to see who the driver was. But as she drew nearer, she could tell it was Eli. And now her emotions were mixed. On one hand, she was greatly relieved. On the other, she was seriously irked.

"Eli," she said calmly as he slowed the wagon to a stop and she pulled Molly up alongside him. "What are you doing here?"

His face glowed with a huge smile. "Coming home." But now his smile faded. "Is something wrong?"

She took in a slow deep breath. "Where have you been?"

His brow creased. "Didn't you get my note?"

"What note?"

"The note I wrote to you on Sunday night. The night before I left. I weighted it down with a stone. It was right inside the doorway of the house, along with a bunch of wildflowers in a tin cup. I thought for sure you would find my note when you came looking for me."

"Inside the doorway of the house...?" She pressed her lips together. "I didn't even go in the doorway."

Now he looked slightly alarmed. "So you didn't know where I was? Where I went?"

She shook her head. Now she felt a mixture of shame and curiosity. "I had no idea where you were...it seemed you'd vanished into thin air."

"I'm so sorry, Elizabeth. I hope you weren't too concerned."

She blinked and swallowed. Be strong. "To be honest, I was quite worried, Eli. I thought some harm had come to you. I searched all over the property for you. Then I thought perhaps renegade Indians had done something to you...stolen the horses and the wagon."

He reached over and put a hand on her cheek. "Oh, Elizabeth. I'm sorry you were worried. But as you can see, I'm perfectly fine." He patted the seat beside him. "Want to ride with me?"

Feeling guilt for doubting him and relief at finding him...as well as many other emotions, she dismounted and hurriedly tethered Molly to the back of the wagon, just as she had often done on the Oregon Trail. Then she came around, and Eli extended a hand, helping her into the wagon seat. Only as she settled into the seat did she think to peek inside the covered wagon, where, to her surprise, she saw a full load of lumber and some other things. "Eli!" she exclaimed, "where did you get all that wood?"

"If you'd found my letter, you'd know that I was journeying over to Empire City." He released the brake and shook the reins to get the team to move.

"To Empire City?" She frowned. "That's a long trip."

"Don't I know it." He rubbed his back. "Much better on horseback than driving a wagon."

"Speaking of horseback…where is your horse?"

"Back in Empire City."

She frowned. "Why?"

"I traded him for the lumber." He smiled but his eyes looked a little sad.

"Eli?" she exclaimed. "Your horse? You traded him? You love that horse, Eli. How could you—"

"I love you and the children more," he said firmly.

Despite her resolve to be strong, tears filled her eyes—but they were tears of joy this time. She slipped her arm into his and pretended to be looking at something alongside the road. She could hardly believe that when she was questioning his loyalties, he was giving up his horse in order to get lumber to build their home.

"I was starting to cut down trees," Eli told her, "and I realized it would be impossible to get very far on our cabin before the rains set in. Then I remembered the Prescotts and how they bought lumber in Empire City and how much more quickly their building went up. And it seemed clear that was what I needed to do."

Elizabeth thought about the beautiful Appaloosa again. She knew Eli would miss that horse. It had always been his source of livelihood, and in some ways it was his ticket to freedom as well. "Well, anytime you need a horse, Eli, you know that Molly is as much yours as mine. And before we left Kentucky I was starting to break Bella and Beau to saddle too. Some people say you can't have both in a horse, but Percherons are special."

He nodded. "Yes, and if your father gets his way, there will be more horses in time. But what we need most of all right now is a house." He grinned at her. "And a wedding."

If Elizabeth could have her way, she would wed Eli right now. Today. They could live in the tent and the wagon just as her parents and Matthew and Jess were doing. However, it didn't seem like it was her place to bring this up. Besides, there were the children to think of. "How long do you think it will take to build a house?" she asked meekly. "Now that you have lumber?"

"I don't know for sure. But it'll be a lot faster than it would have been if I'd had to log all the timber."

"And Father's house is nearly finished. And it sounds like Matthew's is coming right along too. So I feel certain that we can have Brady's help soon. Especially now that Father's rafters have been raised."

At the homesite, Elizabeth ran inside the house's foundation to discover her dusty note and a wilted bunch of wildflowers. Then she insisted on helping Eli to unload the wagon. And as they carried the planks and boards together, he seemed genuinely grateful to have her help—or perhaps he simply enjoyed her company as she filled him in on the latest happenings in and about the settlement. But after they got all the lumber neatly stacked near the foundation, a couple of boxes still remained in the wagon. He slid the first one out. The wooden crate was big and flat, and Eli seemed to be handling it with extra care. She helped him carry it over to the foundation, where he leaned it on its side.

"What is it?" she asked curiously.

"A window."

She blinked. "A *glass* window?"

He laughed. "Is there another kind?"

"Well, most of the settlers have wooden windows."

"Yes, and we will have some of those as well. But we will have one glass window in the front of the house."

She threw her arms around him. "Oh, Eli. Thank you—thank you!"

He leaned down and kissed her, pulling her close and holding her tight. "You're so very welcome."

"This is so exciting!" she said as he released her. Of course, she wasn't sure which was more exciting—being in his arms or having a real glass window. "Ruth will be over the moon when she hears that we have a *real* window."

"Let's just hope it's still in one piece by the time I put it in." Eli returned to the wagon. "Now this next crate is pretty heavy. Why don't you back the wagon up to the house, and I'll attempt to ease it down onto the foundation."

She worked with the team, maneuvering the wagon into a position where the tailgate was right against the front part of the foundation before she pulled on the brake. Then she watched as Eli eased the crate to the back of the wagon and down onto the wall with a clunk. By the time she got back inside of the house, the heavy crate was solidly on the dirt floor.

"What is it?" she asked.

He grinned at her. "What do you think it is?"

She looked at the square, sturdy crate. "Bricks?" she guessed.

"Nope, but you're not far off. Want another guess?"

She shook her head. "I have no idea."

"It's a small cookstove."

Her eyes grew wide as she stared at the crate in wonder. "Really? A cookstove? You found a cookstove in Empire City?"

"It seems someone had ordered it and then changed their mind. It was still sitting on the dock. I actually got a pretty good deal on it."

"A window and a cookstove." She let out a sigh of wonder. "It feels like Christmas, Eli." She smiled happily at him. "But the best part is having you home again."

"And now, since the day is still young, I think I will get to work."

"Why don't I take care of the wagon and the team," she offered.

He nodded. "I'm much obliged."

"And then I'll ride back to Malinda's and fetch you something to eat," she called out. And after that, she would make a run over to her parents and tell them the good news. *Eli was home!*

It was late in the afternoon by the time Elizabeth finally made it back to her parents, where they had already stopped work for the day. As she approached their campfire, she could tell by their glum faces that they were still feeling concerned about her.

"Good news!" she called out as she hurried over. "Eli is safely home."

"Thanks be to God," Clara exclaimed as she hugged her.

Now Elizabeth sat down and told them the whole story—from the lost note to how he'd sacrificed his Appaloosa for lumber—and finally about the window and the cookstove.

"Eli found a cookstove in Empire City?" Clara exclaimed. "Are there more?"

"Now, Clara." Asa shook his head. "We already decided we would wait until next spring to—"

"But were there more?" Clara asked Elizabeth again.

"I don't think so," Elizabeth told her. "It sounded like it was the only one. Someone had ordered it and changed their mind. It was on the dock. And the crate was very heavy."

"Did you open it and see it?" Clara asked eagerly.

"Not yet, Mother."

"Well, I know where we'll be going for Christmas dinner," Clara told her.

Elizabeth laughed. "That's assuming we'll have our house finished by then."

"I'm going to start putting shingles on next," Asa told her. "Brady and I cut down a massive cedar tree last week, and there should be enough shingles for the roofs of all three of our houses."

"That's good to hear. I'll let Eli know."

Asa nodded toward Brady. "And I'll bet Eli would like to have your help now, Brady. Although I'll hate to see you go."

Brady glanced at Elizabeth. "Well, I reckon Miss Elizabeth gets her say on whether I stay or go."

Elizabeth shook her head. "You know you're a free man, Brady. But Eli and I would love having your help. And we already talked about a spot not too far from the creek, but high enough that it should stay dry. And there's enough timber there for you to build a small cabin. Eli wants to help you with it…if you'd like that." She still felt badly that Brady would be unable to claim land as they'd hoped he could. But she also knew that unless he pretended to be their slave, he would be forced to leave. Even with their pretense, according to Oregon law he only had three years to reside here.

But she and Eli had decided to cross that bridge later. Most of all they just wanted to make Brady as comfortable as possible. He was older than her father, and she hoped he could live his final years in peace…and without being uprooted again.

"I'd be much obliged," he told her.

"And we'll section you off a piece of farmland for you to use as you like."

His dark eyes glistened. "I'm most grateful, Miss Elizabeth."

"And I'll help you with your cabin," Matthew offered. "Soon as I finish my house and help Eli and Elizabeth with theirs."

"I'll help too," Asa told Brady. "With all of us working, we'll get it up in no time."

"And we'll share some household goods," Clara told him.

"Ya'll is too kind," he told them. "Better than family."

"We *are* family," Elizabeth assured him. "And now I better get back to Malinda's before it starts getting dark."

Elizabeth felt unbelievably happy as she rode Molly back to Malinda's farm. It was hard to fathom how she had felt so down-hearted and grievous earlier in the day…and now to feel so incredibly hopeful and glad. It was truly amazing. She slowed Molly in order to enjoy the last rays of golden sunlight filtering through the autumn foliage. The air felt so clean and sweet—so full of promise. She was just taking in a deep breath when she heard a rustling off to her right and up ahead.

The hairs on the back of her neck stood up, and she immediately thought of a wild predatory animal. She knew there were bears and wildcats in these parts, but she didn't think they'd want to tangle with a horse. Even so, she nudged Molly to the left side of the road, keeping her eyes trained on the brush where she'd heard the rustling. Just as she was passing, she saw what she was certain was an Indian crouched low in the overgrown brush. Their eyes locked, and Elizabeth's heart pounded with fear. But in the same instant she realized it was a woman. She looked as frightened as Elizabeth felt.

"*Hello?*" Elizabeth called out timidly. And then, just like that, the woman backed away and disappeared. With her heart still thumping hard, Elizabeth stared into the brush, blinking her eyes in disbelief. Had she imagined the young woman crouched down there like that? Or was that for real? But somehow those big dark eyes, so full of fear, burned into Elizabeth's memory. For a moment, she considered getting down off Molly and investigating more closely. But then she remembered what Malinda had said—if Indian women returned to these parts, the men would probably follow. And if that happened, there would probably be more trouble too.

"Gid-up," she told Molly, squeezing her knees into the horse's sides. "Let's get home." As Molly broke into a smooth gallop, Elizabeth tried to decide how to handle this. As badly as she wanted to rush into the house and tell Malinda, she didn't want to alarm her. Malinda seemed to have an unreasonable amount of fear when it came to the Indians in these parts. Perhaps it was rooted in her concern for her children…or perhaps it was more. But Elizabeth decided she would bite her tongue around Malinda. She would, however, tell Eli. Eli understood the Indians better than anyone. He would know what to do.

Chapter Six

On Saturday morning everyone at Malinda's was bustling about, finishing chores and getting ready to go to town. They were all eager to go to the grand opening of Prescotts' Mercantile. Everyone who lived within ten miles was likely to be there. Well, everyone except for Eli, who was determined to work from dawn until dusk on their house. As much as Elizabeth would miss him, she was grateful for his devotion to their future. Right now, every possible building day seemed precious.

She and Malinda were working in the kitchen when Will's wagon pulled into the yard. "That's right," Elizabeth remembered. "Belinda and Amelia are moving in today."

"Yes." Malinda dried her hands on her apron and smoothed her hair. "Will said he'd drop them by before we headed off to the mercantile." She excused herself and hurried out to meet him. Elizabeth watched from the porch, still marveling at how two people who'd recently been complete strangers now seemed so perfect for each other.

"Hello," Belinda called as she lugged a bulky carpetbag into the house. "We have arrived."

Elizabeth smiled and pointed to the ladder stairway. "Your room awaits."

"I wish I could sleep up there too," Ruth said longingly.

"We already went over that," Elizabeth reminded her. "We're not going to crowd you in with Susannah and Emily—and Amelia and Belinda get the other two beds."

"But I'm crowded in with you and Aunt Malinda," Ruth pointed out.

"Why don't you be an angel and go help Amelia with her things," Elizabeth suggested as she watched Amelia struggling to carry a box and a bag up the porch steps. Fortunately, that distracted Ruth for the time being. It wasn't easy being the youngest of the cousins, but someday Ruth might appreciate it.

While the younger girls helped the older girls get settled in and unpack—or more likely to ogle at the lovely clothes these girls had brought with them from Boston—Elizabeth and Malinda returned to fixing food to take to town. The plan was to have a picnic lunch on the church grounds with family and friends.

"Do you remember when we used to go to town on Saturdays in Kentucky?" Malinda asked Elizabeth.

"I certainly do." Elizabeth tucked a cloth down over the biscuits, which were still warm. "But our town had more than just one store and a church."

"This is just the beginning," Malinda assured her.

"That's true. And the Bible says not to despise small beginnings." Elizabeth smiled. "And I do not. After all those months on the trail, I am thankful for our little settlement."

"And I hear that Bert Flanders is planning for his blacksmith shop. Flo told me they want to build a small house with a lean-to that will function as his business."

"I expect Bert will be kept busy too," Elizabeth said. "With so much building going on there's a need for hardware."

"And didn't you mention that Jessica's aunt and her friend might start a business here too?" Malinda asked. "A boarding house and restaurant?"

"That's their plan, and according to Eli, they were doing a good business when he saw them in Empire City last week. I wouldn't be the least bit surprised if they make enough profits to start a nice boarding house here." Elizabeth smiled to herself to think of the business Ruby used to operate back in St. Louis. Jess had said it was a dance hall, where the whisky ran freely. But during the arduous journey, Ruby and Doris had seemed to reform some of their ideals. Still, she wondered what Malinda would think if she knew about St. Louis. Not that Elizabeth had any intention of telling her. Some things truly were better left unsaid.

Everyone chattered happily as they walked to town together, but eventually the younger children hurried on ahead and only Elizabeth, Malinda, and Will's two daughters were walking together. "I can't get over the feeling that this is like a holiday," Malinda said happily. "Having a store within walking distance of my home. It's just wonderful."

"And it's wonderful the weather is so pleasant." Elizabeth looked up at the clear blue sky, the sunshine filtering through the autumn leaves. "It's such a beautiful day."

"Yes, this time of year is exceptionally nice," Malinda told her.

"So far I haven't noticed all that much difference between the climate here and in Kentucky," Elizabeth said. "Autumn in Kentucky was always lovely too. Remember?"

"That's true," Malinda said. "I love autumn in Kentucky too."

"Well, it's a lot warmer here than it would be in Boston this time of year," Belinda told them. "We were usually wearing our heavy coats in early November."

"Will it be warm like this all winter?" Amelia asked Malinda.

"It will get cooler, and of course, the rains will come. But even so, it's still warmer than winters were back in Kentucky." She grinned at the two girls who would become her stepdaughters in December. "And I can assure you that it's much warmer than a Boston winter."

"Does it ever snow here?" Amelia asked.

"I haven't seen snow once since we settled," Malinda told them. "It did freeze one year, but I don't think that's typical."

"Well, I won't miss the snow or ice," Belinda announced.

"But I will miss some things," Amelia confessed. "Like candy stores and bakeries."

Belinda giggled as she pointed at a well-worn shoe in front of her. "And new shoes."

"And buying ready-made clothes," Amelia added.

"Yes, girls, we do understand." Malinda said in a maternal tone. "It takes some adjusting to get used to some of the deprivations of the frontier. But I believe that someday we will have all those amenities too."

"Really?" Amelia asked hopefully. "Even a candy store?"

Malinda laughed. "Well, perhaps it will be a while before we have a store devoted entirely to candy. But surely the mercantile will carry some sweets."

"Oh, I'm sure Aunt Lavinia will have stocked her candy case by now," Amelia told her. "I can't wait."

"I just hope she's got some of the household items I'll be needing to set up housekeeping," Elizabeth said. "I've got quite a list."

"Lavinia told me they'll be taking orders for merchandise," Malinda said. "Although I'm not sure how long it will take for shipments to arrive."

"Eli predicts that the Coquille River will be used to transport shipped goods from the coast someday." Just bringing Eli's name into the conversation filled Elizabeth with a girlish sort of giddiness.

"John used to say the same thing," Malinda told her.

"Imagine how much time that would save," Elizabeth said wistfully.

They were just coming up to the church, and it was fun to see others milling about what Elizabeth hoped would someday be considered a real town. She estimated at least two dozen people gathered between the church and the mercantile. Certainly, it was not much by other standards, but it gave one hope.

After depositing their food baskets at the church and visiting with some of the women there, they ventured over to the new shopping establishment, pausing to socialize along the way. A freshly painted sign was prominently displayed up high on the false front.

PRESCOTTS' MERCANTILE
EST. 1857

"This is a red-letter day," Malinda said with enthusiasm as they went into the mercantile. "Our very own store."

The place was bustling and smelled of coffee and onions as well as many other pleasant scents. People were chattering happily, and Elizabeth estimated at least a dozen adult customers were perusing the interior of the store. Several children, including her own, were gathered around the candy counter and dry goods, eagerly exploring everything. She had warned JT and Ruth to look but not to touch, and as far as she could see, they were heeding her instructions. However, JT looked as if his fingers were itching to pick up a music book that was in the book section.

"Hello, son," she said quietly from behind him.

"Ma." He turned eagerly, pointing out the book to her. "That book has fifty songs in it."

She nodded. "I see that."

"It's got musical notes for piano, but Mrs. Taylor has been teaching us to read music at school. I think I could learn the songs on my guitar."

She put her hand on his shoulder. "Did you bring enough money for it?"

He nodded, looking up at her with earnest eyes. "But do you think it would be wasteful? I know we need things for our home."

She smiled. "Don't you think music would be good for our home?"

He grinned back at her.

"I trust your judgment, son." She patted him on the back and then went to see what Ruth was admiring.

"Look, Mama," Ruth said when Elizabeth joined her. "There's some really pretty pink calico there."

Elizabeth nodded. "Yes, Ruth. But we brought a fair amount of fabric from home, remember?"

"But none as pretty as that," Ruth told her.

"Perhaps not. But until we use up our fabric, I don't see the need to purchase more." She tweaked Ruth's braid. "Although I'm sure it would look very pretty on you. Maybe you can find a pink hair ribbon instead."

Ruth gave her a surprised look. "I didn't mean for me, Mama. I meant for you. Wouldn't it make a pretty wedding dress for when you and Eli get married?"

Elizabeth laughed. "Oh, my. Well...I'm not sure."

"Oh, it would, Mama. I know it would."

Elizabeth looked down into Ruth's sparkling blue eyes. "That's very sweet of you to think so, dear. But I don't plan on sewing myself a new wedding dress. I would much rather spend my time sewing curtains and such."

Ruth looked truly dismayed.

"But if there is time to sew a dress, I think perhaps I'll just use that green calico I brought from home."

"Oh, no, Mama." Ruth looked appalled. "Not green."

"Why ever not? Green is a nice, sensible color. One of nature's favorite shades."

Ruth firmly shook her head. "Haven't you heard the wedding-dress poem?"

"What?" Elizabeth shook her head.

"It goes like this." Ruth stood straight as if she were reciting in school.

> White—chosen right.
> Blue—love will be true.
> Yellow—ashamed of her fellow.
> Red—wish herself dead.
> Black—wish herself back.
> Gray—travel far away.
> Pink—of you he'll always think.
> Green—ashamed to be seen.

Elizabeth couldn't help but laugh. "Well then. I certainly won't wear green!"

"Or yellow or red or black." Ruth got a thoughtful look. "And not gray…I don't want you to go far away, Mama."

"So what does that leave me with?" Elizabeth asked.

Ruth held up three fingers. "White, blue, or pink."

Elizabeth thought. "Well, I wore white when I married your father, but I was just a young woman then. Perhaps…blue?"

Ruth's serious expression broke into a smile. "Yes, Mama, blue."

"And I brought some blue calico too," Elizabeth told her.

"But it's dark blue," Ruth reminded her. She pointed back at the shelf holding the bolts of fabric. "How about that one on the end? It's the same color as your eyes."

"What about the blue fabric we already have?" Elizabeth asked.

"It would make pretty curtains and things," Ruth said hopefully. Elizabeth was about to put an end to this discussion and remind Ruth of the practicalities of living on the frontier when Clara came over to join them. Before Elizabeth could set her daughter straight,

Ruth was emphatically explaining her plans for Elizabeth to have a beautiful blue wedding dress. "The same color as her eyes. And when a bride wears blue it means her love will be true."

Elizabeth sighed. "Oh, Ruth, my love will be true no matter—"

"You're right," Clara said to Ruth. "Your mother *does* need a pretty blue dress for her wedding day."

"But we haven't even set a wedding day," Elizabeth reminded her. "For all I know it might not be until next year."

Clara waved her hand at Elizabeth. "Now, I'm sure you have shopping to attend to. Ruth and I will take care of this little matter ourselves."

Elizabeth just shook her head, and chuckling at how her mother and daughter had just joined forces against her, she went off to see what she could find on her list.

The men, wanting to make good use of the first part of the day, arrived later in the afternoon—just in time for the potluck picnic. Asa and Matthew came in the wagon, and Elizabeth almost asked why Brady hadn't come. But then she stopped herself. Of course, she knew. As a colored man, Brady had not been accepted into the community. And although this wasn't surprising to Elizabeth, she still felt badly for Brady's sake. His life, it seemed, would continue to be an isolated one. Sometimes she wondered if he missed the old days, when James had kept numerous slaves to help with the farm. But even thinking of this felt foreign to her now. And wrong.

"I figured you womenfolk would need a wagon to haul all your wares back," Asa teased as they were sitting out in the churchyard to eat.

"I still want to go back for a couple of things," Clara told him.

"So do I," Elizabeth said. "I got to thinking they might run out of sugar before the next shipment arrives."

"Maybe we should have brought two wagons," Asa teased.

Clara gave him a dismissive wave as they walked away.

"Next year will be different," Elizabeth said to Clara as they returned to the mercantile. "Besides eggs and dairy products, we'll have grown our own produce for trading."

"And perhaps we'll have a couple foals by then as well."

"You think so?" Elizabeth wasn't so sure. Matthew's stallion and their only hope of a sire had foundered on the rich grass shortly after they arrived. "Isn't Storm still having trouble with his feet?"

"He's much improved, but his back feet are still very tender," Clara told her. "However, Asa mentioned that the Thompsons have a very nice stallion that he's considering."

"Really?"

"He's already making arrangements with Mr. Thompson to take Penny over for a visit. I'm sure he could take Molly too."

"Has he seen their stallion yet?" Elizabeth trusted her father's sensibility about horses, but she was surprised he'd agree to a sire he'd never seen.

"No. But Mr. Thompson claims he's a handsome horse."

"Well, as much as I'd love a foal by next year, I'd prefer to hear Father's assessment of the Thompsons' stallion *after* he's seen it."

"That's wise." She chuckled. "Asa might very well get Penny over there and decide to bring her right back home."

"I expect that Storm should be recovered before long."

"And we do know his bloodlines," Clara agreed.

"It would be so wonderful to have foals by next year." Elizabeth was well aware of the value of a good horse in these parts. Selling a yearling could be more profitable than a bumper crop.

They were nearly to the mercantile when Flo came over to speak to them, proudly pointing out where Bert had started to build what would one day be their home and blacksmith shop. "It don't look like much yet, but Bert says it will have a roof by Thanksgiving. And he'll put a tall front on it like the mercantile." She smiled. "Should be right handsome."

"Our town is coming together, isn't it?" Elizabeth said. "The mercantile and the blacksmith...the school and church. We're off to a fine start."

Flo frowned. "Speaking of the church..." She lowered her voice. "Bert flat-out refuses to go no more. Now Ezra won't go neither."

"Oh?" Elizabeth exchanged glances with her mother.

"Why is that?" Clara asked quietly.

"Bert says he doesn't need to give up Sunday mornings just to be yelled at by Reverend Holmes."

Elizabeth pressed her lips together. She was not overly fond of the reverend's fiery sermons either. At first she'd kept her opinion to herself, but eventually she mentioned it to her parents. Asa had reminded her that sometimes preachers went through a season of fire and brimstone, but perhaps it would pass in time. As a result, they'd all decided to wait and see.

"I must agree that the reverend's words can be strong," Clara admitted.

"I defended him at first," Flo told her. "But I'm of a mind to agree with Ezra now. And I hear tell that some other menfolk are quitting the church too."

"Oh, dear." Clara shook her head. "That's a shame."

"The only reason I'm burdening you folks with this is that Bert keeps talking about how much he misses Asa's Sunday services back when we were journeying here."

Elizabeth nodded. "Yes, I miss them too."

Flo looked eagerly at her. "Bert says if Asa was the preacher, he'd gladly come to church."

Clara frowned. "Well, Reverend Holmes is the appointed preacher. Asa can't possibly replace him."

"I know." Flo sighed and then looked over her shoulder as if worried someone was listening. "But we thought maybe Asa could hold church services somewhere else."

"You mean have two churches in our little town?" Clara looked troubled.

"It don't have to be in town. Maybe in somebody's home…or a barn. I recall that party out in Malinda's barn. It could surely house a church meeting, don't you think?"

"Well, that would be up to Malinda," Elizabeth said.

"And Asa," Clara added.

"Well, I'd be much obliged if you folks would give it your consideration."

So before returning to the mercantile, they promised to speak to Asa about the situation. Elizabeth felt sorry for Flo's dilemma, but she wasn't certain that Asa starting a church was the answer. If anything it seemed it would divide the community. She remembered a similar situation on the wagon train. But that had been different—or at least it had seemed so back then. While traveling, they had been a temporary community with numerous Sunday worship services throughout their wagon train. As a result, it hadn't seemed a problem to have more than one group of worshippers in their unit. However, when Mrs. Taylor's husband died so tragically on the trail, Elizabeth regretted not having spent more time getting to know him…or to understand him.

On the ride back to Malinda's, Elizabeth sat in the front of the wagon with her parents. Together they discussed the situation. "I'm well aware that Bert Flanders isn't the only one who's unhappy with the church," Asa quietly told them. "To be honest, I'm not overly fond of anger from the pulpit."

"Why do some preachers feel such a need to shout and carry on like that?" Elizabeth asked him.

He shrugged. "Hard to say. But when I prepare to give a sermon, I usually feel like I'm preaching more at myself than anyone else." He chuckled. "I s'pect if I was in need of chastising I would stand up and yell from the pulpit too."

Clara patted his hand. "I'm most grateful you're not like that."

"So what will you do, Father?"

He adjusted the brim of his hat to block the late-afternoon

sunshine. "I reckon I'll pray about it. And I'm sure the good Lord will show us the best way to go. Never hurts to wait on him."

Elizabeth promised that she would pray about it too. And what he'd said made perfect sense. God would continue to direct their paths just as he always did. And rushing forward without God's blessing would only lead to trouble.

Chapter Seven

Autumn had always been a busy time in Kentucky, and it seemed busier than ever here in Oregon. Elizabeth knew that was to be expected. One couldn't settle the new frontier by sitting about. But sometimes she found herself longing for the quiet of winter. She remembered the peaceful days when there'd been snow on the ground, and other than the usual daily chores, life slowed down immensely. Would it ever slow down here or become quiet again?

Of course, Malinda's house had become even noisier since Will's daughters joined their household on Saturday. The four girls, soon to become stepsisters, shared the sleeping loft upstairs, and JT and his male cousins were sleeping in the barn loft. However, most of the time—when the children weren't in school or doing chores—they chose to reside in the house. It was cozy and busy and loud, but Elizabeth was grateful, especially since the weather had turned wet and windy the past few days. Just the same, she was trying not to count the days until she and her children would need to make other living arrangements. The idea of camping in the wind and rain was not appealing.

"Why don't you go out to check on your property?" Malinda suggested. "You haven't been out there for at least a week now."

"Ten days," Elizabeth clarified.

"Well then, it seems you're overdue for a visit." Malinda peered out the window. "And you're in luck because our little autumnal storm seems to have blown over today."

"I *am* curious to see how Eli's progressing," Elizabeth admitted. "The last time I was there, he and Brady were cutting some logs, and it did give me hope. And Father said that Matthew was going over to help this week. It's possible they've made real progress by now."

"Go on with you," Malinda urged. "Take your men some lunch."

Elizabeth tried not to feel apprehensive as she packed a basket with food. The last time she'd packed a lunch and trekked out to check on his progress, Eli had been missing. However, he'd had good reason to take off, and if she had been more observant, she would have discovered his note. She decided to ride Molly instead of walking. And she would take Flax with her as well. Eli had mentioned that a bear had been sniffing around their property. Maybe with Flax around, the bear would find a more suitable place to live.

She planned to stop by to see her parents as well. She knew they were close to being done with their cabin—at least done enough to start moving inside before long. On Sunday after church, her mother had spoken of little else. And who could blame her? Elizabeth was still sometimes amazed that her parents, especially her mother, had made the incredible trek to this part of the country. Just thinking about it made her feel proud of them...and thankful.

Most of the trees that had recently been bursting with colorful autumn foliage were now showing a fair amount of bare limbs. The recent rain and wind had stripped off many of the leaves. The ground was still a bit soggy from the rain, but the air smelled fresh and clean. Elizabeth pulled the collar of her old barn coat up around her neck to keep the breeze out. Certainly it wasn't very cold, but there was a damp chill in the air.

As the edge of her property came into sight, she felt a thrill of excitement. Flax ran ahead, barking as if he understood this was going to be his home again. She could hardly believe that someday she and Eli and the children would all be living here. There would be a cabin, which could grow larger over the years. And maybe even a barn by next summer. But nothing prepared her for what she saw as she came around the grove of trees—the walls of her house were fully up, logs on the lower part and milled lumber higher up. It was definitely a house, standing tall and straight as if it had every right to be there. And certainly, it did.

She hurried to dismount from Molly, rushing up to where Eli and her father and Matthew and Brady were using ropes to hoist up the first of the rafters. "This is amazing!" she exclaimed. "It looks like a real house."

"It *is* a real house," Matthew called out. "But you better stay out of the way, sis."

"That's right," Eli warned from where he was pulling the rope hand over fist to get the log up into place. "It's dangerous in here."

She stepped back and made sure Flax stayed out of the way too, just watching as the four men worked together so smoothly. They clearly knew what they were doing. And why wouldn't they after the building experience they'd gained the past couple of months? As she examined their progress, she realized the house wasn't set on her stone foundation the way she'd imagined it would be. She wanted to ask why but didn't want to distract the men. They seemed very intent on getting the big rafter into place. And it did look dangerous.

Instead, she walked around, surveying all sides of her house, which had been built just inside the stone foundation. She tried not to be disappointed even though she'd worked hard to gather and stack all those stones. And she felt it would have been handsome to see a cabin set on a stone foundation.

She looked at the square opening where she assumed the glass window would go and felt slightly dismayed to see it was empty. She hoped the window hadn't been broken during all this construction. Then she noticed the familiar crate leaning against some lumber. Eli was probably waiting to put the window in last to ensure it made it up in one piece. She sat down on a pile of lumber and just watched happily. After all those long weeks of thinking she would be homeless this winter, it seemed that she was really going to have a house after all. Even without a stone foundation, it was a house!

Finally, after the rafter was securely in place, the men came down for a dinner break. She greeted them and opened her basket of food. "I hope I packed enough," she told them. "I didn't know Eli had this much help today or I would have packed more."

"No matter," Asa assured her. "Your mother sent food for us."

"Then you shall have a feast today."

Eli grinned at her. "What do you think of the place?"

"I am truly astonished," she admitted. "I had no idea it would go so quickly."

"That's because I have such excellent help," Eli told her. "I don't know what I'd do without this fine team of experts."

"It's also because you got milled lumber," Matthew pointed out. "I can't even imagine how much time that's saving us. At this rate, we'll have this house finished inside of two weeks."

"Truly?" Elizabeth could hardly believe her ears. "That soon?"

"These good straight boards save us a bundle of time," Asa told her. "Even the wet weather didn't slow us down much."

"It also helps that you men know what you're doing," Eli said. "I might be good at hunting and fishing, but I'm no expert at carpentering. Not like you fellows."

Asa pointed at Elizabeth now. "I know you were worried about being the last one to get your house built, Lizzie. But it's plain to see that you and Eli are benefiting from our recent experiences."

"That's right." Matthew reached for an apple. "We made our learning mistakes on our own houses. Yours should turn out the best of all."

"I am truly grateful," she said.

"Looks like you'll have a right fine house," Brady told her.

"It sure does." She smiled at him and then turned to Eli. "I was a bit surprised that the house isn't sitting on the stone foundation I made…"

Eli nodded as he chewed a piece of bread and jam. "I hope you're not too disappointed 'bout that."

"It was my idea to forgo the foundation," Asa told her. "Without mortar, it just wasn't sturdy enough to hold a house up."

"I got us some mortar in Empire City," Eli explained. "But not enough to do a proper job on the whole foundation."

"Besides that," Matthew added, "it would have taken a week or more just to get the foundation ready to build on."

Brady waved over to the house. "And just think, Miss Elizabeth, we'd hardly have any house built at all right now if'n we were still putting them stones together."

Elizabeth nodded. "Well, that makes perfect sense."

"And all those stones you gathered will be just fine for the fireplace," Eli assured her. "I reckon we have enough mortar to do that job properly."

"I bet you'll have the best-looking fireplace in these parts," Asa told her. "Your ma will be jealous." He elbowed Eli. "Clara's already at me to make a trip to Empire City to find her a cookstove like you got for Elizabeth."

Eli laughed. "Good luck with that, Asa. I'm afraid it was a case of plain good timing that I happened along when I did. Otherwise I'm sure someone else would have snatched that stove up first."

"Well, I promised Clara we'd have the Prescotts order us a nice big cookstove by this time next year. That is, as long as we get some crops in and some livestock birthed by then. But I don't see any reason why we won't. This land looks like it's just bursting to produce goodness."

They all chatted hopefully about the future as they ate. Then, as the meal wound down, Eli excused himself, heading back over to the house as if he was ready to get back to work. Elizabeth, eager to have a moment alone with him, followed. "I brought Flax to keep you company," she said as Flax came alongside her. "And maybe he can help make the bears feel a little less welcome."

"Good idea." He leaned down to scratch Flax behind the ears. "You going to scare that bear away, boy?" Flax wagged his tail.

"I'm truly amazed at what you've accomplished here," she told Eli. "I never expected to see this much progress."

"I couldn't have done it without your family."

She ran her hand over the wood that framed where the window would go. "Getting this milled wood has made everyone's work easier. Thank you for doing that."

"I did it for us, Elizabeth. For you and me and the children."

"Is Matthew right? Is this house truly going to be finished in two weeks?"

"If we stay on course."

She looked down at her feet. "So we could set a wedding date?"

He reached for her hand, squeezing it. "I don't see any reason not to."

Their eyes met, and she felt a warmth rushing through her.

"You pick the date," he said, "and I'll be there."

She laughed. "That's just what I'm going to do."

As the men went back to work, she packed up the food basket and bid them goodbye. Then, instructing Flax to stay with Eli, she happily rode over to see her mother. It was still somewhat amazing to see their little cabin sitting proud and square—inhabiting what had been bare land just months ago.

She found her mother outside, sweeping dirt out the front door. She waved and called out a welcome as Elizabeth slid out of the saddle.

"Well, look at you," Elizabeth said as she walked up to the cabin. "You're in your house!"

"That's right." Clara leaned the broom against the house. "Come on in and look around. I'm still getting things unpacked and put away, but we've slept in here the past four days."

Elizabeth tapped her toe on the carpet that was covering the packed dirt floor. "Aren't you glad you brought this along?"

"Oh, my, yes." Clara shook her head. "It's wonderful to finally have a real roof overhead. And I don't want to complain about the dirt floor, but I do look forward to when Asa can put in a real floor. He ordered some lumber through the Prescotts. Sounds like we should have it in a few weeks. Maybe before Christmas."

"Speaking of Christmas, I need to look at a calendar."

"A calendar?" Clara looked around the room, which was cluttered with crates in various stages of unpacking. "I know I have one somewhere. I'm just not sure where."

"That's all right, Mother. I just wanted to let you know that Eli says we can set our wedding date. The house will be finished in about two weeks, and—"

"Two weeks?" Clara blinked. "Why, it seems they only just started it."

"They're making good time. And the milled lumber is speeding it up some too."

"I'm so pleased to hear that. You and Eli could have your wedding in December. Even before Christmas if you liked."

Elizabeth sighed dreamily. "Oh, it would be so lovely to be in our own house…all of us…by Christmas."

"What about Malinda and Will's wedding?"

Elizabeth returned to the present. "What do you mean?"

"Well, I know they're getting married the third Saturday in December."

Elizabeth nodded. "Yes. Their wedding is just a few days before Christmas. And certainly, Eli and I won't pick that date for our wedding."

"Perhaps you could get married on the first Saturday of December—unless that's too soon."

"That would put two weeks between the two weddings." Elizabeth considered this. "But I'm not sure about having our wedding before Malinda and Will's."

"What in the world would be wrong with that?"

"Wouldn't it be stealing the thunder from their big day?"

Clara laughed. "Goodness no, Lizzie. Remember, this is the frontier. Old social conventions don't necessarily apply here."

"It would be so wonderful to move into the house before Christmas." She touched a finger to her chin. "Not only that, but it would get us out of Malinda's house in time for her to put things back together before her own wedding."

"You see," Clara told her as she opened a box of sewing things. "A perfectly good reason to have your wedding first." She pulled out the pretty blue fabric that Ruth had admired at the mercantile on the day of its grand opening. "Looks like I'll need to get busy with this." She stretched out a length of the shiny fabric. "I thought perhaps I'd put some tucks in the bodice, and I have some lovely pearl buttons packed away somewhere. Perhaps a touch of lace on the collar?"

They discussed dress designs for a while, and then Elizabeth excused herself to return to Malinda's. "I can't wait to tell her the good news," she said. "Hopefully she won't mind that our wedding will precede hers."

"If she has any concerns, you can simply point out that you and Eli have been acquainted longer than she and Will. Then just remind her that your marriage will free up some much-needed space in her house." Clara hugged her goodbye.

"Feel free to tell Jess my good news," Elizabeth said as she went to her horse. "I know she's been looking forward to us setting a date."

"Two weddings in one month—what a busy social calendar we keep out here in the frontier!" Clara reached for her broom. "That reminds me, dear, your father and I want to have everyone over for dinner on Sunday after church. To celebrate our new home. He'll invite Eli."

"Wonderful," Elizabeth called out as she got back onto Molly. "Shall I let Malinda know too?"

"Yes, please do!"

As Elizabeth rode back to Malinda's, she couldn't wait to tell her about the wedding plans. It seemed almost unbelievable that she and Eli could be wed in just a few weeks. But it all made so much sense. And she felt so relieved to know that she and the children would be moved into their own home two weeks before Malinda's wedding. Spending this time with Malinda had been fun, but life would become much simpler for both families after Eli and Elizabeth were married.

Chapter Eight

Y ou're planning to have your wedding *before* mine?" Malinda
looked up from her sewing with a creased brow. "What made
you decide to do this?"

As Elizabeth hung her coat on a peg by the door, she regretted
bursting in with her good news. She explained that Eli and the men
were making amazing progress on the house. "I had no idea it would
go so quickly. Having milled lumber has helped immensely." She
described what the house had looked like. "It was so exciting to see
it, Malinda."

Malinda made what seemed a strained smile. "That's wonderful, Elizabeth. I'm so happy for you. But I still don't understand this
rush to have your wedding before mine. What about social conventions and wedding etiquette?"

As Elizabeth warmed her hands on the fire, giving the coals a stir
and adding another log, she realized she'd been foolish to dismiss

her concerns so quickly. As much as she loved her dear friend, she'd known since childhood that Malinda was accustomed to having her way. Growing up as an only child with elderly parents, Malinda had been a bit spoiled. But surely this demanding life on the frontier would have changed some of those old ways. Or perhaps some things never changed. Whatever the situation, Elizabeth was determined to conclude this difficult conversation before the children came home from school even though it was already getting late in the day.

Elizabeth went back over to where Malinda was sitting in the rocker. "Is this going to be a problem for you?" she asked gently.

Malinda frowned. "Well...I realized you and Eli were going to get married eventually, but I didn't realize it would be so close to our wedding date. The same month even. How do you possibly plan to get everything done on time?"

"Everything?"

"Well, your dress and the food for your guests to start with—but besides that, where do you intend to have your wedding?"

"I thought it would be a simple affair. Saturday morning at the church. Perhaps a potluck dinner afterward. And my mother is making my dress."

"Truly? And she'll have it finished on time? I would think she'd have her hands fairly full housekeeping. Have they moved into their cabin yet?"

Elizabeth filled her in on her parents' news, extending the invitation for Sunday. "But even if Mother doesn't finish that dress for me, I'd be happy to wear my good Sunday dress."

"Oh, Elizabeth." Malinda shook her head. "My best friend needs to set her sights a bit higher than that. This may be the frontier, but we are civilized people. Besides, don't you want your wedding to be a memorable occasion?"

Elizabeth bit the inside of her lip. How could she say this without sounding critical of Malinda's values? "Perhaps...because this is my second marriage…perhaps I'm not as interested in the wedding ceremony so much this time. Certainly I want it to be memorable, but I'm content with a small, quiet affair." She sighed. "To be honest, I think my mother is more excited about the wedding preparations than I am."

"I hope you appreciate how fortunate you are to have your mother around to help you with these things."

Elizabeth considered the insinuation. Besides her children, Malinda had no family here in Oregon. But certainly she couldn't fault Elizabeth for that. "I'm here to help you with your wedding, Malinda. And I know my mother and Jess would help too. You must know that. We're your family too. And you also have Will's daughters. Belinda and Amelia are both so excited about the upcoming wedding."

Malinda made a tolerant smile. "But now you're having your wedding just a short time before mine. It seems rather inconvenient timing and…forgive me for speaking frankly, but…not very considerate."

Elizabeth tried not to feel offended. "Why do you feel that having our weddings two weeks apart is such a problem, Malinda?"

"It's a very small community, Elizabeth. So small that everyone will expect to be invited to both our weddings. Surely you know that. So obviously we will have the same people as guests. Have you considered how they might feel about attending two weddings within two weeks? Doesn't it seem an imposition? And right before Christmas too."

"Oh…" Elizabeth thought perhaps she understood now. "Are you worried about gifts? That there will be too much pressure on guests to bring two gifts within such a short period of time? Because I am happy to let everyone know that Eli and I do not expect wedding gifts. I honestly hadn't even thought about that aspect. But I realize this is the frontier. And so many of our friends—the ones we made from the wagon train—are struggling just to get by. I certainly wouldn't want anyone to feel compelled to bring a gift to my wedding. I will insist on no gifts."

"A wedding with no gifts?"

"Yes," she said firmly. "And I will make sure my mother understands this too. No gifts at this wedding."

Malinda still looked uneasy.

Elizabeth pointed out how much simpler Malinda's life would be with fewer people inhabiting her house before her wedding. "Three less people under your roof. As well as one less dog and numerous livestock and chickens. I should think you would be relieved to see us go."

"Yes, I can understand your rationale. It would be helpful if you and Ruth and JT were settled in your own home by then." She brightened. "But why couldn't you and the children move into your cabin without getting married? If it would help matters, I could invite Eli to bunk in the barn with my boys. He could have JT's bed."

Elizabeth stifled her irritation over what seemed like Malinda's incredibly selfish stubbornness. But even as she resented her friend, she felt like digging in her own heels as well. If she and Eli wanted to get married in early December, why shouldn't they?

"I appreciate your generous offer," she told Malinda in a stiff tone. "But I think I would feel greedy to move the children and myself into our lovely new home—the house that Eli is working so diligently to build for us—and forcing him to come sleep in a barn."

"Sleeping in a barn is a sight better than what we had to put up with when we arrived here," Malinda said a bit sharply. "The rains had already started by then, and it was too late in the year to build much of a cabin. And it didn't help matters that we'd sold our team to afford our passage on the ship. Did you know that we spent our first winter in that horrid little sod house that I now use to store my root vegetables? Can you imagine that tiny space with John and me and three children crammed into it?"

"I'm sure it was difficult." She peered curiously at her friend. "I'm surprised you never wrote me of those deprivations. You never mentioned such things in any of your letters. You always made it sound exciting and wonderful here."

Malinda made a funny little laugh. "If I'd told you of all the hardships, how would I have enticed you and James to move out here, pray tell?"

"Don't get me wrong, Malinda. I loved your letters. And I'm very happy to be here now."

"I hope you appreciate that you have it much better than we did. A school and a church and a mercantile and blacksmith. You should be counting your blessings."

Elizabeth looked at the clock on the mantle and realized she should be counting the seconds because the children would be home any minute now. "So if my wedding is a very simple one," she said quickly, "and if I make it plain to the guests that we expect no gifts, would you be amenable to Eli and me getting married the first Saturday of December?"

"Well, certainly, Elizabeth." Malinda huffed as she reached for her sewing scissors. "You can have your wedding whenever you wish. It is after all a free country, is it not?"

Elizabeth couldn't remember ever being in a position as socially awkward as this. She loved Malinda and wanted to please her. But she loved Eli more. "So it seems obvious that you would be much happier if Eli and I waited to marry?"

"Spring is a lovely time for a wedding, Elizabeth. And it comes early in this part of the country. Everything is so lush and green by March, and wildflowers would be in bloom."

"Spring?" Elizabeth took in a deep breath. How could Malinda be so stubborn? But before they could say another word about it, the children came bursting into the house. Suddenly it was time to hear about the happenings at school and to dole out apples for snacks and start preparations for supper. This uncomfortable conversation would have to wait.

Elizabeth had never liked conflict. She tried to avoid disagreements whenever possible, especially with loved ones. For that reason she was tempted to give in to Malinda without a battle. As she checked on a bowl of bread dough that had been rising, she thought perhaps it would be wise to wait until spring to marry. After all, only a year earlier, she felt she'd never be ready to remarry. James had been gone for nearly three years, and her mother had been pushing available bachelors her way, but Elizabeth had felt certain she could never love again.

She gently removed the risen dough, setting it on a floured board. She thought of Eli and how meeting him had changed everything, even if it had taken a while for her to admit to herself that he really was the one. And then she'd felt she'd lost him for good. As she kneaded the warm dough, she considered the freedoms he'd given up just to come back to her. She thought of all he'd done—including giving up his beloved horse—just to hasten their wedding date. And now she had to tell him to wait until spring?

"Goodness, Elizabeth," Belinda said abruptly. "You look as if you want to beat the living daylights out of that poor lump of dough."

Elizabeth gave Belinda a sheepish look. "I suppose I was overly exuberant."

"Are you disturbed about something?"

Elizabeth glanced around and noticed that Malinda wasn't in the house right now, so she decided to speak freely. After all, Belinda was Will's older daughter, and she'd grown up in Boston, where social conventions were respected. Perhaps she could test Belinda's reaction. "The truth is I'm feeling a bit torn about something."

"What is it?" Belinda asked as she tied on an apron and reached for a paring knife.

Elizabeth quickly told Belinda the good news about her house getting finished sooner than anticipated. "And today Eli encouraged me to pick a wedding date." She placed the pummeled dough back into the bowl, covering it with the towel. "I don't want to have a big wedding. Not like Malinda and your father are planning. And I don't want our guests to bring gifts. But I would like to be married before Christmas so that Eli and the children and I can be settled in our house. So I thought the first Saturday in December might work."

"That sounds wonderful," Belinda exclaimed. "Another wedding. What fun!"

"But do you feel that's unreasonable for your father and Malinda? Just two weeks before their wedding day?"

Belinda pursed her lips as if considering this. "I don't know... maybe it would be odd if we were back in Boston. But life was different there. When I think of the weddings on the trail..." She laughed. "Well, I'd never seen anything like that before. But I loved it. I love frontier weddings. I hope I have one someday too."

"From what I've observed with Jacob Levine and how he's always got his eye on you, I'd wager you'll be planning your own frontier wedding before long."

Belinda made an embarrassed smile as she looked down at the potato in her hand.

"But there's no hurry." Elizabeth set the bowl of dough back over by the fireplace. "Perhaps there is no hurry for Eli and me as well."

"But Eli is building the house for you and the children. It's only natural that you'd want to live there with him." Belinda waved her hand to where Susannah and Emily and Ruth noisily burst into the house. "And it probably won't be as crowded there."

Elizabeth smiled. "Not to mention it will be less crowded here if we go."

Eager to look at something Emily had brought home from school, the giggling girls hurried up to the loft.

"I wonder what your aunt would think about this," Elizabeth said quietly. When she'd first met Lavinia, she'd been taken aback by the Bostonian woman's commitment to propriety even though they were on the trail. Of course, it didn't take long before Lavinia set decorum aside.

Before Belinda could answer, Malinda entered the house. But it was too late for Elizabeth to retract her last question.

"Aunt Lavinia's so busy with the mercantile and trying to get into their house up above the store. I truly doubt she'd have an opinion one way or another. Besides that, she loves weddings as much as I do."

"Weddings?" Malinda came over to where they were working. "What are we discussing about weddings?"

"Elizabeth was just telling me that she was feeling conflicted," Belinda said.

"Conflicted?" Malinda eyed Elizabeth.

"About her wedding date being only two weeks before yours. But surely you don't mind about that, especially since you're best friends." Belinda smiled at her soon-to-be stepmother. "Now I have a beautiful idea!" Belinda set the potato and paring knife down and clapped her hands merrily. "Why don't you two have a double wedding? Can you imagine how fun that would be?"

"Oh, I don't think so," Elizabeth said quickly. She could tell by Malinda's face that she was not in favor of Belinda's idea. "I really wanted a small quiet wedding, and Malinda and your father plan to have quite a party out there in the barn." She looked hopefully at Malinda. "Which I am looking forward to. Besides that, I promised to stand up with you at your wedding. How could I do that if I was getting married at the same time?" She put her hand on Malinda's shoulder. "And I never properly asked you to stand up with me—I suppose I took it for granted—but I do hope you will."

Malinda smiled. "Of course I will."

Elizabeth knew this didn't mean that Malinda was resolved to the two-week gap between their wedding dates, but it seemed a step in the right direction. Perhaps in a day or two Malinda would become more reasonable. Elizabeth could only hope.

Chapter Nine

By Sunday Elizabeth felt slightly more optimistic. Although the two brides-to-be had not discussed any further wedding plans—they had barely conversed at all—she hoped that was only because Malinda had finally accepted that Elizabeth was immovable on this subject. Either that or Malinda had simply swept the whole thing under the rug for the time being. And with all that was going on in Malinda's household—her four children, her two soon-to-be step-daughters, and Elizabeth's own two—it was easy to get sidetracked.

It felt wonderful to sit next to Eli with JT and Ruth on either side of them in church, but Elizabeth once again felt dismayed as the service was ending. She was growing increasingly weary of the negativity of Reverend Holmes' sermons. If this was simply a season, as her father had suggested, she was ready for it to be over. The short wiry man was so obsessed with hellfire and brimstone that he seemed to have completely forgotten about God's grace and love and mercy.

She exchanged glances with Flo as they exited the little church building. As usual, Bert was missing, as was Flo's oldest son. Not only that, but Hugh Prescott and a few other husbands appeared to be absent as well. Was it possible that the reverend was slowly driving all the men away, or at least the recent settlers? Perhaps the ones who'd been here longer were accustomed to this sort of church service.

Out in the churchyard, where the heavy-leaden skies were almost as gloomy as the faces of the congregation, no one mentioned the content of the sermon. However, Elizabeth could see that people were avoiding Reverend and Mrs. Holmes as the older couple stood near the front steps. Even Mrs. Taylor, who'd once embraced fiery sermons, looked uncomfortable as she hurried away with Mrs. Levine.

"We better load up and head out," Asa called. "This storm is threatening to break." He'd brought his wagon, and the plan was for his family to ride with him to his newly built cabin for Sunday dinner. Expecting rain, he'd even put the cover on top of the wagon, and now all of them piled into the back of the wagon and under its shelter. Meanwhile, Malinda and Will and their children would ride over in Will's wagon. Unfortunately for them, Will hadn't had Asa's foresight regarding the weather.

Ruth rode up front with her grandparents, but the rest of them sat in the back, where Matthew had placed layers of fir boughs and covered them with a quilt. He'd done it for Jessica's sake, but the rest of them enjoyed the unexpected comfort.

"I don't like going to church anymore," JT said quietly to Elizabeth.

She frowned, knowing she should probably reprimand him for speaking with disrespect. And yet in all fairness, how could she?

"I don't like going either," Matthew told JT.

JT's eyes lit up. "Really?"

Matthew just nodded.

"Truth be told, I'm not enjoying it too much either," Eli confessed. "I found myself wishing I was back at the cabin, fitting in the floorboards."

"Floorboards?" Elizabeth was surprised. "You mean we're going to have a real floor? Not just packed dirt?"

He grinned. "That's right."

"Back to church," Matthew said in a serious tone. "I don't know how much longer I can endure being hammered on by Reverend Holmes."

"Why does he hate us so much?" JT asked.

"He doesn't hate us," Elizabeth told him. "He just thinks it's his job to keep us from going to—well, from straying from the fold."

"Well, if loud preaching could prevent someone from going astray, we'd all be safe from the fire and brimstone," Matthew said. "But that's not the gospel I believe in."

"That's not how Grandpa preaches," JT added.

Elizabeth peeked ahead to see if her parents were listening, but she discovered they were having a conversation with Ruth about what they would be doing for Thanksgiving, which was still a couple of weeks away.

"Is Reverend Holmes going to officiate your wedding ceremony?" Jess asked Elizabeth and Eli. They exchanged glances, but neither of them answered.

"That'll be one strange wedding if he does," Matthew teased Elizabeth. "I don't want to miss it."

"Maybe that's why Malinda wants to have her wedding in her barn," Elizabeth mused.

"Well, couldn't you have your wedding in her barn too?" JT suggested.

"I don't know…I think it might be better to have it in the church." She looked at Eli. "Unless you have other ideas?"

"You tell me when and where and I'll be there," he told her.

Elizabeth didn't want to mention the friction going on between her and Malinda, but she felt certain it would not improve the situation if Elizabeth wanted to have her wedding in Malinda's barn. It truly did not seem like an option.

"Do you think our house would be big enough to hold a wedding?" she asked Eli.

"Depends on how many folks are coming."

"Mother was making a guest list," Elizabeth told him. "And I suspect she's already invited a few people, like Lavinia and Flo and Mrs. Taylor. But she didn't want anyone to feel left out, and last I heard she thought there would be close to fifty people attending."

"That would be mighty cozy in your house," Matthew told Eli. "Unless you didn't have the bedroom walled off and if you didn't have any furnishing in place. Even then it might be tight."

"The barn would be much better," JT tried again.

She smiled at him. "Yes, I agree. But I don't want to burden Malinda with hosting our wedding just two weeks before hers. I don't think she'd appreciate that."

"Then it looks like we'll be getting married at the church," Eli declared. "Makes no matter to me, as long as we're married."

"But I'd like for it to be a pleasant wedding," Elizabeth said sadly.

"With no yelling," JT added.

"I wish Asa could perform the ceremony," Eli said wistfully.

"Now, there's an idea." Matthew pointed at Elizabeth. "Maybe you should go and have a little talk with the reverend. Explain what kind of ceremony you want, and if he's unable to give it to you, ask him if Pa can do it."

Elizabeth nodded eagerly. "Yes! That is exactly what I'm going to do."

"You're a braver woman than I am," Jess teased.

Elizabeth frowned. "Yes, well, maybe I'll invite Mother to go with me."

They all laughed.

Soon they were unloading at her parents' house. "Why is the

tent up?" Elizabeth asked her mother as Brady came out to help Asa with the team and the wagon. "I thought you were all moved into your house by now."

"Asa worried it might be overly crowded in the house, what with all the children and all," Clara explained as the women hurried through the rain to the little cabin. "With Malinda and Will's children, there will be nearly twenty of us." Clara opened the door.

"Oh, Mother, look at how nice it is in here! You've been working hard." Elizabeth went around admiring familiar pieces and shelves and curtains that had been put up since she'd last been here. "Home sweet home."

"Matthew and I just moved into our house this week," Jess told her as they hung their wet coats by the door. "We won't have a party like this, but I'd love to have you come by and visit as soon as we're all settled in. Maybe some sunny day when the children are in school, you and Clara could come for lunch."

"That sounds lovely."

It was fun being in a kitchen with her mother again. Certainly it was nothing like the kitchen she'd left behind in Kentucky, but it was a great improvement over the way they cooked meals on the Oregon Trail. Before long, the men came in along with Malinda and Will and all the children. As Asa had predicted, it was very crowded in the small cabin, and it wasn't long before some of the children opted to go out to the tent to play. But it was plain to see that both Asa and Clara were proud of the house they had built. And in some ways it seemed nothing short of miraculous to Elizabeth.

"God has been good to us," Asa said as they all gathered around for a blessing before the dinner, which would be served buffet style. "For that we are grateful." Then they bowed their heads and prayed. As her father said amen, Elizabeth wished more than anything that he might be allowed to perform her wedding ceremony in December.

After the dinner and a spell of friendly visiting, the sun came out, and it seemed a good time to load up the wagons again. But Elizabeth insisted on staying behind to help her mother clean up, and JT and Ruth went with Eli to see the progress on the house. By the time they returned—with both JT and Ruth suitably impressed with what would become their home in a few weeks—Elizabeth and Clara were just finishing up.

"I'm envious," Elizabeth told Eli. "I haven't seen the house in days."

"Come on." He grabbed her hand. "Let's go see it together."

Asa winked at her. "Off with you. I'll challenge JT to a game of checkers."

"And I'll show Ruth my plans for the wedding dresses."

"Dresses?" Elizabeth looked curiously at her mother.

"One for you and one for Ruthie." Clara grinned. "Didn't I tell you?"

Elizabeth laughed. "No, you did not."

"I get a wedding dress too?" Ruth's eyes grew big.

"Come on," Eli said again. "Let's go while the weather is holding."

It was delightful to be alone with Eli again. It seemed their opportunities were few and far between these days. They had probably spent more time alone together while traveling than since they arrived. He took her hand in his, and they walked blissfully through the cool damp meadow between the two properties. "There's already a path wearing through here," Elizabeth noticed. "That's nice."

"It'll be broken in nicely and I expect it'll be traveled even more regularly once we're all moved in."

"I can hardly wait."

Eli paused in the meadow, and pulling her near, he leaned down and kissed her. "I've been wanting to do this for days now," he declared.

She nodded dreamily. "Me too."

They stayed there for a bit, just enjoying each other, and then Eli frowned up at the dark clouds that were rolling in again. "We better hurry if we don't want to get soaked."

Elizabeth grabbed up the skirt of her Sunday dress, and letting out a whoop, she broke out into a full run. Eli laughed as he hurried to catch her. But they barely reached the house when the sky opened up.

"Come on," he said as he pulled her through the open doorway. "Part of the roof is up on the north side. We can hunker down there and stay dry until this passes."

They went to the back of the house where several stumps were doubling as stools and sat down. "The floor is wonderful," she told him, tapping her toes on the solid board beneath her feet.

"I could easily have the floor done by midweek." He peered up to where the open part of the roof was letting in the rain now. "But I reckon I should make the roof a priority. Your dad and Brady have been making cedar shingles, but when I ran out yesterday, I decided to go to work on the floor instead."

"Well, it's just lovely, Eli. Everything about this house is perfect."

He laughed. "I'm not sure that it's perfectly squared."

"It's a perfect place to bring up a family." She looked down at her wet shoes. They hadn't spoken specifically about the possibility of having more children, but she knew that was likely since they both were young. And being around Jessica today, hearing her talking about the baby that would come in the spring, Elizabeth realized that she would love to have another baby too someday...God willing. But thinking of babies reminded her of something else.

"Eli," she said quietly. "There's something I've wanted to ask you about, but I just never seemed to get the chance."

"What's that?"

She explained about when she'd been riding Molly back to Malinda's just a few days earlier and how she felt certain she'd spied a young Indian woman crouching down in the brush alongside the road. "She looked right at me," she told him. "Straight in the eyes. And then—just like that—she disappeared."

"An Indian woman in these parts?" He picked up a scrap piece of wood, peeling a long sliver from it. "From what I hear, that's not very likely, Elizabeth. I recently heard that all the Indians for miles around were herded to a reservation up north. Fort Umpqua."

She nodded sadly. "Yes, I've heard the same thing."

He looked mildly surprised. "Really? Who did you hear that from?"

"Malinda told me about it."

"Did she also tell you about how inhumane the army has acted toward the Indians these past few years? And how the government broke their treaty? Did she mention how many Indians were forced to walk up the beach for a hundred miles, and how many died just making the journey?" He scowled and grimly shook his head. "And did she happen to say how most of the Indians are starving and dying from sickness on the reservation?"

"No." She stared at him in horror. "Where did you hear all that?"

He reached for her hand. "I'm sorry. I didn't mean to sound irritated at you. But I get so enraged by the unjustness of it." He sighed. "I'd hoped that maybe over here in the far West...well, I thought that perhaps things would be different—that for once there would be enough land for everyone." He made a cynical laugh. "Unfortunately, it seems that wherever the white man goes, the Indians suffer."

She swallowed and then nodded. "I fear you may be right."

"Do you know they won't even allow the Indian men to fish or collect clams on the beach? They won't let the women gather food. They don't even have enough blankets to go around."

"How did you hear all this?"

"Josiah Miller. I picked him up on the road on my way back here from Empire City. Seems he was friends with someone from Indian Affairs, a man by the name of Joel Palmer—"

"Malinda mentioned Joel Palmer. He was friends with James. And it sounds as if he's very sympathetic toward the Indians."

"That's what Josiah said too. But then the army took over the Indian situation and the relocation began, and it seems that no one pays much heed to Joel Palmer anymore." He tossed the piece of wood onto a scrap pile. "Forgive me, my dear Elizabeth, but as you know this is one of my sore spots. As much as I love this country—this brave United States of America—I sometimes cannot comprehend or agree with all of the men in leadership."

"I know," she said quietly. Now she pointed at him. "This country needs leaders like you, Eli. Maybe someday you will hold a political office and straighten them all out."

He laughed heartily, and she felt relieved to see him smiling again.

"Now, back to what you were attempting to tell me before I so rudely jumped on my soapbox and subjected you to my sermon." He chuckled. "One session of fiery words is enough for the day."

"If the reverend's passion had been targeted at the Indian situation, I'm sure I would have listened with much more appreciation." For the second time she described how she'd spotted the Indian woman several days ago. "Her eyes looked so lost and frightened. I really wanted to speak to her. But before I could dismount from Molly, she just seemed to vanish into thin air."

"That sounds typical. She obviously did not want to be seen by anyone."

"But I only wanted to help her."

"Think about it, Elizabeth. Wouldn't you try to hide if someone wanted to herd you and your children off to a death camp?"

"I cannot even imagine that."

"Unfortunately, I can."

The rain had stopped, and the late afternoon sun was glistening through the trees in the west, so Eli suggested it was time to leave. As they walked through the soggy meadow back to Elizabeth's parents' house, she explained what Malinda had told her about Charles Levine offending most of the settlers by taking up with a young Indian woman. "I think she said they've been together a few years. But apparently they're not married."

"Not married by white man's law, which is understandable. But they may consider themselves married."

"Yes…I wondered about that."

"Charles Levine has chosen a difficult path."

"And Malinda said they have a child too."

"Oh…" He let out a long sigh.

"Do you think that was her, the woman I saw that day?" she asked. "And if it was her, do you think there's any way we can help her? Help them? Help the child?"

He shrugged then squeezed her hand. "We can sure try."

"I've been praying for her," she said quietly. "Ever since that day—whenever she comes to mind. Those dark eyes…they were haunting."

He stopped walking and placed his hand gently on her cheek. "You are a good woman, Elizabeth Martin. I am a blessed man."

She smiled up at him but wished she were a better woman. A stronger woman. Because the truth was, even if she could get that Indian girl to trust her enough to accept some help, she had no idea what she could actually do or how much assistance she could truly offer. And what about language? Would she even be able to communicate with the young woman? Furthermore, she feared that her concern for an outcast Indian would be met with severe resistance from the rest of the community. Even her good friend Malinda would probably question the sensibility of that kind of charity. Once again Elizabeth realized her best response to this potentially sticky situation would be to simply pray…to ask God to direct her path.

Chapter Ten

After her mother agreed to pay a visit to Reverend Holmes with her, Elizabeth recruited JT as her postman. She sent a note to school with him on Monday saying she and her mother would like to speak to the reverend about her upcoming wedding. The reverend responded the same day by inviting the two women to tea on Thursday afternoon.

Fortunately the rainy weather gave way to sunshine by midweek, and although the road was muddy, Elizabeth and Clara didn't mind putting on their work boots and trekking to town. "Remember how much we walked every day on the trail?" Elizabeth said. "Sometimes I actually miss it."

Clara chuckled. "You can't be serious."

Elizabeth looked up at the clear blue sky. "I'm not saying I'd like to do the whole trip again," she admitted. "But sometimes I miss the simplicity of having only one goal for the day—getting my family safely down the trail."

"Yes, I suppose that makes some sense."

"Have you ever been in Reverend Holmes' house before?" Elizabeth asked as they came in sight of town—or rather, what was slowly transforming into a town.

"No, but I know they live in that cabin back behind the church," Clara said. "It seems rather small. At first I thought it was a storage shed for the church and school."

"It does seem small," Elizabeth admitted. "And a bit close to the church building. JT said that if the children are too noisy at recess, Reverend Holmes will go out on his doorstep and holler at them to quiet down.

Clara laughed. "Sometimes I'd like to tell the good reverend to quiet down."

They were in sight of the church now, although today it was playing the role of school, and it appeared that class was in session. Elizabeth studied the tiny cabin tucked into the trees back behind. "It's very dark and gloomy back there," she said as they skirted the schoolyard toward it.

"And if I'm not mistaken, it's even smaller than our little cabin," Clara said quietly. "Already I'm planning for Asa to add a lean-to kitchen on the back of it. Wouldn't it be wonderful to have the kitchen housed in its own space?"

Before Elizabeth could respond, Mrs. Holmes opened the door and waved toward them. "Good afternoon, ladies," she said cheerfully. "We've been expecting you."

Soon they were inside the shadowy cabin, and Mrs. Holmes was taking their coats. "We brought slippers for the house," Elizabeth told her as she helped her mother to remove a muddy boot.

"Thank you for your thoughtfulness." Mrs. Holmes waved over to where the reverend was seated in a chair by the smoldering fire. "Please, make yourselves at home while I get our tea ready."

Slightly surprised that Reverend Holmes didn't stand as he greeted them, Elizabeth took the straight-backed chair across from him, and her mother sat down in the rocker to his right.

"Interesting footwear," Reverend Holmes said to Elizabeth.

She looked down at her beaded moccasins and smiled. "My daughter, Ruth, and I got these while traveling the Oregon Trail," she explained. "They make wonderful house slippers."

"Ah, yes…you folks traveled by wagon train. For some reason I thought you came by ship like my wife and I did back in '53."

Elizabeth explained that the last leg of their journey actually was by ship. "It is quite a challenge to get down to this part of the country, don't you think?"

He nodded, pressing his fingertips together as he studied Elizabeth. "So you and your young man are going to pledge your troth to each other. Eli Kincaid, I believe his name is. I've only had the pleasure of his acquaintance once. Does he attend church regularly?"

Elizabeth explained that Eli was relatively new to the area and that he'd made a trip to Empire City for lumber.

"Milled lumber?" The reverend's thin gray brows arched. "That must have cost a pretty penny."

"Yes, Eli traded a wonderful horse for part of it." She smiled sadly. "He felt it was worth the sacrifice to ensure we had a roof over our heads this winter."

"Wise man." The reverend looked around the cramped room. "The parsonage roof was in need of repair last summer. I had been in hopes that the men would enlarge the parsonage as well, but alas, that was not to be." He sighed.

"Maybe next summer?" Elizabeth said with optimism.

"I would be much surprised if that happened." He scowled. "The congregation in this settlement seems to be more concerned for their own welfare than that of their clergy."

"Oh, now, Roland," his wife said as she brought in a wooden tray with some mismatched tea service on it. "Remember what the good book says about—"

"I'm well versed in the good book," he said sharply.

She simply laughed as she set the tray down on a small stool in the center of the chairs. "Roland has very high expectations—both for himself and everyone around him."

"The Lord instructs us to be perfect as he is perfect. I do not intend to settle for anything less."

"The ladies didn't come here for a sermon, Roland." Mrs. Holmes handed a cup of tea to Clara. "I was so pleased to hear that Elizabeth has decided to have her wedding in the church."

"Her first wedding was in a church too," Clara said. "And then we had a big dinner out on our farm. I think there were two hundred people in attendance. We had music and dancing and it lasted late into the night."

"Oh, my." Mrs. Holmes handed a cup to Elizabeth. "That must have been quite a memorable celebration."

"It was," Elizabeth admitted. "But I don't want this wedding to be anything like the other one. I was so young then. And no children. Truly, that feels like another lifetime to me now."

Mrs. Holmes patted her knee. "Well, we're just so pleased you want your wedding to be in the church. Especially after we learned that your sister-in-law is having her wedding in her barn."

"Yes. That was dismaying," the reverend said solemnly. "The Martins have been attending our church since its inception four years ago. I baptized two of the children, and I gave the eulogy for John's funeral. And when I met Malinda's intended, William Bramford, I was quite impressed that he was an attorney of law." He frowned. "But I do not understand why a well-educated man would choose to pledge his marriage vows in the company of farm animals."

"The Lord Jesus was born in the company of farm animals," Clara declared.

"That's true." Elizabeth suppressed the urge to giggle at her mother's boldness. "And we're farmers, so we have the utmost respect for livestock, Reverend."

He cleared his throat. "Yes…I'm sure you do."

"But you *do* wish to have your wedding in the church, do you not?" Mrs. Holmes looked uneasy as she handed her husband a cup of tea.

"Yes. Eli and I would like to be married in the church. On the first Saturday of December, if that isn't a problem."

"Not at all." Mrs. Holmes smiled at her husband.

"We will schedule it for you," the reverend assured her.

Elizabeth tossed a nervous glance at her mother. They'd done some strategizing as they'd walked to town. The plan was for Clara to take the lead.

"But first we have some questions," Clara said in a firm tone.

"Questions?" He set his cup down and leaned forward. "Please, feel free."

Clara took in a breath. "Elizabeth and Eli both want their wedding to be a joyous event. They have both known sadness and grief in their lives, and we all believe it is a wonderful miracle that they found each other the way they did. They wish for their wedding ceremony to reflect that."

His brow creased. "What are you saying?"

Clara glanced at Elizabeth before she continued. "Sometimes your sermons are…well, sometimes we feel rather heavy and somber after a church service, Reverend. We would not care to have their wedding feel like that."

"But a wedding ceremony is a solemn affair," he told her. "When two people pledge their troth before man and God, it is to be taken seriously."

"We do take it seriously," Elizabeth assured him. "Our vows will be genuine. But we would prefer to make our vows in a positive atmosphere. My children are young and impressionable. I want them to remember this as a happy day."

"I think that's a lovely idea," Mrs. Holmes told her.

"Making a vow to God is not to be taken lightly, ladies." The reverend's voice was getting louder. "If you wish to have a wedding that's glib and silly and childish, you will need to find someone else to officiate it."

"We are not asking for glib and silly and childish," Clara told him.

He waved his hand. "You want me to make light of a serious occasion."

"A funeral is a serious occasion," Clara said firmly. "A wedding should be a joyous one. Don't you think?"

"I agree," Mrs. Holmes said.

Mr. Holmes just glowered at all of them.

Elizabeth wasn't sure what to do now. She had suspected this man would be stalwart, but she had not imagined he would be this resistant. However, she was pleasantly surprised by Mrs. Holmes. She seemed entirely reasonable. How was it possible these two opposite sorts of characters lived peaceably—and in such a small space?

"My husband is willing to officiate the wedding service," Clara said quietly.

"Is he an ordained minister?"

"No. But he led our church services on the Oregon Trail," Elizabeth said boldly. "And everyone in our unit felt he did a wonderful job of it. He is a gifted preacher."

"If he is not ordained and he is not a justice of the peace, he cannot conduct a legal marriage."

"I was told that a marriage was considered legal if the couple had a certificate signed by witnesses and filed within the year at Empire City," Clara told him.

"And to do that, you must make two trips to Empire City," he replied. "One to get the certificate, and one to file it. Traveling that distance this time of year can take weeks."

"But we have marriage certificates," Mrs. Holmes said quietly.

"That is because I am an ordained minister," he said a bit smugly.

The room grew quiet again, and Elizabeth could see that the reverend was feeling victorious. And perhaps it was best to simply give in. Even if the wedding ceremony was a solemn, unhappy affair, they would have time to celebrate afterward. She knew her mother would see to that.

"So..." Elizabeth began slowly. "It seems that I am at your mercy, Reverend Holmes. Eli and I do wish to be married in early December. And we certainly do not have time to make the trips to Empire City and—"

"Who will officiate Malinda and Will's wedding?" Clara asked Elizabeth.

Elizabeth tilted her head to one side. "I don't know."

"As a matter of fact, I will be the officiator," he informed them. "Not here in the church as I would prefer. But I did agree to go out to her farm." He cleared his throat. "For the same fee I would charge here in the church, I will perform a simple ceremony in the barn." He looked slightly disgusted now, as if this was beneath him. "And then I will leave the merrymakers to their folly."

"And the reverend prefers that I will remain here at home for the wedding," Mrs. Holmes said sadly.

Elizabeth pressed her lips together. Perhaps this was the reason Malinda wanted to hold their wedding in the barn—so that Reverend Holmes could conduct a quick ceremony and then depart. It made perfect sense. And yet it seemed all wrong. It was as if everyone in their settlement was being held hostage by an angry preacher. Now she wondered...if the settlers were the ones paying for his services, and she knew that was true, shouldn't they have a say about the quality of those services?

"May I ask you something?" she said to him.

"Certainly." The edge of his lips curled into what might be considered a half smile.

"Do you enjoy your work, Reverend?"

He looked somewhat taken aback by her question. "Do I enjoy my work? Well, that is an interesting question. First of all it is not work. It is a calling. A very serious calling. God called me to be a minister more than twenty-five years ago. To preach the gospel to the wicked—to save the sinners from eternal damnation. I do not take this calling lightly."

"Yes," Elizabeth persisted. "But do you enjoy it?"

He frowned now. "I do not believe God intends for me to enjoy myself as I serve him. Teaching about God's judgment is a sobering responsibility. Not to be taken lightly. Not to be done for pleasure. Exposing sin and corruption, rescuing sinners from their wicked ways…it is not meant to be enjoyable."

"My father's understanding of God is different from yours. When my father preaches, he speaks of God's love and mercy. He talks about how God showed us his forgiveness by sending his beloved Son to atone for our sins," Elizabeth told him. "Even during the hardships of the Oregon Trail, whenever my father finished a sermon, we all felt encouraged and strengthened—ready to face another difficult day." She sighed. "How I miss that."

The room grew uncomfortably quiet again. And now Elizabeth felt certain that she had said too much. Her mother's eyes were large, and poor Mrs. Holmes was staring down at her lap. Elizabeth had obviously stepped over some invisible line. But how could she hold her tongue when everything about this "minister of God" seemed foreign to her? Even with the reverend glaring at her, she was not ready to back down.

She took a deep breath and then continued. "The reason I asked if you enjoy your work is that you strike me as a very unhappy man, Reverend Holmes. And with all due respect, that concerns me. I think if someone is called by God to shepherd a flock, he should do it with gladness and joy. However, you seem to be completely without gladness or joy. You seem to be a very sad man."

"Perhaps I appear sad because I take life and death—heaven and hell—seriously." His eyes narrowed and his mouth was grim. "I take my responsibilities in caring for this flock very seriously."

"Is that because you believe that it's all up to you and you alone?" she asked. "Do you believe that your congregation's spiritual fate is in your hands?"

"God has entrusted me with these people."

"I respect that. But it seems to me that you are not trusting God, Reverend. Perhaps if you trusted God more, if you believed more wholly in his love, if you understood the magnitude of his grace, if you felt the power of his mercy, you would be a much happier person. Perhaps you would even enjoy your work—that is, your calling. And if you were happier, I am sure your sermons would be more encouraging and uplifting. And your congregation would look forward to going to church." She took in a quick breath. "But as it is, your congregation is shrinking. And I'm afraid it will continue to shrink."

The only sound was the ticking of the clock. Elizabeth could tell by the sparkle in Clara's eyes that she was secretly pleased with her daughter's audacity. And although Mrs. Holmes looked somewhat shocked with her hand over her lips, Elizabeth thought she could see a trace of a smile there too.

"For a young woman, you certainly have no problem expressing your opinions," he told her in a condescending way. "Apparently you've not learned to respect your elders during your youth. But perhaps when you grow older, you will grow wiser too."

"I am older," Clara said. "And I agree with every word my daughter just said."

"As do I," Mrs. Holmes said with wide eyes.

"Georgia!" He glowered at his wife.

"I'm sorry, Roland, but it's the truth. And it's what I've been trying to tell you, but you refuse to listen. For the past couple of years, your sermons have gotten louder and meaner. You frighten the children. You offend the men—so much so that many of them are refusing to come to church. The women come only out of habit, and then they cannot seem to get away quickly enough. If you continue like this, I suspect they will give up eventually." She had tears in her eyes now. "I don't like to go to church," she confessed to Clara and Elizabeth. "I always have a stomachache on Sundays."

Clearly enraged, Reverend Holmes stood up with balled fists. His face was red and blotchy now, and the whites of his eyes were showing. But without uttering a word, he marched across the room, snatched up his hat and coat, and exited the tiny house, slamming the door loudly behind him. And now poor Mrs. Holmes burst into sobs.

"Oh, you poor dear," Clara said as she put an arm around her shoulders.

"I am so sorry," Elizabeth said as she patted the woman's back. "I never should have said all that."

"No, no," Mrs. Holmes assured her in a shaky voice. "It needed to be said." She blew her nose on her handkerchief. "Someone needed to come forward and say it."

"I…I don't know." Elizabeth's hands were trembling, and she felt close to tears herself. She could hardly believe what she'd just said to the reverend—where had that come from? "I never meant to say that much to him," she confessed. "All I wanted was a peaceful wedding."

"I've been hoping and praying one of the men would come forward and tell Roland he'd gone too far," Mrs. Holmes told them. "But they are so busy with farming and building and whatnot." She smiled sadly at Elizabeth. "I'm much obliged to you for speaking your mind."

"What will Reverend Holmes do?" Clara looked at the door with concern.

"He'll storm around in the forest, walking for miles I s'pect. He'll rant and rave at God, and in time he will come home and be very quiet." She sighed as if the quiet might be appreciated. "After that…

there's no telling what he'll do. He might even vent his wrath from the pulpit on Sunday."

Elizabeth cringed. Because of her the congregation was going to suffer?

"Has he always preached such fiery sermons?" Clara asked her.

"Oh, no. Not at all. Roland used to preach some beautiful sermons. Everyone in the church back in Virginia loved him. But about six or seven years ago, his brother challenged him, saying Roland should become more theological. At first the two of them argued about it. But then his brother got him to read some theology books." She shook her head. "After Roland read those books, he began to see life differently, and he started preaching differently."

"That was back in Virginia?"

"Yes. But the congregation didn't appreciate the change. After a year or so, they decided it was time for Roland to move on." She sadly shook her head. "He was very hurt at first. But then he decided it was God's way of sending us to the Western frontier. We knew the Levine family had settled in these parts, and Roland had been good friends with Wesley Levine when they were growing up."

"Had Mr. Levine passed on yet?" Clara asked.

"Yes, but we hadn't heard about it," she said. "So we sold everything we owned and booked passage to Oregon." She waved her hand. "And here we are."

Clara reached over and grasped Mrs. Holmes' hand. "I'm sure this hasn't been easy for you."

"No...I suppose it's been my cross to bear. But I keep praying that Roland will return to his old way of preaching. I never give up hope."

"Well, I hope we haven't made matters worse for you," Clara said.

"No, don't you worry about me. Roland's bark is much worse than his bite. He truly loves me. And despite his sermons, he loves his congregation too."

"Does the reverend have any close friends? Men he can talk to?"

"I had hoped he and Wesley would rekindle their friendship.

We've been here three and a half years, and so far Roland has yet to make a good friend."

"That's probably because the men are so busy trying to scratch out a living, just as you said."

She nodded. "That and they're probably afraid of him."

"Well, there's one man who won't be scared of him." Clara chuckled. "I'm going to ask Asa to come over and visit the reverend. Now that our house is mostly finished, my good husband can afford to make a trip to town now and then."

"That's a wonderful idea," Elizabeth agreed. "No one could have a better friend than Father. The reverend would benefit greatly from getting better acquainted with him."

Elizabeth and Clara visited a bit longer, staying long enough to see Mrs. Holmes return to her merry little self. But as they were leaving, she stopped Elizabeth with a worried brow. "Oh, dear. Does this mean you won't be having your wedding in the church now?"

Elizabeth tied her bonnet strings. "Why don't we just wait and see what happens with Reverend Holmes. And in the meantime, I'll be praying for him."

"Yes, so will I," Clara told her. "Maybe after Asa talks to him, we'll have a better idea of what to do regarding the wedding."

As they walked back toward home, they noticed a new set of dark clouds rolling in from the direction of the ocean and hastened their pace in order to make it back before the sky broke open. As Elizabeth watched the rain pelting down, she wondered if the reverend would still be stomping around in the woods, ranting and raving. And if so, maybe it was for the best. Perhaps a nice chilly autumn shower would cool him off a bit. Maybe God would use it to wash some of the strange notions out of his stubborn head. Then, as promised, Elizabeth said a silent prayer for the reverend.

Chapter Eleven

After the children went to bed, Elizabeth and Malinda remained seated by the fireside, sewing. Malinda was working on her wedding dress. She'd purchased the beautiful silk brocade from the mercantile. Elizabeth had held her tongue when she saw that it was a silvery shade of green. She had no intention of telling Malinda about the wedding dress poem, and she had warned Ruth to keep quiet on the topic. The bride might be wearing green, but Elizabeth knew she would not be "ashamed to be seen."

"Mother and I had an interesting visit with Reverend and Mrs. Holmes today," Elizabeth said quietly.

"Oh, yes, I nearly forgot about that. How did it go?"

Elizabeth slid the needle into the blue gingham shirt that had once belonged to James. She was altering it to fit JT, shortening the sleeve by placing a tuck just underneath the cuff and then putting in similar tucks along the shoulder seams. At the rate JT was growing, she might be letting out the tucks by spring. As she sewed, she told Malinda about their rather interesting afternoon.

"You truly said that to Reverend Holmes?" Malinda looked flabbergasted.

"That and more, I'm afraid." Elizabeth shook her head. "I was just so upset at him. It was as if someone else was talking—not me."

"Well, I would have liked to have seen that." Malinda put the end of thread to her lips.

"I thought my mother was going to be mortified. But when it was all said and done, she told me she was proud of me. Just the same, I wish I hadn't said quite so much. I truly don't like conflict of any kind. But there seemed to be no getting around it."

"When the Levines told us we were getting a minister back in 1852, we were all so excited. That summer, all the settlers worked together to build the church. Of course, we knew it would also suffice as a school, and that alone was very welcome. But everyone really sacrificed to get that building up. The Levines had spoken so highly of Reverend Holmes that we felt extremely fortunate. And I suppose we all had rather high expectations."

"I see." Elizabeth tied off her thread.

"We knew they were to arrive in September of 1853," she continued. "And although we were all busy with our own farms and homes, we decided to go the extra mile and build a parsonage. We knew it was rather small, but there wasn't much time. Besides, it was better than nothing, and we hoped to add onto it the following year."

"But that never happened?"

"By the summer of 1854, I think we were all feeling a bit disappointed in the reverend. No mention was made of enlarging the parsonage. John told me that some of the men were hoping that Reverend and Mrs. Holmes would leave if we didn't improve their home."

"It is extremely small."

"That was about the time we were having the Indian troubles,"

Malinda continued. "The threat of Indian attacks was an understandable distraction from our clergyman concerns. And I suppose, in light of our fearful circumstances, we were not so opposed to the reverend's style of preaching. Another year passed…and the reverend stayed on. And then we were struck by illness last year…and James died…" She sighed. "I honestly can't remember all of the details of the past couple of years, but Reverend Holmes did not give up. Church attendance fell, and I'm sure the offerings were meager. One would think that alone would have driven them back east. But alas, they are still here. I suppose we all just resolved ourselves to the idea that we would be saddled with Reverend Holmes forever."

"Is he the reason you wanted to have your wedding in the barn?"

Malinda shrugged. "He's still officiating our ceremony. But hopefully we'll all cheer up after he leaves." She gave Elizabeth a sympathetic look. "Are you sure you want to go through with your church wedding now?"

Elizabeth thought about it. "I don't see any way around it. We'll just have to make the best of it."

"If you waited until spring, you could have a very nice wedding in my barn. I would help you with all the details, Elizabeth."

She pursed her lips, considering this offer, but as soon as she thought of Eli and how faithfully he was working to finish their home and how anxious he was to be married and settled—she knew her answer. "Even if Reverend Holmes grumbles and growls and yells throughout our nuptials, I am willing to endure it. For Eli's sake, I will endure it."

❧

On Sunday morning, Elizabeth felt nervous about going to church. She knew her father hadn't been able to carve out the time to go visit Reverend Holmes yet, mostly because he and Brady had been helping Eli with her house all week. So when she walked into the building with Eli and the children, she was bracing herself for whatever wrath might come from the pulpit. She had not told Eli about her visit. He seemed to have enough on his mind with finishing the house, especially now that their wedding date was just less than two weeks away.

They took their seats and waited as more families joined them. As usual, the church was not very full. Elizabeth looked up to where Mrs. Holmes normally sat right in front and was surprised to see that she was not there yet.

"Are we early?" Ruth whispered after they'd sat for a spell.

"No, I don't believe we're early," Elizabeth said quietly.

Other members of the congregation began murmuring among themselves, and everyone was obviously wondering when the service would begin. Elizabeth looked over to where her parents were seated near the front just as her mother glanced back with a concerned expression.

"Excuse me," said a female voice from behind the congregation.

Everyone turned around to see Mrs. Holmes standing in the doorway. Her face was creased with worry. "I'm sorry to tell you that Reverend Holmes will be unable to deliver his sermon today," she announced. "He has taken ill."

Now the congregation made sympathetic and concerned noises.

"I'm sorry that all of you made the effort to come today," she continued. "But we didn't know until this morning that he would not be well enough to preach."

"Asa Dawson can take the service," Will Bramford called out.

"Yes," Hugh Prescott agreed. "Let Asa preach to us."

Mrs. Holmes face brightened. "Would you care to preach this morning, Mr. Dawson?" she asked hopefully.

Asa stood and looked around. "I reckon I could."

"We'd be much obliged," Mrs. Holmes said.

Asa held up his Bible. "I came armed with the sword of the Spirit," he said jovially.

As Asa went to the front of the room, Elizabeth noticed Flo

whispering to Walter, who hurried out. Flo winked at her, and Elizabeth suspected she'd sent Walter to fetch his dad and older brother.

The room grew quiet as Asa stood behind the podium. Elizabeth could see he was a bit nervous, but she knew their friends from the wagon train would be supportive of whatever he decided to say. However, she didn't know about the others. They were so accustomed to Reverend Holmes, they might be let down.

As usual they began with singing, but the songs Asa selected from the hymnal were more uplifting than usual. He led the singing with enthusiasm, and it wasn't long before the congregation seemed to catch his energy and joy. While they were still singing, Elizabeth was relieved to see Walter return with his dad and brother, taking their seats next to Flo and the girls.

When the singing was done, Asa prayed just as the reverend always did before his sermon. But Asa's prayer was gentle and humble and earnest. He asked that God would speak through him and bless everyone in the room with his holy presence.

"Now as ya'll can imagine, I didn't get up this morning knowing I was going to be standing in front of you now." He chuckled as he opened his Bible. "But I've got a mind to share one of our Lord Jesus' parables with you." He flipped through the pages. "I will be reading from the Gospel of Matthew, chapter seven." He moved his hand down the page. "Yes, here it is." He cleared his throat and then clearly and loudly read the parable of the wise man who built his house upon the rock.

Now he looked back out over the congregation. "I s'pect I chose that parable on account of I've been doing some house building myself of late." He chuckled. "I know that all of you know what I'm talking about since you've all had to build your own homes too. You understand the need to build a house that is solid and sound and strong." And now Asa explained a bit about how important it was to square up the house right from the beginning, how the very first logs or boards were like a foundation.

"If you start out wrong on the ground level, if your foundation is crooked or unstable, your house will end up being crooked or unstable. It might even fall down. That's not what you want in a house. You want a house that can stand up to the wind and the rain. A house that can shelter you from wild animals and storms and thieves in the night. A body needs a good strong house out here in the frontier."

Asa paused as if considering his words. "But Jesus was not speaking of an earthly house when he told that parable. He was talking about a man's life. A woman's life. Jesus was saying that when we listen and obey him, it is as if we have built our house solidly upon him. Jesus is the foundation of our lives." Asa pounded one balled fist onto the other balled fist as if to show this. "Jesus is the rock we want to build our lives upon. When we build our lives securely on him, when we listen to his teaching and practice obedience, we will be strong enough to withstand whatever comes our way. And we all know that hard times come to everyone on this earth. Whether it's death or illness or other kinds of losses, storms do come our way. But if our lives are built sturdily on our Lord Jesus, we can withstand those storms."

He preached awhile longer and even shared from his own trials, telling about when their family was struck down by illness and how some of them died. "The storm came at us and it came hard," he said, "but we had our solid foundation of faith beneath us. That's what got us through then. It's what will get us through anything else that might be coming our way. Build your life on the rock, my friends, the rock that is our Lord and Savior, and when those storms and winds of life come crashing down, you will be safe. You will be safe."

Asa took in a deep breath. "Now let us pray." He said another prayer and led them in a couple more songs. Then, before the service was completely over, he told them he had an announcement to make. "My wife will tan my hide if I forget to say this," he said, causing people to laugh. "Clara made me promise to stand up at the end of the service to make this announcement. But since I already have your attention, I just want to be sure to invite every one of you to a very special event that will be happening right here in a couple of weeks." He waved over to where Elizabeth and Eli were sitting. "You kids stand up," he said. And with some embarrassment, they both stood. "I'm sure everyone's heard the news that Mr. Eli Kincaid and Mrs. Elizabeth Martin are going to get hitched, but you may not have heard all the details. On the first Saturday of December they will be repeating their wedding vows right here at eleven o'clock in the morning." He looked over to his wife. "Is that correct?"

"That's right," she said.

"And I know Eli and Elizabeth will be honored if you will be in attendance. And afterward, you are invited to a dinner which we will have right here as well." Now he pointed to Elizabeth. "Anything else you'd like to add?"

She nodded nervously. "Yes. Eli and I request that you bring no wedding gifts. We simply want to enjoy your company as we celebrate our special day. Thank you."

Although the service was over, instead of everyone scurrying away as they normally did, people lingered and visited among themselves. The general feeling in the room was one of pleasantness. And it felt wonderful to see everyone relaxed and even jovial—so different from the way they usually acted. Elizabeth noticed Mrs. Holmes, who had stayed for the service, coming over to speak to Asa. She shook his hand and thanked him with tear-filled eyes before she turned to leave.

But before Mrs. Holmes could go, Elizabeth and her mother went over to catch up with her, both of them warmly greeting her and inquiring as to her husband's health.

"I hope it's not anything serious," Clara said with concern.

"No, no, I don't think it's serious," Mrs. Holmes assured them. She lowered her voice. "Roland came home looking like a drowned rat several hours after you ladies left. He was soaked to the skin. I wasn't the least bit surprised when he came down with a cold the very next day. But it wasn't until today that we discovered he could barely speak. He was as hoarse as an old bull frog this morning."

"Oh, dear." Elizabeth stifled the urge to giggle.

"The Lord does work in mysterious ways." Mrs. Holmes smiled.

"Do give him our regards," Clara said. "And if there's anything I can do to help, please, let me know."

"My mother is very gifted with herbal medicines," Elizabeth told her.

"And you can let him know that Eli and Elizabeth still wish to have their wedding in the church," Clara added.

Mrs. Holmes grasped Elizabeth's hands. "Oh, dear, I was so pleased to hear that."

"And if the reverend is still under the weather, I'm sure my father would be perfectly happy to do the service."

Mrs. Holmes made a knowing smile. "Yes, well, I've never seen Roland be sick for longer than a week. And with your wedding date being just less than two weeks, I expect he'll be all well by then."

Elizabeth nodded. "Please, don't get me wrong, I am not wishing for your husband to be ill."

Mrs. Holmes chuckled. "No, I did not think that was your intention."

Everyone was in good spirits as they went home from church. Her parents acted as if it was because of the sunshine, but Elizabeth knew that it was because of her father's uplifting sermon. If only he could permanently replace the reverend.

Once again, Elizabeth and Eli and the children went to her parents' cabin for Sunday dinner. But today, with just the six of them, it was less crowded, and they were all able to sit at the table together.

"Asa made these benches last week," Clara told Elizabeth as she was admiring the additions to the cabin. "I told him I wanted enough seating to have my whole family here for Thanksgiving this year—and that means nine of us. Naturally, I've invited Brady to join us."

"It will be snug but lovely," Elizabeth said as she stirred the gravy.

"That reminds me, Jess invited you and me to lunch on Tuesday. I told her I'd let you know. She thought we could spend the afternoon sewing on your wedding dress, and I told her I'd be very grateful for the help. I don't know what inspired me to put so many tucks in that bodice, but it's taking much more time than I imagined." She sighed as she removed a biscuit from the pan. "Or else I'm just getting old."

"You're not old," Ruth told her as she set a jar of jam on the table. "You're just right, Grandma."

As Elizabeth and Clara and Ruth worked to get the food on the table, Elizabeth imagined what it would be like to be doing this in her own house—in just two weeks. It was almost unimaginable. To make it even more unimaginable, Eli had told her that she was not allowed to step foot into the house until *after* the wedding. When she complained that she would be unable to sew curtains and what-not, he had promised to write down all the measurements she would need. "But you do not get to see it until we are married," he declared. And so she had agreed, but she was afraid her curiosity would get so strong, she might sneak over there and break her promise. However, she did enjoy the idea of a surprise. Also, she had a hunch—based on various questions her mother had asked recently—that Eli was soliciting help from some of her family members.

Chapter Twelve

To Elizabeth's relief, Malinda had not mentioned anything about the closeness of their wedding dates in the past week. Perhaps she was resolved to it by now. And Malinda had been in church to hear Elizabeth announce they wanted no gifts. That should reassure her that their wedding would be a much smaller affair.

Lavinia had seemed scandalized by this news. "What do you mean by having no gifts?" she'd demanded after church. "What do you intend to do if someone shows up with a gift?" she'd teased. "Will you and Eli throw them out on the street?" Elizabeth had laughed and assured her that no one would be thrown out on the street.

To help keep their relationship moving smoothly forward, Elizabeth was doing all she could to help in the preparations for Malinda's wedding. Every evening, along with Amelia and Belinda, she helped with the sewing on Malinda's dress. At the rate they were going, it would be finished long before the actual date. She and the girls were also helping Malinda with another large quilt, which she assumed was for what would be Malinda and Will's wedding bed. Elizabeth had even donated some of her own favorite fabric scraps to be used in the log cabin design, and as the days and weeks had rolled by, the quilt was turning out to be quite beautiful.

"Are you making a quilt for you and Eli?" Amelia asked Elizabeth on Monday evening.

Elizabeth paused from threading her needle. "I have a nice quilt packed in my wagon that still has lots of wear left in it." She pointed to her sewing basket. "I'd rather put my time into getting those curtains finished," she told her. Certainly it would be lovely to have new things for her new life with Eli, but Elizabeth had no regrets for the way she was going into this marriage. Already she and her children were counting the days until the wedding date.

On Tuesday morning, after finishing with chores, Elizabeth rode Molly over to her mother's house, and from there they walked together to Matthew and Jess' house. "Did you hear about the Thompsons?" Elizabeth asked her mother as they walked.

"The family with the stallion that Asa has spoken of?" Clara said.

"Yes. Their farm is a few miles north of the school," Elizabeth told her. "According to the children, the Thompsons lost their best calf to wild animals on Sunday night."

"Oh, dear. That's too bad. But the stallion is all right?"

"As far as I know."

"I'll tell your father. He may want to bring our stock near the house at night."

"Yes. That's what Malinda and I are doing. She thinks it's a coyote pack."

"All the nights we slept in the tent, I never heard coyotes. Not once," Clara said.

They were on Matthew and Jess' property now. "Oh, look at all they've done," Elizabeth exclaimed as the small cabin came in sight. Built completely of logs, like her parents', it had a stone-lined path and smoke curling from the chimney. "The last time I was out here, the walls weren't even half up. Now it looks like a home!"

"You're here!" Jess called as she came outside to greet them.

"This place is so sweet," Elizabeth said as they exchanged hugs. "I can't wait to see your cabin."

"First I want to show you what I've done outside," Jess said as she pulled on a gray woolen shawl that had once belonged to Clara. She led them around the property, showing where she'd made a good start on some rail fences for livestock as well as a seedling garden similar to Elizabeth's. "And I just planted garlic yesterday." She pointed over to a corner of the garden.

"Wonderful," Clara told her. "It's good for warding off colds."

"And I put onion sets in over there," Jess said proudly.

Elizabeth patted her back. "You're a real farmer now, Jess."

"I can still see you on the trail." Clara chuckled. "Back when I thought you were a boy. Out there riding your horse with your head in your farming book."

Elizabeth laughed. "Yes. I remember how shocked I was to discover you were a girl."

Jess looked slightly embarrassed. "I must have seemed rather pathetic."

"No." Elizabeth shook her head. "You seemed very sweet. A girl who wanted to be a farmer. You won my heart right from the start."

"And Matthew's too," Clara added.

"I still can't believe this is our very own farm." Jess waved her hands. "All this beautiful land. Sometimes I want to pinch myself to see if I'm dreaming."

"I'm sure it's a world different from life in St. Louis," Clara said.

"It will be so exciting to see what kinds of plants will thrive here," Jess said as she led them back to her cabin. "I've read enough to know that this soil might not be as fertile as it looks."

"Asa keeps telling me that our future will be in dairy farming," Clara told them. "But I'm not so sure. With this mild climate, I expect we can grow almost anything."

"It depends on the soil," Jess explained. "I've read about soil amending. And I suspect this soil will require some work."

"I'm already saving ash from our campfires," Clara told them. "Sometimes that's good for soil."

"And I have JT collecting manure to use for fertilizer," Elizabeth said. "But it will take some time to age properly."

"In time, we'll figure it out," Clara proclaimed.

Jess held the door wide open. "Welcome to our home!"

"It's charming," Elizabeth said as she removed her riding hat. "And it smells good too." She recognized one of her mother's rugs over in the sitting area, as well as a rustic pair of chairs that she suspected Matthew and Brady had built. Brady's woodcarving skills were coming in quite handy in the frontier.

"Come see what Jess has done in her kitchen," Clara told Elizabeth. "You won't believe it."

Elizabeth went over to the kitchen area and blinked in surprise. "Wallpaper?" She turned to Jess, who was giggling. "Where on earth did you get wallpaper out here?"

"It's fabric," Jess confessed. "I saw it at the mercantile, and thought it was so pretty, I wanted a way to see it every day. That's when I decided to attach it to the wall. When it gets dirty, I'll just take it down and wash it."

"Very clever." Elizabeth went over to touch the bright red-and-yellow calico. "It's so cheerful."

They visited happily as they ate soup and bread together, and then they sat and sewed on Elizabeth's wedding dress for nearly two hours before Elizabeth knew it was time to go back to Malinda's. "Your house is just perfect," she told Jess as they hugged goodbye. "Tell Matthew his big sister is proud of him."

"And we'll see you on Thanksgiving," Clara reminded her.

There was a chilly breeze blowing as they walked back toward her parents' cabin. "I know we won't have much winter here in Oregon," Elizabeth said as she turned her collar up, "but it does feel like it's getting cooler."

"Your father said it's getting to be perfect hunting weather. But he wants to wait to go out with Eli. And Eli wants to finish your house first. Did you know that they finished the little house for Brady?"

"No, I hadn't heard."

"It's very small. Even smaller than the parsonage. But Brady seemed pleased with it. And he's been building some furnishings for it. I gave him a few things, but with his earnings from the trip, I told him he could probably find a few things at the mercantile to make his place more comfortable." She sighed. "Except I don't think he cares to go into town too much. He's worried that some folks might not be too friendly, if you know what I mean."

"I don't see why Brady should be concerned. He proved himself on the trail. Everyone from the wagon train seemed to be fairly accepting of him by the end of the trip."

"It's the other settlers that concern him." Clara frowned. "No matter how far you go, you can never seem to get away from hatred. Well, that is, until you get to heaven. Brady ought to feel right at home up there."

"I asked him about coming to church a while back, but he told me he holds his own worship services under the trees and the sky."

Clara laughed. "That'd be highly preferable to some of the sermons Reverend Holmes has subjected the rest of us to."

"Well, if you see Brady, tell him that I'm happy to go to the mercantile and do his shopping for him," Elizabeth declared.

"He might be around here," Clara said as they walked toward her cabin. "He's been awfully helpful with Asa lately." She lowered her voice. "And don't tell anyone, but Asa's been teaching Brady to read."

"That's wonderful. But why is it a secret?"

"At first it was because Brady was worried that he was breaking the law. But then he said he just wants to surprise everyone. He hopes that he'll be able to read from the Bible at Christmas."

"I won't tell a soul." Elizabeth spied her father carrying a load of firewood toward the cabin. She greeted him and inquired about Brady.

"I reckon he's working on his own little house today," Asa told her. "Or else he's helping Eli. I'm on my way over there as soon as I fill up the wood box. I promised Eli I'd help him with a door."

"A door," Elizabeth said dreamily. "Just imagine."

"Don't you go imagining too much," Asa warned her. "Might spoil the surprise."

"I'm so anxious to see the house," Elizabeth admitted. "I'm tempted to ride Molly over there right now and sneak a peek."

"Don't you dare!" Asa scolded.

"That's right." Clara shook her finger at her. "Your young man is working as fast as he can. Don't you go and ruin his surprise."

"Yes, yes...I know. Don't worry, I won't break my promise." Elizabeth untied Molly's rein from the hitching post her father had set up in front of their cabin.

"Eli is working so hard." Asa laid his load of firewood in the wood box and then stood straight and looked at her. "I don't know when I've ever seen a man so motivated, Elizabeth."

She smiled. "He's a good man, isn't he, Father?"

"Yep." Now he tipped his hat to them. "And if you'll excuse me, ladies, I will be on my way. I'm sure they're wondering if I'm ever coming back."

"Tell Brady that if he makes a list of things he needs from the mercantile, I'd be happy to shop for him. Also, I have some things I want to give him for his little cabin."

"I will let him know." Asa untied his mare and eased himself up into the saddle.

"And give Eli my best," Elizabeth told him.

"I'll do that." Asa nudged Penny, and as they headed off toward Elizabeth's property, she stood and watched longingly.

"Less than two weeks now," Clara assured Elizabeth.

"Ten more days to be precise." Elizabeth swung into the saddle. "Every morning Ruth reminds me." She laughed. "Almost as if she were counting the days until Christmas."

"I'm sure it'll feel like Christmas for both JT and Ruth—for all of you once you get into your own home."

"Yes. Ruth tries not to complain, but I know she's getting weary of sleeping with Malinda and me. However, JT will probably miss sleeping in the barn with his cousins. He's gotten quite close to Todd and Bart."

"At least they'll be nearby. Speaking of JT and Ruth, that reminds me…" Clara peered up at her. "Would the children like to stay with us for a few days after the wedding?"

"Oh, I don't know." She pulled on her riding gloves. "They'll be so excited about the new house."

"Elizabeth," her mother said firmly. "You and Eli might like some alone time after your wedding. I know you love your children, but you and Eli might be more comfortable if you don't have them with you on your wedding night."

Elizabeth giggled as she pulled her felt hat down more tightly on her forehead. "Yes, Mother, perhaps you're right. I'll ask JT and Ruth if they'd like to visit you after the wedding."

"Or maybe they'd prefer to remain with Malinda and their cousins."

"I'm sure we'll figure it out. See you on Thanksgiving, Mother." Now she kneed Molly, and waving, she was on her way. She really did want to go over and check on Eli and see her house. She was also curious to see where Brady was living and get a list from him. She could think of many excuses to wander on over to her own property. However, she knew she had to keep her word. And so, trying not to feel left out, she turned Molly back toward Malinda's.

As she came to the brushy place where she'd seen the Indian woman before, she decided to slow down. Would she possibly see her again? This spot was close enough to hear the creek bubbling along. And so she slowed Molly to a complete stop and just listened for a spell. She listened to the sound of the wind rustling through the trees, the sound of the creek tumbling along toward the river. She was almost ready to leave when she thought she heard something besides the wind and the water. Or perhaps it was just her imagination.

She held her breath as she strained her ears to listen. Peering into the brushy area where it seemed the rustling sound had come from, she tried to see through the shadows. Perhaps it was simply an animal—a deer or raccoon or rabbit. Or was someone back in there? She was tempted to dismount from her horse, but she worried that she would make a sound and frighten whoever or whatever was there. And so she just waited, quietly stroking Molly's neck lest she make a noise.

Then, just as she was about to give up, the rustling sound grew closer. And suddenly an Indian woman emerged from the shadows. Elizabeth knew it was the same woman, but this time she could see her more clearly. Her long black hair hung limply, and her dark eyes were a mixture of sadness and fear. She wore a dirty threadbare dress, little more than a rag. But it was the small shadow behind the woman that caught Elizabeth's eye. A child perhaps? The Indian woman looked as if she was afraid to move as their eyes locked.

Elizabeth, though startled, attempted to smile and say hello. But the word had barely escaped her lips when the woman backed up and disappeared—just as she'd done before. Elizabeth squinted into the shadows as she tried to decide what to do. Should she dismount the horse and call out to her? Should she attempt to follow her? Or would that only frighten her more? She thought about the small shadow again. She had not imagined it—the woman had a child with her. Elizabeth knew it. But how were they surviving out here? And if this was the woman Malinda had spoken of, where was Charles? And if she wasn't Charles' woman, who was she? Whatever the situation, one thing seemed very clear—the young woman seemed frightened and in need.

Feeling worried for the young woman and her child, as well as frustrated that she'd failed to win the woman's trust, Elizabeth nudged Molly into a gallop. She wasn't comfortable telling Malinda about seeing an Indian nearby. But she really wanted to take something back to share with Indians. And she wanted to get it to them as quickly as possible, before they had a chance to get too far away.

The children were just getting home from school, so after greeting JT and Ruth and seeing that they were off to do their chores, she went to the corner of the barn, where she had stored some of her own goods—items she'd brought along with her when they'd first moved into Malinda's. There were spare blankets and some other things. She removed a blanket and then went into the kitchen, where Amelia and Emily were excitedly telling Malinda about something they'd seen on the way home from school.

"It looked like a cougar had sharpened its claws on the tree," Emily told her mother with wide eyes.

Amelia held her hand high over her head. "But it was this tall."

"So the cougar would have to be really, really big," Emily said.

"And we didn't see those marks there this morning," Amelia explained.

"So it must be around right now," Emily said in a frightened voice.

"Do you think that's what killed the Thompsons' calf?" Malinda asked.

"That's what the boys said," Amelia told her. "They think there's a cougar on the prowl."

As interested as Elizabeth was in this conversation, she was grateful for the distraction because it allowed her to take a bread loaf and tuck it inside the blanket. She'd made three loaves yesterday, and they still had enough for supper tonight. However, this meant she'd need to bake again tomorrow.

"I wonder if one of the boys should take a gun with him to school tomorrow," Elizabeth said to Malinda as she tucked the rolled blanket under her arm.

Malinda's brow creased. "I suppose I could let Todd take the rifle. He's a good shot."

"JT is a good shot too," Elizabeth said. "But our guns are still packed in the wagon."

"Todd's the oldest," Malinda told her. "He should be the one to carry a gun."

Elizabeth nodded. "Yes. That sounds best."

The girls continued telling Malinda about the "giant wild cat" as Elizabeth slipped out the door. She hurried over to where her horse was still tethered by the barn.

"I've got to run an errand," she told JT as he and Bart emerged from the barn, each one with a pail in hand. "I'll be right back."

He just nodded.

She felt guilty for not being fully honest with her son as she nudged Molly into a trot. But at the same time she didn't want to tell her children she was helping an Indian—who knew what kind of problems that could create for them at school? No, it was better this way. And the next time she saw Eli, she would ask him for his counsel.

Before long, she was back at the brushy spot by the creek. She slowed Molly to a walk and then stopped. As she slid down from the saddle, she remembered the girls' fears about the cougar in the area. However, she felt fairly safe with her big horse so close by. Not many cougars would go after a horse.

"Hello?" she called out again, waiting to see if she could hear anything. "I leave this gift in friendship," she said loudly, hoping the woman was listening—and that she understood some English. She knew the woman and child could be far away by now. But maybe they weren't. "I'm sorry I don't have more to share right now," she said as she set the bundle in the exact spot where the woman had stood, looking up with such frightened eyes. "God bless you," she said finally as she went back to her horse.

As she rode back, she prayed for the woman and child. She prayed that God would show her an even better way to help them. For some reason—probably that look in her eyes—they seemed to need help.

Chapter Thirteen

By the time she got back and made herself busy helping with supper preparations, the big talk in the house was about the cougar. "Eli could hunt it down," Ruth was telling her cousins. "He's the best hunter in the whole world. Even my grandpa says so."

"Do you think we should tell Eli about the cougar?" Malinda asked Elizabeth.

"That's not a bad idea," Elizabeth confessed. Now she wished she'd thought of this earlier. She could easily have made it over to her property when she'd taken the bundle to the Indian woman. She could have told him all about it.

"I wouldn't be concerned," Malinda said. "Except that the place where the children spotted the claw marks is less than a mile from here. And that's nearly four miles from where the Thompsons live. It sounds like it's moving this way."

"But we don't know for sure that the cougar killed the calf, do we?" Elizabeth asked.

"No, not for sure."

"Remember when the coyotes killed one of our calves?" Susannah reminded her.

Malinda nodded. "I nearly forgot about that." She turned to Elizabeth. "We lost a calf to a pack of coyotes a couple years ago."

"Pa was so mad," Susannah told her. "He and Todd took turns standing guard at night. On the third night, the coyotes came back. By the light of the moon, Pa could see them almost as plain as day, and he shot two of them."

"And the rest of the pack never came back," Malinda finished for her.

"And Pa saved the coyote skins and Ma made them into fur collars for me and Emily for our winter coats," Susannah proclaimed.

"We need Eli to come shoot that cougar," Ruth declared. "Then I can have a fur collar too."

"He's so big you could probably have a whole fur coat," Susannah told her.

Malinda gave Elizabeth a worried look.

"I'll ride over and let Eli know about this," Elizabeth said quietly. "But I should leave straight away."

"Maybe we should send one of the boys instead," Malinda suggested.

"Except the sun will set before they could get back here. I sure wouldn't want JT riding out by himself in the dark. Especially if there's a cougar on the prowl."

Malinda frowned. "What about you? We don't want you riding around in the dark either."

"I can carry a lantern," Elizabeth told her.

Just now the boys were coming into the house. Like everyone else, they were talking about the cougar as well. "We think we should take turns watching over the livestock tonight," Todd told his mother.

"Aunt Elizabeth wants to ride over to tell Eli," Malinda explained.

"Yes," JT said. "Let's get Eli."

"He's the best hunter in the world," Ruth bragged.

Elizabeth tossed her a warning look. "Not in the *world*," she corrected her.

"Even so, he could get that cougar," Ruth said with confidence.

"I can ride over and fetch Eli," JT offered.

"I want to go too," Todd said. He was three years older than JT and several inches taller.

"Me too," Bart added.

"You're too young," Malinda told Bart.

"I'm the same age as JT," Bart said defiantly.

"I don't know if I will let JT go," Elizabeth said protectively. "The plan was for me to ride over to fetch Eli. And I should get going now."

"Please, Ma," JT begged. "I rode with the men all the way down the Columbia River and helped drive the livestock to Vancouver. Sometimes we even rode late into the night. You let me do that with them, and this is just a little ride."

She smiled at her man-boy. "That's true, son. Well, I suppose it's all right for you to ride over to speak to Eli. But take a lantern with you. And get our guns while you're there. And don't dillydally along the way. Come straight back here. I don't want to be worrying about you."

After more urging, Malinda let both her boys go as well. Equipped with lanterns and some slices of bread and butter in their pockets, and with Todd carrying a gun, they set out on horseback to get Eli.

"Godspeed," the women and girls called out as the boys rode off into the late-afternoon shadows. Elizabeth looked around the farm, suddenly feeling even more concerned for her chickens and livestock. She turned to Malinda. "I think the boys' idea of guarding the livestock might be wise if that cougar is really that close by. Especially since it's getting dark. Do you have a gun I could use?"

"You're going to stand guard?"

"I most certainly am," Elizabeth declared. "I didn't work that hard to get these animals across the Oregon Trail only to lose them to a cougar attack out here."

Malinda nodded. "You're right. Emily, run and fetch Aunt Elizabeth your father's shotgun from under my bed."

"I'll get my coat and hat," Elizabeth told her.

"And I'll send one of the girls out with your supper," Malinda said as they went inside.

"After the boys get back, we can take shifts throughout the night," Elizabeth told her.

"Just like they used to do on the wagon train," Ruth said in an excited tone. "Except they only let the men and boys do it."

"Well, here in Oregon, we let the women help out too," Elizabeth told Ruth. "As long as they're old enough."

"Amelia and I can do some watches," Belinda said to Elizabeth as she opened the door. "That way everyone will get a little more sleep."

"Are you sure?" Elizabeth asked with uncertainty. "Can you girls even shoot a gun?"

Belinda nodded eagerly. "Our father gave us shooting lessons on the trail. Amelia's an even better shot than I am."

"I'll work out a schedule for everyone," Malinda promised as Elizabeth was closing the door.

The sun was fully down when Elizabeth set up a wooden crate to use as a chair on the backside of the barn. They'd gathered the livestock in on Monday, so she could see most of the animals from this vantage point. Or at least she could see their shadows. But as it grew darker, it became harder to see. She would need to rely more on sound than sight. And if she heard something suspicious and felt the need to shoot the gun, she would probably just aim it into the air. That alone should scare off a cougar. Besides, she didn't want to take the chance of hitting an animal. She would make sure the rest of the watchers would do the same.

After an hour or so, Emily came out with a hot bowl of stew and a chunk of bread for her. "Ma thought you might want a lantern." Emily held out the kerosene lantern.

"No thank you. I'd rather watch from a dark spot. My eyes adjust better that way."

"That makes sense."

She thanked Emily, and then, keeping her ears tuned into the sounds around her, she quietly ate her supper. She was just setting her empty bowl down when she heard something. Silently reaching for the gun, she froze in place, listening carefully. After a few minutes, she realized it was the sound of horses' hooves. And now she could see lantern light as the riders came back into the farmyard.

"Hello," she called out as she went over to see them.

"Elizabeth." Eli slid down from what looked like Beau, although it was hard to tell in the dim light. "What are you doing out here by yourself?"

"Keeping watch," she told him. "We're going to take turns all night."

"Oh." He nodded, smiling at her in the lantern light.

While the boys took the horses into the barn to remove their saddles, she asked Eli if he thought the cougar was very dangerous.

"That all depends. If this is the same cougar that killed the Thompsons' calf, like the boys are claiming, the answer is yes. He could be very dangerous. Once a wild animal goes for livestock, it's time to put it to an end."

Elizabeth felt a shiver go down her back as she looked over to where their animals were penned in near the barn. "I doubt I could shoot it in the dark," she admitted, "but I think I could scare it away."

"I'm sure you could. And hopefully this cougar is just passing through," he told her. "But sharpening his claws on a tree right next to the road where humans travel regularly...well, that seems pretty bold. Even for a cougar."

"Yes, I wondered about that too." She reached up to stroke Beau's mane. She hadn't seen either of her team for some time now. But Beau was still as sleek and handsome as ever. She couldn't imagine how sad she'd be if one of her horses was taken down by a cougar.

"It's possible that this is an older cougar," Eli said. "To be honest, they can be the most dangerous because their hunting skills are rusty. If they're hungry and desperate, they aren't so picky about what they eat. That's when they become a very serious threat."

She sighed. "I told Malinda that after working so hard to get my livestock all the way to Oregon, I don't care to lose them to a cougar now."

"Can't blame you for that. Now I wish I'd brought Flax over here with me. He could help keep watch over these animals."

She thought about the other half of her team. "No, I'm glad you left him there, Eli. Flax can protect Bella if need be."

"That's true enough."

Now the boys emerged from the barn. "There's stew inside," she told them. "I'm sure they're keeping it warm for you." She pointed at Eli. "And I'm certain there's plenty for you as well."

Eli went inside but soon returned with a bowl of stew. "Thought I'd help you keep watch while I ate."

"Thank you."

"I'm going to stick around here for a while," he told her between bites. "Maybe get a little shut-eye. The boys offered me a bed in the barn. Then a couple hours before daybreak, I'll set out and see if I can track that cat down in the predawn light."

Elizabeth thought that sounded dangerous. However, she knew Eli well enough to know that this was a lifestyle he was comfortable with. She was not going to question his skills. "Just be careful out there," she said quietly.

"You know I will."

"I know."

With six of them sharing guard duty, no one had missed out on too much sleep by the following morning. Everyone got up in time to do morning chores. And thankfully, all the livestock were safe and sound.

"Eli set out while it was still dark," JT told Elizabeth as she handed him a bowl of oatmeal. "I offered to go with him, but he said no."

"That's on account you have to go to school," Ruth reminded him.

"Hunting a dangerous cougar is more important than school," JT shot back.

"Which is exactly why Eli is out hunting that cougar," Elizabeth assured them both.

"But shouldn't he be back by now?" JT asked. "He told me that cougars sleep during the day."

"Who knows how far he may have tracked it." Elizabeth handed Bart a bowl of oatmeal.

"And maybe he got tired and took a nap," Todd suggested.

Before long it was time for the children to go to school. As planned, Todd carried a gun. "Don't use it unless you really need to," his mother warned as they were heading out.

"I can't imagine a cougar would want to take on a pack of eight kids, half of them mostly grown," Elizabeth said as they watched them trekking off toward school.

"Yes, I do believe there is safety in numbers," Malinda concurred.

Elizabeth looked around the farm. "I do wish Eli would stop by before he goes back to work on the cabin. I'd like to hear if he had any luck or not."

"I'm sure you're worried about him," Malinda said, "and my best cure for worry is to keep busy."

"Yes, and there's plenty to keep us busy around here," Elizabeth agreed. However, as she worked, she longed for the day when she'd be investing her energies into her own farm and her own housekeeping. And even though Ruth had forgotten to give her the day count until the wedding, Elizabeth knew it was nine more days. Just the same, she was grateful for the time they'd been able to stay with Malinda. Certainly, not everything had gone smoothly, and she would be glad when their visit came to an end, but she was still thankful.

It was midmorning when, just as she was finishing churning butter on the porch, she spied a black horse with a rider coming down the road. She knew at once it was Eli, and since the butter was nice and stiff, she hurried out to meet him. Of course, she was not prepared for what she saw slung across the back of her big black Percheron.

"Oh, my!" Her hand flew to her mouth to see the giant lifeless animal behind Eli. "You killed it."

He gave her a tired nod. "I had to, Elizabeth." He extracted himself from the saddle, and once his feet were on the ground, he stretched his arms and back.

"I'll bet you're hungry," she said suddenly.

He grinned. "Now that you mention it."

"Come on in," she told him. "I'll cook you up some eggs, and you can tell us the whole story." She hurried into the house, calling out to Malinda. "Ruth was right," she announced. "Eli is the best hunter in the world."

Elizabeth handed him a cup of coffee, and as she cooked him a late breakfast, he told them about riding along the river until he found what appeared to be cougar signs not far from the Thompsons' ranch. "I wasn't sure if it was from Sunday night or last night. But it made sense that the animal might go back there for another meal. The sun was just coming up by then, so I wasn't feeling too hopeful. I figured the cougar had probably bedded down for the day. But I decided to go check out that ridge that runs alongside the Thompsons' place. Seemed a good spot for a cougar to hide out."

He paused as Elizabeth put a plate with eggs and biscuits and gravy in front of him. "Maybe I ought to go cougar hunting every morning." He hungrily smacked his lips. "This looks delicious."

"Come on," Malinda urged him. "Tell us the rest of the story. You got me on pins and needles here."

He chuckled as he took a big bite, taking his time to savor it. "So I got to the rocky part of the ridge, tethered Beau to a bush, and walked around a bit. I had my rifle loaded and ready. After a while I decided to climb on up and have a look around from a higher spot. And I was just about to scale up the rocks when I heard something above me." He took another bite, and both Elizabeth and Malinda waited anxiously for him to chew and swallow. "When I looked up, there was the cat, perched and ready to pounce." He gave Elizabeth an uneasy look. "Right over Beau."

She grimaced.

"So I had no choice but to take aim and shoot." He stuck his fork back into his eggs. "The cat tumbled down, landing about ten feet away from Beau." He chuckled. "You should have seen your horse, Elizabeth. He just looked at the dead cat and then went right back to munching the grass. Calm as anything."

She laughed. "First of all, he is *our* horse, Eli. And he obviously knew he was in good hands with you."

"Oh, my." Malinda refilled Eli's coffee cup.

They peppered him with questions as he finished up his breakfast. "Thanks for the meal," he told them.

"The children are going to be so thrilled to hear this story," Malinda said.

"Well, you ladies will have to relay it to them. I've got work to do."

They both walked him outside, pausing to look at the enormous cougar. "Does anyone eat cougar meat?" Elizabeth asked cautiously.

"Most people wouldn't care for it," he told her. "But I've known mountain men who think it tastes like pork. And when the other game sources are scarce, some Indians are known to eat it. I reckon if you're hungry enough you'd eat most anything."

Malinda wrinkled her nose. "I do not care to be that hungry."

Elizabeth cautiously reached over to touch the fur. "The fur's very soft."

"What are you going to do with the hide?" Malinda asked.

He shrugged. "I don't rightly know yet. But you can be sure it won't go to waste."

Malinda excused herself, told Eli goodbye, and then returned to the house.

"Before you go," Elizabeth said quickly, "I want to ask you something." She told him about seeing the Indian woman and the child and taking the bread and blanket. "Was that silly to leave it there like that?"

He smiled. "I think it was very kind."

"I got to thinking…what if Charles is sick or hurt? Or maybe he abandoned her. Or maybe he just can't provide for them. But for some reason I feel like she and her child are in need." She pointed to the cougar carcass. "Do you think they could use any of that meat?"

He shrugged. "I think with the abundance of fish and deer in these parts, we could find her some better food than this."

"Really?" she asked hopefully. "We could share food with her?" Though she contributed from her own staples, Elizabeth was hesitant to take any more food from Malinda's home.

"I don't see why not. I've got plenty of smoked salmon and venison. I'd be happy to share some of that. Why don't you send JT over after school? I'm sure he'll want to see the cougar anyway. I'll send a package of salmon and venison back with him for you to use however you like."

"Thank you." She looked into his eyes, feeling so very grateful that they were in agreement about something like this, something that other people might not understand, might even condemn them for. She was thankful to God that she was about to marry a good and kind and generous man.

Chapter Fourteen

On the afternoon before Thanksgiving, Elizabeth slipped away on her horse without telling Malinda where she was going. Fortunately, Malinda was too caught up in her own ever-growing Thanksgiving plans to pay much heed. First Malinda had invited Will and his family. Then, of course, they decided to include the Prescotts. But the Prescotts had already invited the Flanders family because Julius Prescott was marrying Mahala Flanders after the New Year. Consequently, Malinda felt compelled to invite them as well. As it stood now, Malinda was expecting twenty-one guests to fill her table and give thanks. Because of the size of the crowd, she had decided to set up the dinner in the barn, and she was determined to make it a dinner to remember.

Meanwhile, Elizabeth was thankful that she and her children and Eli would be gathering with Matthew and Jess and Brady in her parents' humble home. And today as she rode Molly toward her property, her plan was to make a quick trip to where she'd left the blanket and bread a few days earlier. If the items were gone, Elizabeth would leave a second blanket, this time wrapped around a parcel of smoked fish and deer meat—the food that Eli had sent by way of JT. She had no idea if the woman and child were still there, but if her first bundle was gone, it would be a good sign. And she figured she could always pick up the bundle tomorrow if it remained there untouched.

When she got close to the brushy spot alongside the road, she slowed Molly to a stop and silently dismounted. Walking quietly, she approached the spot in the brush and was relieved to see that her previous bundle was gone. Like before, she spoke aloud. "I come in friendship," she said clearly. "I want to share this food and blanket with you. Please, know that I am your friend." She stood there for a long moment, wishing that the woman and child would come out and reveal themselves. And then she wondered if they were even within hearing distance. "God bless you," she said as she set the bundle down in the same spot.

Feeling like that was all she could do—besides pray—she got back on Molly and rode back to Malinda's. More than anything, she wanted to just keep on going on to her own property. She wanted to walk around and inspect Eli's work. She wanted to make sure he was watering her seedlings even though the rain came almost every other day now. Mostly she just wanted to see his face. However, she intended on keeping her promise to him. Not until after the wedding.

"Where have you been?" Malinda asked as she walked in to discover Elizabeth removing Molly's saddle in the barn.

"I had a Thanksgiving errand to attend to," Elizabeth said absently.

"Did you sneak over to look at your house?" Malinda asked with suspicion.

Elizabeth made a sheepish smile as she let Molly join the other livestock outside the barn. "I am dying to go take a peek. I can hardly stand it. But a promise is a promise."

Malinda nodded. "That's right. Now, how about if you give me a hand setting up these tables and benches." She pointed to a pile of long boards. "Will brought these over while you were gone. He got the lumber to use for the floor of Julius and Mahala's house, but he thought we could put the boards to good use here first."

Elizabeth examined a board. "This is probably wide enough for a bench—a rather narrow bench. Maybe you could set them on crates or stumps. But wouldn't you have to nail the boards together to make them sturdy enough for a table?"

Malinda showed her the smaller pieces of wood that Will had brought. "He said to attach them to this to make the tables. Maybe the benches too. We'll just leave them fastened together until our wedding."

"Why don't you let JT do the carpentry for you," Elizabeth suggested. "He's helped so much with building houses these past months that he's gotten quite handy with a hammer and saw."

"Good idea. We'll put the boys onto it as soon as they get home." She pointed at Elizabeth. "And you promised to make pies for my feast."

"That's right. I should probably get to it." Elizabeth considered reminding Malinda that the pies were for her family's feast too. After all, she was using her own flour and sugar, and Ruth had picked most of the berries. However, the pumpkins had been grown on Malinda's farm. And she was using Malinda's kitchen and butter. Oh, for the day when she would have her own house again.

Elizabeth was elbow deep in pie filling by the time the children came home from school. And now the house, which had been relatively quiet, suddenly grew noisy, filling as if it were about to burst at the seams as Malinda began giving everyone special jobs to complete before supper. These were in addition to their usual after-school chores. And after some expected complaining, the children shuffled off to their various assignments.

❧❧❧

Before going to bed, Elizabeth had told JT and Ruth that they would leave for their grandparents' house as soon as their morning chores were finished. And she was pleasantly surprised at how quickly they completed their usual tasks the next day. It wasn't long until they were dressed in their Sunday best and preparing to leave. However, as Elizabeth reached for the basket containing the pies she was taking to her parents' house, she could see that Malinda's household was in a frenzy.

Elizabeth knew that Malinda was trying too hard to impress the Bostonians, but she had no intention of mentioning this. She'd already suggested that Malinda might enjoy the day more if she kept her preparations a bit simpler, but Malinda had not appreciated that advice.

"Have a wonderful Thanksgiving dinner," she told Malinda as she made her way to the door.

"Oh, dear." Malinda wiped a floury hand across her forehead. "I just hope I'll be ready in time."

"I'm sure you will," Elizabeth told her. She knew that if she volunteered to stay and help out, Malinda would not refuse her offer.

Before they could leave, Susannah pointed at JT. "You're taking your guitar with you?" she asked.

He shrugged at his cousin. "Yeah. We like making music together. Uncle Matthew will bring his fiddle, and I hope Eli will have his guitar."

"If he doesn't, we'll make him go back and get it," Ruth declared.

"I wish we could have music at our Thanksgiving dinner," Susannah said to her mother.

"Instead of wishing for what we don't have, come over here and chop these walnuts for me, Susannah Marie."

As Susannah groaned, Elizabeth ushered her two toward the door. "We'll be back before bedtime," she promised as they went out. Her parents had asked if she and the children would like to spend the night, and although it was very tempting, she knew they would be crowded in their little cabin. Besides that, the children had school in the morning.

As they walked down the mucky road, still wet from last night's rain, Ruth led them in cheerful singing. Despite the mud, the morning sun was clear and bright, and Elizabeth soon felt light and happy and free. As much as she loved her sister-in-law, sometimes she grew weary of her high expectations. And sometimes it seemed that Elizabeth's wedding day could not get here quickly enough. Of course, these were thoughts she kept to herself.

As they walked and sang, she kept something else to herself. She slowed her pace when they came to the brushy spot alongside the creek. Without saying a word to the children, she paused to see that the offering she'd left yesterday was now gone. She sighed in relief, feeling certain the Indian woman and her child were the ones who were benefiting from her gift. Just knowing they were a bit more comfortable made her feel much more like celebrating this special day with her family.

"Happy Thanksgiving!" Ruth proclaimed as Clara led them into the house. Hugs were exchanged, and Elizabeth and Ruth were happy to enlist as volunteers in Clara's cheerful kitchen. Meanwhile, JT opted to go outside and find his grandpa and Brady.

"Remember you have on your Sunday clothes," Elizabeth reminded him.

"This is truly a special day," Clara told Elizabeth and Ruth. "Our first Thanksgiving in Oregon. So much to be thankful for."

"Most of all, I'm thankful for my family," Elizabeth said as she hung up Ruth's coat and her own.

"Me too," Ruth chimed in as she removed her bonnet. "We have the best family in the whole world."

Elizabeth chuckled. "Yes, well, I must agree with you on that."

"When will everyone be here?" Ruth asked.

"Matthew and Jess will come around one," Clara told them.

"And Eli too?" Ruth asked.

"Yes, Eli too," Clara assured her.

Ruth sniffed the air. "Are we having turkey, Grandma?"

"Oh, Ruth," Elizabeth said. "You know there are no turkeys in Oregon."

"But she's not too far off," Clara told Elizabeth with a twinkle in her eye.

"What are we having?" Ruth asked.

"Goose." Clara pointed to the cast-iron roaster positioned over the fireplace coals.

Ruth clapped her hands. "A goose!"

"Where in the world did you get a goose?" Elizabeth asked.

"Eli brought it over last night," Clara explained. "Otherwise we would have only had a venison roast. But now I'm fixing both."

"What a feast!" Elizabeth exclaimed. "Our first Thanksgiving, and we get to have roasted goose."

"And Jessica is baking yams with apples."

"And Mama made pies," Ruth told her.

"And now I need someone to peel potatoes," Clara said to Ruth.

Together they worked, but not at the frenzied pace Elizabeth suspected was taking place at Malinda's house. Instead, they enjoyed one another's company—talking and laughing and remembering Thanksgivings past and planning for ones in the future. It was a little past noon when Jess joined them. But her company only made the house merrier. Elizabeth felt truly blessed to be with her family like this, and even more so when Eli came into the house with her father, her brother, her son, and her dear friend Brady. This was truly a Thanksgiving to remember.

Although they were in high spirits, chattering happily as they gathered around the table, the room grew quiet, when Asa held up his hands. "As has always been the tradition of this family—in good times and in bad—we will go around the table expressing gratitude for something we are thankful for." He nodded to Ruth. "As usual we will start with the youngest and end with the oldest."

Ruth smiled, revealing where she'd recently lost a front tooth. "I'm thankful for my school and my teacher, Mrs. Taylor."

Asa looked at JT. "I'm thankful that I'm finally getting to know my cousins Bart and Todd."

"What about Susannah and Emily?" Ruth asked.

"They're girls," JT told her. Everyone laughed.

"I am thankful to be part of this wonderful family." Jess smiled at Matthew. "And thankful that our little family is growing."

"I'm thankful for Jessica," Matthew looked adoringly into her eyes. "And that our cabin is finished."

Jess nodded eagerly. "Yes! Me too."

Elizabeth knew it was her turn now. "I'm thankful for so many things. Where do I begin? I'm exceedingly thankful that we all made it safely to Oregon, thankful to be settling here with my family. I'm thankful for my upcoming marriage to Eli." She laughed. "I could go on and on."

Eli nodded. "I feel thankful for many things too." He looked around the table with genuine appreciation in his eyes. "For the way you've all welcomed me into your family. For all the help Asa, Matthew, Brady, and JT have given me." He turned to Elizabeth. "For my bride-to-be, Elizabeth."

She swallowed and smiled.

"My turn," Clara said. "Well, my list isn't so different. I am very thankful for every one of you at this table. I am thankful and somewhat amazed that an old woman like me made it all the way across the Oregon Trail in one piece." They all laughed. "I'm thankful my little house is finished." She smiled at Asa. "And thankful that God is allowing me to grow old surrounded by my loved ones."

Asa looked at Brady now. "You're a little older than me, Brady, so I reckon I go next." Brady looked relieved. "I'm thankful for all of you. And thankful for our safe passage to our new home in Oregon. I'm thankful for all our friends and neighbors in this settlement. Most of all I am thankful for God's continued goodness to this family."

They all looked at Brady. Sensing he was feeling uncomfortable, Elizabeth smiled. "Your turn, Brady."

He nodded with misty-looking eyes. "I'm thankful for each and every one of you folks. Ya'll been like kin to me. You took me on a journey I won't never forget. I'm thankful for my cabin. And most of all, I'm thankful to be a free man."

Asa nodded. "Now let us bow our heads and give thanks to our generous Father in heaven." He prayed a heartfelt prayer of thanksgiving and gratitude to which everyone added a hearty amen.

⁂

After dinner some of them went outside to enjoy the afternoon sunshine and to admire the split-rail fence Asa and Brady were building. "Now that Eli is working on the inside of your cabin, he doesn't need our help so much, so we have more time on our hands," Asa told Elizabeth. "At the rate we're going, I s'pect we'll have a couple of acres fenced in by Christmas. Don't you reckon, Brady?"

Brady nodded. "I sure hope so."

"Well, since your fenced pasture is so much bigger and better than ours, we just might be wintering our livestock over here," Elizabeth teased her father.

"That's not a bad idea," he said. "Then when you get your pasture fenced in, we could move them over there and give this grass a chance to replenish itself."

"And come summer, you can move 'em on over to our place if you like," Jess suggested.

Now Asa pointed over to a sunny rise midway between the cabin and the fenced pasture. "I want to put my barn right there," he explained. "As big as I can afford to build it, and with room to grow it even bigger on down the line. I've got this notion in my head that we're going to be a dairy farm." He continued pointing at his imaginary barn. "And there'll be a big sign right there above the door, saying Dawson's Dairy."

"I wouldn't be a bit surprised," Elizabeth told him. "Maybe we'll all want to become dairy farmers someday." She looked at Eli, wondering how he felt about seeing these fences going up.

"The grassland along the river seems just about perfect for cattle," he said. "I'm not opposed to the idea of raising dairy cows." He grinned at her. "I like milk and butter and cheese."

"And my Clara knows how to make some mighty fine cheese." Asa smacked his lips.

"That's true," Elizabeth said. "Mother's cheeses are the best."

"Cheese…" Jess sighed. "That sounds wonderful."

"I'll bet that next Thanksgiving, if not sooner, we'll have cheese at the table," Elizabeth proclaimed.

As Asa, Jess, and Brady continued walking around the fence line, Elizabeth lingered back with Eli, shyly slipping her hand into his. It felt so good to be here with him right now. She could hear the sounds of Matthew's fiddle and JT's guitar as the two warmed up for their after-dinner music. Meanwhile Ruth was helping Clara to serve the dessert. A perfect day.

"Brady was talking to me on our way over here," Eli began. "There's something that I need to talk to you about."

"Oh? Is something wrong?" She studied his profile as he gazed over the pasture, admiring his straight nose and firm chin.

He turned to look at her. "Not really wrong. But Brady would like to live over here…on your parents' property."

"Brady wants to live with my parents?"

"Not with them. But he'd like to have his house near them."

"But he has a house on our property."

Eli nodded. "And he feels badly about that."

"Why?"

"Because he wishes he'd said something sooner. Otherwise I never would have pushed to get his little cabin up. But I had the leftover lumber, and I thought, why not use it to get a roof over Brady's head? I didn't like the idea of him living in your father's tent when the weather gets wetter and colder. He's an old man."

"Yes, that makes perfect sense. But Brady doesn't want his little cabin?"

"He's willing to live in the tent…just to be closer to your parents."

"I wonder why he wants to be closer to them."

"Partly because he feels they could use his help. He talked about how they were all getting older and how they can help each other. But more than that, Brady really admires your father. And they've been turning out some nice-looking pieces of furniture together."

"Yes, I've seen some of it."

"I reckon Brady feels like they could work together more easily if he was living over here."

"It would save him a lot of walking," Elizabeth admitted.

"And he is getting older."

"So are my parents." She nodded. "I suppose it does make sense. Too bad you went ahead and built that little cabin."

He shrugged. "Maybe we'll think of a use for it." He peered at her. "Brady is worried that you'll be hurt if he moves over here."

She considered this. "Well, I might have been hurt if you hadn't explained it. But it does make sense."

"And there's another thing." He lowered his voice. "Nobody's supposed to know, but your pa is teaching Brady to read."

She grinned. "I heard about that already."

He smiled. "Well, keep it under your hat."

She looked to where Asa, Jess, and Brady were coming back toward them now. "So should I tell Brady that I don't mind him moving over here?"

"Not right now. I promised him I'd speak to your parents too. But if you don't mind, I can let Brady know that you understand. I know that will be a comfort to him."

"Yes, of course. And let him know that I appreciate knowing he'll be over here to help my parents if they need it. And after all, like he said at the table, he's a free man. He can live wherever he wants to live."

"Well...not exactly." Eli frowned.

She nodded, remembering Oregon's recently passed legislation—the three-year limit for Negroes to reside here. However, if Brady kept to himself as he'd been doing, if he avoided town and other settlers, perhaps no one would notice. They could only hope.

Chapter Fifteen

I do not understand you," Malinda said to Elizabeth on Saturday evening. As usual, they were sewing by the fire. The children were all in bed except for Belinda and Amelia, who were spending the night with Evelyn and Lavinia in town. The Prescott men had decided to make the most of a recent dry spell by traveling to Empire City to pick up some supplies for the mercantile.

"What is it you don't understand?" Elizabeth asked as she stitched the hem of the curtains she was sewing for the front window of her house. She still hadn't seen the window, but Eli had given her the measurements. She'd found the red and white gingham fabric at the mercantile and felt it would look charming in the cabin. She'd gotten enough fabric for additional curtains for the kitchen cupboards as well as a tablecloth.

"I do not understand how you can appear so calm and nonchalant with your wedding less than a week away."

Elizabeth just laughed. "Oh, is that all?"

"Well, my wedding is three weeks away and I'm a bundle of nerves."

"Perhaps that's because your wedding is a bigger, fancier affair than mine."

Malinda frowned. "When you say it like that it feels as if you are judging me."

"I'm sorry. That's not how I meant it. The truth is I'm really looking forward to your wedding. I think everyone is."

"But you're not looking forward to your own?"

"Of course I am." Elizabeth set her sewing aside. "But maybe I'm looking more forward to the marriage…settling into our house… feeling like a family again."

"Oh." She nodded. "Yes, that makes sense."

"Remember how you felt when you came to Oregon? How you looked forward to putting down roots, moving into a real house?"

"I most certainly do."

Elizabeth returned to hemming the curtain.

"Even so," Malinda persisted. "Are you not a little bit excited about your upcoming wedding?"

Elizabeth laughed again. "I most certainly am."

"But you don't show it." Malinda peered at her.

Elizabeth pursed her lips, unsure of how much to say. "Do you want the truth, Malinda?"

"Yes, of course I do. We're best friends. Why wouldn't you tell me the truth?"

"The truth is I've been trying to play my wedding down for your sake."

"For my sake?" Malinda looked shocked.

"You were so opposed to the date," Elizabeth told her. "You wanted me to wait until spring and—"

"Oh, I'm all over that now." Malinda reached for her scissors. "I don't mind if you get excited over your wedding."

"Thank you," Elizabeth said calmly. "But perhaps I'll wait for a few days before I get overly excited."

Malinda laughed and then held up the quilt top she was working on. "Look, it's all done."

Elizabeth studied the colorful piece. "Oh, Malinda, it's beautiful. Do you think you'll have it finished before your wedding?"

Malinda's brows arched. "Oh, I should say so. I invited a dozen women over here for a quilting bee on Thursday."

"Really?" Elizabeth frowned. "Was I not invited?"

Malinda shrugged. "I thought you'd have your hands full with your own wedding preparations by then."

"Oh." Elizabeth tried not to feel hurt. But missing out on a quilting bee felt like a real slight. "Yes. I suppose I could go to my mother's and help her with—"

"Your mother will be here," Malinda said. "Working on the quilt with me."

"Oh." Elizabeth felt more than slighted now. She felt hurt. "Well, perhaps I'll go visit Jess and—"

"Jess will be here too."

Elizabeth was about to insist that she should participate in the quilting bee as well, but that would be like inviting herself to a party. Bad etiquette. But what sort of manners was it for Malinda to invite Elizabeth's family and leave her out?

"I'm very tired," Elizabeth said quietly. "I think I will turn in."

***

On Sunday, Elizabeth was trying to put her best friend's thoughtlessness behind her. It was silly to be offended by the slight. Besides, she felt certain that if she told Malinda she wished to come, Malinda would probably welcome her with open arms—or at least she'd welcome her help in serving lunch. However, Elizabeth felt just stubborn enough not to mention it. She felt even more stubborn after sitting through Reverend Holmes' sermon about Daniel in the lion's den. To be fair, it was probably the most positive sermon she'd heard him preach. But it was nothing compared to her father's.

Even so, she shook hands and thanked him. "I was greatly relieved to hear you were feeling much better this week," she said. "And that was a fine sermon, Reverend."

He looked slightly surprised. "Thank you, Elizabeth."

Now Eli stepped up to shake his hand, also praising his sermon.

"I look forward to your wedding on Saturday," the reverend told them both.

"We're looking forward to it too," Eli assured him.

Asa and Clara came up to the reverend next as Eli and Elizabeth went outside to where the children were playing in the yard.

Before long, Eli was enticed to go over and visit with some of the men. They wanted to hear his story of how he'd hunted down the cougar. Then Elizabeth, seeing that Lavinia was standing by herself, went over to talk with her. As they chatted about the mercantile, Elizabeth got an idea. "Will you be open for business on Thursday?" she asked.

"Oh, yes, of course. We're always open on Thursdays," Lavinia assured her. "In fact, Hugh and Julius should be back from Empire City by Tuesday or Wednesday at the latest, and I'm sure we'll have the shelves freshly stocked by Thursday."

"Good." Elizabeth nodded. "Then I shall come and do some shopping."

"Do you need things for your new house?"

"Oh, I'm sure that I do. I plan to go through my things this week and make some lists."

"I've heard that Eli won't let you see your house until after the wedding." She chuckled. "I told Hugh that could be a bad sign."

"A bad sign?"

"Yes—that is, if Eli were trying to get you married before showing you the house because it is a complete disaster." She laughed. "Although I'm sure that's not the situation, Elizabeth. But it would be funny, don't you think?"

Elizabeth frowned. "I'm not sure it would be very funny. But I am fairly certain that Eli has built us a fine home. My father and brother and JT have helped him with it, and I cannot imagine—"

"Yes, dear…I'm sorry. You'll have to forgive my humor."

Elizabeth patted her arm. "Don't give it a thought." She sighed. "I suppose with the wedding less than a week away, I'm finally starting to feel a bit nervous."

"That's only natural." Lavinia's cheery countenance faded slightly as she lowered her voice. "Although I still find myself regretting that you're not marrying our Will."

"But you do get on well with Malinda, don't you?"

Lavinia made a small shrug. "I suppose I haven't had the opportunity to get very well acquainted yet, whereas you and I solidified our friendship on the Oregon Trail. I still don't know what I would have done without you and your family."

Elizabeth nodded. "Friendships made on the trail are lasting ones." She was tempted to ask Lavinia if she'd been invited to Malinda's quilting bee, but she knew that was rather meddlesome. "So will you be working at the mercantile on Thursday afternoon?" she asked.

"You can count on that." Lavinia glanced down the street to the imposing building. "And if it's not busy in the store when you come, perhaps you will want to come upstairs and have a tour of our new living quarters. Not everything is finished yet, but we are trying to make ourselves at home."

"I would love to see it, Lavinia."

"Maybe we can have tea."

Elizabeth nodded happily. "I would enjoy that."

Now JT and Ruth, accompanied by Tillie and Walter Flanders, came over to Elizabeth. "Mrs. Flanders invited us to stay in town with them for lunch," Ruth said with bright eyes. "It's Tumbleweed Tillie's birthday today."

Elizabeth laughed. She hadn't heard Tillie's nickname for some time. "Happy Birthday, Tumbleweed," she told her.

"Thank you, Mrs. Martin."

"And I gave her my hair ribbon." Ruth pointed to the blue bow tied around Tillie's wavy blond hair, which had grown out to her shoulders. "Isn't it pretty?"

"Very pretty." Elizabeth tugged Ruth's now-barren braid. Ruth had bought that ribbon with her own money, and it was touching to see her generosity.

"Is it all right, Ma?" JT asked.

"Ma made a cake," Walter said proudly.

"It's just fine," Elizabeth told her children. "Just mind your manners. And I'll expect you home in time for afternoon chores." They agreed to this and then ran off to rejoin their other friends just as Eli came over to join her.

"I see that Hugh and Julius aren't back from Empire City yet," he said to Lavinia.

"No, I don't expect them until midweek."

He nodded.

"Perhaps Elizabeth can pick up your order for you when she comes to town on Thursday," Lavinia told him.

"You're going to town on Thursday?" Eli asked.

"Yes. Lavinia and I might even have tea."

"Good for you. How about if I bring the wagon over to Malinda's on Thursday morning? You can drive it to town and use it to pick up my order."

"What did you order?" she asked curiously.

He just grinned. "Never you mind. But it's heavy enough to need a wagon."

Lavinia laughed. "What I wouldn't give to see your face when you walk into your new home, Elizabeth."

"It won't be long now," Eli assured her.

"And once we get settled, we will invite our friends over," Elizabeth said. "Maybe for a Sunday dinner since the mercantile is closed."

"Let's make it a potluck," Lavinia suggested.

"Wonderful." Elizabeth looked at Eli. "Perhaps a week after our wedding? Or do you think that's too soon?"

"That is entirely up to you."

Elizabeth nodded. "Then we shall plan on it," she told Lavinia. "Feel free to tell any of our friends who come into the store. After church on the second Sunday, the Kincaids will host a potluck at their new house."

"And that gives me an idea," Lavinia said suddenly.

"What's that?"

"Oh…you'll find out." She made a sly smile and waved goodbye as she hurried away.

Elizabeth explained about Tumbleweed Tillie's birthday. "So we can head back whenever we like."

His eyes twinkled. "Just you and me?"

She nodded eagerly as he took her hand and led her down the road. "As much as I love my family and friends, I do enjoy your company," she told him.

He squeezed her fingers in his. "I am counting the days until Saturday," he said. "And the hours too."

She laughed.

"But as much as I'm looking forward to it, I do want to have our house finished. Or nearly."

"I'm certain that it would be fine just as it is right now."

"Oh, sure, it's livable enough."

"Are you living in it?"

He shook his head. "No, my dear, I'm waiting for you."

"Oh, Eli, you can live in it if you like."

"Not without you."

Not for the first time, Elizabeth had to ask herself if this was real or just a delightful dream. But the musty smell of decaying autumn leaves and the sound of the birds twittering in the trees told her it was authentic. And for some reason this reminded her of the Indian woman in the woods. "I didn't have a chance to tell you that the second blanket and parcel of food I left for the Indian woman and child were gone the following day. So I can only assume they got it."

"Yes, if it had been taken by animals, the blanket would probably still be there."

"So it makes me believe they are living somewhere near there."

"At least for now. It's possible they are on their way to somewhere else." He shook his head in a dismal way. "Although, for the life of me, I cannot imagine where that would be. No place is safe for Indians in these parts. Any that are found are rounded up and herded up north like animals."

"I'm sure that's why she looks so frightened," Elizabeth said sadly. "Her eyes looked so empty and hopeless and scared. I wish I could get her to trust me."

"And then what would you do?" He peered at her.

"To be honest, I don't know." She sighed. "But I will keep praying. I believe that God will show me."

"Now, not to detour our conversation, but is there anything I need to know or to do before next Saturday?"

She shook her head. "Not that I can think of."

"I assume you don't want me to show up in my buckskins," he said teasingly.

She laughed. "I would not complain if you did, Eli. That's what you wore the first time I met you, and I happen to think you look very handsome in your buckskins."

He chuckled. "I'm glad to know that because I'm reluctant to give them up."

"However…" She pointed to his Sunday clothes. "What you have on would probably be more appropriate for a church wedding. Don't you think?"

"I am in complete agreement. And I'm content to save my buckskins for other activities like traveling and hunting."

"Speaking of hunting, I know that my father is most eager to go on an elk hunting trip with you."

"Yes. He and Matthew both. I promised them we would go the week before Christmas—if that's agreeable to you."

"Yes, as long as you won't go before Malinda's wedding. I'm sure she'd want to tan my hide if all my menfolk went missing on her big day."

"We'll keep that in mind."

"Speaking of my father, did you have a chance to speak to him about Brady yet? I meant to ask, but we must have gotten distracted."

"As a matter of fact, I did tell him about Brady."

"What did Father say?"

"Both your parents were very touched. And they said that if you were all right with this, they would gladly welcome Brady to live on their land. Brady can continue using the tent, and Asa even offered to help Brady build a new cabin. I expect Brady will move back over there by tomorrow."

Elizabeth had mixed feelings. As much as she wanted Brady to be happy and free and to live where he liked, she would dearly miss having him close by. He'd been in the Martin family for as long as she could remember. And he'd been with her and James from the first days of their marriage, overseeing their farm. Even after she and James decided to free the other slaves, Brady had asked to stay on with them. And then, during the years following James' death, Brady had been as dependable as the sun. Just seeing him about her farm each day, checking on livestock, hitching a wagon, bringing her firewood…it had always been so reassuring.

However, she knew circumstances were different now. This was the Oregon Territory, not the State of Kentucky. Furthermore, she had Eli to depend upon. And really, what more could she ask? Plus, she reminded herself, her parents were getting older. Having Brady around to help her father carry the load was a great comfort. And Brady was getting older too. Why shouldn't he live out the last of his days however and wherever he wished? So truly this was for the best. It was time for her to let Brady go.

Chapter Sixteen

By Thursday morning, Elizabeth harbored no ill feelings about being left out of Malinda's quilting bee. She tried to make herself useful as well as doing her regular chores, but Malinda resembled a small whirlwind as she ran from task to task.

Grateful for an excuse to get out of the house, Elizabeth hurried out to talk to Eli when she saw him arriving with the wagon and her team. He kissed her hello and seemed happy to see her, but she could tell he was eager to get back to the house. For that reason she encouraged him to ride Molly back home.

"It will save you time," she said. "And then you can ride her back when you pick up the wagon at the end of the day."

"I'll see you tonight," he promised. "Have a good day in town."

For the next hour, eager to stay out of Malinda's way, Elizabeth remained in the barn, sorting through crates of goods she'd brought with her to Malinda's. She wanted to have everything ready to load into the wagon before Eli drove it back.

Satisfied that all was organized, she returned to the house only to discover Malinda still scrambling about, trying to get her house into perfect order and her "luncheon" meal prepared. Elizabeth didn't dare to point out that Malinda still hadn't changed out of her work clothes and that her guests would soon arrive. Elizabeth was tempted to offer some additional help, but knowing Lavinia was looking forward to her visit, she simply wished Malinda a good day and made her getaway.

Elizabeth felt relieved to be driving the wagon to town. Her team looked sleek and handsome. Her wagon without the canvas covering was sturdy and strong. Dressed in her Sunday best, she looked forward to getting some much-needed supplies for her first week of married life. She also looked forward to a friendly visit with Lavinia. She had no regrets about missing out on Malinda's gathering and hoped the quilting bee was enjoyable for the ladies, but reminding herself of how much of her spare time was spent sewing, she decided that she'd been lucky to miss out on it.

Besides that, she told herself as town came into view, she would have a quilting bee of her own someday. She would hold it in her own home. And she would be sure to invite Malinda—and anyone else who had the slightest interest in coming.

As she came in sight of the school and mercantile and blacksmith shop, she slowed the team. She wanted to take a good long look at the scene before her. Someday the virtually empty street would be just a memory. In time the town would grow and change. It would become noisy and busy and be transformed into something altogether different. And she and her family could say they remembered when there was nothing here.

She paused to admire the slowly moving river just south of town. She smiled to think that it was one thing that would never change.

She pulled the wagon in front of the mercantile and, removing her driving gloves, held out her skirt as she carefully climbed down. It hadn't been necessary to wear her Sunday dress today, but it had felt good to put it on. And she knew Lavinia would appreciate the effort. As she went up to the store, she looked up at the sky. She'd noticed clouds rolling in from the ocean and suspected that the fair weather they'd enjoyed the past few days was about to disappear. She hoped it wouldn't be wet and gray by tomorrow, although rain on a wedding day was always considered to be good fortune—at least among farmers.

"Hello, hello," Lavinia hailed as Elizabeth entered the store. "I was just telling Mrs. Levine that you were coming to visit me."

"Good day, Elizabeth," Mrs. Levine said. "Are you looking forward to your wedding? Just two days away now."

Elizabeth smiled. "Yes, I can hardly believe it's almost here."

"I was just telling Lavinia that the upcoming year will most likely be filled with even more weddings."

"That's right," Lavinia told Elizabeth. "We predict that Belinda and Jacob will be engaged by Christmas."

Elizabeth nodded. "That would not surprise me."

"And Mahala and Julius have decided to be married in April," Lavinia said with excitement. "That will give me enough time to plan for a proper celebration."

"I hear that springtime is lovely here," Elizabeth said as she perused a basket filled with colorful spools of thread. "Lots of wildflowers to choose from." The three of them chatted congenially for a bit, and finally Mrs. Levine excused herself and, taking her parcel, exited the mercantile.

"Perhaps we should take advantage of this lull and go upstairs," Lavinia said. "I suspect customers will be having their dinners now anyway." She hurried to close the front door, putting the We Will Be Right Back sign on the door. Then she led Elizabeth to a staircase in the back. "Right this way, my friend."

When they emerged from the stairwell, Elizabeth was surprised to see how light and bright the rooms up there were. "Oh, my," she said. "Look at all these windows."

"Yes." Lavinia nodded. "I told Hugh that the last thing I wanted was to be stuck up here in a dreary attic. He made certain that did not happen."

"It's lovely." Elizabeth admired the fir floors in the main room. "And your furnishings!" she exclaimed over the padded settee and chairs. "They obviously came here by ship."

Lavinia laughed. "Well, yes. I had to leave so much furniture behind, but I insisted on a few comforts." She led Elizabeth around, showing her their home, which by frontier standards was quite luxurious.

"I told Hugh that everything we brought for our own use could always be sold in the mercantile should times get hard." She grinned. "It's a bit like living in your storeroom."

"A very lovely storeroom."

Lavinia even showed Elizabeth the bedrooms—all three of them. "One for Augustus and one for Evelyn. Although I imagine Evelyn will not be living her for more than a year or two."

"Has Evelyn found a beau too?"

"I do believe she's got some fellows with their eyes on her."

"I shouldn't wonder."

"When Evelyn marries, we will turn this room into a study."

"Very nice." Elizabeth nodded, trying not to be overly impressed with the advantages that wealth could provide. Even if her own house was rustic and meagerly furnished, she would be wholeheartedly thankful for it. And she knew it would be filled with love. Not that the Prescotts' home was not filled with love. She had no reason to think that. But she also had no reason not to rejoice with Lavinia over her new home. "This is a truly beautiful place to live," Elizabeth said finally. "The Lord has blessed you and your family, and I could not be happier for you."

Lavinia smiled happily. "Oh, that makes me feel so glad to hear that." Her smile faded. "I do worry sometimes that our situation might make others jealous. In fact, Hugh warned me not to invite just anyone up here. And I do understand his rationale. But it is such fun to share it with someone. And I felt that you would be more understanding than most."

"My mother would delight in seeing your home too," Elizabeth told her. "She left a very fine house behind in Kentucky. Although she won't admit it, I know she misses certain things, such as her china dishes and her beautiful bedroom furniture."

"The very sort of items I someday hope to carry in our mercantile."

"That day may be a long way off. At least for most settlers."

"Oh, mark my word, Elizabeth, it's not that far off. This is beautiful country, and I feel certain more settlers are coming. I have no doubts that all of us—or at least most of us—will have very fine houses again someday."

"You already have one," Elizabeth reminded her.

Lavinia shrugged. "Yes, well, this is quite livable for now. But in time, after our town grows and our business prospers, I want a real house built on our land. I want a place where my grandchildren can run and play."

"Yes." Elizabeth nodded. "I understand that."

Lavinia led her to the kitchen area. "As you can see, I am cooking on a real stove now. However, I must confess my cooking skills have not greatly improved since we were on the trail. Thanks to you and your mother, Evelyn has become quite adept at cooking—something, I'm sure, some young man will be most appreciative of someday."

"I hope you're not in a hurry to get Evelyn married off," Elizabeth said.

"Not at all. That girl is too valuable here."

"Isn't she just barely sixteen?"

"She will be seventeen in May. And she is still attending class with Mrs. Taylor. Did you know that Mrs. Taylor not only speaks Latin, but French and German as well? Who would have known?"

"Besides the languages, JT is delighted that she is teaching the children to read music. And my Ruth practically thinks that Mrs. Taylor hung the moon. I had no idea she had so much to offer."

"I suppose it was a blessing in disguise…" Lavina sighed as she checked a pot that was on the stove. "I mean…that she is with us now."

"Most certainly."

"Evelyn insisted on helping me to make us a soup," Lavinia told Elizabeth.

"Oh, my…and I only expected to come for tea."

"Well, certainly you must be hungry. Evelyn was sure you would be."

"As a matter of fact I am," she admitted.

"It's potato and sausage." Lavinia moved the pot to a cooler part of the stove.

"Sounds delicious." Elizabeth looked over to where the kitchen table was set with fine china dishes and silver. "The table looks beautiful too."

"That was my idea," Lavinia declared. "It makes me feel so festive to use my good dishes. But I hope you don't mind eating in the kitchen. It seemed more sensible than the big dining table."

"Not at all. It's very cozy in here."

Soon they were seated, and Lavinia invited Elizabeth to ask the blessing. "Your family seems so much more experienced at that than we are," she said quietly. Elizabeth prayed, and they both began to eat.

"This soup is wonderful," Elizabeth told her.

Lavinia nodded. "It is good, isn't it? I'll be sure to tell Evelyn you liked it. She was so happy to hear you were coming." Lavinia's mouth puckered into a frown. "Although I must confess that we were very disappointed about your insistence that no one bring gifts to your wedding. Why in the world did you do that? And mind you, I am not only asking as a businesswoman, but as a friend."

Elizabeth didn't want to say anything to diminish Malinda in her soon-to-be sister-in-law's eyes. "It just seemed the right thing to do. Most of the settlers can barely feed their families, let alone try to come up with two wedding gifts in a month. Eli and I are not in need of gifts."

"But perhaps your friends and neighbors should have been the ones to decide that."

"Perhaps." Elizabeth buttered her biscuit. "Seeing this butter reminds me, my mother is a very good cheese maker."

"Cheese?" Lavinia's eyes lit up. "Oh, how I miss cheese."

"I wonder if it would sell well in your store."

"Oh, I'm sure it would. I would certainly buy it."

"Well, we have decided that as soon as our cows begin giving milk—mind you, it won't be until a year from now, if we are lucky—my mother and I will begin making cheese."

"That is wonderful. Consider me your first customer. And I will sell it in the mercantile too."

After their meal, they got back downstairs just as Flo came into the store. And while Elizabeth shopped, Lavinia and Flo visited together like old friends. Sometimes Elizabeth found it hard to believe that these two women, who would one day be sharing grandbabies, had come from such completely different economic situations. But the Oregon Trail and the frontier eliminated some of the social barriers that were common in the eastern part of the country. Not all of the barriers, of course, but many. At least for the time being. Elizabeth had no idea how all the various relationships would fare on down the line. But for now they all needed one another. And the tighter their little community remained, the greater their chances for success. Or so it seemed to Elizabeth.

"Your shelves seem better stocked than the last time I was here," Elizabeth called out to Lavinia.

"Yes. Hugh and Julius got back yesterday. We spent the evening unloading and stocking all the merchandise."

"You are making it rather hard on me," Elizabeth admitted.

"What do you mean?" Lavinia came over to where Elizabeth was admiring a coffeepot. Her coffeepot from the trail was dented and stained and lidless. The idea of this shining new red enameled pot was rather appealing. Even so, she did not need it, and it was not on her list. She reluctantly set it back down.

"I made myself a list that I plan to stick to, but some of your lovely items are tempting." She smiled. "And once we start producing cheese and other dairy products, my purse strings will loosen up some." She held up her shopping basket. "As it is, this will do me for today. Well, along with these dry staples." She handed Lavinia her list, waiting as she measured and weighed flour and sugar and salt and coffee and beans and all the other staples necessary to feed a family of four.

While Lavinia was packaging her things, Elizabeth peered outside and noticed that the dark clouds were indeed converging overhead. "Oh, dear," she said. "I hope I make it home before those clouds burst open. I fear the road will turn into a bog soon."

"I'm glad Hugh and Julius made it back." Lavinia frowned at the window. "I told them they were pushing it. They could have easily been wading through mud by now."

Elizabeth hoped she wasn't going to be wading through mud.

"Hello, Elizabeth," Hugh said as he came into the mercantile.

"Good afternoon," she replied.

"I was helping Julius with his house today," he said as he brushed sawdust from his trousers. "Had to quit before the rain came."

"Not in here," Lavinia warned. "I just swept."

He made a sheepish grin. "I'll take this outside."

"And can you help Elizabeth with Eli's order," Lavinia called out the open door. "But don't tell her what it is. Eli said it's a secret."

"Will do." Out on the boardwalk in front of the mercantile, he was busily brushing the sawdust off. "In fact, I'll be happy to load everything up for you, Elizabeth," he called into the store. "And I'll loan you a tarp to keep it dry too. Looks like we're going to have a deluge."

"Thank you," she said appreciatively. "I better get going."

"Take this to JT and Ruth," Lavinia said as she handed Elizabeth a couple of peppermint sticks.

"Thank you." Elizabeth tucked them into her skirt pocket, wondering if she should give the children a ride home, but when she looked at the clock, she realized they would already be well on their way. Perhaps she would pick them up on the road.

"All loaded and ready to roll," Hugh said as he returned to the store. "If I were you, I would roll in haste." He grinned. "And judging by those horses, I'll bet you can too. At least you can go a lot faster than when the wagon was fully loaded on the Oregon Trail."

"That's for sure." She laughed. "And you're right, that team can go fairly well when I let them." She thanked Lavinia again and then, saying goodbye, hurried out to climb into the wagon. The clouds seemed to be getting lower and darker by the moment. She snapped the reins and commanded the team to go, urging them to a faster pace than usual as they got onto the rutted road. It was not a smooth road by any means, but if one kept the wheels in the ruts, and if there was no mud, it was not too terrible.

However, she was only halfway home when the sky opened up and the rain came pouring down, falling so heavily it felt as if it were being dumped by the bucketful. In no time, Elizabeth could feel herself being soaked clear down to her underclothes. She glanced over her shoulder, thankful that Hugh had thought to protect her purchases. Hopefully the dry goods would make it home without being ruined.

"Gid-up," she shouted, urging the team to continue even though the road was quickly turning to gooey mud.

Finally, she realized that it was useless to try to go fast. Beau and Bella were struggling to get their footing in the slippery mud, and the wagon wheels were so coated that the mud was splattering all over the wagon. At one point, she considered just stopping and waiting it out. But who knew how long this downpour would last?

Eventually, she knew it was futile to remain on the road, and seeing a meadow off to one side, she wondered if that might provide a firmer surface. However, the team seemed unable to move. Thinking she could lead them over to the grass, she climbed out of the wagon and immediately slipped in the mud. Now she was not only soaked to the skin, but covered in mud as well. Climbing back to her feet, she went to the horses' heads and grabbed Beau's harness. "Come on," she urged, pulling him toward her.

But their footing, like hers, was slipping. And the more she worked with them, the more she realized she was putting them in danger by asking them to do the impossible. The wagon was so mired down in the mud, it was going nowhere. Now she decided her only goal was to get Beau and Bella safely away from the wagon before one of them fell and injured a leg. In the pouring rain, she spoke calmly to her team, struggling to get them out of the harnesses and finally free from the wagon.

"Easy does it," she said as she slowly led them away from the mud. "Come on, Beau and Bella, let's get you to firmer ground." She finally got them somewhat sheltered under a stand of fir trees. And when she looked back to the road, she was stunned to see that the belly of the wagon was nearly touching the mud. No wonder the team could not budge it.

"Let's see if we can get you home," she said as she led the horses through the grass. The ground was soft and the going was slow, but it wasn't nearly as mucky and sticky as the road had become. She found the going was easier if she kept them moving on the higher ground. But at the same time, she felt worried that she was getting too far from the road. What if she got lost?

She paused beneath another stand of trees, stopping to check her team. She ran her hands down their legs, making sure they were sound. Fortunately, other than being tired, they seemed just fine.

She stroked their sleek heads, talking soothingly to them. "You two are worth much more than all the flour and sugar and coffee in the whole mercantile. And I'm sorry I put you at risk just to get my wagon home."

She looked out over the grassy slope she was leading them on. She would prefer walking them on flat land when it was slick like this, but all the flat land seemed to be turning to mud. As it was, she knew if she took it slow and easy, they should make it back all right—as long as she wasn't lost. She wondered what it would feel like to spend the night out here. If she could make a fire—which was doubtful—she might be able to dry out her clothes and make it to morning. She wondered what Eli would say to her. Certainly, he would not allow himself to be caught in a situation like this. What kind of frontier woman was she, anyway?

Chapter Seventeen

I n all our days on the Oregon Trail," she said aloud as she trudge along, "I never ever saw anything like this rain and mud." Bella shook her head up and down as if to concur with her. Traveling this off-road route was taking much longer than it would to simply wade through the mud on foot. However, she knew it didn't matter as long as she got her team home in one piece.

Eventually, she found her way back to the road again, and she recognized the land as part of Malinda's property. Feeling somewhat hopeful but exhausted, she encouraged the team to keep going. It was dusky by the time Malinda's farm finally came into sight. Elizabeth couldn't remember when she'd been so happy to see the warm golden light through a window. As she plodded toward the barn, she tried to remember when she'd felt this weary. Probably on the Oregon Trail—although that seemed impossible at the moment.

"Come on," she urged her horses, leading them through the muddy farmyard and into Malinda's pasture. "You're home for now."

She watched as they wearily went through the gate. She knew they were all right, and she planned to send JT out to check on them. But in all likelihood, they would recover more quickly than she would. However, they couldn't have possibly pulled that wagon all the way home. And she did not even want to think about her dry goods, which would probably turn to mush by morning.

Feeling as if she could barely plant one foot in front of the other, she trudged over to the house, but when she opened the door and saw the shocked faces of Amelia, Malinda, and Susannah, she knew she couldn't go inside the house like this.

"What happened to you?" Malinda demanded.

Elizabeth held up a tired hand. "Excuse me a moment," she said hoarsely. Then she turned and walked over to where one of the water troughs was overflowing from the rain and, knowing she looked perfectly ridiculous, plunged herself into the trough, washing the caked mud from her outer clothes as if she were bathing. She could hear the girls laughing from the porch. She didn't blame them because she knew she looked foolish, but at the same time they had no idea how cold she was.

Shivering and weak, she climbed from the trough and made her way to the covered porch, where she slowly peeled off her dripping outer clothing, dropping it down on the bench by the door. She would deal with it later.

"Here," Malinda said as she wrapped a blanket around Elizabeth's shoulders. "Get inside before you catch your death of cold."

"Thank you," Elizabeth muttered with chattering teeth, allowing Malinda to guide her toward the fire. There, with the help of the older girls holding blankets as a screen, Elizabeth removed the last of her wet clothing and then wrapped herself up in Malinda's warm woolen robe.

"Sit down," Malinda said as she shoved a straight-backed chair beneath Elizabeth.

"Put these on." Amelia knelt down, pushing Elizabeth's white icy feet into a pair of thick socks.

"And drink this," Malinda handed her a cup of hot coffee with cream.

"What happened, Mama?" Ruth asked her with wide eyes. "Susannah said you jumped in the water trough."

The girls laughed, and Elizabeth couldn't help but giggle despite herself, or maybe it was something in the coffee. And then she explained about going to the mercantile and getting stuck in the mud and how she had to get her team away from the wagon to get them safely home.

"You left our wagon out on the road?" Ruth sounded shocked.

"I had to," she explained as she sipped the odd-tasting coffee. "It was the wagon or the horses. And the wagon will survive the mud. I wasn't so sure about the horses." She turned to Malinda. "Honestly, in all our days and all our hard times on the Oregon Trail, I never ever encountered anything like that horrid mud."

"I should have warned you about downpours like this. You should never take out a wagon this time of year—not unless you've got a good shovel and a bunch of wood planks with you." Now Malinda explained how the men would sometimes dig out the mud and place planks in the road for the wheels to roll onto. "Even that is an enormous undertaking."

"I can imagine."

"You're much better off on foot," she told Elizabeth.

JT and the boys came into the house now. "Ma," he called out, "I noticed our team was here. Are you all right?"

"Yes," she told him. "Did you see to the team?"

He assured her he'd done that. "Did you see Eli on your way here?"

"Eli?" she peered over her coffee mug at JT. His hat was dripping, and he looked nearly as soaked as she'd been. However, seeing he was wearing his father's old waxed barn jacket, she knew his clothing would remain dry underneath.

"He came through here with Grandpa's oxen team about an hour ago."

She blinked. "Eli brought the oxen here?"

"Yeah. He knew you'd need some help to get the wagon home." JT frowned. "Where *is* the wagon?"

Once again, she explained her recent dilemma. "But where is Eli now?"

"I expect he went on down the road looking for you."

"Oh…" She sighed.

"Don't worry about Eli," JT assured her. "He can take care of himself."

"Did he have a shovel with him?" Malinda asked as JT was heading back out the door.

"Yep. And a couple of planks of wood too," he said as he left.

"See," Malinda told Elizabeth. "Your man's got a good head on his shoulders."

Elizabeth just nodded.

"Okay, we're going to get some soup into her," Malinda told the girls. "And then we'll get her to bed. Susannah, you get those warming stones heated up for her. Amelia, you make her some tea."

Elizabeth watched almost as if she were dreaming as they all scurried around, chattering among themselves. She wasn't sure if Malinda had put something in her coffee, but she felt surprisingly warm and relaxed when Amelia and Susannah finally helped her into bed.

"I'll come to bed and read to you after supper," Ruth promised as she tucked the quilt snugly under Elizabeth's chin.

"Thank you, sweetheart," Elizabeth murmured as she closed her eyes and sighed.

"Our bride-to-be is awake," Malinda said in a teasing tone as Elizabeth came out into the front room and looked around.

"Where is everyone?" She buttoned the cuffs of her chore dress.

"Off to school." Malinda handed her a cup of coffee.

Elizabeth peered suspiciously into the coffee. "What's in this?" she asked.

"Cream and a bit of sugar," Malinda said innocently.

"What about last night's coffee?"

"Just a drop or two of *medicine*," Malinda chuckled. "To ward off a cold or chill."

Elizabeth took a cautious sip and was relieved to discover it tasted normal.

"And it seems to have done the trick," Malinda told her. "You look none the worse for wear."

Elizabeth sighed and sat down at the table. "Thank you, Malinda," she said gratefully. "I'm sure that you and the girls saved my life last night."

Malinda grinned. "Well, we couldn't very well let our bride expire just two days before her wedding. Goodness, if I'd known you were going to go out and try to drown yourself, I would have forced you to stay for the quilting bee."

"How was the quilting bee?" Elizabeth looked down at her coffee.

"Successful. We finished it up in time for the ladies to get home before the rain let loose."

"May I see the finished quilt?"

Malinda frowned. "I'm sorry. It's all wrapped up in paper to keep it clean and safe until the wedding day."

Elizabeth nodded. "I'm sure it's beautiful."

"Eli came by last night to check on you." Malinda set a bowl of oatmeal in front of Elizabeth. "You had already gone to sleep."

"Was he all right?" She poured some milk over her oatmeal.

"Well, other than being soaked, he was fine. He used the oxen team to pull the wagon from the mud. However, he said they were worn out. So he left them and the wagon here. He thought you might want it for tomorrow—if the road dries out by then." She pointed to some bundles sitting on the bench by the fireplace. "He brought those into the house to dry out. I think most of your purchases from yesterday will be just fine." She pointed to a large bowl of damp-looking oatmeal. "Except that one. It must not have been as well covered as the others. But we fixed a big pot of oatmeal for breakfast. And I thought perhaps I could make a big batch of oatmeal and molasses cookies out of the rest of it." She smiled. "I could bring them to the wedding dinner tomorrow."

"That would be nice. Thanks." Elizabeth ate her breakfast as Malinda bustled about the kitchen. But when Elizabeth started to do her normal morning chores, Malinda held up a hand. "Not today, my friend."

"But I want to help."

Malinda just shook her head. "Do you feel well enough to go to your mother's like you planned to do today?"

Elizabeth nodded. "I feel perfectly fine."

"Perhaps you could ride Molly."

"Yes. That might be a good plan. And if the road is too bad, we'll just cut across some fields."

"The rain seems to have moved eastward, but after yesterday's downpour, it's still rather soggy out there."

"I'll be sure to wear my heavy boots and barn coat this time."

"And don't overdo," Malinda warned her.

Elizabeth patted Malinda on the back. "Thank you for caring."

Now Malinda reached out and hugged her tightly. "Of course I care. You are my oldest and dearest friend."

To Elizabeth's surprise, she felt tears welling up. "I'm so glad we're still friends."

Malinda pulled her an arm's length away and looked into her eyes. "I realize I've been a bit harsh at times," she admitted. "I hope you'll forgive me. I've given it some thought, and I suppose I can be a bit self-centered at times."

Elizabeth just shrugged.

"And then, living out here in the frontier, I've also gotten rather self-reliant. It occurred to me last night after you'd gone to bed that being too self-centered and too self-reliant weren't the best qualities in a friend. I want to try harder."

Elizabeth patted Malinda's shoulder. "I suspect we both have much to learn about friendship—especially out here in the frontier," she told her. "But I'm very thankful that I have you, Malinda." She noticed that her wet clothes from yesterday were washed and hanging by the fireplace to dry. "And thank you again for taking such good care of me last night."

"What time do you think you'll be back here?" Malinda asked with an arched brow.

"In time to help prepare supper," she assured her.

"Good. I will expect you then."

ஒஐஒ

As Elizabeth rode Molly through a wooded area, she noticed how dirty her fingernails were from yesterday's mud bath. Now if Malinda had allowed her to wash up the breakfast dishes as she usually did, her nails would be clean. Maybe she could offer to wash her mother's dishes or do some laundry, although she was fairly certain that wasn't going to happen. She knew her mother and Jess planned to spend their time sewing and cooking today.

Her mother planned to do a final fitting of the wedding dress and do the finish work on Ruth's dress. At the same time, they wanted to bake some cakes and pies for dessert. Tomorrow, Asa would go early to the church and set up a fire pit to roast venison and salmon. Elizabeth wasn't sure about all the other food details, but she wasn't worried about them either. Her mother had assured her that she was handling them, and Elizabeth trusted her.

She looked up at the sky as she rode. Through the overhead branches, it looked clear and blue. She hoped the fair weather would hold out through tomorrow. Perhaps the road would have a chance to dry out and firm up by then. And if not...well, she expected they would simply make the best of it.

Clara and Jess welcomed her into the snug little cabin, and it wasn't long until Elizabeth was trying on her dress. "That shade of blue is so pretty with your eyes," Clara told her. "Ruth was smart to pick it out."

"It reminds me of the color of the river on a clear day," Jess said. "Very pretty."

Clara stood back to look at Elizabeth. "My dear, you look just beautiful."

"Thank you. And this dress is beautiful too. The prettiest dress I've had since...well, since losing James." Elizabeth sighed as she admired the carefully stitched tucks in the bodice, fingered the delicate lace collar, and smoothed her hands over the silky fabric of the skirt.

"And the fit looks perfect," Jess said.

"I believe you're right. I don't think we need to adjust a thing." Clara nodded with satisfaction.

"It's such a lovely dress that after the wedding, I'll probably be afraid to wear it," Elizabeth confessed.

"Of course you'll wear it," Clara said as she helped her out of it.

"You can wear it to church," Jess said.

"And other weddings."

"But not on a rainy day." Now Elizabeth told them the details of her harrowing trip home from town the day before.

"My goodness!" Clara gasped. "I had no idea. Eli came by here for the team, but I didn't realize you were in such dire straits."

"I learned some important things," she told them. "First of all, we need to be just as prepared out here as we were while traveling the Oregon Trail." She explained what Malinda had told her about carrying shovels and planks. "I also learned never to take this seemingly mild climate for granted. The weather here can change quickly. From now on I will take a very good look at the sky before heading out in the wagon. Getting stuck in the mud like that was a valuable lesson for me. One that I do not care to repeat."

"Couldn't you have simply ridden one of the horses home?"

"Not on the road. They were worn out from trying to pull that wagon. And they were slipping and sliding, and I did not want to risk a broken leg." She shook her head. "Can you imagine how devastating that would be? After getting them safely here from Kentucky only to lose them a couple miles from home?"

"Oh, my." Jess shook her head. "I plan to tell Matthew about the shovels and planks. Not that we'll be taking our wagon out much."

"I can understand now why everyone kept telling us to get our houses built before the rains started."

"Not to mention having roofs over our heads," Clara said. "It rained so hard here last night that I was very concerned about Brady in the tent."

"Oh, dear. I forgot about that. How did he fare?"

"He was a bit damp, I'm afraid." Clara shook her head. "He and Asa and Matthew are working hard to get him a small shelter built, but I doubt it will be as nice as the cabin on your property."

"He is still welcome to it," Elizabeth told her.

"He knows that." Clara smiled. "But he truly wants to be here with us. I have to say, I was very touched. I do hope you don't mind, dear."

"Not at all. I actually believe it is a sensible idea. But I do wish Brady would have spoken up earlier. Then he would have a nice little cabin all built."

"I told him that if it got too wet and cold in the tent, he is welcome to come in here to sleep." Clara pointed to the braided rug by the fireplace. "It's not much, but it would be warm and dry."

The three of them continued working together into the afternoon. By the time they called it quits, they had finished both dresses and baked three cakes and six pies. "And I made two cakes yesterday," Clara assured Elizabeth as she handed her the parcel she'd wrapped, containing the two dresses for tomorrow's wedding.

"And I have two more pies at my house," Jess said.

"And Malinda is making oatmeal and molasses cookies," Elizabeth told them.

"Your father got a big bag of potatoes from the mercantile," Clara told her. "He plans to bake them in the barbecue pit while the venison and salmon cook. Besides that, he has several crates of corn. He asked if the children could come to the church early to help with the husking."

"I'll be sure and tell them," Elizabeth promised as she pulled on her riding hat. "And now I should be on my way because I promised Malinda I would be home in time to help with supper."

Clara glanced at Jess. "Say...before you go, Elizabeth," she said quickly. "Your father wanted you to run down to where they're building Brady's cabin. He wants to ask you something. I believe it has to do with tomorrow. Do you mind, dear?"

"Not at all."

They all hugged goodbye, and Elizabeth tied the precious parcel of dresses onto the back of her saddle and rode on over to the spot her mother had described. A small stand of fir trees were behind what was the beginning of a very small log cabin. "Hello," she called as she slid off her horse and went over to where her father was notching one end of a log and Brady was notching the other.

"Elizabeth," Asa said cheerfully. "What brings you out here—and on the eve of your wedding day?"

"Mother said you wanted to speak to me." She waved to Brady now. "Looks like your cabin is coming along."

Asa's brow creased as he rubbed his chin. "What did she say I wanted to speak to you about?"

She shrugged. "I don't rightly know. I assumed it was something about the wedding."

He still looked slightly confused. He went over the same details her mother had just told her about the venison and salmon. "Brady and I caught the salmon, and Eli and Matthew got three deer this week. We got several good-sized roasts hanging for tomorrow, and the rest is getting smoked." Then he told her about the potatoes and corn. "Oh, that's right, I did want the children to come help husk the corn. Maybe that's why your ma sent you over here."

"But Mother told me that." She frowned. "So there's nothing else to talk about?"

Asa shook his head. "Nothing that I know of." Now his face lit up. "Except that I couldn't be happier for you and Eli. And I'm plum delighted that I get to walk you down the aisle again tomorrow. It will be a grand day."

"Thank you." She turned to Brady again. "And you will be at the wedding too, won't you?"

He made an uncertain smile. "Well, now…I ain't so sure."

"Oh, please, *do* come, Brady." Then she realized the reason for his hesitation. "I mean, I want you to come if you want to come." She put her hand on his shoulder. "I will understand if you don't want to be in town. But if you don't come, you must promise to join us for a wedding celebration at our new house. That will be just for family."

"Just for family?" He tipped his head to one side.

She smiled. "Yes, and that means you too, Brady. You know that. And you will have to promise to bring your harmonica too."

He grinned. "You can count on it."

"And if you don't make it to the wedding, I'll be sure to bring you home a big plate of food," Asa promised.

"I'd be much obliged."

"But I do want you to know that you are very welcome at the wedding," Elizabeth said as she slipped a boot into the stirrup. "Either way I will understand."

He nodded. "Thank you, Miss Elizabeth."

As she rode back to Malinda's, she wished that the laws were more welcoming to people like Brady and the Indians. She felt certain that someday, with the help of education and good Christian values, these laws would change, both in the Oregon Territory and in the United States of America. But she just didn't know how long it would take. She prayed that this change would occur in Brady's lifetime, but considering his age, she realized that might take a miracle.

Chapter Eighteen

When Elizabeth got back to Malinda's, the house seemed to be more lit up than usual, and a lantern was hanging outside on the porch. Very inviting. She was just slipping down from Molly when she saw JT and Bart hurrying from the barn.

"Hello, Ma," JT called to her. "We'll take care of your horse for you."

"Thank you very much," she said as she handed him the reins.

"And Bart and Todd and me got the wagon and Beau and Bella all cleaned up after school," JT told her.

"They'll look real nice for the wedding tomorrow," Bart told her. "Those are real nice horses, Aunt Elizabeth."

"Well, thank you again," she said as she removed the parcel containing her wedding dress. "And I agree, they are wonderful horses. I felt badly for working them so hard yesterday. That was very thoughtful of you boys to take care of that for me."

"It was Aunt Malinda's idea," JT told her.

"Thank you just the same. I'm sure it was quite a chore."

"And Todd took the oxen team back to your pa," Bart said.

"Well, I am most grateful to all you fine young men," she said happily. "I hardly know what to say."

JT tipped his head toward the well-lit house. "Maybe you ought to go inside now, Ma."

"Yes." She nodded. As she went, she thought she heard the boys giggling, but she didn't care to investigate the reason. She was so thankful for the generous help with the team and so thankful that Malinda had thought of it. She pushed open the door and then blinked to see a room full of females. They were circled around the door as if they expected her.

"Surprise!" they all yelled.

"What?" She looked at the merry faces.

"We're having a bridal shower," Malinda explained as she reached for the parcel and then helped to remove Elizabeth's coat.

"A *what*?" Elizabeth frowned down at her still dirty nails. "I realize I had a mud bath yesterday, but I did intend to clean up before—"

"No, no..." Lavinia laughed as she came over to hug Elizabeth. "Although I did hear about your misadventures in the mud. But no, that is not what a bridal shower is for. I will explain that later. First you must greet your guests."

"Mother and Jessica—how did you get here before me?" Elizabeth peered curiously at her female relatives. "Ah...so that's why you sent me to speak to Father—so you could beat me back here. No wonder he was confused."

Clara giggled as they hugged. "I felt terrible for tricking you like that."

"That's all right. As it turned out, I wanted to speak to both Father and Brady." She looked around to see not only Belinda, Amelia, Susanna, Emily, and Ruth, but also Evelyn and Flo and Mahala and Hannah and Tillie. Even Mrs. Taylor was there. Elizabeth took time to greet each of them one by one. "What a delightful houseful of women," she declared.

"Since you were opposed to receiving any wedding presents, I decided to make a plan of my own," Lavinia explained to Elizabeth.

"Yes, this was all Lavinia's idea," Malinda told her. "I thought maybe it was her way of drumming up business for the mercantile, but she assured me that had nothing to do with it." They all laughed.

"Now come and sit here, Aunt Elizabeth." Emily led her over to the rocker.

As Elizabeth sat, she looked at Lavinia. "You still haven't told me what a bridal shower is."

Lavinia stood up, folding her hands in front of her as if she were getting ready to recite. "The tradition of a bridal shower comes from Holland," she began. "According to my mother, who was Dutch, there was a young woman who fell in love with a kindhearted miller back in the 1600s. Now the miller was a hard worker, but because of his kind and generous heart, he often gave bags of wheat away to those in need." Lavinia chuckled. "Not very profitable for a businessman to give merchandise away for free."

"Not like our Aunt Lavinia," Amelia teased.

Lavinia smirked at her niece. "So as you can imagine, this kindhearted miller was rather poor. In fact, he was so poor that the young woman's father refused to let her marry him. Both the miller and the girl were devastated." She paused long enough for the women to express their dismay. "To make matters worse, the young woman's father decided his daughter must marry the pig farmer, who was very wealthy but not nearly as nice as the miller."

"Oh, no!" Ruth said. Once again everyone laughed.

"What happened, Aunt Lavinia?" Belinda demanded.

"Well, when the good miller's friends heard his sad news and remembered how generous he had always been to them, they naturally wanted to help him out. They decided they would raise money to provide a dowry for his beloved." She paused as the younger girls cheered.

"However, the miller's friends, like him, were rather poor. Alas, they did not have enough money to make a respectable dowry."

Now the girls expressed their disappointment.

"Then they came up with another idea. Instead of giving them money, they decided to shower the couple with goods. They gave them linens and china and all sorts of things to set up housekeeping. And so the miller and the bride were allowed to marry and lived happily ever after."

Now everyone clapped and cheered.

"So in some places, like Boston, it has become a custom to shower the bride-to-be with gifts, and that is exactly what we are doing."

And now the women and girls came to Elizabeth and began to present her with a variety of wonderful presents. Susannah and Emily gave her a fine set of embroidered bed linens. "We were working on them in secret," the sisters explained.

"They are beautiful," she said as she thanked them.

Next she was presented a tea set from Amelia and Belinda. "We got it at the mercantile," Belinda whispered.

"It's lovely! Thank you."

On the gifts came…a vase from Flo, four teaspoons from Evelyn, a set of kitchen linens from Hannah and Tillie, a pair of knitted slippers from Mahala, a set of pillows from her mother, a kerosene lantern from Mrs. Taylor, a braided rug from Jess, an embroidered wall hanging from Malinda that featured a little cabin and said "Home Sweet Home," and from Lavinia, the enameled red coffeepot that Elizabeth had admired in the mercantile just yesterday. Once again she expressed her sincere gratitude to everyone.

"You're not done yet, Mama." Ruth handed her something wrapped in paper. Elizabeth opened it up to see a hand-drawn picture of a cabin nestled in the trees with a blue river flowing in front of it.

"This is beautiful, sweetie." Elizabeth held it up for all to see. "My daughter is an artist."

"I made the frame too," Ruth said shyly.

"I love it!" Elizabeth pulled Ruth in for a hug. "You are all so wonderful," she told everyone. "I am so very grateful for all my lovely friends, just as the miller surely was for all of his. You are all worth more to me than a dowry." She held up the coffeepot and grinned. "I can assure you that Eli and I will put these items to good use, and we will think of all of our dear friends whenever we do. Thank you all so much!"

"One more thing," Malinda said mysteriously. She nodded to Susannah and Ruth, and the two girls dashed to the bedroom and soon emerged carrying a big bundle between them. It was wrapped in brown paper and tied with string.

"That is from all of us," Malinda proclaimed as the girls set it in Elizabeth's lap.

Elizabeth untied the string and unwrapped the paper and then gasped to see it. "This is your quilt," she said to Malinda, holding the beautiful log cabin design up for everyone to see.

"We were making it for you," Malinda told her. "That was the plan all along."

Elizabeth held it up to her cheek. "It is beautiful. Thank you all so much."

"That's why we didn't want you here when we finished it," Malinda explained.

"Oh, my." Elizabeth just shook her head. "I don't even know what to say."

"That must mean it's time to serve the food," Malinda declared. "But first let's all ask the good Lord's blessing and invite him to bless Elizabeth on her special day tomorrow."

❧

Good food, good fun, good friends...it was an occasion to remember always. Elizabeth could not recall the last time she'd had such an enjoyable evening. "A bridal shower is a lovely tradition," she told Lavinia as the women who'd come from town were preparing to leave. They'd all come together in a wagon that the boys had hidden behind the barn.

"I'm not sure that we'll do this for all the upcoming weddings," Lavinia confided. "But when I heard you and Eli were not allowing wedding gifts...well, I knew something had to be done about that."

Elizabeth thanked everyone again. "I'll see you all tomorrow," she called out as the wagon started to move.

Just as it was leaving, another wagon pulled into the farmyard from the opposite direction with lanterns hanging on both sides. Elizabeth was relieved to see that Matthew had come for Clara and Jess.

"How was your shower?" he asked her in a teasing tone. "Did you get all wet?"

"I got wet yesterday," she told him. "Tonight's shower was much more pleasant. Goodness, you should see the lovely gifts these women brought for Eli and me."

"Anything you want us to take in the wagon? I could run it on over to Eli."

"That's a good idea," Clara said. "If you take these gifts up to Eli, she won't need to trouble herself with it tomorrow."

"And I have some crates and things as well." Elizabeth remembered what she'd stowed in the barn. "Would you mind taking them too?"

"Not at all."

With the help of the girls, they soon got the wagon loaded up, and Matthew and Jess and Clara were on their way. "See you tomorrow," Elizabeth called out.

Back in the house, the girls were already cleaning up, and no one would allow Elizabeth or Malinda to help. "This was such a wonderful night," Elizabeth said to Malinda as they sat together. "Thank you so much."

"It really was Lavinia's idea," Malinda said.

"The quilt was your idea," Elizabeth pointed out.

"Well, yes, that's true."

"I love it, Malinda. I don't even know how to thank you."

Malinda smiled. "Just enjoy it."

"Matthew is taking everything up to Eli." Elizabeth shook her head. "I feel a bit envious though. Eli is up there in our house. Do you think he'll put things away?"

"I don't see why. Most men would think of that as women's work."

"I hope he does." Elizabeth sighed. "I am just itching to start keeping house—I mean in my own house."

"Yes, I can imagine." Malinda made a sad sigh. "Although I am going to miss you, Elizabeth. And Ruth and JT too."

Elizabeth laughed. "You'll still have a fairly full house, Malinda. With your four and Will's two girls, you are not hurting for companionship."

"That's true. But it's not the same as having my best friend right here."

Elizabeth tried not to remember the times when she had felt like anything but Malinda's best friend. "And don't forget that in just two weeks, you'll have Will here as well. I expect he'll become your best friend…in time. And, of course, we will just be down the road. I predict our families will have many wonderful times to look forward to in the years to come."

Later that night, after everyone had gone to bed, Elizabeth lay still, listening to the sounds of her daughter's and best friend's even breathing as they peacefully slumbered. And yet, as tired as she was, sleep was evading her tonight. Her mind seemed unwilling to quiet down as she pondered her life and how different everything had been just one year ago. She remembered being awakened in the middle of the night last December, feeling again as if James were leading her. She remembered her recurring dreams about traveling to Oregon. It all seemed so far away now, like a different world.

And indeed it was. But it was about to change again. Marrying Eli and moving into their home together—tomorrow! As much as she wanted this, had been waiting for this, she suddenly felt uneasy. The more she thought about it, the more distraught she felt.

If she hadn't been sleeping in the middle of the bed, wedged between Ruth and Malinda, she would have gotten up and slipped out. She would have sat by the fire to think…and think. As it was, she didn't want to disturb them.

Finally, after what felt like hours, she remembered the way her mother taught her to put herself to sleep as a child. She would count her blessings. And so she started with each member of her family and then moved on to friends and even livestock, until finally she was thanking God for every single little thing she could think of—from ladybugs to forget-me-nots to hummingbirds—until eventually she felt herself drifting away.

Chapter Nineteen

When Elizabeth woke up the next morning, she was alone in the bed, but it still seemed dark outside, so she didn't think she'd slept in. But when she poked her head out the bedroom door, it was clear that everyone else was up and busy. And when she saw the clock, she realized it was nearly nine.

"Oh, dear," she exclaimed. "I didn't know it was so late."

"There's our bride," Malinda announced. "You were sleeping so soundly, we thought perhaps you needed it."

"Bless you," Elizabeth said. "I did have a restless night. But now I better get moving."

"Is it time for me to get on my wedding clothes?" Ruth asked hopefully.

"Yes." Elizabeth waved. "Come on in here, and we'll get at least one of us ready."

Ruth entered the room, pushing the muslin curtains aside to let in a little light. "There sure are a lot of dark clouds out there today," she announced sadly. "Do you think it will rain?"

Elizabeth peered out to see that the sky was gray and somber looking—the reason it had seemed dark even though it was late in the morning. "Don't worry, Ruth." She reached for Ruth's new blue dress. "Rain on your wedding is supposed to be good luck." She slid the dress down over Ruth's head and shoulders.

"How can rain be good luck?" Ruth asked as her head popped through the neckline.

"If there's been a dry spell and your crops need water, you consider yourself lucky when it rains. Remember?" She buttoned the back of her dress.

"Yes, but we haven't had a dry spell. And last night when I prayed before bed, I asked God to keep the rain away today," Ruth told her.

"Well, come rain or shine, Eli and I are getting married this morning," Elizabeth declared. "And it will be a very happy day. You can count on it." She tied the sash in back of Ruth's dress, fluffing it out into a big bow before she turned her around. "Ruth Anne, you look lovely. And your grandmother will be relieved to see that the dress fits you just right."

Ruth spun around to make the full skirt flare out. "And it will be good for dancing too!"

"Hold still now, and let's do your hair." Elizabeth reached for the hairbrush.

As she brushed and braided Ruth's hair, she gazed out the bedroom window. Malinda was fortunate that their house had more than just one glass window. Still, Elizabeth would happily move into a house with no glass windows if it meant that she and Eli and the children could be together.

However, her daughter was right about the weather. It did look as if the sky might open up at any moment. Even so, Elizabeth was not going to let that get her down. Today was a happy day regardless of the weather.

"There," she proclaimed as she tied the big blue satin ribbon at the bottom of Ruth's braid. "You are pretty as a picture."

Ruth frowned up at her. "But you are still in your nightie, Mama."

Elizabeth laughed. "Yes—and I can't very well get married in my nightie, can I? You go and remind Aunt Malinda that Grandpa wants the boys to come to the church early to help him, and I will get dressed."

"Yes, Mama!"

With the bedroom to herself, Elizabeth layered her corset over the chemise and bloomers and stockings, and then she put on her best petticoat. Finally she removed the new dress from where she'd hung it last night after she and Malinda had used the sadiron to smooth it out. She slipped the full skirt on, fastening it at the waist. She slid her arms into the long sleeved, fitted bodice, taking her time to button the long row of pearly buttons up the front and along the cuffs of the sleeves.

"Need any help in here?" Malinda peered in. "Oh, my. Don't you look pretty!"

"Thank you." Elizabeth reached for the hairbrush. "I just need to put my hair up and I'll be ready."

"The boys ate breakfast and are just finishing chores, and then they'll head for town to help Asa."

Elizabeth pointed to the window. "The weather looks formidable."

"Yes. In fact, JT asked if you plan to take the wagon to town."

Elizabeth cringed. "Oh, I don't think so. I don't want to go through that again. I suspect that my father will be taking his wagon though. They had so much to carry."

"Well, at least he has his oxen. Will you ride your horse to the church?" Malinda asked. "Or walk?"

Elizabeth looked down at the pretty dress, imagining the hem soaked with mud. "Perhaps I should have waited to put this on in town."

With a finger resting on her chin, Malinda made a thoughtful look. "Here is what I think you should do. Take the wagon into town unless it is already raining. But if it's not, we could all go in the wagon. Then if it's raining after the wedding and dinner, when it's time to go home, you and Eli could simply ride your Percherons." She chuckled. "That would be a lovely picture. The bride and the groom on the beautiful black horses. And the wagon could just remain in town until the weather gets better. I'm sure Lavinia and Hugh wouldn't mind if you left it parked at the mercantile."

"That's a good plan." Elizabeth twisted her long hair into a roll, securing it with pins. "If the rain can hold out long enough, that is just what we'll do."

"So should I tell the boys to hitch up the team before they go?"

"Yes. And tell them to put my saddle in. I guess Eli will have to ride bareback, although perhaps we can borrow a saddle blanket from you."

"I hope you won't need it," Malinda said. "But just in case, I'll tell JT."

Elizabeth looked out the window and shook her head. "I can't imagine that we won't."

"Ruth and Susannah are praying diligently."

Elizabeth checked her image in the small mirror above Malinda's dresser. Her hair seemed to be smoothly in place. "Do you think it looks all right?" she asked Malinda. "In back too?"

Malinda came over and fussed with it a little before she proclaimed it perfect. Then, after she set the brush on her dresser, she opened a small wooden box and extracted a pair of pearl drop earrings. "Do you remember these?" She held them up to the light.

"Yes. From your wedding to John."

"Why don't you wear them today?" Malinda held them up to Elizabeth's ears so she could see herself in the mirror.

"Oh, no, Malinda, I couldn't. They're too precious."

Just then Ruth came back into the room. "Ooh, Mama, you look so pretty."

"How about these earrings?" Malinda asked her.

Ruth's eyes grew wide. "Those are beautiful."

"Have you forgotten the rhyme?" Malinda asked Elizabeth.

"What rhyme?" Ruth asked with her usual interest.

"Something old, something new, something borrowed, something blue, and a silver sixpence in her shoe," Malinda told her.

"What does it mean?" Ruth asked.

"It's to bring good luck to the bride," Malinda explained. "A bride needs to have each of those things. Old and new and borrowed and blue."

"And a sixpence in her shoe," Ruth added.

"That's right."

"Will you do that, Mama? Everything in the rhyme?"

"It was something your aunt and I both did at our first weddings." She stroked Ruth's hair. "With your father and your uncle."

"Do it again today," Ruth urged. "For luck."

Malinda held the earrings out. "These could be something old since they belonged to my mother first."

"Yes, yes," Ruth declared. "Now you have something old, Mama. And you already have something blue—your dress!"

"And it's new too," Elizabeth pointed out.

"Can a dress count as two things?" Ruth asked. "Both new and blue?"

"It has two parts to it," Elizabeth reminded her that the skirt and bodice were separate.

"Good," Ruth said. "Now you just need—something borrowed."

"Do you have a clean handkerchief I can use?" Elizabeth asked Ruth.

"You want to borrow something from *me*?" Ruth's eyes lit up.

"Yes. I would like that very much."

Ruth hurried to find a clean hanky and pressed it into her mother's hand, and Elizabeth slid it inside her cuff.

"Now, what about a silver sixpence?" Ruth asked. "What is that, and where do we get one?"

Elizabeth smiled at her daughter's persistence. "That's a British coin. I suppose it was a bit like six cents."

Ruth features twisted into a frown. "I have a half dime and a penny. That makes six. You could put the half dime in one shoe and the penny in the other. Will that work, Mama?"

Elizabeth laughed. "Yes, I'm sure that will work just fine."

Ruth hurried to find her coins and handed them to Elizabeth, watching as she slipped one into each shoe. "There," Elizabeth proclaimed. "I believe I'm nearly ready."

"Not until you have your breakfast." Malinda ushered her out of the bedroom. "The girls fixed something special."

"With all this attention, I am beginning to feel like a queen," Elizabeth said as she sat down at the table.

"You should be the queen on your wedding day. After that...well, I'm sure you'll be dethroned quickly enough." Malinda laughed.

After a breakfast of pancakes and syrup, it was time to proceed to the church. And to Elizabeth's relief, the dark clouds had not opened up yet. In fact, it almost looked as if they were rolling eastward. "Did JT hitch the team to the wagon?" Elizabeth asked Malinda.

"He certainly did." Malinda pointed toward the barn, where Elizabeth's team was just rounding the corner. Behind the shining Percherons was the wagon. Not only was it cleaned up, but someone had gone to the trouble of draping the sides with evergreen garlands and large bows made of white muslin.

"It's beautiful!" Elizabeth clapped her hands.

"All the children worked on it last night," Malinda told her.

As Elizabeth climbed up to drive, Malinda offered to take the reins, but Elizabeth just shook her head. "No thank you. I would prefer to drive."

Malinda just laughed, climbing into the seat beside her. Meanwhile the girls, all five of them, climbed into the back.

"Gid-up!" Elizabeth called out happily. "We have a wedding to attend."

Thankfully, the road had firmed up in the past couple of days. Still, Elizabeth was relieved to see that someone—probably Eli—had the foresight to leave a shovel and some planks in the back of the wagon.

"And now we shall sing you the wedding march song," Ruth proclaimed from behind Elizabeth.

"The wedding march song?" Elizabeth asked. "What is that?"

"Mrs. Taylor taught it to us," Ruth declared.

"It was written by a German composer named Richard Wagner," Amelia explained.

"And it was written in German," Belinda explained. "But Mrs. Taylor taught it to us in English."

"Because we don't speak very good German," Susannah told her.

"Mrs. Taylor said that the song is from an opera," Emily added.

"We just learned it last week," Ruth said.

"But we've been practicing it every day on our way to and from school," Amelia said.

"Well, I would love to hear it," Elizabeth told them.

"So would I," Malinda said.

After a bit of giggling and adjusting of their positions in the back of the wagon, the five girls began to sing.

> Faithful and true, we lead thee forth
> Where love, triumphant, shall crown ye with joy!
> Star of renown, flow'r of the earth,
> Blest be ye both, far from all life's annoy!
> Champion victorious, go thou before!
> Maid bright and glorious, go thou before!
> Mirth's noisy revel ye have forsaken,
> Tender delights for you now awaken;
> Fragrant abode enshrine ye in bliss;
> Splendor and state in joy ye dismiss!

"That is perfectly beautiful," Elizabeth told them when they finished. "Thank you so much, girls! In fact, that was so delightful, I would love to have you sing it in the church too."

"Can we, Mama?" Ruth asked hopefully. "Would it be all right?"

"I do not see why not. We always sing in church. Why not sing at a wedding?"

"We could sing it while you walk up the aisle," Belinda suggested.

"Yes. That would be lovely."

When they reached the church, both Matthew's wagon and her father's were parked in front. Elizabeth looked up at the cloudy sky, hoping now more than ever that the rain would hold off long enough so that all the wagons wouldn't be stuck in town.

They were just getting out of their own wagon and walking up to the church when Elizabeth spotted Mrs. Holmes rushing toward them with an urgent expression.

"Oh, Elizabeth," she said breathlessly. "I am just in time."

"What is wrong?" Elizabeth asked with concern.

Mrs. Holmes smiled. "Oh, nothing is wrong. But I was asked to bring you to my house, and I nearly missed you. You are to stay with me until they are ready to begin the wedding ceremony." She took Elizabeth by the arm. "Come along, dear."

Elizabeth didn't argue, and the girls all giggled as if they were in on this too.

"I have made us a nice pot of tea," Mrs. Holmes told her as they walked back to the parsonage. Inside the tiny house, Mrs. Holmes took Elizabeth's coat and hat and gloves. And soon they were seated by the fireplace, and Mrs. Holmes was handing Elizabeth a teacup.

"I want to assure you, dear, that I have been speaking to the reverend—morning, noon, and night—about how he needs to continue bringing God's goodness and love and mercy into his sermons. Just the way your father did when he preached that time."

"Oh, that is so good to hear. And how does the reverend respond to your encouragement?"

"At first he pretended not to listen to me. But then your father came by to speak to him. They have met several times now. And I do believe there is the making of a solid friendship between the two men."

"That is wonderful to hear." Elizabeth sipped her tea, trying to keep her eyes off the small mantle clock as it ticked steadily toward eleven o'clock. Was it truly possible that within the hour, she would become Mrs. Eli Kincaid? And furthermore, was she truly ready for it?

Chapter Twenty

It was a quarter past eleven, and Elizabeth was starting to feel a bit uneasy, when she and Mrs. Holmes both startled at a loud knock to the door.

"Hello?" called what sounded like her father's voice. "I have come to fetch the bride."

Elizabeth laughed as she stood. "I'm coming, Father."

He grinned at her. "Why, don't you look pretty."

"Thank you."

"Are you ready?" He peered into her eyes.

She nodded nervously. "I believe I am."

"The groom awaits." Asa took her arm and led her to the church with Mrs. Holmes following. He paused at the door, allowing Mrs. Holmes to slip in first. Then he looked at Elizabeth again. "You have chosen well with Eli. He is truly a good man. And I know he will be a fine husband and a good father. I have utmost confidence in him."

She blinked back tears. "That means so much to me, Father."

"It means everything to me, daughter." He leaned over and kissed her cheek. "Ready?"

She nodded with confidence. "Now I am."

Asa opened the door, leading her into the crowded church. She waited as he closed the door, taking in the faces that were eagerly looking back at them. And then, as Asa took her by the arm again, the girls began to sing their lovely wedding march song. As she and her father slowly walked down the aisle to the sweet lilting sound of the girls' voices, she noticed that someone had hung evergreen garlands clear down the aisle and then up over a graceful arch in front. White muslin ribbons were tied here and there. And a pair of candelabras glowed on cloth-covered tables on either side of the podium. She had never seen the little church look more beautiful than this.

But what captured her attention more than anything was the tall, handsome man standing beneath the evergreen arch. Eli's gaze was fixed on her, and although his expression was solemn, she could feel the warmth in his clear blue eyes as she stepped forward to take his hand. Standing next to Eli was Matthew. And standing next to Elizabeth was Malinda. Before her father sat down, Reverend Holmes invited him to say a prayer. And that's when Elizabeth knew the wedding ceremony would be perfect.

Just as Elizabeth had requested, it was a simple, straightforward wedding ceremony. But as she and Eli repeated their vows, she knew that it was heartfelt for both of them. And suddenly it was over and the reverend was proclaiming them man and wife, and after a shy kiss, the couple walked back down the aisle to the sweet singing of the wedding march song again. Perfect, Elizabeth thought as they went outside. Just perfect.

"You are the most beautiful bride in the world, Mrs. Kincaid," Eli whispered as he leaned over to kiss her with more passion than they'd shared in the church. "And you have made me the happiest man in the world."

Before she could respond as she would like, their friends and family began pouring out of the church. Gathering around the newlyweds, they extended their hearty congratulations. Many commented on the wedding ceremony and how much they enjoyed it. A few even mentioned their relief that the reverend didn't yell at anyone.

It wasn't long until Matthew and JT and Paddy McIntire were playing music, and the celebration grew even merrier as young couples started dancing outside and the women set up the food inside the church—just in case the weather changed.

"It hasn't rained," Ruth happily told Elizabeth. "God must have heard my prayer."

Elizabeth leaned over to kiss her daughter's cheek. "And why wouldn't he?"

Thanks to Clara's organization skills, people brought their own place settings, and many of the older people brought chairs to make themselves comfortable. And for the next couple hours, people were eating and dancing and merrymaking.

"We have plenty of food," Asa told Elizabeth with relief. "With so many people in attendance, I wasn't sure."

"Don't forget to take a plate home for Brady." Elizabeth sighed. "I wish he could have come."

Asa shook his head. "I'm afraid he made the right decision."

Elizabeth glanced around the crowded yard and knew her father was right. Everyone who lived within ten miles had come to this celebration, and they were all happy to eat of the wedding feast, but many of them would not approve of a Negro in attendance. As disturbing as that was, Elizabeth was determined not to let it spoil this day. Her reconciliation was that her family, including Brady, would celebrate with them next Sunday when she invited them all for dinner at her new house.

Eli and Elizabeth were just finishing up dessert when the first raindrop fell. She looked up at the gray sky and then laughed. "Well, like I kept telling Ruth, rain on your wedding day is good luck."

He chuckled. "Then it looks like we're about to get very lucky."

"Do you think we should try to leave?" she asked. "In order to get the wagon home?" She'd already told him of Malinda's idea to leave the wagon behind if it rained hard.

"I think we should honor our guests with one last dance," he told her.

She grinned. "Yes. I agree."

"And tell me, Mrs. Kincaid, what would you choose for your last wedding-day dance?"

She thought for a moment. "Would you mind if it was the Virginia reel?"

He laughed. "Would I mind? It's my favorite."

Now Eli went over to the musicians, who had been rotating off and on during the celebration in order to give everyone a chance to eat and dance. He requested a tune for the Virginia reel. Then he hollered to get everyone's attention as he rejoined Elizabeth, and the crowd got quiet.

"My wife and I wish to thank each and every one of you for helping us to celebrate today," he told them. Now he pointed to the sky. "As you can see, the weather is turning, and we do understand if some of you will need to make a run for home. But for the adventurous among us, we are going to enjoy one last dance. Who would like to join us for the Virginia reel?"

To Elizabeth's delight at least two dozen couples, including everyone in her family, came out to form several lines. Once they were ready, despite the raindrops that were falling more liberally, Eli waved to the musicians standing under the tarp awning that Asa and Matthew had constructed, and the lively song began.

Laughing and dancing in the rain, Elizabeth knew this was a day she would remember always. Seeing her parents and her children and everyone else enjoying themselves was the perfect way to end this celebration.

"Oh, my!" she exclaimed when the song ended. "Thank you all very much!" she called out. "Now we all better make a run for cover!"

Already, people were gathering chairs and dishes and belongings and making their hasty departures. Elizabeth and Eli offered to help her parents and family, but they shooed them away. "Not this time," Clara told her. "Off to your honeymoon." And so Elizabeth kissed her children goodbye, and she and Eli made their exit.

By the time they reached the wagon, it was raining hard enough that Elizabeth did not want to risk her team by taking them home. "Do you mind if we just ride horseback instead?" she asked Eli. "I've got my saddle."

"Not at all," he said as he started to unhitch the horses. "And I'm sure the wagon won't go anywhere parked right here in front of the church."

She laughed. "No, I think not."

Before long, they had saddled Bella, and Eli gave Elizabeth a hand getting up. Fortunately, her skirt was so full that she could easily straddle the horse without being indecent. Next he put the saddle blanket onto Beau, and using the wagon wheel hub for height, he mounted the horse. "Ready to go home?"

"Am I ever!" she declared.

People called out to them, wishing them well, and some teased as if they planned to follow the newlyweds, but thanks to the rain, no one seemed very serious. And before long, they were well on their way out of town. Although the road was getting muddy, it wasn't nearly as bad as on Thursday. And when they were about halfway home, the rain let up considerably. Even so, they were both fairly well soaked by the time they reached their property.

Elizabeth looked eagerly as they rounded the corner near the stand of fir trees and the cabin came into view. "Oh, Eli!" she cried out. "It is so beautiful."

He smiled. "Home sweet home."

She stared happily at the boxy cabin. The lower part of the walls consisted of solid logs, and the upper part was milled wood. The sloped roof was covered in cedar shingles, and she could see the top of a stone chimney in back. But what really got her attention was the big glass window on the left side of the front door. "It looks like a real house," she said with wonder.

"Wait until you see the rest." Eli slid off his horse and then helped her down from Bella. "You go on inside and get warmed up while I see to the horses."

She started to go but then stopped. "But you must carry me over the threshold," she declared stubbornly. "It's tradition."

He chuckled.

"What is so funny?" she demanded.

"You sounded just like Ruth when you said that."

She grinned at him. "Well then, it's about time you learned that every woman has a little girl inside of her."

"All right then. I'll carry you over the threshold. But would you like me to tend to the horses first?"

"Yes, please do."

"In the meantime, you could at least go up on the porch and stay out of the drizzle."

"I'll do that." As she walked up the stone-lined path leading to the porch, she spied what looked like an outhouse off to the right. Eli seemed to have thought of everything. On the covered porch there was a washing-up table with a bucket of water and a towel. Next to that was a bench, which looked like a handy place to remove muddy boots. And since she'd sent her carpetbag filled with clothes, including her moccasins, with Matthew the other day, she decided to remove her good shoes, which were now in need of a thorough cleaning.

She had just gotten her shoes unbuttoned and off when Eli came onto the porch. "Are you ready to be carried into your new home?"

She pointed out her stocking-clad feet. "I most certainly am." And before she could stand up he leaned over and scooped her up into his arms, nearly taking her breath away as he did so.

"Goodness!" she exclaimed as he opened the door.

"Right this way, my lady." He carried her into the warm room and closed the door with his foot. She was tempted to remind him that his boots were muddy too, but she stopped herself. Mud was not that difficult to clean. "What do you think?"

She stared in wonder at the big room. She wasn't sure if it was her imagination or wishful thinking, but it seemed even larger than Malinda's house to her. "Oh, Eli," she gushed. "It's the most beautiful house in the whole world."

"Beautiful?" He eased her down to the wooden floor. "You really think so?"

"I do," she said sincerely. "It is truly beautiful." As she removed her coat and hat, her eyes attempted to take it all in, which was impossible. Certainly this house was more rustic than her home in Kentucky, but the golden brown wood walls and floors seemed to glow with warmth. And the recently sawn lumber smelled clean and fresh. "I love every inch of it."

He grinned. "I'm glad to hear that. But maybe you'll want to see more of it before you make that claim."

"Of course, I want to see every bit of it." She hung her coat and hat on a peg on the door.

"So do you want me to show you around?" He lit a lantern and carried it over to the fireplace. "Or should I go out and call for Flax?"

"Flax?" She suddenly remembered. "Where is he anyway?"

"Probably off chasing a rabbit. He's not used to being left on his own too much. He and I have gotten quite close, you know."

"Yes, please, do go call him. And if you don't mind, I'll make a fire and look around. I want to admire your workmanship."

"This is your house, Elizabeth. Make yourself at home."

Chilled from the rain and feeling slightly damp, she went straight to the hearth, where sticks of kindling and wood shavings were stored neatly in a wooden crate. She stacked them carefully and found a box of matches on the mantle. She lit the shavings and blew a bit just to get it to catch. And then, with the light from the lantern, she admired the fir grain of the sturdy mantle. She ran her hand over a smooth round stone in the fireplace, one of the same stones she and the children had begun gathering from the creek after they'd first arrived. She thought they were for the foundation, but they were just perfect for the fireplace.

With the kindling crackling and snapping, she put on some large pieces of wood, and after warming her hands, she continued touring her new home. The rug she'd brought from Kentucky was just where she would have put it—in the sitting area near the fireplace. Her old rocker as well as a roughly hewn chair were in place as if waiting for the master and mistress of the house to hold court. Certainly, the area could use a woman's touch, but that would come. She went to the kitchen area, where the table and chairs she'd brought from her previous home were set into place. Directly across from the table was the large window. And hanging from the ceiling, directly over the table, was another kerosene lantern, which she lit. In the center of the table was a hand-carved wooden bowl filled with apples. On top of the apples was a note that appeared to have been written by Ruth. "To Mama and Eli. Love, JT and Ruth. PS. I picked the apples and JT made the bowl. Brady helped him."

Next it was the cookstove that captured her attention. New and black, it was spotless and ready to put to use. Resisting the temptation to light it, she examined the cupboards instead. Eli had given her the measurements for these, and she'd made some curtains she planned to hang on them to keep things tidier.

She was relieved to see that other than a few food items, some coffee and sugar and flour, the shelves and cupboards were still bare. The boxes of her household goods and the items she received at her bridal shower were stacked neatly against the wall. She could hardly wait to start putting everything into place.

Next to the stack of goods was a rustic but sturdy-looking dry sink. And on top of the dry sink was a little piece of paper. She immediately recognized her father's handwriting. "Lovingly made for Eli and Elizabeth by Brady." She ran her hand over the smooth surface. Unless she was mistaken, it was maple. Where had Brady found maple? She bent over to examine the cupboard space below. Nice and deep. She would hang a curtain over the front for now, and maybe someday it would have wooden doors.

She resisted the temptation to delve into the boxes containing her kitchen supplies and start putting the space into order. First she wanted to see everything in this sweet little house. She paused to look out the window, curious as to whether Eli had found Flax yet. Where could that dog have gone? As she peered out the shiny new window, she wondered why Eli had positioned it on this side of the house. She had assumed he would have placed it in the sitting area near the fireplace.

No matter, she told herself as she went to the rear of the house, where a rustic set of wooden steps, almost as steep as a ladder, was situated. Still in her stocking feet and holding her damp skirt up, she gingerly climbed the rungs. She knew this would be the children's sleeping quarters. She expected to emerge into a large open loft where her children would make beds on the floor out of blankets and quilts. But to her surprise, the loft space had been divided into two separate bedrooms, each complete with a small bed made from rough-hewn logs. Next to each bed was a bedside table, created from a wooden packing crate, with a small lantern on it. Along the dividing wall was a row of clothing pegs. Eli had thought of everything!

Curious as to how the beds had been constructed, she decided to investigate. Ropes were wrapped around the logs and then woven together to provide springy support for the mattress that rested on top. But where had Eli found mattresses? And what were they stuffed with? She gave the mattress a squeeze to discover that it was probably filled with straw. Perhaps it had been gathered from the dry grass that grew down by the river—back before the wet weather had set in. But how did Eli have time to do that?

On closer inspection, seeing the fine stitches on the mattress ticking and the colorful crazy quilts created from some familiar fabrics,

Elizabeth realized it had to be her mother's doing. Of course—Clara would want to ensure that her grandchildren had comfortable places to sleep. The dear woman had even made them pillows. What more could anyone ask of a bedroom?

However, the most amazing and impressive part of these two sweet sleeping places was that each room had a small glass window above the bed and centered in the gable. It was a way to let light in, and thanks to the wooden hinges, which must have taken some time to carve, the windows could be opened to let in fresh air as well. Elizabeth was touched that Eli went to so much trouble for her children. And she couldn't wait until JT and Ruth saw everything.

Chapter Twenty-One

E lizabeth?"

"I'm up here," she called as she went over to the stair ladder.

"Taking a nap, are you?" he teased.

"Oh, Eli," she exclaimed as she came down the steps. "That loft is simply wonderful!"

He grinned as he reached for her hand. "You like it?"

"I never dreamed the children would have their very own rooms. Not at first anyway."

"I wanted to make the roof sturdier, and building a privacy wall seemed a good way to kill two birds with one stone." He helped her down to the floor. "Besides, we might have more children someday. The girls could be on one side and the boys on the other."

She laughed. "You have thought of everything."

"Oh, I'm sure there are some things I forgot."

"All the pegs for hanging clothes," she said. "And the bedside tables and lanterns. JT and Ruth will be over the moon when they see what you've done."

"I'm so glad you're pleased." He beamed at her.

"I'm beyond pleased," she proclaimed. "Everything is just perfect."

"And I found our dog down by the creek. He'd trapped some critter inside a hollow log and seemed determined to remain there until it came out." Eli chuckled as he pointed to where Flax was lying next to the fire. "I'm afraid he's plum worn out."

"Hello, old friend." She went over to pet Flax, but the tired dog didn't even bother to stand. However, his tail slapped happily against the floor. "We're finally home," she told him as she stood. "We'll all be back together soon."

"Did you see everything in the house?" Eli asked.

She smiled shyly at him. "Not everything…yet."

He pointed to her damp skirt. "Your personal things that Matthew brought over are in the bedroom. You should probably get into some dry clothes before you catch your death."

She looked over at the only interior door inside the house. It was just opposite the kitchen and she knew it must lead to their bedroom. "Yes," she said slowly. "Dry clothes would help keep the chill off."

"Meanwhile I'll stoke up this fire," he told her. "Get it nice and warm in here."

Elizabeth took in a deep breath as she slowly slid the wooden latch on the door that led to the bedroom—the room she would be sharing with Eli from now on. She had no idea what she was expecting to find, but when she saw the sweetly furnished room—with a bed similar to the ones upstairs except bigger—she felt a wave of relief wash over her.

Somehow, and to her amazement, this room felt very welcoming to her, as if she were truly home. On top of the bed was the beautiful quilt with the log cabin design. She felt the mattress to discover it was her own feather bed that she'd brought from home. And her feather pillows were here as well. All were covered with the new bed linens that Will's girls had given her at the shower. And beneath the feather mattress, resting on top of the rope supports, was yet another straw-filled mattress. They would sleep comfortably in this.

As wonderful as the bed looked, she was even more impressed that just like the bedrooms upstairs, this room had its own window. She went over to peer out, seeing that it looked toward the stand of fir trees behind the house. Hanging over the window was a lovely curtain that she felt sure had come from her mother's home in Kentucky. She fingered the crocheted lace and smiled. A very nice touch indeed.

Next she examined the washstand beneath the window. Like the dry sink in the kitchen, this piece was made of roughly hewn wood, which appeared to be maple. But on the front was a carved rose. Hanging on the towel bar were some fresh white linens, and positioned in the center of the cabinet was a creamy white pitcher and bowl—with water in the pitcher.

She picked up a bar of soap from a small china soap dish and sniffed it—lavender. Her mother had brought dried lavender from Kentucky with the plans of making soap once they got settled. She suspected this too was her mother's doing. Beneath the bar of soap was a slip of paper that said, "To Eli and Elizabeth with love from Father and Mother." They had obviously put the washstand and everything on it together. Bless them!

She looked back at the handsomely made bed. On one side sat a rustic chair—a good place to remove one's boots. On the other side was a small table covered in linen with lace trim. But on closer inspection, she discovered it was actually a crate. On this bedside table sat her small silver lantern as well as a little crystal vase that held a fragrant arrangement of evergreens and pretty dried grasses, giving it a feminine feel. Also there was a colorful rag rug on this side, perfect for keeping feet warm on a cold winter's night. Because of the more feminine touches, she suspected that this side of the room was meant for her. She had no complaints whatsoever.

At the foot of the bed was the trunk she'd brought in the wagon with her from Kentucky. As far as she knew, it was still packed with blankets and fabric and miscellaneous items of clothing for the children and her. But it looked nice at the foot of the bed. All in all, this room was unexpectedly sweet, albeit a little chilly.

And that reminded her that she'd come in here to get into a dry dress. Before long, her pretty blue wedding dress was hanging from a peg, and she had on her green calico and her moccasins. Putting her woolen shawl over her shoulders, she emerged to find Eli sitting by the fire.

"Are your clothes wet too?" she asked.

"My trousers are a little damp," he said as he stood.

"Well, you don't want to get a cold either."

"What did you think of the, uh...the bedroom?" He sounded slightly uneasy, which she found charming.

"It is beautiful," she told him. "And quite homey too. Although it is a bit chilly in there. Do you think we should leave the door open?"

"That's a good idea." He went to open it. "And the way the room is positioned, right across from the kitchen here, I expect that using the cookstove will help to warm it up some too."

"I'd love to try out the cookstove," she told him. "I'm not very hungry after our wonderful wedding feast, but perhaps I could make us some coffee or tea."

"Coffee would be good to warm up on. And I think your mother brought some over the other day, as well as some other staples she thought we might need. And she was very helpful in getting the bedding on the beds all put together. I couldn't have done it without her."

Elizabeth smiled. "I suspected she'd had a hand in some things."

"And that rug in our bedroom was made by Jessica. She just brought it by a few days ago."

"I wondered about that. It's so pretty."

"And I'm sure you saw that Brady made the dry sink and your

father made the washstand. They found an old maple that had fallen a year or more ago. The wood had plenty of time to dry and was in perfect condition for making furniture."

"I wondered where they'd gotten the maple."

She held up the red coffeepot that Lavinia had given to her. "I'll put this pretty thing to good use now."

"And while you're doing that, I'll put on some dry trousers," he told her.

It wasn't long until Elizabeth had a little fire going in the cook-stove. Then she filled the pot with water and measured out some coffee. Just as she was setting it on top of the stove, Eli emerged. He'd changed into a clean pair of work pants, but he still had on his good shirt. She blushed to think of how handsome he looked.

"You have no idea what a thrill it is to put a coffeepot on a real stove again."

"That's right, Malinda still cooks in the fireplace, doesn't she?" Eli sat down at the table, just watching her as she continued to explore her new kitchen.

She nodded. "I'm sure she'll be envious when she sees this one." She opened the iron door to poke at the fire before she slipped in some additional pieces of wood.

"I expect it'll just be a matter of time before Will buys her one, don't you think?"

"I'm sure you're right." She looked out the big window from where she was standing by the stove and sighed. "That window is just lovely. But I am curious as to why you put it over here instead of near the fireplace."

"Seemed to me you would enjoy it more over here. You can look out when you're cooking. And we can all look out when we're sitting here at the table and eating. But when we're sitting by the fire in the evening, it will be dark outside, and a window would be wasted."

She laughed. "You really did think of everything, didn't you?"

"I did my best."

She removed a parcel wrapped in brown paper from a cupboard and held it up. "Do you know what this is?"

"Something your mother left here yesterday."

She unwrapped the paper to find a loaf of bread, a crock of butter, and a jar of jam. "Looks like she thought we might want some supper tonight. Are you hungry?"

"I'm not very hungry, but I wouldn't mind some bread and jam with my coffee," he said.

She glanced around the homey-looking house, curious as to what time it was getting to be. Her best guess, based on the darkening sky, was that it was past five. Not too early for a light supper. Her livestock was still at Malinda's and her children were at her parents', so there wasn't much in the way of chores to be done this evening. She knew she should make the most of this unexpected bit of leisure.

"I have a clock packed somewhere," she absently said as she sliced some bread. "From Kentucky. If it still works, it might look nice on the mantle."

"I'm sure you'll have fun putting everything into place."

"I will. I am so eager to unpack my things and get settled. To make this our home."

"We *are* home, Elizabeth." He stood and came over to where she was buttering the bread. "Can you believe it?" He slipped his arms around her waist and pulled her close. "We are home at last."

"It feels a bit like a dream," she confessed. "A very sweet dream."

"Mr. and Mrs. Kincaid in their new home." He kissed her. "This is for real."

After a bit, she moved the coffeepot to the soapstone slab in the back of the stove, where it would stay warm without scorching. She suspected that they would have their light supper a little later.

On Sunday morning, Mr. and Mrs. Kincaid rode Beau and Bella

back to the church, where they were warmly greeted by family and friends. Sitting with Eli and JT and Ruth, listening to Reverend Holmes' sermon, which was even more positive than the last one, Elizabeth felt very nearly perfectly happy. She probably would have been completely perfectly happy if she hadn't noticed something on the way to church.

Just as they were passing the brushy section near the creek, she'd observed the foliage moving. Eli had suggested it was the wind, although there didn't seem to be any breezes blowing. Then he said perhaps it was simply her imagination. And although she conceded that was possible, she felt fairly certain that wasn't it either. Somehow she knew that woman was still there. And the child. And somehow she was going to reach out to them. In the meantime, she would keep praying for them.

After church, while Eli was hitching the team to the wagon, Clara told Elizabeth that the children were welcome to stay with her and Asa for a few more days. "If you and Eli would like some more alone time."

"I don't think that's necessary," Elizabeth quietly told her. "Eli and I are both anxious to have the children settled in the home with us. I can't wait for them to see their rooms."

Clara smiled. "What did you think of everything?"

"It's all so wonderful and amazing. I could hardly believe it." Now Elizabeth began to gush, thanking her mother for all her sweet little touches. "One week from today, I want to have you all over for a thank-you dinner."

"That will be fun," Clara told her. "But I thought today you might want to join us for Sunday dinner. We had so much food left over from the wedding! We shared some with Matthew and Jess, but we want to send some of the food home with you. Also, the children's clothing and things are at our house. You'll need to pick them up."

"I'll check with Eli, but I'm sure we'd like to come," Elizabeth said. "Especially since I haven't got our kitchen very well set up yet.

However, we might not linger much afterward. Eli hopes to get our livestock moved from Malinda's this afternoon." Elizabeth waved to her sister-in-law, who was approaching. "I know she'll appreciate it."

"Are you all settled in yet?" Malinda asked as she joined them.

"I haven't unpacked much," Elizabeth admitted. "But I feel completely at home. And we're taking the children home with us today."

"Already?" Malinda frowned. "I thought they were going to spend a few days at your parents'."

Elizabeth shrugged. "I'm eager to have my family all under one roof." Now she told Malinda about the loft bedrooms. "One for JT and one for Ruth."

"Oh, my. I look forward to seeing this house. When will I be invited over?"

"Give me a few days to get unpacked," Elizabeth told her. "How about coming over for tea? Sometime when the children are in school? I think I should have everything unpacked and put to order by midweek. How about Thursday?"

"I'll be there with bells on," Malinda promised.

"And Eli and JT will be by your place later this afternoon to pick up our livestock," Elizabeth promised. "And we've got the wagon, so we'll pick up the chickens and anything else we left behind on our way home from church."

It wasn't long until they were on their way home, with Elizabeth and Eli in front of the wagon and JT and Ruth in the back. Ruth was as chatty as a magpie, talking about yesterday's wedding and how many days until Christmas and a dozen other unrelated things. Meanwhile, JT seemed to be unusually quiet. Finally, worried that he might be coming down with something, Elizabeth decided to get to the bottom of his sullenness. "Are you feeling quite well, JT?"

"I feel fine, Ma."

"You seem rather quiet." She turned to peer at him, seeing that he had a slightly perplexed expression. "Is something wrong, son?"

"No. Nothing's wrong."

"It's about Eli," Ruth blurted out.

"Ruth!" JT glared at his little sister.

"I'm sorry," Ruth told him. "But you should tell Mama and Eli about what's troubling you."

Elizabeth glanced at Eli to see that he was looking a little uncomfortable. She wondered if JT could be having second thoughts about their marriage. However, it was a little late for that. Even so, perhaps this wasn't the best time to have a conversation like this. She wasn't sure what to do.

"Go ahead and tell them, JT," Ruth said. "Or else I will."

"Ruth!" JT sounded truly irritated.

"If you have something to say," Eli began slowly, "maybe you should just get it out in the open, JT. I'm sure it's something we can all sort out together. We're a family now."

"Come on," Ruth urged.

"All right," JT grumbled. "I was just wondering, now that you and Ma are married, what are we supposed to call you? Do we still call you Eli? Or do we call you Pa?"

Eli's countenance relaxed. "Well, I think that's up to you and Ruth," Eli said. "I'm comfortable with you calling me Eli if that's what you'd prefer. And I'd be rightly honored if someday you feel like calling me Pa. I realize I have some big shoes to fill, but I do want to be your father. When I married your mother, I married you children too. We are a family now."

"Well, I want to call you Pa," Ruth declared.

Eli turned to smile at her. "I am truly honored, Ruth."

"I reckon I should call you Pa too," JT said. "If you really don't mind."

"I do not mind in the least. Like I said, I am honored."

Elizabeth let out a relieved sigh. Well then, that was settled.

Chapter Twenty-Two

After dinner at Elizabeth's parents', they loaded up the wagon and continued on toward home. Elizabeth tried to act calm, but she was so excited about how JT and Ruth would react to the finished house. "Here we are," she said as Eli pulled the wagon in front.

"Oh, my!" Ruth exclaimed. "It's bigger than Grandma and Grandpa's cabin, isn't it?"

"Yes, but there are four of us and only two of them," Elizabeth pointed out as they climbed from the wagon. "And instead of unloading everything right now, do you want to go in and look around first?"

The children didn't argue, and she and Eli exchanged glances as they followed them into the house. Their reactions were similar to Elizabeth's, although Ruth was much more vocal and JT used his comments sparingly.

"And now you need to go up the stairs," Elizabeth told them. She and Eli waited down below, listening as the children exclaimed over the two separate bedrooms. A short argument erupted over who got which room, but eventually both JT and Ruth decided that the spaces were identical, and JT flipped a coin to determine who got what.

"I love my room," Ruth declared as she came down the stairs. "And the bed is really comfortable."

"I didn't know we'd have our own rooms," JT said happily as he rejoined them. "Thanks, Eli." He chuckled. "I mean, Pa."

"Yes! Thank you, Pa!" Ruth told Eli.

Although Elizabeth was glad the children accepted Eli enough to call him Pa, it was a bit unsettling too. The last man they'd called Pa had been James. And, the truth was, she wasn't sure she was ready for this. And yet she didn't want them to keep calling him Eli either. Really, she should be thankful.

"Let's get the wagon unloaded," Eli said to JT. "And then we'll change out of our church clothes and go fetch our livestock."

Elizabeth pointed at Ruth. "And let's get changed out of our Sunday clothes too. Then you can help me get those chickens all settled."

"Do you think they're glad to be home, Mama?"

"I'm sure they are."

"I think so too. Especially since some of Malinda's hens were bossy toward ours," Ruth said. "As if they thought they were better."

"Well, our hens were newcomers. Maybe they didn't like that."

"Or maybe they were jealous."

"Jealous?"

Ruth giggled. "Because of Reginald."

"The rooster?"

"Yes. Because Reginald probably liked our hens better than Aunt Malinda's."

Elizabeth laughed, thinking that could be beneficial to increasing their numbers. "Say, Ruth, now that we're home and settled, we won't collect the eggs for a while—maybe even a whole week."

"No eggs for a whole week?" She frowned. "What will we have for breakfast?"

"Oatmeal. Or biscuits and gravy."

"Like on the Oregon Trail?" she asked.

"A little like that. But don't worry, we won't starve. And it'll only be one week without eggs. Maybe not even that."

"But why don't you want to eat eggs, Mama?"

"Because I'd rather hatch some chicks."

"But it's not springtime."

"That's true. But the climate is mild here. I think we can raise some young chickens in the winter. And thanks to Reginald the rooster, we might have some fertile eggs in the next few days. And if we let the hens sit on the fertile eggs, we'll have baby chicks right around Christmas."

"Christmas chicks!" Ruth clapped her hands. "Yes! Yes! Yes!"

On Wednesday morning, after the hens had three undisturbed days of egg laying, Ruth carefully collected about a dozen eggs, and she and Elizabeth began candling them to see if any were fertile.

"See?" Elizabeth held the first egg up to the bright light of a kerosene lamp. "This one doesn't show any veins, so it's not fertile," she explained. "Put it in the bowl for later." Ruth handed her the next warm egg, and to their delight, it showed the faint traces of veins inside. "This one goes back in the basket," Elizabeth told her.

"Should we keep the basket near the stove to say warm?" Ruth asked. "Until we're done candling?"

"Yes. But not too close. We don't want to cook our chicks."

By the time they finished candling, they had discovered eight fertile eggs. Elizabeth marked each one with a spot of ink. "So when you see the spotted egg, you know not to bring it back in the house again," she explained to Ruth. "Now take these precious eggs back to the hens, and hopefully we'll get a few more before the week is out."

Elizabeth knew that it was unlikely that all the fertile eggs would safely hatch into chicks. But the more eggs they left with the hens, the greater the chance their chicken flock would grow. And at least one of the chicks was sure to be a cockerel. It was exciting to see that their farm could become productive. Besides the possibility of chicks, Elizabeth was hopeful that Goldie might be with calf, but they wouldn't be sure for a few more weeks.

She stood on the porch, watching as JT helped Ruth onto Molly's back. Then he climbed up behind her, taking the reins as they both called goodbye. "Have a good day at school," she called back.

Because they'd had several rainless days, Eli had the team out today, felling timber to use for fence rails. Elizabeth went back inside the house, which she'd spent the past two days putting to order. She smiled in satisfaction at how much homier it looked with curtains up, dishes on shelves, the clock on the mantle, and all the other housekeeping amenities that made a house a home.

She went to the dry sink, and removing the washtub from beneath, she filled it with hot water from the kettle on the stove and then happily went to work washing the breakfast dishes. Elizabeth had never disliked housework—not like some women she'd known—but she usually preferred being outdoors. However, she was so thankful to be in her own home, she relished every mundane little chore these days. Just the same, she had promised to join Eli by midmorning. She wanted to help him get as many fence rails into place as possible today. "It's like making hay while the sun's shining," she told him at breakfast. "I'll do whatever I can to help get our fences up. As long as I don't have to wade through the mud."

After she finished her housekeeping, she put on her split riding skirt and barn jacket and work boots. Then she wrapped a couple of buttered biscuits in a piece of linen and slipped it into her pocket for Eli. And grabbing her old felt hat and riding gloves, she headed out to where Eli was felling timber.

By the time she got there, he already had a load of wood ready to go. Because these logs were much smaller than what they'd used on the cabins, Eli had been using the wagon to transport them. "Looks like you've been busy," she said as she handed him the biscuits.

"Thanks." He pushed his hat back from his forehead, wiping his glistening brow as he took a bite. "Do you want to drive the wagon back and unload it? The poles aren't too heavy, and they slide out fairly easily."

"I'd be happy to."

He grinned at her. "I always liked seeing you in that outfit."

She looked down at her working clothes. "Truly?"

He nodded. "Oh, yes. You caught my eye many a time out on the Oregon Trail. I could spot you from almost a mile away, Elizabeth."

"That's rather hard to believe."

He chuckled. "Well, that might be an exaggeration. But believe me, Mrs. Kincaid, I kept my eye on you."

She reached over and touched his cheek. "And I'm so glad you did."

She got into the driver's seat of the wagon and drove the team over the hill and down toward the river, where they were constructing the fence. Eli's plan had been to use this section of river as part of the fence because the livestock wouldn't be likely to cross it and because they would have access to drinking water.

As the wagon slowly rolled along, she surveyed their land. There was so much potential here, so many possibilities. She wondered how long it would take to fully realize it. Perhaps in her children's lives...or her grandchildren's.

As she was gazing out over the meadow that led down to the river, she noticed a figure moving alongside a grove of trees—a woman. She squinted into the sunlight, thinking it could be Jess or her mother. But then she saw the smaller figure trailing behind the woman and realized it was the Indian woman. Without really thinking, Elizabeth pulled off her hat and waved, calling out what she hoped sounded like a friendly greeting.

But just as quickly, the woman and small child both ducked into the shadows of the trees. Elizabeth knew she'd probably frightened the poor woman. Yelling out like that must have sounded threatening. But didn't the woman know that Elizabeth was the one who'd taken her blankets and food? Even just yesterday, Elizabeth had walked a loaf of bread down to the place where she'd seen them before. She'd wrapped the loaf in one of her old dresses—a brown-and-black calico that she'd nearly worn out on the trail. It hadn't been easy to part with fabric because she had thought of using it for quilt pieces, but if it would keep the woman and her child warm, it was worth it. From the distance, it was impossible to see whether the woman was wearing the dress. And Elizabeth hadn't been back to the drop-off spot to check.

She pulled the team to a stop, set the brake, and climbed down to unload the poles. Eli had been right—they did slide fairly easily from the wagon. After she dropped a small pile, she moved the team farther on up, where she unloaded some more, spacing them out so they wouldn't need to be carried so far. She did this until the wagon was empty and then headed the team back to where Eli was working.

Using the crosscut two-man saw, they were able to cut down trees much more quickly. As they sawed back and forth, she told him about seeing the Indian woman and child again. "I called out to her," she admitted. "But I'm sure it frightened her."

"Did she have on your old dress?"

"I couldn't tell from the distance."

After they'd felled a number of trees, they used axes to chop off the limbs and make them into poles. Eli, much more adept than she, cleaned branches off four trees to her one. Still, she felt she was doing her part. Then they loaded them into the wagon together, and she took the second load. She decided to take this load over to the far side of what would be their livestock pasture—over by the trees where she'd spotted the woman and child.

Like before, she unloaded a few poles in one spot and then moved the wagon on up to the next, distributing the fencing materials evenly along the fence line. Every once in a while, she paused to catch her breath and glance around. She was curious if the woman was nearby because for some reason, Elizabeth felt she was being watched. After she dropped the last of the poles, she took off her hat and pushed the hair that had come loose from her bun back into place. And then she looked around again.

"Hello?" she called out in what she hoped was a cheerful sounding voice. "Is anyone there? Hello?" She waited quietly and then she heard a rustling sound back in the trees. "Hello?" she called again. "I want to be your friend. I want to help you if I can. Hello?" She stood still now, unsure of what to do. "Do you need my help?"

A small part of her questioned her behavior—and she could almost hear what Malinda would have to say. "What on earth are you doing standing out here like this calling out to an Indian?" And for all Elizabeth knew, there could be a whole bunch of them back in the woods. They could be very angry at the white men for taking over their land. For all Elizabeth knew, this land she considered her own might have truly belonged to the Indians. That thought alone made her feel slightly sickened. She closed her eyes and prayed silently. "Dear God, please help me to know what to do. Help me to help this woman…if she wants my help."

"Hello?" said a low voice.

Elizabeth opened her eyes to see the Indian woman standing at the edge of the woods. Her long black hair hung limply over her shoulders, and she was wearing Elizabeth's old dress, with her bare feet poking out from beneath the dirty hem. She peered curiously at Elizabeth with dark, somber eyes.

"Hello," Elizabeth said nervously.

"You need help?" the woman asked in a flat tone. "I hear you say help."

"No, I don't need help." Elizabeth made a stiff smile. She was tempted to approach this woman, but knew that might make her run. "You speak English?"

"Some."

Elizabeth pointed to herself. "I'm Elizabeth," she said slowly. "E-liz-a-beth."

"Elizabeth." The woman nodded as if she understood.

"You are?" Elizabeth pointed to her. "Charles' wife?"

The woman's eyes lit up ever so slightly. "You know Charles?"

"I know who Charles is. Are you his wife?"

"Yes. Charles' wife."

Elizabeth's smile grew bigger. "I'm Eli's wife."

"Eli?" The woman nodded toward where the sound of the ax was ringing.

"Yes." Now they stood just staring at each other. Elizabeth was trying to think of the right words when the woman glanced over her shoulder as if she were frightened. Was she about to run?

"I want to be your friend," Elizabeth said slowly. "Friend."

"Friend?" Her dark eyes looked suspicious as she folded her arms across her front.

"I think you need a friend," Elizabeth said gently. "You need help."

The woman pressed her lips together as if she understood the meaning, and yet she seemed somewhat confused. Probably she was unaccustomed to being befriended by white people. How had she met Charles?

"Charles is a good man?" Elizabeth asked.

"Yes." The woman nodded.

"Not all white men are good," Elizabeth said slowly. "Some white men hurt your people."

The woman nodded even more firmly. "Yes."

"Eli and I," she pointed at herself. "We want to be friends to Indians."

The woman narrowed her eyes, studying Elizabeth closely as if taking in every small detail.

"I want to help you," Elizabeth told her. "Do you need help?"

"You help me." She waved down at the hand-me-down dress. "You give food. You give blankets. You give clothes. You help."

"Yes. I gave those to you and your child. To help you. To be friends."

"Yes." Her features softened slightly. Almost as if she were trying to believe Elizabeth…to trust her.

"What is your name?" Elizabeth asked quietly.

"Marakeenakanaha."

Elizabeth attempted to repeat the name.

"Mara," the woman said.

"Mara." Elizabeth nodded.

"Your boy? Girl? What name?"

Elizabeth smiled. Mara had obviously been watching their whole family. "The boy is JT. The girl is Ruth. What is your child's name?"

"Rose."

"That is a pretty name. Rose."

Mara looked over her shoulder, calling out some words in her own language, and in the same moment a tiny barefoot girl emerged from the shadows.

"Hello, Rose," Elizabeth said warmly. The child looked to be about three years old. Her long hair was light brown and wavy, but she had her mother's eyes.

"Where do you live?" Elizabeth asked Mara.

Mara pressed her lips together and scowled.

"Do you have a home? A place to stay dry and warm?" Mara shook her head no.

"Where is Charles?"

Mara's eyes lit up again. "Charles go find gold."

"Gold mining?"

"Yes." She nodded eagerly. "Charles go find gold."

"Has he been gone for long?"

Mara looked uncertain.

"Did he leave in the summer? Or last year?"

Now Mara ran her hand over her midsection, which Elizabeth suddenly noticed was very well rounded despite Mara's overall thinness. Charles had obviously been here in the last nine months. But where was he now? Did he know his wife was with child? Did he know she was homeless? Did he even care?

Chapter Twenty-Three

Elizabeth looked up at the sky, realizing it was well past midday. Although she'd taken Eli those biscuits earlier, he was probably hungry for his dinner by now. For that matter, she was too. She pointed at Mara and Rose. "Are you hungry?"

"Yes," Mara muttered.

"Will you come with me?" She pointed to the wagon, wondering if she was expecting too much for them to ride with her, but to her surprise, Mara took Rose by the hand, and soon they were all loaded in the front seat. "I have food at my house," Elizabeth said simply as she drove the team toward home.

Elizabeth attempted to make small talk as she drove her impoverished passengers toward her cabin. Rose's dress was little more than a rag and couldn't possibly be enough to keep her warm. By the time they reached the house, Elizabeth had made a plan to alter one of Ruth's old dresses to fit the child.

Seeing Eli and Flax striding toward the house but peering curiously in her direction, she waved to let him know that everything was all right. "That's Eli," she told Mara and Rose. "And Flax is our dog."

"Dog," Rose pointed at Flax. "Dog."

"Yes," Elizabeth told her. "Dog. Flax."

"Flax." Rose repeated. "Flax. Dog."

"Rose is a smart girl," Elizabeth told Mara.

"Yes." She nodded.

"Hello," Eli said in a friendly tone as he approached the wagon.

"This is Mara and her daughter, Rose," Elizabeth said politely. "Mara and Rose, this is Eli, my husband."

Eli reached out to help them down from the wagon. First he gave Mara a hand, and then he simply lifted Rose, holding her high in the air until she giggled, and then he carefully set her on the ground. Then he helped Elizabeth down.

"Mara and Rose are joining us for dinner, Eli."

He nodded and smiled at Mara. "Good. Welcome to our home."

They went up to the porch, where they took turns washing up. The whole time, Elizabeth chattered cheerfully at her unexpected guests. She knew it was a strange situation, but she wanted them to feel at home. However, when it was time to go inside the house, Mara refused. "We stay here." She pointed to the porch.

"You are welcome to come in the house," Eli said.

"We stay here."

Elizabeth nodded. "I'll leave the door open," she told Mara. "If you want to come inside, please do."

While Elizabeth prepared food, Rose looked longingly into the house, but Mara spoke to her in their native language, and Rose did not step past the threshold. Instead, she played with Flax, who was happy to get this unexpected attention. Meanwhile, Mara went over to sit on the porch bench.

"They need help," Elizabeth quietly told Eli as he filled a coffee cup.

"I'm sure they do."

"They have no place to live, and it sounds like Charles has gone gold mining—probably down at the Rogue River. I hear that's where men go seeking their fortunes of late. Anyway, I'm not sure how long he's been gone, but Mara is with child, and I expect her baby is due in just a month or two."

"Oh…" He shook his head with a dismal sigh as he reached for the sugar bowl.

"But I have an idea."

"An idea?" He stirred some sugar into his coffee.

"Brady's cabin."

His eyes lit up. "Ah-ha."

"Is that all right with you?"

"It's perfectly fine with me. But you know you'll have to keep it a secret from everyone else."

"Even from the children?"

He shrugged. "I don't know, Elizabeth. Is that too much to expect of them? To keep a secret like that from their friends at school, their cousins, their teacher?"

"They know that they're not to speak of Brady in town."

"That's true."

"What is one more secret?" She smiled as she handed him a plate of smoked salmon, two slices of buttered bread, and one of the apple fritters she'd made last night.

"I'll leave that to your discretion."

She picked up the plate she'd made for Mara and Rose to share and carried it outside. "Here." She smiled as she handed it to Mara.

"Thank you," Mara muttered.

"You are most welcome." Elizabeth patted Rose on the head.

When she went back into the house, Eli handed her plate to her. "Why don't we go out and eat with them? It's a nice day today."

She grinned. "Good idea."

So it was that the four of them ate their picnic dinner out on the porch. And when Mara and Rose's plate was empty, Elizabeth went back inside and got them more food. After a while, Eli excused himself to return to work. "I'll take the wagon, and if you don't make it back out there to help me, I'll understand." He winked at her then tipped his hat to the porch. "Goodbye, ladies."

"Goodbye, Eli," Mara said politely.

"Goodbye, Eli," Rose said, imitating her mother.

Satisfied that Mara and Rose had eaten enough, Elizabeth took their plate, but once again she invited them to come inside her house. "You are my friends," she told Mara. "You can come in my house."

Mara looked uncertain. "Charles say no. I no talk to white man. I no go in white man house."

"I am a white *woman*," Elizabeth told her. "You can come into my house. Besides, I think I may have a dress for Rose."

"Dress for Rose?" Mara's eyes lit up.

"A dress that belonged to my little girl, Ruth." Elizabeth tipped her head toward the door. "Please, come inside."

"Yes." With a determined expression, Mara took Rose by the hand and cautiously followed Elizabeth into the house.

Elizabeth set the dirty dishes on the dry sink and then went to her bedroom and opened the trunk, where she had stored all the clothes that were too small or too big or only for special occasions. She dug until she found the blue-and-gray gingham dress that Ruth had nearly worn out on the Oregon Trail. It was patched and mended in places, but it was clean. She carried it out to where Mara and Rose were standing by the door waiting. She held the dress up to Rose. "It's too big now," she said to Mara, "but I can make it smaller so that it fits." She opened her sewing basket.

"I can sew," Mara declared.

"You can?"

Mara held up her hands in a helpless gesture. "No needle. No thread. No cloth."

Elizabeth took a spool of thread, slid a needle down into the side of it, and then wrapped it into the dress and handed it to Mara. "Yes. You can sew."

Mara held the dress to her chest. "Thank you."

"Now I want to get some food for you to take with you," Elizabeth told Mara. While Rose followed Flax to his favorite spot by the fireplace, Elizabeth went into the kitchen and began to fill a basket. Uncertain of Mara's cooking abilities, she put in smoked venison and fish and apples and bread. She also put in two drinking cups and a few other basic household items. Just enough to get them started. She had no idea whether Mara would even accept her offer. But she suspected by their soiled clothes that they'd been camping along the creek. She could imagine how miserable that would be in the rain.

She turned to Mara. "Let's go now."

Mara just nodded, still clutching Ruth's old dress to her chest. She called out to Rose to come—this time in broken English.

Elizabeth went outside with them, and still holding the basket of goods, she nodded in the direction of Brady's cabin. "I have a house for you to use," she told Mara.

"House?"

"Yes. You and Rose can stay there until Charles comes back for you."

"House?" Mara said again.

Elizabeth patted Mara on the back. "A very small house."

As they walked, Elizabeth tried to explain that her friend Brady was going to live in the small house but that he changed his mind.

"The dark man?" Mara asked.

"Yes. That is Brady. He lives with my mother and father now." She pointed in their direction.

Mara nodded as if she understood.

"Did Charles teach you English?" Elizabeth asked as they walked through the meadow.

"I learn some from Charles. I learn some at mission."

"What mission?"

"When I girl, many people die from white man sickness. My father die. Mission take village children. Girls learn to sew. Learn to cook white man food."

"Oh?"

"I go school. Learn English. Learn read and write."

"You can read and write?" Elizabeth tried not to sound too shocked.

"Some. Then school no more. Troubles start."

Although Elizabeth hadn't actually seen Brady's cabin, she knew exactly where it was because she was the one who had originally picked the spot as a good place for him to live out his final years. It was near the creek so that water would be handy, but not so low that it would flood. Set in a grove of fir trees, it was somewhat protected from the elements. Most of all, it was private. Walking up to the tiny cabin encased by tall evergreens, she was reminded of a fairy tale— as if she expected gnomes and fairies to emerge from the shelter.

She opened the door, which was barely her height, and peered inside. Like her house, it smelled of recently cut wood. But unlike her house, it had a packed dirt floor and no glass windows or new cookstove. It didn't even have a fireplace. Indeed, there would be no room for a fire in here. However, she had noticed the campfire area outside where she assumed Brady must have done his cooking during the short time he'd lived here. The cabin's interior, which was about the size of the bedroom she and Eli shared, was bare except for a shelf, a couple of clothes pegs, and a wooden bed that was attached to the wall.

"This is it," Elizabeth waved her hand. "If you want, you are welcome to make yourself at home."

"Home." Mara's dark eyes glistened as she looked around the tiny space.

"It is very small," Elizabeth said apologetically.

"Thank you," Mara said earnestly. "Thank you, thank you."

"Thank you," echoed Rose happily.

Elizabeth smiled in relief. "Do you still have the blankets I gave you?"

"Yes. I hang in sun. Dry."

"Good." Elizabeth looked around, wondering what more she could bring to make them more comfortable here. Perhaps another blanket. Maybe a pot to cook in. A bucket for fetching water. And yet she didn't want to interfere too much or overwhelm them with too many things. She suspected that Mara was accustomed to taking care of herself.

"We had house," Mara said quietly.

"You and Charles?"

"Yes. White men burned. Big fire."

"White men burned your house?"

Mara nodded sadly.

"I am so sorry." Elizabeth put her hand on her bony shoulder. "I think you are safe here. I will not tell anyone about you." Of course, this reminded her that her children would soon be home. And for the time being she had no intention of telling them either. Not only could it put Mara and Rose in danger, it might endanger her family as well. Hearing that white men had burned Mara's home was disturbing to say the least.

Elizabeth excused herself, promising to come back and visit in a day or two. Mara thanked her again, and then Elizabeth hurried away. As she walked back to her house, she experienced a mixture of conflicting emotions. On one hand, she was greatly relieved that Mara and Rose had accepted her offer of help and were now safely settled into Brady's little house. That in itself felt like a godsend. But on the other hand, she was greatly grieved to learn that white men had burned down Mara's house. How could supposedly civilized people be so thoughtless and selfish and cruel?

However, she wasn't only torn over Mara's situation. Now

Elizabeth felt somewhat conflicted about returning to her own beloved home. As grateful as she was for her delightful cabin, it was unsettling to think that what she considered her land had probably belonged to Mara's people first. Suddenly home sweet home felt more like stolen treats.

Chapter Twenty-Four

On Thursday morning, Elizabeth wished she were more excited about Malinda's visit. Originally she had planned to make this visit into a memorable occasion. She'd planned to get out the tea set and silver spoons and linens and make Malinda feel like Queen Victoria. As it turned out, right after the children left for school, Elizabeth ran around the house gathering up items she felt would be useful to Mara and Rose. Loaded with a water pail, a cooking pan, two tin plates, some utensils, a tin bowl, another blanket, and more food, she was nearly out the door when she remembered Mara and Rose's bare feet.

Elizabeth knew that even the shoes Ruth had outgrown would be too large for Rose. But she could take her a pair of Ruth's stockings to keep her warm in the house. But what for Mara? That was when Elizabeth spied her moccasins by the fireplace. As much as she loved those, she knew that Mara needed them more.

Knowing that Malinda could very well arrive before she finished this errand, Elizabeth hurried as quickly as she could over to the little cabin. When she got there, she didn't see Mara or Rose around, so she knocked on the door. "It's me," she called out. "Elizabeth. I have some things for you. I'll just set them out here."

The door opened, and Mara smiled. "Come in my house," she told Elizabeth.

As much as Elizabeth wanted to make her excuses to get back home, she knew she needed to honor Mara by going inside. As her eyes adjusted to the dim light, she could see the blankets on the bed. She smiled. "I brought you some things." She set some of the supplies on a corner of the floor and then looked at Rose. She was wearing Ruth's old dress, and Mara, true to her word, had made some alterations. Certainly, they weren't the way that Elizabeth would have done it, but the child was clothed. "You look very pretty."

She pulled out the black stockings and handed them to Rose. "These are to keep you warm in the house." Rose stared at the stockings as if she didn't know what to do with them. "For your feet and legs." Elizabeth pulled up her skirt to show Rose her own stockings.

Now she handed the moccasins to Mara. "These are for you."

Mara stared down at the moccasins and then back up at Elizabeth. Her dark eyes grew misty. "Thank you," she said.

"I need to go back to my house," Elizabeth told them. "But I will come back again."

"Thank you," Mara said once more. "Thank you, *friend*."

"You are welcome, dear friend."

As Elizabeth hurried back to her house, she wondered what Malinda would think if she knew what her best friend and sister-in-law was up to this morning. Not that she had any intention of telling her. In fact, she had made up her mind that no one, besides her and Eli, would be in the know as far as Mara and Rose went. It just wasn't safe. However, she wouldn't mind having Will's legal counsel in this matter—as long as it could be done with confidentiality. She remembered how Will had offered her some advice in regard to Brady's emigration to Oregon. Of course, she hadn't appreciated all the answers or the narrowness of the new laws. But she did appreciate his legal knowledge.

To Elizabeth's relief, she managed to get her morning housekeeping chores finished and to set up what seemed a very respectable tea party before Malinda arrived. The table was covered in her best lace-trimmed tablecloth and set with her new china tea set and the silver teaspoons. A small plate of molasses cookies that Ruth had made yesterday graced the center. A cheerful fire glowed in the fireplace, and Elizabeth had just hung up her apron when she heard a knock at the door.

"Your little cabin is charming," Malinda said as she came into the house.

"Thank you." Elizabeth closed the door. "And welcome."

Malinda untied her bonnet, handing it to Elizabeth. "And I noticed you have quite a large glass window." She frowned. "But it seems oddly placed, over there by the kitchen."

"Eli thought we would enjoy it more there. As it turned out, he was right. I love looking out while I'm working in the kitchen. Or when we're eating."

"I'm surprised you have wood floors." Malinda tapped her toe on the solid floor. "Most newcomers must settle for packed dirt the first few years." She made a funny laugh as she removed her coat. "Perhaps that's why we call them *settlers*."

"Well, I don't feel that I've had to do much settling in that sense." Elizabeth took her coat, hanging it on a peg. "Eli thought of just about everything."

Elizabeth showed Malinda about the house, listening as her friend examined and commented on everything. But something about Malinda's tone made the comments feel more like complaints than compliments. It seemed that everything was either not good enough or too good. Elizabeth could not make heads or tails of her good friend.

"Glass windows in the loft?" Malinda questioned as they stood in Ruth's bedroom. "That seems awfully extravagant."

"Eli felt the children needed the light."

Malinda pointed to the bedside table, where Ruth had set her favorite bedtime storybook. "Lanterns provide good light."

"Yes, well, Eli thought the children might want fresh air in here too," Elizabeth explained.

"Do the windows *open*?"

"Oh, yes. Eli made wooden latches. See?"

"For a wagon train scout, he seems to know a fair amount about carpentry." Malinda gave Elizabeth a slightly suspicious look. "Did he learn that on the wagon train?"

"My father and Brady have helped him with some of the woodworking. Eli said he learned a lot while building the house."

"This ladder is a bit steep," Malinda said as they scaled down.

"Yes, I must agree. But the children don't mind it at all. They scurry up and down it like little mice. And it takes up so little space down here. I appreciate that." Now Elizabeth opened the door to their bedroom, and Malinda peered in.

"Another window?" Malinda's brow creased.

"It is awfully nice to have the sunlight coming into the room."

"Well, windows are lovely, but they don't put food on the table, Elizabeth. Don't forget, this is the frontier. Your priority is to feed your family—not impress people with your house."

"I'm not concerned for food. Eli is an excellent huntsman. He's providing us with plenty of venison and fish." Elizabeth almost reminded Malinda of how many times Eli and other members of her family had shared these sources with Malinda's household while Elizabeth and the children stayed with her. Instead, she simply smiled at Malinda. "Besides, as you and I know, God is our provider. We trust in him."

"Yes, yes, I know that as well as anyone. But I do want my best friend to be practical and wise and frugal. When hard times hit us, we need to be prepared to face them."

Elizabeth nodded as she removed the teakettle from the stove. "Yes, that's true…" As she poured a bit of hot water in the teapot, swishing it around to warm the china, she wondered why she was being lectured like this. And why was Malinda out of sorts? Surely it didn't have to do with Elizabeth's wedding. That was all over and done, wasn't it?

"When sickness runs through an isolated community such as ours, you realize how vital it is to be prepared for any sort of calamity."

"I feel that we are fairly well prepared." Elizabeth poured black tea leaves in the pot and added more hot water.

Malinda was staring at that cookstove now. "Does that little thing really work? It seems much too small to be useful."

So Elizabeth set the teapot aside and gave Malinda a quick lesson on how the cookstove worked. "The oven is large enough for two big loaves of bread or a large venison roast. And I'm sure it could hold a good-sized goose. Anything larger can always go in a roaster on top. It's actually quite convenient, and it helps to take the chill off the house. Sometimes we don't even use the fireplace. Also, the stove doesn't use very much firewood. Perhaps that's because it's smaller."

"Well, you don't have a large family to feed. Not like I do," Malinda smoothed her skirt. "I suppose when I get a cookstove, I will want a larger one."

"Yes, I can understand that." As Elizabeth moved to the table, she tried to stifle her irritation. Why was Malinda being so ungracious?

"This is an interesting piece." Malinda paused to examine the wet sink.

"Yes, it's very handy."

"Quite rustic. Did Eli make it too?"

Elizabeth almost mentioned that Brady had made it but stopped herself. She did not want Malinda to launch into a lecture about how Brady didn't really belong here and how he wouldn't be allowed to stay. "It was a wedding gift—from my family."

"Ah, yes. So much for your plans to have no wedding gifts. Honestly, I think you and Eli made off like bandits."

Elizabeth stared at Malinda. Why was she being so rude? "Would you like to sit now?" she asked in a stiff voice.

"Yes, of course." Malinda came over and took her seat at the table. "This looks very pretty, Elizabeth. Thank you." She made what seemed a strained smile.

"Malinda," Elizabeth began slowly as she filled Malinda's teacup. "Is something bothering you? Have I done something to offend you in some way?"

"No, no, of course not." Malinda reached for her teaspoon.

"Because you just seem a bit unhappy to me," Elizabeth said gently. "As if something is troubling you."

Other than the ticking clock and an occasional sound from the fire, the room grew very quiet. Elizabeth passed the plate of cookies to Malinda and then filled her own teacup with the hot amber liquid.

"I'm sorry," Malinda said contritely. "I suppose that I was being rather persnickety, wasn't I? Please, forgive my bad manners."

Elizabeth made an uneasy smile. "Certainly. But I'm concerned. You don't seem yourself today. Are you unwell?"

"No, my health is perfectly fine." Malinda made a small smile, but her eyes looked sad.

"I know something is troubling you." Elizabeth leaned forward. "You can tell me, Malinda. I'm your best friend."

Malinda set down her teacup with a loud clink then shook her head.

"Is it something with the children? No one is ill I hope…"

"The children are all fit as fiddles."

Elizabeth pondered the situation, wondering how hard she should push. "Does this have to do with Will?"

Malinda nodded sadly. "I'm afraid so."

"Is he ill?"

"No…but it's all coming apart."

"What is coming apart?"

"Everything."

"What do you mean?" Elizabeth peered at her friend with concern. She could see that Malinda was close to tears.

"Will wishes to postpone our wedding."

"Postpone it? Why?"

"Oh, Elizabeth!" She let out a sob. "I am devastated!"

"You poor dear." Elizabeth reached across the table and took her hand. "But I don't understand. Why postpone the wedding? I thought you were both eager to marry before Christmas. And you've made so many preparations."

Malinda retrieved a lace-trimmed hanky from her skirt pocket and dabbed her eyes. "Will is afraid we may have rushed into this without giving it sufficient consideration."

"Oh, dear." Elizabeth bit her lip. She had wondered about the same thing after they'd gotten engaged within days of meeting each other. It had seemed overly fast, not to mention that Malinda had not even been widowed for a year. Naturally, these were opinions Elizabeth kept to herself.

"I will admit that we don't know each other terribly well. But I do love him, Elizabeth. I know that I do. I felt it almost from the start. These are not things one imagines."

"I'm sure you do love him," she agreed. "And that's how I felt about Eli quite early on too. It just took a while for my heart to convince my head."

"So tell me, are you enjoying married life?"

"Very much so." Elizabeth smiled happily. Her first few days of marriage had been wonderful—far better than she'd even imagined. "But we are still newlyweds. I expect we'll have a disagreement before long. But I will not let it trouble me. Two people cannot always agree on everything."

There was another long silence, and Elizabeth regretted boasting about her marriage. Surely that was not what Malinda needed to hear just now. Elizabeth tried to think of a way to encourage her. "Remember how you encouraged me to consider a spring wedding? Perhaps that's what you will have. I can hardly wait to see how beautiful it will be here in the spring. I'm sure the wildflowers must be blooming profusely by—"

"There's more to this than postponement," Malinda blurted.

"What is it?" Elizabeth studied Malinda's troubled expression.

"Will feels he is not suited for pioneering."

"What do you mean *not suited*?"

"It seems that he's been a failure at cabin building. Even Jeremiah, who is only eighteen, has far better carpentry skills than Will. Lavinia confided that Hugh has been going out to help Jeremiah, and he comes home to tell her that poor Will is all thumbs."

"But that shouldn't matter to you," Elizabeth assured her. "Your house is already constructed. Your barn as well. You even have most of your fences up. Will won't have to build much of anything."

"I told him this very thing." She wiped her nose. "But Will pointed out that he is not a good hunter or fisherman or farmer. He feels that nothing in his life has prepared him for living in the frontier."

"And yet he was determined to come here." Elizabeth remembered when she'd first met the Bostonians—right from the beginning she'd been concerned that they would encounter problems. "I wondered whether the Prescotts and the Bramfords would even survive the Oregon Trail," she confessed. "And yet they did, whereas many did not. Will certainly proved himself a pioneer on the wagon train."

"Yes, but he had help."

"There are those who can help him here." She pointed to Malinda. "You yourself are a fine frontierswoman. You can certainly help him."

"I'm afraid there's more to it than that, Elizabeth." She sighed.

"Will sees the Prescotts prospering with their store and their lovely home up above. Meanwhile he and Jeremiah have struggled so hard with their cabin—the cabin that Jeremiah and Mahala were supposed to live in after their wedding. But now Will even questions that."

"What does he question?"

"He's worried that Jeremiah is marrying beneath him."

"Mahala is a wonderful girl."

"Yes...but the Flanders...well, they are a bit rough around the edges."

"They are *good* people, Malinda. And if Jeremiah marries Mahala—and I hope he does—the Flanderses will be your in-laws too. Well, that is if you and Will marry." She frowned. "You say Will wants to *postpone* the wedding. For how long?"

"I don't know how long. Truly, Elizabeth, it feels as if he is questioning just about everything. He doubts himself and his ability to be a pioneer. He's worried that his choice to come out here has hurt his children. He frets that he has kept them from having a proper education. He is concerned that we made our decision to marry in haste." She threw up her hands. "Nothing...absolutely nothing seems to be working out for him—or for us."

"It's no wonder you were feeling a bit negative about my house this morning."

Malinda looked around the room and sighed. "Your home is perfectly lovely, Elizabeth. You are so very fortunate to have found a man like Mr. Eli Kincaid. I have no doubt that I am severely jealous. I wanted to find fault...just to make myself feel better. But in all honesty, there is nothing wrong with your dear home. The fault lies in me."

Despite her relief at hearing that her friend approved, Elizabeth felt sad. "What can be done for Will?"

Malinda sadly shook her head. "I don't know. We have talked and talked. It seems to get us nowhere. I suspect that if Will lasts here until springtime, he will be making a plan to move. He has mentioned San Francisco. He feels that attorneys would be welcome there."

"They will be welcome here too," Elizabeth declared. "In time." She almost divulged how she'd been wishing for his legal advice just yesterday, but she knew she couldn't.

"So now, besides feeling heartbroken, I have the additional humiliation of needing to inform everyone that there will be no wedding next week. Do you know how difficult that will be? And I feel so embarrassed when I consider how much trouble I created for you regarding your own wedding." She blew her nose. "And come to find out, my wedding was nothing more than a pipe dream all along. I am such a fool."

"Oh, my." Elizabeth didn't know what to say. "I am so sorry, Malinda."

"You made a lovely tea party for us," she said quietly. "A party that I have completely spoiled."

"You've not spoiled any—"

"Yes, I have! And I should probably just go home because I can't bear to—" She broke into fresh sobs.

Elizabeth went over to wrap her arms around Malinda. "You poor dear," she soothed. "If there's anything I can do to help, I will."

"Just keep being my friend," Malinda said softly. "That is most valuable."

"You know I will." She patted her back as Malinda stood. "Are you sure you don't want to stay and talk about this some more?"

"Will and I have talked it nearly to death." Malinda went for her coat and bonnet. "Mostly I want to just forget about it. Forget about the whole thing. Perhaps a year from now it will be just a distant memory."

"Would you like me to let people know about the postponement?"

Malinda brightened slightly. "Oh, Elizabeth, that would lighten my load considerably."

"I will get right to it. Perhaps I should ask Reverend Holmes to make an announcement on Sunday."

Malinda sighed. "Yes…please do that."

"And I won't give specific details when I tell people," she promised. "I'll just say that you realized you needed more time. After all, having a wedding right before Christmas was quite an undertaking. People should understand the sensibility of waiting."

"Yes. Hopefully they will. But Hugh and Lavinia are aware of the troubles we're having. No need to make up any excuses for Lavinia."

"Do Belinda and Amelia know?"

"I think they have their suspicions. But no, they are in the dark about the wedding getting called off. So are my children. Emily and Susannah will be so disappointed. They were looking forward to it. And they love their new stepsisters-to-be. I feel this is tearing our family apart." She sniffed. "A broken engagement is very much like a divorce."

"Perhaps it is only a postponement," Elizabeth reminded her.

"No…I fear that we are calling it a postponement simply because it feels less painful. But the truth is I do not think Will and I shall ever marry." As she went out the door she started crying all over again.

Elizabeth grabbed her coat and hat and insisted on walking Malinda partway home. She was unwilling to let her friend leave feeling so distraught. Linking arms with her, she was determined to remain with her until she appeared somewhat recovered. Eventually Malinda assured her that she would be fine.

"I just needed a shoulder to cry on," she confessed. "Thank you." She pointed to the sky, which was growing dark and foreboding. "You best get yourself home before it rains, dear one."

As Elizabeth hurried back toward home, she felt very thankful for Eli. Not only was he a dear husband and good father, he was a very capable frontiersman too. In fact, as she went into the house, she wondered if he might be able to help Will Bramford.

Perhaps Eli could invite Will to go hunting and fishing with him. He could teach Will some valuable skills and possibly help the frustrated attorney to feel more confident about himself. Perhaps Eli could even ask Will for legal counsel in regard to their Indian friends.

Chapter Twenty-Five

On Saturday morning, Elizabeth and Ruth walked over to her parents' house. Leaving Ruth to visit with her mother, Elizabeth set out to find Brady. She wanted to inform him that his cabin was being inhabited. And she hoped that he wouldn't mind. She found Brady and Asa working on a very similar-looking cabin.

"Good morning," she called out.

They paused from chinking a log to greet her, and after some polite exchanges, Elizabeth asked Brady if she could speak privately with him. But then seeing her father's puzzled expression, she decided to include him. If she couldn't trust her father, she couldn't trust anyone. She quickly poured out the story of Mara and Rose.

"I thought I saw an Indian woman and child," Asa said. "A week or two ago. I mentioned it to Clara, but she thought I'd imagined it."

"You didn't imagine it, Father."

"Do they like my little cabin?" Brady asked.

She nodded. "Very much so."

Brady grinned. "Good. Musta been meant to be."

"Yes. That's exactly what I thought too."

"I never got a chance to make a table and chair for that cabin like I meant to do," Brady told her. "But maybe when I get this one all done, I can make Mara and Rose some furnishings too."

"I'm sure they would appreciate it. But in the meantime, I know they are just happy to be in out of the weather." She looked up at the gray sky. "Speaking of weather, I wanted to make it to town before it rains. I'll let you get back to your work."

"I'll walk back to the house with you," Asa said.

As she and Asa walked, she told him about Malinda and Will. Without going into much detail, she explained about the change in wedding plans.

"That's too bad," Asa said. "I know how much Malinda was looking forward to her wedding."

"Yes. She was fairly devastated." And now, since this was her father and she knew she could trust him, she confided some of the reasons for the "postponement." Her hope was that perhaps he would have some answers for the unhappy couple. "So Malinda feels that if Will felt more confident about hunting and fishing and farming, perhaps he would be more confident about their marriage as well."

Asa rubbed his chin. "I reckon that makes some sense. No man wants to feel as if he can't provide for his family and protect them."

"So I've spoken to Eli about it. And I thought perhaps you and Matthew could extend your friendship to him as well."

"I consider Will to be my friend. But I reckon I haven't reached out to him much. Everybody has been so busy."

"Eli wondered about inviting Will to go hunting with you men."

"That's right—we've been trying to plan our big hunting trip. In fact, Will and Malinda's wedding was complicating our plans. I reckon we don't need to be concerned about that now."

"Would you mind if Will went along too?"

"Not in the least." Asa paused a ways from the cabin. "Before we go inside, I want to talk to you about your Indian friends."

"Yes?"

"Well, I understand why you wanted to tell Brady. It would have been mighty awkward if he'd gone over there for something and found he had squatters."

"Yes. That was why I told him. And I suspected he'd be understanding."

"And I know we can trust him not to speak of it to anyone." Asa frowned. "I assume you don't plan on telling anyone else."

"No." She firmly shook her head. "Besides you and Brady and Eli and me, no one will know."

He put his hand on her shoulder. "That's wise. You do understand that keeping Indians on your land could be dangerous. And not just to the Indians."

She told him what Mara had said about white men burning her house down. "I felt so sorry for her. It was plain to see that she was terrified by the experience."

"She speaks English?"

She filled him in a bit more about the mission and how Charles had been teaching her. "She seems quite intelligent."

"Did she say when Charles is coming back?"

"She doesn't seem to know. But she is expecting another child."

"Oh, my." He shook his head.

She glanced over at their cabin now. "I wouldn't really mind if Mother knew about Mara and Rose. I know I can trust her."

"If you like, I'll explain the situation to her."

"Thank you."

"I expect she'll want to help them too."

Elizabeth nodded. "Well, they can certainly use it." She sighed. "Perhaps I should tell Matthew and Jess too. Just in case they've seen them."

"You know you can trust them not to speak of it. And I know Jess is a very compassionate young woman. She would probably want to help too."

"So feel free to tell them if you see them. And, please, tell them about the wedding postponement too. That is my task today. I'm going to town to let everyone know. I plan to ask the reverend to make an official announcement from the pulpit tomorrow."

"You are a good friend." He nodded toward the house. "I expect your ma will want to walk to town with you. She said she wanted to visit the mercantile."

"Then we had best be on our way." She glanced at the clouds. "Or we may have to stop and take shelter at Malinda's."

"And I'll get back to helping Brady."

"I thought you were going in the house."

He chuckled. "Sorry. I had to make an excuse to speak privately with you about my concerns for your Indian friends."

She nodded. "Well, they truly are friends, Father. They are both very dear."

⚜

Before long, Elizabeth and Clara and Ruth were on their way to town. As they walked, she told her mother about the postponed wedding.

"Oh, my—poor Malinda. She'd had her heart set on having the wedding before Christmas."

"But Mama said they might have a spring wedding now," Ruth said hopefully. "And there will be lots and lots of flowers then."

"That's true enough."

"So perhaps you can help me spread the word in town," she told her mother. "You don't need to say too much. Just that it's been postponed. That way it won't be so shocking when Reverend Holmes announces it at church tomorrow."

They walked at a fast pace, making it to the mercantile shortly after the rain began to fall. Shaking off moisture on the front porch, Elizabeth greeted Mrs. Taylor, who was just coming out. After exchanging pleasantries, Elizabeth told Mrs. Taylor about the change in wedding plans.

"Oh...well," Mrs. Taylor said. "You know the old saying."

"What's that?" Ruth asked.

"Thus grief still treads upon the heels of pleasure," she recited. "Married in haste, we may repent at leisure." She smiled. "William Congreve wrote that."

"Yes, well, perhaps waiting a bit is the wise route," Elizabeth told her.

As they shopped in the mercantile, the news of the postponement spread quickly. And although some expressed disappointment—ones who had been looking forward to the festivities—most were very kind and understanding.

Evelyn and her cousins Belinda and Amelia were helping to mind the shop, so Lavinia invited Elizabeth and Clara and Ruth to come upstairs. "Elizabeth has seen our home, but you two haven't," she told Clara and Ruth as she led them into the apartment.

"It's so beautiful," Ruth gushed.

"Oh, my." Clara clasped her hands. "I don't feel that I'm on the frontier anymore."

Lavinia laughed. "Yes. That's exactly my intention. Civilization in the midst of the wilderness. Would you ladies like some tea?"

Clara and Ruth both were happy to accept this unexpected invitation, but Elizabeth decided to use this opportunity. "I need to pay a visit to the Holmeses," she told Lavinia as she peered out the window. "And it appears the rain has let up. Perhaps Mother and Ruth could have tea with you while I run over to the parsonage."

"Mama's going to tell Reverend Holmes about Aunt Malinda," Ruth explained.

"Oh, yes," Lavinia said. "By all means go now, Elizabeth. We will be just fine here."

So Elizabeth hurried on over to the parsonage, and since the reverend was out, she explained the situation to Mrs. Holmes. "Malinda would appreciate it if the reverend could make an announcement."

Mrs. Holmes promised to relay the message, and then the two women visited for a while. For some reason Elizabeth felt that she could trust Mrs. Holmes, and although she didn't intend to tell her about the Indians, she wanted to question her about Mrs. Levine. "I know that you and the reverend are close friends with the Levines," she began. "I have only had a few limited conversations with Mrs. Levine, although I feel I have some commonality since I too have been a widow. Are you very close friends with her?"

"Oh, yes. Martha is my very best friend here. I don't know what I would do without her."

"I'm sure you must be a valued friend to her as well." Elizabeth weighed her words. "It must have been difficult for her when her Charles married an Indian woman. I'm sure she must have relied on your friendship then."

"Oh, they are not married, dear," Mrs. Holmes said quietly. "It's not legal, you know."

"Yes, I realize that. But I suspect they consider themselves married, don't you?"

She looked uncertain. "Well, I don't know. That all happened shortly before the reverend and I arrived here."

"So you don't know Charles then?"

"Certainly, I know him. Our families have been friends for quite some time."

"Were you shocked when you heard the news about him?"

"I was a bit surprised. But then I'd heard that happens sometimes. Especially in the frontier, where the white men often outnumber the white women and, well, you understand how it can be."

Elizabeth nodded. "Do you think that's how it was for Charles?"

"To be honest, I don't rightly know. Martha hasn't told me all the particulars. I suppose I've come to my own conclusions."

"What sort of man is Charles? I mean what sort of character?"

Her brow creased. "Oh, I always felt he was a fine young man. Charming and well-spoken and polite. Although Roland always felt that Charles was a bit willful. And he said that Charles had wild oats to sow."

Elizabeth nodded. "What are Mrs. Levine's feelings toward Charles now? Is their relationship broken beyond repair?"

"Oh, no, not at all. Martha loves Charles. Truth be told, I believe he was her favorite son. She calls him her prodigal, and I suspect if he asked to come home, she would welcome him with open arms."

"And his wife and child too?"

Mrs. Holmes put her hand over her lips.

"I take it that his wife and child would not be welcome in her home?"

"Oh, dear. I'm not sure what Martha would do. As a good Christian woman, she might wish to take in the woman and child, but she would be putting herself and her family in harm's way if she did."

"What would happen to her?"

"Goodness, I'm not altogether certain." Mrs. Holmes looked distressed.

"Are there people in our settlement who would make trouble for her?"

Mrs. Holmes simply nodded. "I'm afraid so."

"Would their actions be legal?"

"Legal?" She sighed. "In the frontier, there are laws…and then there are other laws, if you get my meaning."

"I think I do."

Mrs. Holmes peered curiously at her now. "Why are you asking these questions, dear? Why are you so interested in the Levines?"

Elizabeth had prepared an honest answer for this. "Being a newcomer here, I want a better understanding of my community," she explained. "I know that the Indians have been removed from these parts. And I'd heard bits and pieces about Charles Levine. I was simply curious as to the local sentiments."

"The local sentiments are divided. There are a few settlers who felt that removing the Indians was unfair and unkind, but they are not a majority. They believed that the Indians, for the most part, were peaceful—just like we believe that the settlers, for the most part, are peaceful. However, it only takes a handful of angry men to stir things up. And that is what happened."

"Would you and the reverend be in the minority of folks who hold no ill feelings toward the Indians?"

"We do believe that the Indians, like us, were created by God—in his image. Certainly, they are different from us. But they are not savages like some people claim."

"I'm relieved to know that, Mrs. Holmes."

"But be assured, this is not something that you will hear the reverend mention from the pulpit," she said firmly. "Don't expect him to."

"Why not?"

"He tried to voice his concerns. He'd seen and heard some things that were disturbing—some of it was related to Charles and his Indian woman. Roland preached on the subject shortly after our arrival here." She sighed. "Unfortunately, his sermon led to some severe disagreements, and the church nearly came to an end."

"I see."

"It has been a source of frustration for him."

"I can imagine."

"I hope that you will keep my confidence in these matters." Mrs. Holmes' brow creased. "I don't usually speak so freely about such things. And Roland might not approve."

"You can trust me to not say a word." She eyed the older woman. "I feel certain I can trust you too."

She nodded. "If you would like to become better acquainted with Mrs. Levine, I would be happy to arrange for us to meet. Perhaps you could come for tea."

"Or perhaps you and Mrs. Levine would like to come to my house for tea."

Her eyes lit up. "Oh, my. That would be delightful."

And so they set a date. The two women would come for tea on Tuesday morning at ten. "Unless it is raining," Elizabeth said. "In that case, I will understand."

"Then I shall pray that Tuesday breaks with no rain."

"And if it does rain on Tuesday, why don't we plan on Wednesday, whichever day is fair?"

"Yes." Mrs. Holmes smiled. "I like that plan."

"And speaking of rain, I see that the sun is out. I think I'll make a run for it and gather up my mother and daughter and hurry on home."

As Elizabeth went back to the mercantile, she wondered what she was getting herself into. Did she really intend to let Mrs. Levine know that her granddaughter was living nearby? No, Elizabeth decided, she could not betray Mara like that. First she would have to become thoroughly acquainted with Mrs. Levine. She would have to find out the woman's true character. Then she would try to do whatever was best for Mara and Rose.

Chapter Twenty-Six

The ladies were unable to come for tea until Wednesday. But thankfully, the day broke sunny and clear, and at just a bit past ten, Mrs. Holmes and Mrs. Levine showed up at her door.

"Welcome," Elizabeth said warmly. "Isn't it a fine day we're having?"

"It most certainly is," Mrs. Holmes said as she removed her bonnet.

"I hardly needed my shawl," Mrs. Levine told her.

"I cannot believe it's December," Elizabeth said. "It feels more like springtime to me." The three women made polite small talk as Elizabeth showed them through her home. Both of her visitors were suitably impressed. After Malinda's moody evaluations the previous week, Elizabeth appreciated her guests' kind and appreciative comments. Soon they were seated at the table, which was set just as grand as it had been for Malinda, and Elizabeth was pouring tea.

"It's such a pleasure getting to know you better, Mrs. Levine." Elizabeth handed her the plate of sugar cookies that she and Ruth had made the other day.

"Please, dear, if I am to keep calling you Elizabeth, you must call me Martha." She smiled. "After all, this is the frontier. We don't have to be overly prim and proper out here."

"And if you're going to call her Martha, it's about time you started calling me Georgia," Mrs. Holmes said.

"Thank you."

"I told Martha that you were curious about her son Charles," Georgia said a bit carefully.

"And naturally that aroused my curiosity," Martha admitted. "But Georgia assured me that you had no ill motives."

"Not at all," she told her. "In fact, you and I have some commonalities I believe. First I thought it was because we were widows, but when I learned more about Charles, well, I felt that I could take you into my confidence." She glanced at Georgia. "And I know I can trust you as well."

"Certainly." Georgia nodded.

Elizabeth had told Eli her plan several days ago, and he had given her his blessing to tell his story. "You see, my dear husband has had an experience similar to your son Charles," she said to Georgia. "And I felt it might comfort you to hear about it." And now she told them the story of how Eli had rescued the Indian woman and how her people had helped him and how Eli had fallen in love and married the woman.

"My goodness," Georgia exclaimed. "I had no idea."

"And they had a child," she told her spellbound guests. "A son." She described how happy the young family had been, how much at home Eli had felt with her people. And finally she explained how the mother and child had both died from a white man's disease. "Eli was brokenhearted over it."

"Oh, my." Martha wiped her damp eyes with her handkerchief.

"Such a sad tale." Georgia sniffed.

"Now I wouldn't share this story with just anyone," Elizabeth said to Martha. "But after hearing more about Charles and how much you love him, I felt that you especially needed to hear it."

Martha nodded. "I do believe I did need to hear it. Although it's a sad story, it does give this mother's heart hope. I admire your husband, Elizabeth. If he made a mistake like that but is living such a fine life now, well, it gives me hope for Charles."

Elizabeth bit her lip. This was not exactly the response she was looking for. "Eli did not consider his first marriage to be a mistake, Martha. He loved his first wife."

"Oh, well, yes…I suppose he thought he did. But don't you think his life would have been mighty complicated—wouldn't it have made things more difficult if his wife and child had survived?"

"Certainly, it would be more difficult for me." Elizabeth frowned. "But that's not my point. What I'm saying is that Eli is a good man. And I believe your Charles is a good man too."

"Yes, yes, he most certainly is," Martha assured her. "He was always a good boy. A little lively at times, but he had a good heart."

"And marrying an Indian woman doesn't make him less good, does it?"

"That all depends on who you're talking to." Martha shook her head. "Some folks round here would just as soon a man marry his horse rather than an Indian woman."

"Oh, Martha." Georgia shook her head with disapproval.

"It's true and you know it." Martha frowned. "And some folks have good reason to dislike Indians." She launched into a horrible story about how the Indians staged a brutal attack in the Rogue River War. "And that was just a couple of years ago."

"And wasn't that why the Indians got moved up north?" Elizabeth asked. "Although they didn't just move the warriors, but innocent women and children as well."

"That's true," Martha confirmed. "But I'm sure the women

wanted to be with their men. But for all we know some of those same violent Indian warriors could still be lurking anywhere—even in these parts. I don't think the trouble with the Indians is over by any means."

Elizabeth studied Martha. She didn't seem to be a hateful woman, but she was apparently overly fearful of Indians. And yet how could she possibly be afraid of anyone as harmless as Mara or Rose? "Your son has a child, doesn't he?"

Martha made an uncertain nod. "Yes…I heard there was a baby, although I've never seen it. To be honest, I'm not sure I would want to see it."

"Your own grandchild?"

She twisted her handkerchief. "I just don't see what good could come of it."

Georgia patted Martha's hand. "You are caught between a rock and a hard place, my dear."

"I'm sorry to be so persistent about this," Elizabeth said as she refilled their teacups. "More than anything, I want you to realize that you are not alone. Eli and I have great compassion for you, Martha. And we want you to know that we are your friends. And if Charles should ever return from—from wherever he has gone—we would treat him as a friend as well."

Martha smiled. "That is a great comfort to me, Elizabeth. Thank you."

Feeling a bit guilty for being so intrusive, Elizabeth was determined that the duration of their tea party would remain cheerful and uplifting. They shared funny stories about their children and compared ailments and just laughed like girls together. And by the time the ladies left, Elizabeth felt certain that a strong friendship was being forged. However, she did not feel certain that Martha would welcome an Indian daughter-in-law and granddaughter.

The week before Christmas, the men planned to take off for a few days of hunting. But the night before they left, Eli shot a deer, leaving the best cuts of meat for Elizabeth and the children. "If you don't mind, I will take the rest of the meat as well as the skin to Mara and Rose."

"Thank you," she told him. "That will take a load off my mind."

The next morning, Eli went over to her parents' well before daybreak in order to help Asa pack the wagon and hitch up the oxen. Then, according to Clara, while it was still dark, the five hunters—Eli, Asa, Matthew, Brady, and Will—set out.

"I was so surprised when I heard that Will wanted to go hunting with your fellows," Malinda told Elizabeth. The hunting "widows" had gathered at Malinda's house to work on a quilt that was meant for Mahala and Julius' wedding. Thankfully, the young couple had dug in their heels, making it clear to everyone that their wedding was still scheduled for the first Saturday of February.

"Eli said they were grateful to have Will join them," Elizabeth told Malinda. "Last week, Eli scouted a nice herd of elk, and he hopes they'll bring home two cows. According to Eli, that's a lot of meat to pack back to the wagon. Will's muscles will come in handy."

"I appreciate that there are some young men along," Clara said. "Asa thinks he can keep up, but he's getting older. He needs to slow down."

"I feel like I'm slowing down," Jess admitted. "I've been so sleepy lately. Sometimes I feel like I can barely keep my eyes open."

"That's because of the baby," Elizabeth told her. "I had the same thing. Not when I was carrying Ruth so much, but with JT. Of course, maybe I had it with Ruth, but I was so busy chasing after JT that I didn't notice."

Now they all started comparing pregnancy and birthing stories. Malinda, having birthed four children, seemed to have the best ones. Or perhaps she just was a better storyteller. "Unfortunately, we don't have a doctor nearby," Malinda told them. "But I've helped with a number of births."

"Mother is a good midwife," Elizabeth said.

"And she's promised to help me when my time comes." Jess looked at Clara. "Right, Ma?"

Clara grinned. "You can count on it."

"I'm not as experienced as Mother—unless you're birthing animals." Elizabeth laughed. "But I'm happy to help too, Jess."

"And if by some weird stroke of bad luck they are both unavailable, you tell Matthew to come and fetch me," Malinda told her. "I'd be happy to deliver your baby."

Jess smiled. "I feel very well taken care of."

"Do you think Ruby and Doris will come in time for your birth?" Clara asked.

"I just got a letter from Ruby," Jess told her. "They don't expect to make it here until early fall next year. Her plan is to keep the business in Empire City going throughout the summer because so many settlers come through there. But in midsummer she expects to have enough profits to send out a carpenter to begin building an inn right next to the mercantile."

"Wonderful!" Malinda said happily. "Our town is growing by leaps and bounds."

Elizabeth was relieved to see Malinda in such good spirits today. She had been worried that her friend would be fretting over the wedding that never happened last Saturday. That was the very reason she'd suggested that they gather like this while the men were gone.

"I'll bet you all have plans for Christmas," Malinda said. "But I've been daydreaming about a little get-together I'd love to have here."

Elizabeth exchanged glances with her mother. Their plan was to have their family at Elizabeth and Eli's house. They hadn't invited Malinda because they weren't sure about the Bramfords and Prescotts, and Elizabeth knew her house wasn't big enough to contain all those people for that long.

"What sort of get-together?" Clara asked Malinda.

"I thought it would be lovely to have everyone here on Christmas

Eve. I imagined a big bonfire, and we could have music and dancing in the barn. I suppose it's because I'd been dreaming of our December wedding," she confessed.

"I think that sounds like fun," Elizabeth said. Fortunately, their plan was to gather on Christmas Day. "I know the children would love it."

"So would Matthew," Jess told them. "He had been so looking forward to the…well…" She grimaced.

"The wedding," Malinda finished for her. "It's all right. You can say it. I'm resolved to my fate by now. You know what they say, the best laid plans of mice and men—and I suppose we could add overbearing brides to the list."

They all laughed.

"I'll promise you all this," Malinda continued. "If it turns out that Will and I do decide to get married—which is probably not going to happen, but if it does—I will try to follow Elizabeth and Eli's example."

"What example?" Elizabeth asked.

"Being more concerned about the marriage than the wedding."

"Oh." Elizabeth chuckled. "Well, a wedding is one day. A marriage, hopefully, is forever."

"Do you think the men will encounter any wild cats or wolves or bears where they are hunting?" Jess asked.

"If they do, you probably don't need to be worried," Elizabeth assured her. "Besides, I know Eli wouldn't mind bringing some skins or furs home. He's almost got that cougar skin ready to become a rug." Of course, as soon as she said this, she regretted it. The rug was meant to be a Christmas present for her parents, to go in their bedroom, to help cover their hard-packed dirt floor. So now she quickly changed the subject. "What can we bring to your Christmas Eve party?" she asked Malinda. And suddenly they were making plans for what was sure to be a fun evening for all.

❧❈❧

Elizabeth tried not to feel worried when Eli didn't come home on the day she expected him. She assured JT and Ruth that it was probably something as mundane as a broken wagon wheel. "Or perhaps they were having such a good time, they decided to stay an extra day." And she couldn't blame them because the past two days had been exceptionally good weather. But when she finally blew out the lantern and went to bed, she felt a little concerned. And as usual, she prayed for the safety of all of the hunters.

"What if they don't get home in time for the Christmas party tomorrow?" JT asked as he picked up his guitar case the next morning.

"I'm sure they'll be home by today," she told him.

"In time to come to our Christmas program at school?" Ruth asked hopefully.

"I'm not sure about that." She tweaked a braid, adjusting the red bow that Ruth had insisted was necessary because they were doing their program. "But I am sure that Grandma, Aunt Jess, Aunt Malinda, and I will all be there. And I'm also sure that if you don't get going, you will be late for school."

After the children left and after she finished with chores as well as delivering some food to Mara and Rose, Elizabeth focused her attention on finishing some Christmas presents for the children and Eli. For Ruth, she had sewn a school dress from some of the green calico she'd brought from Kentucky. And then she'd made a matching dress for Ruth's doll. For Eli and JT she had sewn matching chambray shirts in a nice shade of blue. Just as she finished the last buttonhole on JT's shirt, it was time to go hitch up the team. She had promised to give her mother and Jess and Malinda a ride to school. She hoped that perhaps the men would be arriving at her parents' house by now, but to her dismay, there was no sign of them.

"You don't think anything went wrong with the hunters, do you?" Elizabeth asked Clara as she sat down on the seat next to her.

"I expect they've had good luck and it's just taking longer."

"Or they might have had a breakdown on the wagon."

"Your brother took tools. If they break down, he will fix it."

"Yes. I'm sure you're right." Elizabeth saw Jess waiting for them on the edge of her property. "And I won't act worried around Jess."

Before long, they were standing in the back of the school with the rest of the parents, watching as Mrs. Taylor led the children in a number of lively songs. Some, like JT, had instruments to play, and all in all, it was quite a nice production. But Elizabeth couldn't have been prouder than when Ruth sang "O Come, All Ye Faithful" accompanied by JT. It was so beautiful that tears filled her eyes. She wished Eli could hear it. Malinda's girls along with Will's older daughters sang a lovely rendition of "Hark! The Herald Angels Sing," and some of the older boys bellowed out "Joy to the World."

For the finale, all the children joined in to sing "Deck the Halls," and then the parents were treated to goodies that were provided by Mrs. Taylor, the Holmeses, and Prescotts' Mercantile. All in all, it was a very nice program. Considering they were just a little one-room frontier school, Elizabeth was impressed.

"We are so fortunate to have you," she told Mrs. Taylor afterward. "If you don't have plans for Christmas, we would love to have you join us."

"Thank you," Mrs. Taylor smiled happily. "But I promised to spend Christmas at the Levines. Reverend and Mrs. Holmes will be joining us."

Elizabeth squeezed her hand. "Merry Christmas!"

After visiting with the other parents and explaining more times than she cared to about why Eli and the other men were missing, Elizabeth suggested that it was time to go home. "Those clouds look like they could let loose before long," she told Malinda. "And we'll have a heavy load of people to get home."

The children insisted on singing Christmas songs in the back of the wagon. And for a while their merriment seemed to displace her concerns about the missing hunters.

"Susannah and Emily want to know if I can stay overnight at their house tonight," Ruth said when they reached Malinda's house. "There's no school in the morning."

Elizabeth glanced at Malinda. "Is that all right with you?"

"Sure. I'll put her to work helping prepare for tomorrow's party."

"What about JT?" Bart protested. "If Ruth gets to stay, can JT stay too? Please, Ma?"

"I'm fine with that," Malinda said as she climbed down.

"Ma?" JT asked hopefully. "Do you mind?"

Elizabeth made a tolerant smile. "Not at all. But both of you mind your manners and help Aunt Malinda."

They assured her they would, and suddenly it was just her and Clara and Jess. "Do you ladies want to keep singing?" Elizabeth asked tentatively as she drove the team on toward home.

"Not particularly," Jess answered solemnly.

"Yes, I think I've had enough music for now," Clara said. "Although it was a lovely program. And when JT and Ruth sang "O Come, All Ye Faithful"...oh, my. That was so beautiful. JT is such a musician and our dear Ruth has the sweetest voice."

"I just wish Eli and Father and Matthew could have heard it." Elizabeth sighed.

"Perhaps the children can do it again on Christmas Day," Clara suggested.

"Yes." Elizabeth nodded. "Of course."

"Do you think the men are all right?" Jess asked suddenly.

"Oh, sure," Clara told her. "I expect they're home by now. Probably dividing up the meat."

They speculated on this for a while, but when they reached Clara's there was no sign of Asa's wagon. "I'll walk from here," Jess told Elizabeth as she climbed down with Clara. "You better hurry and get that wagon home before the rain comes."

"Thanks," Elizabeth called out. "I don't want to get stuck in the mud again." She waved to them, and trying not to feel too dismayed over the missing men, she kept the team moving quickly, getting home just as the sky opened up.

By the time she'd unhitched and tended to the team, checked on the rest of the livestock, and gotten the hens safely into the henhouse, she was soaked to the skin. At least she had a safe and dry house to go to, albeit a house with no children and no Eli. But she did have a dog. "Hurry up," she told Flax as they were going inside. "Let's get ourselves dry."

She tried not to worry about the hunters as she busied herself making a fire in the cookstove and quickly changing out of her wet clothes. Since she was home alone, she simply put on her nightie and a shawl. But she missed having her moccasins. She brewed a pot of tea and then made herself some porridge. Then, to help take the chill off her and the house and to help her wet clothes to dry, she made a fire in the fireplace.

She tried to stay busy, but her eyes kept wandering to the window. But the darkness came quickly, and it wasn't long until all she could see outside was inky blackness. And now her imagination started to run away with her. As she pulled the curtains closed and returned to her chair by the fireside, she was gripped with an oppressive sense of fear. She tried to focus on the baby blanket she was knitting for Matthew and Jess' baby, but she kept dropping stitches and finally set it aside.

Something was wrong. She knew it. The men would not purposely stay away this long. Not unless something was wrong. She had already considered the various possible reasons that the men were late coming home. She wasn't all that concerned about wild animals. She knew that Eli was savvy about hunting in the wilderness and that he was a good shot. A wagon breakdown could explain a delay. And Eli had told her that because of the terrain, they could only take the wagon partway to the area he planned to hunt. But most breakdowns were repairable within hours, so that would only slow them by a day at most.

The next explanation that came to her was sickness. She knew this was only because of what her family had suffered from cholera back in 1853. She had not heard of any cholera outbreaks in this part of the country, but she knew that could change in a moment—and that cholera could come on quickly and without warning. But finally she had to assure herself that her family was unlikely to be ravaged by cholera again. Wasn't that a bit like lightning striking twice?

And so the peril that concerned her more than anything else seemed to be Indians. Fueled by Martha Levine's bloody tale about the Indian attacks on the Rogue and at Battle Rock, it was easy to imagine a band of displaced warriors hiding out from the army. And how outraged might they be, knowing their women and children had been forced off their land by the invasive white men? In all fairness, it would be a righteous anger too. But what would be the dire consequences if these incensed warriors encountered five white hunters invading their territory and killing their game? She couldn't bear to imagine. All she could do was pray.

Chapter Twenty-Seven

Elizabeth was still praying by the fireside when she heard the clunk of the door's latch. Jumping up and just inches from grabbing the old shotgun hanging above the fireplace, she watched as the door swung open—and Eli walked in.

"Eli!" she cried out, running to him. "You're safe!"

"Shhh," he hushed her as he held her in his arms. "The children."

"The children are at Malinda's," she said, choking back sobs of relief. "I was so worried."

"I'm sorry." He smoothed her hair. "Oh, Elizabeth, it's so good to be home."

"Welcome!" Regaining composure, she stepped back and looked at his face. He had the beginning of a beard and a happy grin. "Are you hungry?"

He nodded, unlacing his soggy buckskin shirt. "And wet. And cold."

She hurried over to the fire, tossing a couple more logs on. "Get undressed here by the fire, and I'll bring you something dry to put on."

She bustled about, happy to be tending to her husband, happy to have him home. Before long he was in dry clothes and sitting by the fire with two fat slices of bread and butter and jelly and a cup of coffee. "Your eggs are almost ready," she called out.

"Eggs?" He sounded disappointed.

"You don't want eggs?"

"What about the chicks?"

She laughed as she spooned the scrambled eggs onto a plate. "We already saved the fertile eggs—nineteen altogether. The hens are sitting on them. We won't get any more fertile eggs until we have our own rooster." She handed him his plate. "Now I want to hear the whole story, from beginning to end, and try not to leave anything out."

Between hungry bites, Eli explained why their hunting party was late. "It started out to be an uneventful expedition. We got the wagon up to the campsite just like I planned, and the weather was with us. On the first day your father shot a bull elk." He took a sip of coffee. "We ate like kings that night. The next day we were hunting for a cow because the roasts are so good, but no luck. So on the third day we split up. Brady seemed worn out, so Asa suggested he stay at camp and be our cook. Your pa went with me, and Matthew and Will set out together. I got a real nice cow early in the day, but it took Asa and me until midday to pack it back to camp. I left Asa and Brady to tend to the meat, and I went back to where I'd seen sign of turkeys. By the time I got back it was close to dark, but I got three turkeys." He paused to eat his last bite of eggs and then looked at her.

"Still hungry?" she asked.

"We haven't eaten since breakfast."

"You keep telling me your story and I'll make you some more eggs."

"So night came on, and it was just Asa and Brady and me at camp. None of us had seen hide nor hair of Matthew and Will. And we didn't let on, but I know we were all feeling a mite concerned."

"Oh, my." She cracked an egg. "Were they all right?"

"You said to tell the story from beginning to end," he reminded her. "So it was dark and late, but I decided to set out with a lantern to look for them. I knew which direction they'd taken, but I finally realized it was useless and returned to camp." He paused to refill his coffee cup.

"Oh, dear." She handed him another piece of bread with butter and jam.

"The next morning, the day we'd meant to go home, Will and Matthew weren't back. So Asa and I set out on horses to look for them at daybreak." He shook his head as he chewed. "We all knew that Will was the least experienced outdoorsman, and I couldn't help but think maybe he'd gotten lost or hurt or something."

"Yes." She nodded as she put the second portion of eggs on his plate. "I was just thinking that too."

"Your pa and I were calling and whistling, and I'm sure we were both praying, but it wasn't until midday that we found them."

"Oh, good." She sat down in the chair across from him.

"Your brother had fallen down a small ravine and broken his leg. Will was carrying him out."

"Oh, dear!" Her hand flew to her mouth. "Poor Matthew. Is he all right?"

"He's fine. Well, excepting for that broken leg. But thanks to Will, it looks like he will heal up just fine."

"Thanks to Will?"

"Turns out that Will knows a little about doctoring." Eli grinned. "Now, bear in mind that Will made us swear to secrecy, but I think I can trust you with this."

"Of course." She leaned forward with interest.

"Seems that Will started out to be a doctor. But when he was studying medicine, he discovered that he didn't have the stomach for working on cadavers."

She grimaced. "Can't fault him for that."

"So he switched from medicine to law. But apparently he had enough medical training to know how to set a bone and make a splint. Not only that, but Will shot a couple of rabbits to roast for their supper the previous night—otherwise they'd have gone hungry. Matthew swears that Will saved his life."

"Thank goodness for Will."

"So we loaded Matthew on a horse, but because he was in pain, it was slow going. By the time we reached camp it was too late in the day to head out. So this morning, we ate a hasty breakfast and broke camp first thing. I could tell the weather was about to turn, and I wanted to get back before it let loose. We were making good progress. But then just as we were crossing a creek, the axle broke."

"Oh, dear."

"Unfortunately our best mechanic was indisposed. So with Matthew's guidance I was doing my best to repair it, but I have to say that Will stepped right up, and if it hadn't been for his help, we'd probably still be out there."

"Did you tell Will that?" she asked eagerly.

"Sure did. We all did. In fact, by the time we made it back to Asa's, we all decided to adopt Will into the family." He gave her a sleepy smile. "You all right with that?"

She laughed. "That's fine with me. I just hope that it makes him want to marry Malinda now."

Eli let out a yawn, and she took him by the hand. "If there's any more story to tell, it will have to wait until morning," she said firmly. "It is time for bed, my dear."

"You won't get any argument from me."

The gray dawn light was already coming in the bedroom window by the time Elizabeth awoke, but Eli was already up. She dressed quickly, hurrying out to get a fire going and the breakfast started, but when she got out there she discovered the cookstove was hot and a pot of coffee was sitting on the soapstone. She set out some breakfast things, and then, remembering that Ruth was not home, she went out to tend to the chickens. It was still too early for eggs to hatch, but it wouldn't be long. According to her calculations, a few days after Christmas the first chicks could begin to hatch.

As she returned to the house, she spotted Eli and Flax coming toward the house. Eli was carrying something big and bulky. She paused to see better and realized it was an evergreen tree.

"Merry Christmas," he called out as he got closer.

"A Christmas tree!" she exclaimed as she went out to meet him.

"I thought we could surprise the children."

"Perfect." She peered at the tree. "And that is a beauty."

He leaned over to kiss her, and she stroked his smooth cheek. "You appear to have found your razor."

He chuckled. "Well, after all, it's Christmas Eve."

"Speaking of that…" As they walked to the house, she told him about Malinda's Christmas Eve party. "She was hoping you would bring your guitar tonight."

"I'm happy to."

"I expect poor Matthew won't be able to play fiddle now."

"It's his leg that's broken, Elizabeth, not his arm."

While Eli made a stand for the tree, Elizabeth fixed breakfast. Then, just as he carried the tree into the house, she set a stack of pancakes on the table. "I thought you could put the tree right here," she pointed to the center of the room. "That way we can admire it from every direction."

After breakfast and chores, Eli drove their wagon over to her parents' to help Asa with the meat as well as to bring some home. Most of it would be smoked, but some would be shared with friends in the community, and the best section of roast as well as a turkey would be used for their Christmas dinner tomorrow. While Eli was gone, Elizabeth looked at the Christmas tree. As pretty as it was, it seemed to be in need of some decorations, but all of hers had been left behind in Kentucky. She went to her trunk and her sewing basket, and before long she had crafted a few things. And she left some materials out for when Ruth got home because she knew she would want to help. She also took time to wrap the presents she'd recently finished, placing them under the tree.

JT and Ruth got home in time for dinner and, as expected, they were both delighted to see the Christmas tree. However, they were even happier to see Eli. After they all ate tender elk steaks and fried potatoes together, JT went out to help Eli with chores, and using fabric, paper, ribbon, sticks, and string, Ruth and Elizabeth proceeded to decorate the tree.

When it was time to get ready for the Christmas Eve party, Elizabeth decided she and Ruth would wear their wedding dresses. And why not—this was a time to celebrate. The men had made it safely home, and this was their first Christmas in Oregon. Why shouldn't they all kick up their heels tonight? She was only slightly disappointed when she realized that because of the slate-colored afternoon skies, they would not be taking the wagon and team to Malinda's. In all likelihood they would be walking in the rain.

"Perhaps we should wear our old dresses to walk in," Elizabeth said to Ruth as she watched the rain pelting against the big window. "Maybe we could change at Malinda's."

Just then Eli came into the house. "I forgot to tell you that your pa left the cover on their wagon, and he's double teaming just like we did on our hunting trip. He wants us to all ride together over to Malinda's."

Ruth clapped her hands. "And we will sing all the way!"

Within the hour, she and the children were all bundled into the back of Asa's wagon. Jess and Clara had brought blankets and quilts to keep everyone comfortable. And Matthew, with his leg wrapped in wooden splints and resting on a pillow, seemed in fairly good spirits. "Pa and Brady made me a set of crutches," he told them.

Up front, Eli was sitting with Asa, and Brady, bless his heart, had insisted on helping as well. The plan was to deliver the family members to the barn, and then Brady would park the wagon around back. After that Brady planned to tend to the teams and stay with the wagon.

"But you could play music with us," JT told him when it was time to unload.

"Yes," Ruth insisted. "Please, come to the party, Brady."

He smiled at them. "Truth be told, I'd druther stay out here and take a nap in the wagon. I'm plum wore out from hunting."

Asa slapped Brady on the back. "That sounds like a right smart plan. When I bring out your plate of food, I might just take a nap out here myself."

The barn was well lit and bustling with guests by the time they got inside. A few musicians were just starting to warm up, but the music became much more lively after JT and Eli pulled out their guitars. Then, after Matthew got situated on a chair with his leg resting on a crate and tuned up his fiddle, the music got into full swing.

"I'm so relieved to see the hunters are home," Malinda said as she joined Elizabeth.

Elizabeth stared at her friend in wonder. Dressed in the pale green gown that had been meant for her wedding, Malinda's dark hair was piled on her head, and her pearl drop earrings glistened in the lamplight. "Oh, Malinda, you look as beautiful as a portrait!"

"Really?" Malinda frowned down at her dress. "Just this morning, Ruth told me that green was not the best color for a wedding dress. She said green meant 'ashamed to be seen.'"

Elizabeth made an uneasy laugh. "Oh, well, that's a silly old rhyme."

"Maybe. But I realized that I truly had been ashamed to be seen.

As you know, I didn't show my face in church last week. But this morning I thought, not only am I not ashamed to be seen, but I shall wear my wedding dress tonight. And I shall dance to my heart's content!"

"Good for you." Elizabeth patted her on the back. "And I suppose you've heard about Will's role in the hunting trip by now."

Malinda's eyebrows arched. "No…I haven't seen Will. Is he all right?"

"Yes. He's fine—"

"Come on, Ma." Bart grabbed his mother by the hand. "You promised to dance the first dance with me. Let's go."

Malinda laughed and waved as she and Bart hurried over to join in a circle dance that was just starting. Elizabeth went over to where her mother and Jess were standing on the sidelines, tapping their toes to the music and watching as merrymakers started the dance.

"Malinda hasn't seen Will yet," Elizabeth told them. "I wonder if he is even coming tonight."

"Maybe he wasn't invited," Jess said. "After all, Malinda made plans for this party while the men were out hunting."

"But wouldn't Jeremiah have told his father?"

Clara shook her head. "I expect we will have to wait to see."

"We don't have to wait long." Jess nodded toward the door.

Elizabeth glanced over her shoulder to see Will, dressed in party clothes, entering the barn behind the Holmeses and with Mrs. Taylor by his side. He looked around the barn, and then his eyes stopped as he spotted Malinda dancing with her son. And that was when he smiled. It was such a nice smile that it made Elizabeth giggle. Will still loved Malinda! She knew it.

When the dance ended, Will went over to greet Malinda, and the two of them disappeared. However, as Elizabeth took a turn dancing with Bart, she was not concerned. After a couple more dances, Will and Malinda reappeared in the barn, but now they went their separate ways. Malinda headed for the musicians, and Will, with a serious expression, returned to where the Holmeses and Mrs. Taylor were standing near the door. Was he going to leave and go home?

"Excuse me, folks," Eli said loudly from where he was standing with the other musicians. "We have an important announcement to make. If you could all gather round and give us your attention for a moment." Malinda was nowhere to be seen now. Had she gotten upset? Had she decided to put an end to this celebration? Surely not.

The partiers, caught off guard, grew quiet and looked at Eli. Meanwhile, Will was leading Reverend Holmes through the crowd. Once they got up front with the musicians, Will said something to Eli and then turned to face the guests.

"I have an announcement," Will spoke in a loud and clear voice. "As you all know, we had intended to hold a wedding here just one week ago. But that wedding was postponed. Now, if you would oblige us, we would like to hold that wedding tonight."

The surprised crowd began murmuring among themselves as Eli started to lead the musicians in playing a song—not one with a lively dancing tempo, but a quieter piece that seemed suitable for a wedding. At least for a barn wedding. And now Malinda, escorted by her older son, Todd, was coming forward and wearing the sweetest smile ever.

Reverend Holmes appeared to be prepared for this unexpected occasion, and opening his Bible, he proceeded to perform a simple ceremony. It wasn't long until the happy couple was repeating their wedding vows, and then the reverend pronounced them man and wife and the whole barn erupted into cheers and clapping.

Toasts were made and congratulations were shared, and the barn grew noisier and happier than ever. Young couples crowded around to dance while the older ones went to the house to fill their plates. All in all it was one of the merriest Christmas Eves that Elizabeth could remember.

Chapter Twenty-Eight

O n Christmas Day, Elizabeth's family gathered at her house as planned. They opened presents first, and for a while the room was noisy and lively, but it slowly quieted down. And compared to the previous evening it was a calm celebration. Clearly everyone was a little worn out. Especially the men, still recovering from their hunting excursion. But Christmas dinner was tasty, and no one went hungry. Afterward, Ruth and JT performed "O Come, All Ye Faithful" for the family, and then they all sang some familiar Christmas carols together. Finally Asa opened the Bible—but then he handed it to Brady.

The room grew quiet as Brady cleared his throat. Haltingly but clearly, he began to read. "And it came to pass...in those days, that there went out...a decree from..." But he had to stop when he reached the name Caesar Augustus. Smiling shyly, he handed the

Bible back to Asa while everyone clapped. And then Asa continued with the beloved story of the first Christmas.

⚜

Just a few days after Christmas, Ruth burst joyously into the house. "Mama, Mama, we have four baby chicks," she declared. "*Four!*"

Elizabeth paused from stirring biscuit batter. "That's wonderful, Ruthie. Do they appear to be in good health?"

"Yes. They are so sweet, Mama. Can I bring them in the house to show you?"

Elizabeth thought. "Perhaps not. But I will go out and see them right after breakfast."

When Elizabeth went out to survey their increasing flock, she could see that Ruth was right. All the chicks appeared to be sound and healthy. "Hopefully this is just the beginning," she told Ruth.

Seeing the baby chicks reminded Elizabeth that she needed to check on Mara and Rose. Between Christmas festivities and having the children on break from school, it had been difficult to slip away the last few days. But today JT was out helping Eli build the fence, and Elizabeth knew the perfect excuse to distract Ruth for an hour or so.

"We really have more eggs than we need," she told her. "And I don't plan on going to the mercantile until Friday. Why don't you take this basket over to share with Grandma and Grandpa? And perhaps you could take half of the eggs to Uncle Matthew and Aunt Jess. And of course, you will have to tell everyone about the new additions to our farm family."

Naturally Ruth was delighted to run this errand. She was barely out the door when Elizabeth began loading some food staples as well as the remainders of an elk roast into a basket. She hurried over to the cabin, but just as with each other time she'd gone, she felt uncertain as she went. What would happen if some of their Indian-hating neighbors found out? But as always, when she saw Mara's face as she opened the door, her fears evaporated.

"Come in," Mara insisted.

"Hello." Elizabeth stepped inside.

"Hello!" Rose declared loudly.

"Don't you look pretty!" She leaned down to stroke the little girl's head. Today her brown hair was smoothed into two tidy braids. Mara had obviously put the comb Elizabeth had given her to good use. She stood and began to unload the basket into Mara's arms and onto the crate that Mara was using as a small table. After the basket was empty, Elizabeth looked at Mara. "How are you?" she asked looking down at Mara's well-rounded tummy. "How is the baby?"

She rubbed her belly. "Good. We are good."

"Good. I'm glad to hear it."

Mara smiled faintly. "He is boy child."

Elizabeth blinked. "How do you know?"

"He kick like warrior."

"Oh." Elizabeth laughed. "It was my girl child that kicked most."

Now Mara laughed.

Elizabeth looked around the crowded space. "Do you need anything?"

Mara pressed her lips together then nodded. "Knife."

Elizabeth frowned. She had given her a knife already, though not a very good one. "I thought you had a knife."

"Yes." Mara nodded firmly. "I want *sharp* knife. Hunting knife."

Now Elizabeth felt slightly alarmed. Why would Mara need a sharp hunting knife? Surely she didn't plan to hurt anyone.

Now Mara went over to a corner of the room, picking up a skin of some sort. "I want to cut." She held it up. "To make moccasin for Rose."

"Oh." Elizabeth nodded eagerly. Now she understood. "Yes. That's a good idea. I will bring you a sharp knife."

"Thank you."

Elizabeth reached for the door. "I'll go get one and bring it right back," she promised. Mara thanked her again, and Elizabeth hurried back to the house. She wished she could send JT back on this errand, but she knew that was impossible. As it was, she wanted to get the knife to Mara before Ruth returned and got curious.

꧁꧂

In the next few days, nine more baby chicks hatched. "Thirteen chicks," Ruth proclaimed proudly on the last day of December. "That's a baker's dozen."

"And I suspect that's all we can hope for," Elizabeth told her. "The other eggs should probably be thrown out by now."

"But maybe the chicks are still coming," Ruth said hopefully.

"You can let them sit a bit longer if you like, but remember what a rotten egg smells like when it gets accidentally broken," Elizabeth warned.

Ruth wrinkled her nose. "I'll get rid of them tomorrow," she promised.

On the first day of 1858, Ruth buried the six unhatched eggs back behind the chicken coop. Elizabeth was only mildly surprised to see that Ruth had planted a little wooden cross over the freshly dug grave. Then at around noon, the four of them traipsed over to her parents' for a New Year's Day dinner. Matthew was still on crutches but seemed to be in a little less pain than previously, and Jess' waist was just starting to thicken, which reminded Elizabeth about Mara. After dinner, seeing that Matthew and Brady were involved in checkers and the others had gone out for a stroll, Elizabeth remained behind to help her mother with the dishes.

"I think Mara's baby is not too far from arriving," she said quietly.

"Oh?" Clara looked at her. "Do you plan to help her when it comes?"

"I don't know exactly." Elizabeth glanced over to the checkers players, but they were oblivious. "Certainly, I'm willing. But she wouldn't have any way to send for me. Rose is too small."

"Yes." Clara nodded. "That is a problem."

"I'm not sure what to do."

"In all likelihood she won't need help." Clara frowned.

"Unless…she does need help." Elizabeth scrubbed the pot harder. "And what about poor Rose? She will be terrified if her mother is in great pain. And what can she do to help?"

"Oh, dear. I hadn't even thought about that."

"If they were in a village, other women would be on hand to help Mara and watch out for Rose."

"That's true."

"Well, she is in a village," Elizabeth declared. "You and I will have to be her village."

"What will we do?"

"I'm not sure." Elizabeth tried to think of a plan. "You are more knowledgeable than I am about birthing babies. Is there any way to know how far along she is?"

"Does she know?"

"She didn't seem to. But just looking at her and how much larger she's gotten these past few weeks convinces me that it can't be too far off now. I suppose it could be as much as a month…or as little as a few days." She set the pot down. "I don't know. And it's been difficult to spend much time with her when the children are out of school. And I really do not want them to know about her."

"Why don't you take me to visit Mara," Clara suggested. "The first day the children are back in school, you and I will go."

Elizabeth agreed. She just hoped that Mara didn't have her baby before that. In the meantime, she would be praying faithfully for her.

The day for school to be back in session broke rainy and gloomy, and Elizabeth almost didn't want to send the children out in it. But they were eager to be back with their teacher and friends. And

JT put on his waxed coat, and Elizabeth insisted on wrapping her thick barn coat around Ruth before the two climbed up onto Molly. Sometimes she wondered if snow wasn't preferable to rain.

"Don't worry," Eli said as he joined her on the porch. "Those two are made of sturdy stuff. Besides, they have the heat from Molly to keep them warm. And once they get to school, Mrs. Taylor will have the stove cranked up and they will soon be toasty." He chuckled. "Or steamy."

She nodded. "I know you're right."

"Are you going to check on Mara this morning?"

"Yes." She peered in the direction of her parents' property, but thanks to the drizzling rain, she could barely see. "Although I won't blame Mother if she doesn't make it over."

"Come have a cup of coffee with me," he said. "Give her some time just in case she's coming."

It was pleasant to sit and share coffee with Eli. It had been some time since the two of them had been alone in the house. They were just finishing up when Clara arrived looking somewhat drenched. "Oh, Mother," Elizabeth exclaimed. "Let's get you in here and dried out." She peeled off the soggy coat and ushered her over to the chair by the fire, where she helped to remove her wet muddy boots. "At least your dress is dry."

"It really looks much worse than it is," Clara said as Eli handed her a cup of hot coffee. "But thank you."

After Clara was somewhat dried out and the rain shower had moved on, the two women bundled up and headed over to Mara's cabin. As they walked, Elizabeth confessed her fears to her mother. "I always wonder what would happen if someone in the settlement found out. Would they make trouble for Mara? Or burn down the cabin? Or come after Eli and the children and me?"

"Oh, goodness. I hope not."

"If you had seen the fear in Mara's eyes when she told me about how they burned down their cabin…you would understand."

"Poor dears."

Elizabeth knocked on the door, calling out to Mara. As soon as Mara opened the door, Elizabeth introduced her mother, explaining how Clara knew about babies and giving birth. At first Mara seemed uncertain, but as Clara began talking to her, Mara visibly relaxed.

"Can I take Rose outside with me?" Elizabeth asked Mara. "While you two talk?"

Mara looked unsure, but then nodded. "Put on your moccasins," she told Rose. Elizabeth watched as the little girl hurried to find her shoes.

"You made them," she said to Mara as she helped Rose tie the laces. "They are very nice." Soon Elizabeth and Rose were outside exploring and getting some fresh air. Rose seemed to appreciate this time, and Elizabeth was relieved that her mother was with Mara. She completely trusted her mother's wisdom and intuition when it came to things like health or childbirth.

After a while, Clara called them back inside, explaining to Elizabeth that Mara was close to giving birth. "It could be today or a week from today. But I don't think it will be much longer."

Elizabeth nodded, taking this in. "How does she feel about giving birth…alone? Or with only Rose here?"

Clara smiled at Mara. "Mara has agreed to come with me. She and Rose will stay with your father and me until her time comes."

Elizabeth was surprised. "Really? She wants to stay with you?"

Mara looked at Elizabeth with frightened eyes. "My mother… she die…when I birthed." Mara put a protective hand on Rose's head. "No good be alone."

Soon they packed up a few things and walked back toward Elizabeth's, and from there Clara, Mara, and Rose continued. Elizabeth prayed as she watched them walking through the soggy field. She prayed for all of them.

Then she went home and finished the baby blanket she'd been making for Jess' baby. However, she knew there was plenty of time to make another one before April. Mara would need it sooner. Elizabeth made a few other baby things as well. Nothing overly frilly or silly, just practical and warm.

Three days later, Mara gave birth to a small but healthy baby boy.

Chapter Twenty-Nine

January came with exceptionally mild weather that made the newest of the settlers imagine that it was spring. Mara and her baby, Charles Jr., continued to thrive, and after several days, the family of three moved back to their tiny cabin, where for the next couple of weeks, Elizabeth checked on them daily. But still there had been no sign of Charles Sr., and Elizabeth began to fear that harm may have come to the young man.

When February came, it brought enough rain and wind to down a number of trees and close the school for a few days. Not only that, it postponed Jeremiah and Mahala's wedding.

"The good news is that this delay has given Jeremiah and Will a chance to put some nice finishing touches on the cabin," Malinda told Elizabeth as they had tea at Malinda's house. It was the first time Elizabeth had been off of her property for nearly two weeks, and it was much needed.

"Have Will's carpentry skills improved?" Elizabeth asked curiously.

"Ever since that hunting trip, everything in Will's life seems to have improved," Malinda told her. "Truly, your father, brother, and husband were like a tonic for Will."

"I'm glad to hear it." This was the first time they'd been able to catch up since the surprise wedding on Christmas Eve. "I'm sure Will told you how he saved my brother's life."

Malinda waved her hand. "Oh, to hear Will talk, it was nothing special at all. But Jess took me aside after church a few weeks ago and thanked me. She told me what happened—in detail." She smiled proudly. "I felt as if I had married a real hero."

"You did."

"Well, he never would have had a chance to be a hero if the men in your family hadn't taken him in like they did. I am so thankful."

"So your marriage agrees with you?"

Malinda nodded. "Oh, there's some adjusting, I'll admit that. Will and I both have strong personalities. And as you know, I can be a bit stubborn at times. But I believe we are making progress." She seemed to be studying Elizabeth now. "How about you? How are things with you and Eli?"

Elizabeth smiled. "I have no complaints."

Malinda frowned. "And you are feeling well?"

Elizabeth looked down at her teacup.

"Elizabeth?"

She looked up and shrugged. "I've been a little under the weather. I blamed it on the weather. Wasn't it ghastly? Although Eli is using the fallen trees for our—"

"Don't change the subject, Elizabeth." Malinda peered at her. "You look pale and drawn to me. Are you sure that you are not unwell?"

Elizabeth took in a deep breath. "If you must know…and only if I can trust you."

"You can trust me, Elizabeth. I may be a bit willful and outspoken at times, but I am loyal to my best friend."

"All right." Elizabeth sighed. "I haven't said anything to Eli yet. And Mother doesn't even know. But I suspect I am with child."

"Oh, Elizabeth!" Malinda reached for her hand. "I'm so happy for you."

She made a weak smile. "Thank you. But I don't remember feeling so ill with JT or Ruth. My stomach seems to be upset every morning. In fact, that is what made me first suspect I was pregnant."

"I wasn't sick with my first three children, but oh, my, I couldn't keep anything down for the first three months with Susannah. John got quite worried."

"But you got better."

"Yes. By my fourth month I was hungry as a horse."

They visited for a while longer, and when Elizabeth left, she felt encouraged. Walking home in the sunshine, she tried to imagine what it would be like to have a baby in her arms next fall. She wondered what Eli would think. Or her children. Ruth would be thrilled. And Jess would be happy to find out that her baby would have a cousin close to the same age. Still, she was determined not to tell anyone until she'd reached her third month. If Malinda hadn't pressed her so, she never would have told her. As it was, she felt she could trust her.

On Saturday, everyone gathered at the church to celebrate the marriage of Mahala Flanders to Jeremiah Bramford. Elizabeth couldn't help but chuckle at the irony of this match. She remembered when she'd first met the Bostonians and how she'd felt they were stuffy and superior. And when she'd met the Flanders, she'd felt they were a bit loud and rough. Who would have guessed back then that the oldest Bramford son would wed the oldest Flanders girl? Yet here the two young people were, pledging their vows before God and their families and friends.

Afterward a lively potluck celebration was held at Will and

Malinda's barn, and it seemed that everyone within a fifteen-mile radius was in attendance. Elizabeth danced with her husband and children and father, finally sitting out as the evening was drawing to an end. "How are you feeling?" Malinda asked with some concern. "You look a little pale."

"To be honest, my stomach is feeling a little sour," Elizabeth admitted. "Usually I get over this by midday."

"Just rest and take it easy," Malinda said. "I'll go get you some tea. That might soothe your belly."

Unfortunately, the tea didn't help. And by the time Eli was driving their wagon home, Elizabeth was feeling quite ill. To her dismay, Ruth seemed to be sick too. "Do you think you girls ate something bad?" Eli asked as he helped her into the house. JT was helping Ruth.

"I really don't know," she said weakly. "But please see to Ruth. I can take care of myself." With wobbly legs, she got a pot from the kitchen and went to her bed. If Ruth were not feeling ill, Elizabeth would assume this was related to her pregnancy. But as she continued to be violently ill, and knowing that Ruth was sick as well, she feared it was something more serious. The next hours passed in a painful blur.

By the time Elizabeth felt able to sit up in bed and sip some broth, it was late in the afternoon of the following day, and her mother was sitting with her. "How is Ruth?" Elizabeth asked in a hoarse voice.

"Ruth is just fine now. She's already eating solids," her mother assured her. "But I believe you both ate something tainted at the wedding potluck."

"Oh." Elizabeth let out a weak sigh.

"Unfortunately for you, it seems to have hit you harder than Ruth. Eli was so worried that he sent JT for me early this morning." She spooned more broth into her.

"Thank you for coming."

"I sent JT to check on Jess," Clara continued. "I was worried that in her condition she could be in trouble if she'd eaten something tainted. Thankfully, she is fine."

"Oh, I'm so glad to hear that."

Clara reached for Elizabeth's hand now. She had tears in her eyes. "But you, my darling, did not fare so well."

"What?" Elizabeth looked curiously into her mother's face.

"You lost your baby, Lizzie."

Elizabeth took in a jagged breath and then looked down at her lap as tears began to roll down her cheeks. They both just sat there in silence for a while.

"I'm so sorry, dear. I didn't even know. Nor did Eli."

Elizabeth looked back up. "Did you tell him?"

"I'm sorry if that was wrong. I just assumed he knew."

"No, I hadn't told him yet."

Clara squeezed her hand. "He is sad. But he was so worried about you…well, I think he's so relieved that you're all right." Now she started to cry, and they both just hugged and cried.

❧

It took a full week before Elizabeth felt like leaving the house. Eli and the children were thoughtful and helpful, but a cloud seemed to hang over her head. Finally on a sunny Monday in March, she forced herself to go and check on Mara and her children. Clara had been checking on them, and Eli had been taking them food, but Elizabeth knew she was long overdue for a visit.

Mara greeted her warmly, inviting her in to her tiny cabin. She showed her baby Charles, and wrapped in the blanket Elizabeth had knit, he was growing nicely. Rose's hair was neatly braided. Despite their rather impoverished conditions, this little family seemed fairly content.

"I am sorry," Mara said quietly. "Clara told me."

Elizabeth just nodded.

"I have something." Mara turned now, going over to a corner of the room and then returning with something in her hand. "I make for you." She held out a pair of deerskin moccasins. "You wear. You get better."

Elizabeth hugged Mara. "Thank you. I will wear them. And I will get better."

As Elizabeth walked back to her house, she wondered at the strength Mara had to live in that cabin with her two young children, hoping that her husband was going to return to her. But the more Elizabeth considered the missing Charles Sr., the less she felt that he was likely to come back…or that he was even alive. And yet Mara was not giving up.

She looked at the moccasins Mara had painstakingly made for her. Mara was right—she would wear them, and she would get better. Like Mara, she would become strong again. And God willing, she and Eli would have another baby…someday. In the meantime, spring was coming on with lush meadow grass and bright green foliage and wildflowers blooming profusely along the river. Elizabeth's fruit tree seedlings had fared well over the mild winter and would be ready to transplant in the fall. Only about a fourth of them didn't survive, and that was better than she had expected. The other good news was that Goldie would calve by summer, and Molly would foal in the late fall. Besides that, their chicken flock was increasing regularly. Their farm was growing.

In mid-April, Jess delivered her first baby, a precious little girl whom they named Maude Ruby. Elizabeth and Ruth went over to visit the next day, taking a baby blanket and a few other things Elizabeth had made for the new addition to their family. Clara welcomed them into the house, holding her finger over her lips. "Jess is sleeping, but the baby is awake." Soon they were taking turns holding and admiring the newborn.

"She's so tiny," Ruth said as she held her new cousin, examining her fingers.

"So were you once," Elizabeth told her.

"And so was your mother," Clara said. "We all start out that small."

"Her hair is dark like Jess'," Ruth said.

"How is Jess?" Elizabeth asked her mother.

"Just fine. She did very well."

"How is Matthew?" she asked.

Clara chuckled. "I think he's recovering. He was mighty thankful to get outside this morning."

"What's wrong with Uncle Matthew?" Ruth asked.

"It's not easy being a father for the first time," Elizabeth explained. "But he'll get used to it."

"Will you have a baby, Mama?"

"God willing." Elizabeth nodded. "In his time." And as Elizabeth rocked her tiny niece, she did not feel in any hurry to have another baby. Really, there was so much to do with spring coming on. She would much prefer to put her energy into improving their farm.

❧

On Sunday, they went to church as usual. But after the service, as they were visiting out in the sunshine, Elizabeth overheard some of the men talking. She could only hear bits of their conversation, but she was certain they were speaking about Indians. Excusing herself from the women she was chatting with, she went over to where Eli was talking with Asa.

"Excuse me," she said. "But the men over there, the ones gathered around Mr. Walters, seem to be talking about Indians. I couldn't catch all of it, but Mr. Walters seems to believe there are Indians nearby. And the way he was talking, it almost sounded like he wanted to round them up."

Eli's brow creased. "Mr. Walters always seems to be looking for a fight."

"Do you think he may have seen Mara? I know she takes the

children out for sunshine now and then. She used to be afraid to go out in daylight, but she's gotten more comfortable lately."

"I suppose it's possible she's been seen," Eli conceded. "The Walters' farm is out past ours, and they go by our property on their way to town. But the way the cabin is placed, Walters would have to be well on our land in order to see Mara—unless she's wandered out a ways."

"I doubt she goes too far from the cabin," Elizabeth said. "And I'll warn her to be more careful."

"In the meantime, why don't we see if we can find out what Walters is talking about," Asa told Eli. "Maybe we can put a lid on it before it starts to smoke."

Elizabeth thanked them and casually walked over to where the older ladies were visiting. "Good day, Georgia and Martha," she said politely. "What do you women think of this glorious spring weather?"

"We were just saying how lovely it's been," Georgia told her. "I have daffodils and tulips blooming."

"Daffodils and tulips?" Elizabeth was surprised. "Where did you get bulbs?"

"I brought a few when we came out here. They have multiplied over the years. I'll be happy to share some bulbs with you in the fall."

"Oh, that would be delightful."

Elizabeth looked at Martha. "Have you had word from Charles?"

Martha sadly shook her head.

"I'm sure you must miss him. I want you to know that he's been in my prayers."

"Thank you," Martha told her. "I appreciate that more than you know."

"You are fortunate to be blessed with three fine sons," Georgia told her.

Martha brightened. "I s'pect you've heard that my Jacob and Belinda Bramford have set their wedding date for June," she said to Elizabeth.

"Yes, Malinda told me. That's wonderful news."

"June is such a nice time for a wedding," Georgia said.

"And now my youngest boy, Joseph, appears to be setting his cap for Belinda's younger sister, Amelia. So perhaps it won't be long until we have another wedding in the family."

"I still remember the day you ladies came to tea at my house," Elizabeth told them. "I hope you will come out again sometime."

"You just name the time and day, and I will be happy to come," Georgia said.

Martha nodded. "I would like that too." She lowered her voice. "Not everyone understands my…my suffering."

Elizabeth thought about Baby Charlie, as she'd taken to calling the infant. Such a sweet baby, contented and happy and getting cuter by the day. What would Martha think if she knew what she was missing out on?

"I just got to thinking, Elizabeth," Georgia said suddenly. "If you like flowers, you might want to come take a start from my violas."

"You have violas?"

"Oh, my, do I have violas!" She glanced at Martha.

"Yes, she certainly does. They grow in profusion behind the parsonage."

"They like the shade," Georgia explained.

"I would love to get some violas," Elizabeth told her.

"Why don't you get some today?" Georgia urged her. "No time like the present."

"And I should be getting home by now," Martha said. "Mrs. Taylor and I have invited the Prescotts for Sunday dinner."

Elizabeth told Ruth to let Eli know that she'd be right back, and she and Georgia hurried to the parsonage, where she was soon handed a trowel. After she dug up a good start of violas, Georgia gave her an old tin to contain them. "Thank you!" Elizabeth sniffed the fragrant blooms. "I know exactly where I'll plant these." Now she studied Georgia carefully. "Can I trust you with something that is extremely confidential?" she asked suddenly.

"I certainly hope so. I have not broken a confidence yet." She peered curiously at Elizabeth. "Is something wrong, dear?"

Elizabeth took a deep breath and said a silent prayer, but somehow she felt this was the right thing to do. "Georgia, I have been hiding Charles' Indian wife on my property."

Georgia blinked as her hand flew up to her mouth. "Oh, my word!"

"Her name is Mara, and she is a dear girl. She speaks English and was educated at a mission. I can understand why Charles fell in love with her."

"Oh, my…oh, my…" Georgia glanced around as if worried someone could be listening, but it was clear they were alone.

"Mara told me that Charles left to find gold, and then some of the settlers burned down the cabin that she and her daughter, Rose, were staying in. I found them in early December. They were living outside and suffering considerably. Mara had her second child—"

"She has two children?"

Elizabeth nodded solemnly. "Rose is about three or four. Baby Charlie will be four months soon. They are dear children. A sweet little family. But I am in constant fear for them." Now she explained what she'd overheard Mr. Walters saying.

Georgia scowled. "That man has always been a troublemaker."

"The reason I'm speaking to you of this is because I had hoped that I could somehow win Martha over by showing her these darling grandchildren. I thought perhaps she could be of some help to Mara." Elizabeth held up her hands. "I really don't know what else to do. It's not that Eli and I mind having Mara and the children on our property. But I worry they are not safe. I know Mara worries too. And hearing Mr. Walters just now…" She shook her head.

"That is certainly a conundrum. To think you've had them with you all these months, Elizabeth…and no one knew?"

"My parents know. And my brother and Jess know. But I haven't told my children. I feel that's too dangerous."

Georgia nodded.

"You know Martha much better than I do, Georgia. How do you think she would react if I presented her with her grandchildren?"

Georgia pursed her lips. "Martha has a good heart. I am certain she would love her grandchildren."

"But would she try to take them from Mara?" Elizabeth studied Georgia closely, looking intently into her gray eyes.

"I do not know for sure. I suspect it would depend…"

"Depend on what?"

"Her impressions of Mara. If she felt the girl was a savage or not fit to be a mother—"

"Mara is a wonderful mother. She loves her children dearly. I am certain she would die for them."

"Hopefully she will not have to."

"Do you think that if I could present Mara and her children to Martha in a way that would show Martha they are good people… would Martha consider helping them or taking them in? With two of her three grown sons living so nearby, perhaps Mara would be safer. And if they were out in the open, it wouldn't appear as it might now…as if we are hiding refugees." Elizabeth hated to think of what men like Walters might do if they were all worked up into an indignant rage—not only to Mara and her children, but to Elizabeth's family too.

Georgia grasped Elizabeth's hand. "I think your plan could work. But I will discuss it with Roland first. Do you mind?"

"I want to believe he can be trusted with this confidence, but I do not know him as well as I know you."

"The reverend can be a bit stern at times, but he is wholly trustworthy, Elizabeth. I promise you."

Elizabeth knew she could trust Georgia with this dilemma. But as she returned to rejoin her family, she silently prayed that God would help all of them to find a good solution for Mara and her children. Somehow that little family needed to carve a life for themselves in this hostile frontier—a land that had once belonged to their ancestors. However, Elizabeth knew that the odds were probably against this plan. The Indians had been removed, many were dead or dying, and still people like Mr. Walters continued to brim with hatred. It did not bode well for Mara and her children.

Chapter Thirty

On Monday morning, as soon as her children were on their way to school, Elizabeth paid a visit to Mara. After she shared a loaf of bread and some venison and played with the children, she turned to Mara with a serious expression. "We need to talk," she told her.

Mara made a worried frown and Elizabeth looked at Rose. "Can you stay here with Baby Charlie while your mother and I go outside to talk?"

Rose nodded solemnly.

Elizabeth smiled at her, patting her head. "You are a good big sister."

Now Rose smiled.

Outside, Elizabeth quietly told Mara about the conversation she'd overheard and how Eli and Asa had learned more. "It's possible that some of the men have seen you. Do you ever go far from here?"

"I gather. Along creek." She looked uncertain.

"You *must* be careful. These men are dangerous."

"I know."

Elizabeth sighed. "Of course you know." She put her hand on Mara's shoulder. "It's just that I worry about you."

"You good friend."

She nodded. "I have a plan, Mara. But you will have to help me."

"Me help you?"

Now Elizabeth explained how she wanted Mara and her children to look and act more like white people, but even as she said this she felt embarrassed. What right did she have to tell Mara how to live? But Mara's life could be in danger if she didn't. "I wish there was another way, Mara. But I'm afraid there is not."

Mara looked down at her hand-me-down dress. "I wear white-woman clothes."

"Yes. But we must do more. And we must work on your English. We have to do this to show the white man that you are a good mother."

"I am good mother."

"I know you are." Elizabeth stifled her frustration over the unfairness of this. "Will you do this with me?"

Mara looked confused. "I do not know how."

"I will help you. And my mother will help you too."

Mara agreed, and so for the next few days, Elizabeth and Clara took turns helping Mara and her children to fit in better with white society. They altered one of Elizabeth's dresses, a pretty blue calico, to fit Mara. They taught Mara how to comb and pin up her hair. They gave her shoes and a shawl and a new bonnet to wear. They altered one of Ruth's dresses as well—a red-and-white gingham that Ruth had outgrown. All the time they spent with Mara and her children, they insisted that Mara practice her English skills, speaking full sentences and practicing good grammar. Sometimes Mara complained, but all it took was one reminder that her efforts could very well save her children's lives, and she would comply.

By the end of the week, Mara had made good progress, and Elizabeth felt hopeful. After church on Sunday, she consulted briefly with Georgia. Encouraged that her plan was sound, Elizabeth then invited Georgia and Martha to come for tea on Thursday. She wished she could take more time, but seeing Mr. Walters and his cronies clustered together again warned Elizabeth that time might be of the essence.

Elizabeth and Clara had three more days to work on refining Mara. On Wednesday morning, they had a mock tea party. By now Mara was well aware that she would be meeting Charles' mother tomorrow. And she was trying her best to cooperate. By the time they finished, Mara not only poured tea and folded her napkin properly, she managed to converse a bit about the weather as well.

"I am so proud of you," Elizabeth told Mara as she walked her back to her cabin.

"Thank you," Mara said quietly.

"You will do just fine tomorrow," Elizabeth assured Mara before she left. "Just be sure to be ready before my mother comes to fetch you in the morning. Just like today."

"I will be ready," she promised.

The plan was to have Mara and the children at Elizabeth's before the ladies arrived. Mara would wait in the bedroom while Elizabeth and Clara had the children in the main room. As she walked back home, Elizabeth prayed that the plan would work.

᠃᠃᠃

"Welcome," Elizabeth said as she opened the door to let the ladies inside. "My mother and two young friends are joining us today." She led Georgia and Martha inside, and Clara greeted them from where she was sitting in the rocker, holding Baby Charlie.

"This is Rose," Elizabeth told Georgia and Martha. Rose looked very sweet in the red gingham dress. Her hair was in two neat braids, each tied with a red ribbon. On her feet were the moccasins Mara had made, but even that did·not seem too unusual since many of the settlers' children went barefoot. And Ruth often wore her moccasins. "Rose, this is Mrs. Holmes and Mrs. Levine."

"Hello, Mrs. Holmes. Hello, Mrs. Levine." Rose repeated her lines just as she'd been instructed, even adding the curtsy Clara had taught her to do.

"Hello, Rose," Georgia said. "A pretty name for a pretty girl."

"Hello, young Rose," Martha said with a curious expression. "Where did you come—"

"Now you must come meet my little one," Clara called out. "Come and say hello."

"Oh, my," Georgia gushed as she went to see him. "What a beautiful baby!"

"Goodness," Martha exclaimed. "This cannot be your grandbaby, Clara. He is much too big."

"You're right, the young lad is not my grandchild," Clara confirmed. "But isn't he adorable?"

"May I hold him?" Georgia asked eagerly.

"Certainly." Clara stood and passed the cherub to her. "He is a most good-tempered baby."

"Where did these children come from?" Martha asked. "Are their parents new to the settlement? I haven't heard of any newcomers lately."

"They are not new to the settlement," Elizabeth told her.

"What's your name, little one?" Georgia cooed to the baby.

"This is Baby Charlie." Elizabeth watched Martha as she said this, but the woman did not seem to register any recognition at all. "He is four months old."

"He is a doll," Georgia gushed. "A sweet little doll."

"I'm confused," Martha told Elizabeth. "You say their parents aren't new. But I don't recall these children. They didn't come with the wagon train families last fall."

"Would you like to meet their mother?" Elizabeth asked, trying not to feel too nervous.

"Certainly." Martha nodded.

Elizabeth went to the bedroom door, slowly opening it and giving Mara an encouraging smile, but she could see a look of pure terror in her eyes. "Come and meet some friends." She linked her arm in Mara's, leading her out into the room. Once again, Martha didn't seem to understand.

"Georgia and Martha, I want to present Mara to you. Mara, this is Mrs. Holmes and Mrs. Levine."

Mara stepped forward just as she'd been taught, extending her hand to Georgia first. "I am pleased to make your acquaintance, Mrs. Holmes," she said in a shaky voice.

Georgia clasped her hand and smiled warmly. "I am pleased to meet you too, Mara. You have lovely children."

"Thank you." Now Mara extended her hand to her mother-in-law. "I am pleased to make your acquaintance, Mrs. Levine."

"Pleased to meet you too." Martha's brow creased. "But I did not catch your last name."

"I'm sorry," Elizabeth said. "I forgot to mention it. This is Mara Levine."

Martha's face visibly paled, and Clara hurried over to ease her into a chair by the table. "We did not wish to shock you," she said kindly. "But we felt it was time for you to become acquainted with your grandchildren and your daughter-in-law."

"I…I…don't know what to say." Martha's eyes were wide as she first stared at Mara and then Rose and finally the baby. "*Charlie*," she whispered. "For Charles." She looked back at Mara. "Where is Charles?"

"Charles went to find gold," Mara said simply.

"He left last summer," Elizabeth explained. "He wanted to get gold in order to care for his family. But Mara has not heard from him since then."

Martha looked at Charlie again. "The baby looks like his father."

"Mara and her children have been staying on my property," Elizabeth explained as she poured Martha a cup of tea. She glanced at Mara. "Perhaps you'd like to take Rose to see the chickens now." They had already worked this out. Elizabeth didn't want Rose to be exposed to all of their conversation. As soon as the two were out of earshot, Elizabeth told Martha about how settlers had burned Mara and Rose out of their home last fall.

"Naturally, Charles wouldn't know that his little family was homeless. I doubt that he even knew that Mara was with child. I'm sure if he did know, he would return to care properly for them."

"Yes," Martha said quickly. "I'm sure he would. Charles was always a good boy."

"I haven't minded having Mara here with me," Elizabeth said. "I consider her a friend, and her children are delightful."

"You have lovely grandchildren," Georgia told Martha. "Look at this little fellow."

"May I?" Martha asked.

Georgia handed over the baby, and soon Martha was talking and cooing to him. The other women exchanged hopeful glances.

"As you can see, Mara is a fine woman," Elizabeth told her. "A daughter-in-law that anyone could be proud of."

"I certainly would be," Clara said.

"She is an Indian," Martha said stubbornly.

"That's true," Elizabeth agreed. "And her people have been driven off their land by the white man. If men like Mr. Walters have their way, Mara and Rose and Charlie will be driven off as well. Or worse." She locked eyes with Martha. "It's possible that if they are discovered they will be burned out of their home again. And they might not survive this time."

"But that's wrong," Martha declared. "These children have Charles' blood in them. They cannot be treated like that. I won't allow it."

"Perhaps if we band together," Clara said. "If we could get enough settlers to stand by you and your grandchildren and daughter-in-law, perhaps we could stand up to the likes of Mr. Walters."

"Where is Charles in all this?" Martha asked in a slightly desperate tone. "He should be here to protect his family."

"I agree," Elizabeth said. "But perhaps he felt it was more important to provide for them. Mara said that he wanted to get enough money to get them away from here…to take them someplace safe."

With the baby still in her arms, Martha stood, looking at all of them with a defiant expression. "They will be safe with me."

"All of them?" Elizabeth asked. "Because I have promised Mara that I will let no one take her children from her. I want you to understand that."

"And I back her on it," Clara said.

"As do I," Georgia added. "And the reverend too."

Martha frowned but then looked back into her grandson's chubby face. "Yes. I will take all of them. I'll take them home today. My sons and I will keep them safe until Charles returns."

Elizabeth took in a sharp breath. She knew it was possible—maybe even likely—that Charles would never return. However, she did not intend to say this. Mostly she was relieved. Mara and her children would be cared for and protected—by their own kin.

"Georgia Holmes," Martha said a bit sharply. "You were in on this from the very beginning, weren't you?"

Georgia made a sheepish smile.

"That is why you insisted I drive the wagon out here today, wasn't it? You don't really have an ingrown toenail, do you?"

"I must confess…I told a falsehood. Please forgive me. It was for a good reason."

"Shall we load them up and go home now?" Martha asked.

"First we will have tea," Elizabeth told her. "Mara and Rose have been looking forward to it." She nodded to her mother. "Can you play hostess for a bit? I'll go ask Eli to get Mara's things loaded into Martha's wagon."

Elizabeth felt like dancing as she went out to where Eli was working to level a piece of land where their barn would eventually be located. "It worked!" she called out to him. "Martha is taking all three of them home with her."

Eli grinned. "I knew if anyone could pull that off it would be you, Elizabeth."

"Would you mind gathering up Mara's things from the cabin? She promised to have them packed up and ready to go."

"I would be happy to." He came over and hugged her. "Job well done, Elizabeth."

As she returned to the house, she knew that the job was not really done. Her friendship with Mara and her children would continue. She would continue to support this little family, helping them to fit into school and church and life in their town for as long as they remained here.

Chapter Thirty-One

In early June, shortly after school broke for the summer, Belinda Bramford and Jacob Levine were married. By the time of the wedding, everyone in the settlement was aware that Mara and her children were living at the Levines'. Reactions varied. Some settlers accepted them. Some seemed unsure. And a few, like Mr. Walters, were antagonistic. But Elizabeth was glad to see that Mara and the children attended the wedding in the church as well as the reception in Malinda's barn.

"I want you to meet my best friend, Malinda," Elizabeth told Mara as she linked arms with her and walked her over to where Malinda was standing with Will. Elizabeth made introductions, even introducing the children. And Mara, still practicing her English, graciously shook their hands.

"Mara and her children lived with us for a while," she said even

though Malinda was well aware of this by now. "And I still miss her."
She grinned at Mara. "We were neighbors, weren't we?"

"And friends," Mara said simply. "We miss you too."

"Well, now you will have my daughter for your neighbor," Will
said in a friendly tone. "Belinda has spoken warmly of you."

"Belinda is a good girl." Mara smiled. "She is good with children too."

"She certainly loves your children," Malinda said. "She talks
about them all the time."

Mara nodded down to Rose. "She made the dress for Rose."

"Very pretty," Malinda said.

Now Elizabeth changed the subject, telling Malinda that Goldie
had calved several days ago. "A healthy heifer."

"I'm glad to hear it," Malinda told her. "I've had two heifers and
a bull this spring."

"Do you have any interest in selling the bull?" Elizabeth asked.

"Now, now, ladies…" Will held his hands up. "Is this a wedding
or a livestock auction?"

They both laughed, and soon they were joining in with the merriment, eating and dancing and congratulating the happy newlyweds. However, Elizabeth felt determined that somehow, between
her father and brother and herself, her family would pool their
resources to purchase that bull from Malinda.

<hr/>

As summer progressed, the town expanded. Will Bramford
built a law office next to the mercantile, and because of his medical
knowledge and the community's needs, it doubled as a pharmacy.
On the other side of the mercantile, which now had a lean-to on
one side for a post office, a large building was going up. This impressive structure would house a hotel and restaurant that would be run
by Ruby and Doris before the year was out. Down the street a ways
was Flanders' Blacksmith, and next to that was the new livery stable

that Ezra Flanders was running with his new brother-in-law, Julius Prescott.

In just one year's time, their settlement had grown dramatically. And if the rumors were true, it would be twice as big by next year. As happy as Elizabeth was about these changes, she was even happier about a tiny change going on inside of her. She'd kept the news of her pregnancy within the confines of her family at first, but by early fall, her midsection had increased enough that people in town had begun to suspect her family would be growing too.

In mid-October two delightful surprises occurred. Actually, one was not a complete surprise, although it did arrive earlier than expected. Molly had a foal—a sweet little filly that Ruth named Pansy and claimed as her own. The second surprise was that Charles Levine came home. However, Charles was probably more surprised than anyone when he discovered that Mara was living with his mother.

"And when Charles saw his children," Martha excitedly told Elizabeth at the mercantile, "well, he was just beside himself. He had no idea he had a son." Then she happily boasted that Charlie, who wasn't even a year old yet, was trying to walk. "And Rose has been helping Mara with the garden, and I've never had such produce growing." She grasped Elizabeth's hands and squeezed them. "Thank you, dear."

"Thank you," Elizabeth told her.

By late October, the hotel was finished, and Doris and Ruby began to get settled in. "We made good money in Empire City," Ruby told everyone as they all enjoyed a happy reunion dinner at Eli and Elizabeth's house.

"But we never felt at home there," Doris finished for her.

"Doris had a suitor though," Ruby teased as she bounced Baby Maude on her knee. "A businessman named George Johnston. And I would not be surprised if we have a hardware store here by next summer."

"We told a lot of folks at Empire City about our plans to come help develop this town with our friends," Doris said. "But the problem was, this town does not have a name." She frowned. "Don't you locals think it's about time to name this place?"

"As a matter of fact, that's been a hot topic in these parts," Asa told her.

"Some families want to name it after themselves," Matthew said glumly.

"Like the Walters family," Ruth said.

"And they're not a real nice bunch," JT added.

"Then there's the Thompsons," Eli said. "They claim they were here first."

"Naturally, it's causing some arguments," Elizabeth explained.

"Some want to name it after the river, but seems there's a town east of here already going by that, although they're not incorporated."

"Not that we want to incorporate," Asa said.

"Some folks are trying to name it after plants or trees or fish, but that hasn't gone over too well," Clara explained.

"I suggested the name Riverside at the last meeting," Elizabeth said. "That's one thing most of us have in common...the river."

"I like that," Ruby said. "Riverside."

"Unfortunately, the Walters and Thompson families didn't like it," Eli said.

"And so the debate goes on."

"Why don't they put it to a vote?" Ruby asked.

"Good question," Asa told her. "That's what we keep encouraging them to do."

"Mr. Walters is afraid he'll lose," Ruth said.

"Godfrey Walters goes to our school," JT told her. "He's always bragging that his dad runs this town."

"Maybe someone should challenge him on that." Ruby pointed to Asa. "Like you. I think you'd make a good mayor." She looked around the crowded room. "Anyone else here willing to vote for Asa?"

Naturally, they all raised their hands.

Asa laughed. "Well, I don't think we need to be concerned about that. Our nameless town isn't big enough to need a mayor yet."

"Give it time and it will," Doris said. "From what we heard, Empire City has grown like a weed."

"That has to do with its location," Eli pointed out.

The energetic discussion about their nameless town and its uncertain future continued on into the afternoon until they finally realized it was getting late, and although it was Sunday, there were still chores to be done.

✢

It wasn't until December, just a week after Eli and Elizabeth's first wedding anniversary, that a town meeting was called. All the men who lived within five miles were invited to attend, and after what Eli described as a rather loud and disagreeable evening, a vote was taken and the town's name was decided upon.

"What is it?" Elizabeth asked anxiously, keeping her voice low since the children were in bed. "Please tell me it's not Walters."

He grinned. "Or Thompson."

"What then?"

"Riverside."

"Riverside?" She grinned. "That was *my* idea!"

He nodded. "I know. It was your dad who suggested it. And he put forth a very convincing argument for it, saying some of the same things you said that day we were all talking about it right here."

Elizabeth felt torn. Of course, she liked the name and was relieved their town hadn't been named after a disagreeable family. But at the same time it seemed unfair that just because she was a woman, she had not been allowed to speak in behalf of the town's name. Would that ever change?

"After the vote had been taken and the town's name was secured, your pa let on that you were the one who thought of the name Riverside."

313

"He did?"

Eli chuckled. "Sure. He told everyone that he'd stolen the idea from you, but he was pretty sure you wouldn't mind."

She laughed. "Did they want to take another vote?"

"Oh, I'm sure that some of them did."

"Yes, I'm sure."

So it was that the little town of Riverside, Oregon, was born just before winter in 1858, a little more than a year after Elizabeth and her family settled there. To celebrate the town's name as well as the opening of its first hotel and restaurant, Ruby and Doris hosted a party at the Riverside Inn. Naturally, it was well attended and the event of the season.

The Dawson and Kincaid families had been blessed with four calves during the summer, and they'd gone in together to purchase Malinda's young bull. The calves were weaned and the grasslands were unlimited, so the cows were producing rich, creamy milk. And Asa's dream of Dawson's Dairy was beginning to be realized. Clara and Elizabeth were making two kinds of cheese, and Jessie was making butter. Not only that, but Elizabeth's ever-increasing flock of chickens was producing eggs by the dozens. All these wholesome food products were being sold and traded at the mercantile under the label of Dawson's Dairy. From what they could see, with more hard work and gumption, the future for their family and the town of Riverside was sunny and bright.

Chapter Thirty-Two

After a spell of wonderful springlike weather the first three weeks of January, the weather turned gray and grim and wet. Elizabeth, late in her pregnancy, felt clumsy and awkward trying to do farm chores, and after she took a bad spill, Eli put his foot down.

"I don't want to see you out here floundering around in the mud again," he said firmly. "Not until our baby is at least a month old. Understand?" He gently pulled her up from where she'd slipped just outside of the chicken yard. "Are you all right?"

"I'm sure my pride is a bit wounded." She made a lopsided smile.

He leaned down to kiss her. "I'm sorry. But I mean what I said. You are to stay in the house. The children and I will see to all the outdoor chores."

She shrugged. "Fine by me." Looking down at her muddy dress, she frowned. "But I still need to do laundry, and I normally do that outside."

"Yes, but you can do that on the porch. And in weather like this, you'll have to hang it in the house to dry anyway."

Elizabeth didn't really mind being housebound, but the gray weather was a bit dreary. However, she knew she could fill her time with knitting and sewing and getting ready for the new addition to their family. But in the next few days, she started to grow concerned, and on Saturday, she asked Ruth to take a note to her mother.

"Is it an invitation to a party?" Ruth asked excitedly.

"No, dear. It's just a note. I've missed her lately."

"Oh." Ruth nodded as she buttoned up her coat.

Elizabeth peered out the window at the darkening sky. "Don't dilly dally on the way, and maybe you will make it back before it rains."

Ruth hurried on out, and Elizabeth hoped that her mother wouldn't be too alarmed by the letter. Mostly she just wanted Clara to answer her questions. She'd described her symptoms in the note, reminding Clara that her baby was not due until early March. It wasn't even February yet. If the baby came too soon, it would not be good. Elizabeth had not had problems like these with JT or Ruth. But she had been considerably younger then. And though she didn't like to think of it, the two pregnancies after JT and Ruth had both ended sadly. To be fair, the first baby she'd lost was due to cholera. The second one…well, she didn't know for sure.

She sat down in the rocker, rubbing her rounded belly. "Be well, little one," she whispered. "And be patient. Don't come too soon." Then she picked up her knitting and attempted to distract herself with the pale blue blanket she was making for her unborn child. She hoped the baby would get to enjoy it.

"I brought Grandma with me," Ruth announced as they both came into the room.

"Oh?" Elizabeth looked up from her knitting. "That wasn't necessary." She started to push herself to her feet. "But I am happy to see you, Mother."

"Stay put," Clara demanded. "I've come to see *you*."

"Want to put on the teakettle, Ruth?" Elizabeth called out.

"How about if Ruth takes a snack out to the fellows," Clara suggested. "I said hello to them, and they looked hungry."

Elizabeth looked at the clock. "Oh, my. It is about dinnertime."

"Dinner can wait," Clara told her.

"Take them those doughnuts we made last night," Elizabeth told Ruth. "They can finish them off."

"Can I have one too, Mama?"

"Sure."

"Hurry now," Clara called "Before they come in here demanding to be fed."

Before long, it was just the two of them. "What is it, Mother?"

"What you wrote me." Clara sat down across from her frowning with concern. "You've got me worried, Lizzie." Now Clara began peppering her with questions. And she felt her forehead as well as her belly. "I brought you some red clover tea. That might help some. But as your mother and midwife, I am going to recommend bed rest for you until the problems you described to me stop. Or the baby is born."

"But the baby isn't due until early March."

"It's possible that your calculations are wrong."

"I do not think so, Mother."

"Well, that's even more good reason to get you to bed, my dear." Clara stood and then helped Elizabeth to her feet. "To bed with you. And do not argue with your mother."

"But I don't feel—"

"Elizabeth." Clara said sharply.

"Yes, Mother."

"I'll make you some tea. And then Ruth can help me fix dinner for your men. You just go get into your nightgown and climb into bed."

Elizabeth felt foolish going to bed in the middle of the day. Perhaps she'd been mistaken to call on her mother. And yet…she didn't want to put this baby at risk. She was just getting into bed when her mother appeared with a cup of red clover tea. "Drink this all up."

Determined to be a good patient, she drank the tea and remained in bed. She could hear them in the house, and she knew that Eli was probably concerned for her as well as the baby. After a bit, Ruth brought her a tray of food. "How are you feeling, Mama?" she asked with worried eyes.

"I feel just fine," she said. "I would like to get up and take care of—"

"Grandma says you have to stay in bed to keep the baby safe."

"Yes. I know."

"And I am to take care of you when I'm not at school. But while I'm at school, Grandma is going to be here."

"Oh, I don't think that's necessary."

"Grandma said you have to mind us, Mama." Ruth shook a finger at her. "We are all going to make you stay in bed. So you shouldn't argue about it."

Elizabeth laughed. "Well, I can see that your grandmother is ruling the roost now."

"Grandma and me."

Elizabeth had never been so bored in her life. It hadn't been too bad the first day or two, but after that, being confined to bed started to feel like a cruel punishment. But because her symptoms did not seem to be improving, she knew better than to question her mother's advice. And by now her whole household seemed to have turned against her. If she even made a move to get out of bed, they would scold her and show no mercy. Even the dog seemed to be keeping guard at the bedroom door.

On the third day, her father came to visit, bringing her some books to read. "Be patient," he told her. "Before you know it you'll be out on your feet and wondering why you didn't enjoy this respite a bit more."

"I don't think so, Father."

"You're a strong woman, Lizzie, but sometimes even a strong woman needs to let others help her." And then he asked if he could pray for her. Naturally, she didn't protest. By the time he left, she felt considerably better in spirit, but not well enough physically to be on her feet. Not if she wanted the baby to born healthy.

Word of her confinement began to spread in the community, and unless Elizabeth was mistaken, the women had made a schedule to ensure that she had a female visitor calling every afternoon. This provided a diversion in Elizabeth's boring days and allowed Clara to go home and see to her own household.

Her first visitors were Jess and Baby Maude. "See how big she's getting," Jess said as she held Maude up to stand on her little feet. "And she's only nine months old." She nodded to a small pile of baby clothes that she'd set on the washstand for Elizabeth. "She outgrew those a couple of months ago. And now she's crawling all over the place. Matthew says she'll be riding a horse in no time." Jess chattered cheerfully, telling Elizabeth the news from their farm and how Matthew was putting in a corral. "He's getting ready to start training our colt."

"I can't wait until I can be out there working with our filly."

"Don't be in a hurry." Jess nodded to the window. "There's mud everywhere right now. You might as well enjoy this break." She laughed. "Sometimes I think what I would give to take a nap." She looked at Maude. "This little girl only sleeps about an hour during the day now. But at least she sleeps soundly all night."

Jess continued chattering away, and Elizabeth couldn't help but remember the somber girl on the horse—the girl they all thought was a boy—and how she kept herself apart from everyone. And just look at her now. "Well, Jessica," Elizabeth said when they were finally getting ready to go. "You are a fine mother. And I am proud to have you for my sister."

Jess leaned down and kissed her cheek. "You take care of yourself. And mark my word, you'll be on your feet and chasing your little one in no time."

Malinda came the next day, presenting Elizabeth with a small quilt that she'd just finished for the baby. Like Jess, she chattered cheerfully almost nonstop. But Elizabeth sensed that underneath the happy chitchat, her friend seemed uneasy. It was clear that someone, probably her mother, had told these women that Elizabeth had been feeling a bit down in the dumps. And of course, that made Elizabeth feel a little guilty. "So how are you?" she asked Malinda finally. "Is it just my imagination, or do you seem a bit troubled?"

"Troubled?"

Elizabeth peered closely at her friend. She seemed to have shadows under her eyes. "And tired too. Malinda, are you all right?"

Malinda waved her hand. "I'm fine. It's you we're concerned for."

Elizabeth studied her. "Malinda Bramford—are you expecting?"

Malinda looked embarrassed.

"You are, aren't you!"

She shrugged. "To be honest, I'm not sure. I thought perhaps I was just getting old. You know I'll be thirty-five in June. I honestly felt I was too old to have another child."

"Mother had Matthew when she was in her early thirties."

"Yes, well…like I said, I'm not sure. I haven't said a word to anyone."

Elizabeth remembered the time she'd confided in Malinda…and how it turned out. "Don't worry," she told her. "Your secret is safe with me."

Belinda and Amelia came on the next day. They gave Elizabeth two sweet little nightshirts for the baby. And then they talked about how Belinda was helping Amelia to plan her wedding. "She's getting married in June, just like we did."

"Sisters marrying brothers," Elizabeth said. "One big happy family."

"It does make family gatherings simpler," Belinda admitted. Then Amelia asked Elizabeth's opinion on wedding dress colors, and Elizabeth told her to talk to Ruth about that.

On the following day Lavinia came, bringing a lace-trimmed christening gown for the baby. "Of course, I didn't sew it myself," Lavinia admitted. "But isn't it just fine?"

"It is beautiful. Thank you." They talked about new developments in town and how some of the businesses felt they should consider incorporating, but others, including the Prescotts, felt it was premature. "However, I do wish we had a mayor. Someone to help lead us in a good direction. I worry that a saloon will come to town. Can you imagine?"

Elizabeth grimaced. "That would be too bad."

"But Hugh says it's bound to happen."

They discussed the town's future at length until it was time for Lavinia to leave. Elizabeth sighed. She didn't like feeling sorry for herself, but it was strange feeling as if everyone and everything was moving right along and passing her by.

Mrs. Taylor came to visit on Saturday. She brought a pair of booties she'd made for the baby. She told about the latest goings on at school and how she hoped that Belinda and Amelia might start taking over for her more. "I still want to be involved, but to be honest, I am not getting any younger. I don't think I can keep up with the youngins the way I'd like to."

"You have done a wonderful job," Elizabeth assured her. "My children both love you. JT wouldn't be able to read music if you hadn't worked with him."

"Yes, and that is exactly what I've been wondering about. I think I could give music lessons to the children if the parents were able to pay. I would happily trade too. What do you think?"

"I think it's a great idea. I know my children would be happy to have lessons with you." They talked at length about how Mrs. Taylor could do this, and by the time she left, it seemed they had put together a good plan for next year.

On the women came throughout the next week, all of them bearing gifts for the baby. Doris and Ruby, Evelyn Prescott, Georgia Holmes, Martha Levine...but Elizabeth's favorite visitors were Mara and Rose. Dressed prettily in matching pink calico dresses that Mara and Martha had sewn, Mara and Rose looked happier than Elizabeth had ever seen them. "These are for your baby." Rose handed Elizabeth a tiny pair of deerskin moccasins with intricate beadwork.

"They are lovely," Elizabeth told her.

"Ma made them," Rose proclaimed proudly.

"Thank you."

"You're welcome," Rose said politely.

"And these are for you," Rose handed Elizabeth a beautiful pair of oyster white moccasins, also decorated with beadwork—delicate roses in shades of pink and red. They were very similar to the ones she'd given Mara.

"Oh, Mara, these are beautiful. Absolutely beautiful. Thank you so much."

Mara leaned over and grasped Elizabeth's hand. "Thank you, Elizabeth. I feel that you gave me a life."

⸎

On Monday, Elizabeth woke up with a backache and a sense of foreboding. But she tried to act cheerful as the children prepared to go to school.

"I have all my valentines finished," Ruth told her. "One for every person in school. Even the teachers."

"Good for you."

"I'm not giving valentines," JT said. "That's girl stuff."

Elizabeth smiled at him. "Well, someday you might have a sweetheart, and you might want to give her a valentine."

He wrinkled his nose.

"JT *does* have a sweetheart," Ruth teased. "He just doesn't want anyone to know."

He tossed his sister a dark look.

"If he doesn't want anyone to know, Ruth, why would you tell?"

"We better go or we'll be late," JT warned.

"Have a good day," Elizabeth called. But as soon as they were gone, she was in pain. "Mother," she called weakly.

Clara came quickly, tending to Elizabeth in every way she knew how, but it seemed clear that this baby was on its way. "I sent Eli for Malinda," Clara told Elizabeth as she urged her to drink some cool tea.

It wasn't long until both Malinda and Clara were with Elizabeth, doing what they could to make her comfortable and trying to cheer her. "This is only a couple of weeks early," Clara told her. "And it's possible you got the dates wrong."

"That's right," Malinda said as she wiped her forehead with a cold cloth. "Just look how big you are. That baby must be plenty big."

And when it came time for the baby to be born, Elizabeth had to agree with her friend. The baby was plenty big. And when it emerged into the world, screaming loudly, it sounded perfectly healthy too.

"You have a boy," Clara proclaimed. "A big, beautiful, baby boy."

As Clara worked to clean the infant off, Malinda announced that she was going to tell Eli the good news. It wasn't long until Clara handed the precious bundle to Elizabeth. The moment she looked into his wrinkled little red face and examined his fingers and toes, she burst into tears of happiness. "He looks just fine," she told her mother. "Just fine."

Soon Eli was in the room with them, inspecting his son with awe and relief. He leaned down to kiss her forehead. "You did well."

"She certainly did," Clara said.

"What are you going to name him?" Malinda asked.

Elizabeth looked up at Eli. "His name is Eli Dawson Kincaid."

Eli smiled.

"And he will grow up to be a good man in the Oregon frontier."

It wasn't until two weeks later, when Elizabeth was up and around and able to care for her household again, that some surprising news reached the small town of Riverside. It was a mild day, and Elizabeth had taken Eli Jr. outside with her, safely nestled in a basket, as she took down the dried wash. Meanwhile Eli was working nearby on the ever-expanding chicken yard. A scene of bucolic peace and contentment.

But suddenly their serene day was shattered when the children came running and shouting. "We have news!" they cried out together.

"Big news!" Ruth shrieked.

With his saw still in hand and a worried expression, Eli hurried over to see what was wrong.

"Let me tell it," JT said reaching them first.

"Wait for me!" Ruth cried as she hurried to join them.

"We have *big* news," JT said breathlessly. "Big, big news! It happened on February fourteenth—"

"That's Valentine's Day," Ruth exclaimed.

"Yes. And the same day our baby brother was born," JT added.

"But that's not the news," Ruth said.

"No." JT shook his head. "The news is that on that same day, the thirty-third state was added to the Union."

"Oh?" Elizabeth wasn't sure why that was such news.

"Our state!" Ruth told them.

"*Oregon!*" JT declared. "Oregon is the thirty-third state in the Union."

"We are a state!" Ruth shouted.

Eli and Elizabeth exchanged looks. "We are a state," she said with wonder.

"Imagine that," Eli said. "The state of Oregon was born on the same day Eli Jr. was born."

Elizabeth smiled down at her baby and then at her family. "May God bless them both—our new baby and our new state."

"And our family," Eli added. "God bless our family."

"And God bless our friends and neighbors," JT declared.

"And our animals," Ruth added as Flax came over, wagging his tail eagerly. "God bless them too."

OREGON STATEHOOD, FEBRUARY 14, 1859

Discussion Questions

1. While on the Oregon Trail, most of the pioneers couldn't wait for the arduous journey to end. Yet many hardships were still ahead. What do you think was the best thing about settling? What was the worst?

2. Imagine that you were a pioneer just arriving in the western frontier. What do you think you'd miss the most from your old life back east?

3. What was your initial reaction to Eli's disappearance with Elizabeth's wagon and beloved team? What did you imagine had happened to him?

4. Malinda is Elizabeth's best friend, and yet they sometimes seem at odds. Why do you think their relationship was so strained?

5. Imagine again that you're a new settler. What, besides food and shelter, would be your first priority in creating your homestead? How would you go about securing it?

6. Elizabeth's stay with Malinda was necessary but stressful. Fortunately it only lasted for a season. Describe an era in your life when you had to endure some discomforts for a spell. What helped you to get through that time?

7. Malinda seems driven to have the perfect wedding. Why do you think she was so obsessed with this?

8. What was your initial response to Reverend Holmes? To Mrs. Holmes? How did you feel about them later on, after you got to know them better?

9. When Malinda planned her quilting bee, she seemed to intentionally leave Elizabeth out. How did you react to her seemingly bad manners? How did you feel later on when you discovered she was actually making the quilt for Elizabeth?

10. Although the Indians were "relocated" from the area, Elizabeth manages to find one of the few still remaining. Considering the other settlers' opinions on these matters, as well as the welfare of her own children, do you think Elizabeth was wise to reach out this woman? Why or why not?

11. There are a number of strong women in this series. Elizabeth, Clara, Jessica, Malinda, Lavinia...to name a few. Describe the qualities you think best sustained women in the western frontier.

12. After Eli and Elizabeth wed, Elizabeth finally got to see the home Eli had built for her and her children. Naturally, she was ecstatic over every little detail. What did you like best about their rustic cabin?

13. Elizabeth knew Mara and her children would survive only if they integrated into White culture. How did you feel when

Mara was getting her "makeover"? Describe your reaction to the tea party where Mara met her mother-in-law, Martha.

14. Confined to bed rest toward the end of her pregnancy, Elizabeth was understandably antsy and anxious. For a hands-on frontier woman, doing "nothing" was a challenge. Describe a time when you felt your hands were tied and all you could do was wait. What helped you get through that era?

15. Eli and Elizabeth's first son together was born on the same day Oregon became a state. What do you imagine Eli Jr. would have been doing 40 years later—in 1899?

16. Did anything in this series change the way you look at life? If so, describe.

Westward Hearts

The Oregon Trail—
Hardship or Happiness? Loneliness or Love?

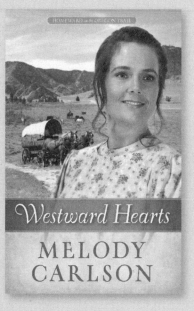

Kentucky, 1856—Elizabeth Martin has mourned her husband's death for three years, but now she feels ready to fulfill the dream they had shared—to take their two children west. The dream becomes reality when her middle-aged parents and bachelor brother surprise her with the news that they want to go as well.

After converting three of their best wagons for an overland journey and thoroughly outfitting them with ample supplies and tools, the family travels from Kentucky to Kansas City, where they join a substantial wagon train. Elizabeth soon draws attention from fellow traveler Will Bramford as well as Eli Kincade, the group's handsome but mysterious guide.

Will Elizabeth's close-knit family survive the challenges they face on the Oregon Trail? And is this young widow truly ready for new love —even as she pursues the dream once shared with her late husband?

A Dream for Tomorrow

Life on the trail was challenging.
Will settling down prove just as difficult?

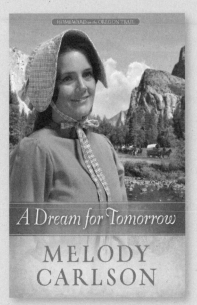

It's the summer of 1857, and Elizabeth Martin is pursuing the dream she shared with her late husband—to take their two children west and start a new life. Along with her parents, her newly married brother, and even her devoted farmhand, she has joined a substantial wagon train and successfully completed the first half of the long trip from Kentucky to the southern Oregon Coast. And along the way,

Elizabeth has caught the eye of fellow traveler Will Bramford, a wealthy and charming widower from Boston, and also of Eli Kincade, the handsome but mysterious scout for the wagon train.

Now the time has come for the train to divide as some travelers head south to California. Several emigrants, including Will and his children, have decided to settle near Elizabeth and her family, but Eli is chosen to lead the southbound group. Elizabeth must decide whether to do the prudent thing—to accept Will's proposal and the security he can provide—or to follow her heart and fall in love with a man who seems wed to life on the trail.

Romance, adventure, and faith are on display in this second book in the Homeward on the Oregon Trail series.

To learn more about Harvest House books and
to read sample chapters, log on to our website:

www.harvesthousepublishers.com

HARVEST HOUSE PUBLISHERS
EUGENE, OREGON